"Faces, Souls, and Painted Crows powerful setting."
> J. Rios, Vice-President
> Fox Television

"For a novel I find "Faces, Souls, and Painted Crows" quite an achievement, bringing together an arresting character, many original plot situations and contrasting settings. The story affords the opportunity of dramatizing interesting and important themes, i.e., the relationship of physical appearance and the soul (which I don't remember having seen presented quite so concretely)."
> Leonard Tourney, Santa Barbara Writers' Conference
> Faculty of Comparative Writing
> University of California, Santa Barbara

"What makes this a great book are the thoughtful themes and the symbolism that are woven into the story. . . . I couldn't help but be drawn in by all the deeper parts and I found myself thinking about the many themes despite myself."
> Clinton McKenzie, author, "The Edge of Justice"
> Random House

"Faces, Souls, and Painted Crows" is the best writing by a first time author that I've read in a long time."
> Frank del Olmo, Senior Editor, LA Times

"Good stuff. Exceptionally well written."
> Robert Goulet, Broadway Star

"This is a novel of expiation – of old fashioned penance and atonement. Its main strengths are the powerfully conflicted main character, his wonderfully sane and sensible wife, and the novel's most unusual setting."
> Andreas Schroeder, Head of Department of
> Department of Comparative Writing, UBC
> Vancouver, B.C., Canada

"Faces, Souls, and Painted Crows" touches the most basic aspects of life portrayed by Paul Reiter's riveting journey between Hollywood and the wild shores of the Baja Peninsula. Rudi Unterthiner's fictionalized memoir is a masterpiece."
> Gary Quinn, Author and Motivational Speaker

" . . focusing on the doctor's story makes the book attractive as a film possibility. The elements are there: a heroic physician, his lovely wife and family, moral conflicts, temptation and struggles of conscience, questions of the value of his profession."
> Nancy Peters
> City Lights Books
> San Francisco, California

"Once I started reading "Faces, Souls, and Painted Crows" I couldn't put it down. I was drawn into the powerful and yet humane character. . . Excellent. Every chapter comes alive and we get a picture of the protagonist, more vivid with every page. He is what the reader relates to. The woman who died beautiful . . fascinating character.

Jess Stearn, Best selling author

"Paul Reiter, the pilot, is the protagonist of "Faces, Souls, and Painted Crows," and yet he is not. Reiter is actually Unterthiner, the 64-year-old Rudi from the Tyrolean town of Sterzing in Italy, who started out in the coal mines and ended up as one of Hollywood's top plastic surgeons. Unterthiner, who is married to a half-breed, could well be the star portrayed in his book."

Helmut Sorge, US. Correspondent,
Spiegel Magazine

"Faces, Souls, and Painted Crows" is a page turner that chronicles Reiter's journey through three different worlds. Best seller material."

Baldour Freek,
ZDF German TV
Bonn, Germany

"Rudi Unterthiner's fictionalized memoir, "Faces, Souls, and Painted Crows" sweeps the reader into extraordinary places as they travel along an extraordinary journey between contrasting cultures and picturesque characters."

Kim Duke
Producer, Documentary Division
BBC, London

"Real good writing, Rudi. It's a hell of a story.

Ernie Borgnine, Oscar award film star

"Faces, Souls, and Painted Crows" is an exceptional, inspirational story: A journey of an underprivileged youngster from nowhere into the precarious heights of wealth and glamour without losing sight of life's moral implications. It is a story of human triumph and perseverance. I see the book as a powerful message in the form of a fictionalized memoir. The writing is riveting, the background fascinating, filled with vivid imagery and characters."

Sebastian Ritscher, Mohrbooks, Zurich, Switzerland

Faces, Souls, and Painted Crows

Rudi Unterthiner

Chronicler Publishing

This is a work of fiction. All of the characters, organizations, and events portrayed in this novel are either products of the author's imagination or are used fictitiously.

Faces, Souls, and Painted Crows

Chronicler Publishing

For information address:
Chronicler Publishing
Jones Beach,
RR 1 Evansburg,
Alberta, Canada, T0E 0T0
www.chroniclerpublishing.com

ISBN: 9780980953411

Cover Image: Painted Crow by Clayton Pidcock, used with permission.

Dedication

To my wife, Linda, from the Ute Mountain tribe who found her way back to her culture and with her native patience spent countless hours typing and retyping my manuscript.

To my children and grandchildren, who remind me to live every minute to the fullest.

There are many people and events who have altered and enhanced the course of my life; I would like to give special thanks:

To the people of my hometown, "Sterzing" in South Tyrol, where my journey began.

To the faculty and students of Carleton College, who introduced me to America as a Fullbright Scholar.

To Whitworth College, for giving me a safe harbor in the storm.

To the Faculty of Medicine at the University of Alberta who made my dream of becoming a doctor a reality. They made me a family doctor first and a surgeon second.

To Hans Peter Frisch, my ski instructor on the banks of the Saskatchewan River, who sustained me during difficult times.

To William Austin and the Starkey Foundation, who gave me the gift of hearing and whose mission "So the World May Hear", has taught me to listen.

To the Swarovski family of Austria, for their longstanding friendship and because their world famous crystals bring so much beauty to the world.

To Red Crow Westerman for nurturing my wife's roots and for his philosophy of gratitude to "Takoye Oyassin". All our relations: the earth, sky, animals and mankind.

To Dean Pananides, Leonard Turney, Andreas Schroeder, Richard O'Connor and others, who read the manuscript and offered suggestions and encouragement.

To Phil Fontaine, National Chief of First Nations and his special advisor, Ken Young, for their support of Linda's culture and their exemplary struggle for their people

To William Plested, my friend and President of the American Medical Association, a true healer.

To the people of the We Wai Kai Band of Cape Mudge who have given me a new home where the journey ends and to Captain Johnny Chickite and the memory of his father.

To my editor and publisher, Charles Goulet, who encouraged me to tell my story.

Dear Reader,

I'm humbly honored that you decided to come with me on this meandering journey. Writing this account of parts of my life was a journey in itself that took over twelve years. You see, I must confess that I'm not a writer and that made it a bumpy road.

Few of the words I put down were final—I wrote and re-wrote the manuscript more than fifty times. For example, the first chapter was revised twenty-one times, the chapter on Alicia's birth was rewritten seventeen times, and the painted crows close to thirty times.

The book is based on my diaries, although I have fictionalized some people, places, and events to represent typical compilations that affected me deeply.

I ask for your generous understanding not to judge the writing style or the contents too harshly and to remember I'm an amateur who tried. So tighten your seat belt and enjoy the ride.

Rudi Unterthiner

PROLOGUE

Austrian Coal Mine, 1956

Paul Reiter ignored the oppressive gloom of the coalmine as he opened his water canteen. He drank sparingly and caught a glimpse of himself in the shiny lid he used as a cup. He shuddered in disbelief. Trying to make sense of what he'd seen, he adjusted his headlight and stole another look at the old face. As if to dismiss the sudden panic he felt, he reminded himself that he'd just turned eighteen. With a trembling hand, he traced a path across the deep furrows in his forehead, down hollow cheeks embedded with soot. Beads of perspiration trickled over smudges of coal dust, and the eyes were streaked fiery red. He wanted to believe that the old face wasn't his, because if there was any connection between the face and the soul, he was afraid that the mine could destroy more than his body.

Whether the thought was just a fleeting aberration that careened through his mind in the middle of that night shift, he didn't know. Nor did he know that the connection between faces and souls would haunt him for years.

With a sense of dread, he replaced the lid and hooked the canteen back on his belt. His mind drifted back nearly a year to a bitter cold Monday at the end of October. He'd had no qualms signing up for the job at the mine that morning, but when he showed up for his night shift, he had the feeling he'd walked into a graveyard. Waves of doubt curdled his stomach when he saw the hopelessness etched in the faces of the other miners, all pale and unshaven. They reminded him of ghosts digging graves in the mountains.

Not sure what to do, he'd followed them into one of the larger sheds of the compound. There, they struggled to pull on work clothes with sleeves and pant legs so stiffened by coal dust they looked like stovepipes that had been cobbled together. Someone pointed to a jacket dangling from a hook, and Reiter slipped into it, wondering whose it was. Then everyone put on hard hats and stepped into the bitter cold night. Hacking coughs burst into white puffs that rose through the beams of the headlamps.

The jacket he'd ended up with was no match for the icy wind blowing off the snow-capped mountains, but it struck him as odd that he was the only one shivering. Instinctively, he reached for the buttons at the top of his coat and cursed when he discovered they were missing. All the miners hunched their shoulders and turned sideways as they waded through the snow, seemingly oblivious to the cold. No one wore gloves, and even raising their hands to their mouths looked more like a reflex than a real attempt to warm them. The strange waves curdling his stomach came back when he saw the chopped off fingers and the clusters of warts on their grimy hands.

For the rest of his life he would remember the crunching sound of rubber boots trudging over hard-packed snow and how his mind had often wandered to his friends and family. He'd imagine them playing cards and laughing in some cozy house with smoke curling out of the chimney while he was shuffling through a graveyard.

Falling in line with the others, he overheard two miners whisper the name "Willy" as they stole glances at a man who walked by himself. One of them tugged on Reiter's sleeve. "That guy is a bastard," he mumbled, nodding toward the loner. Reiter didn't react. "He'd drag his own mother down here for an extra bucket of coal," the man added.

Willy turned around as if he'd overheard them although he was several yards away. Suddenly, he stumbled on a sheet of ice and struggled for balance. Immediately, someone reached out to steady him. "Leave me alone," Willy growled as he righted himself and shoved off the helping hand. "God damn shit," he muttered. Then he jammed his hands into his pocket and stomped down the road into the biting wind.

That first night the supervisor assigned Reiter to be Willy's helper. They'd been working together ever since, backbreaking nights that melted into days of exhaustion. The routine was so grueling that Reiter had no desire to note the time of day or night.

The sound of rivulets trickling somewhere through black seams disrupted the flow of his troubling thoughts. He listened to the faint rumble of a conveyor belt propelling chunks of coal toward rusty carts waiting on hastily laid tracks. As he reached for a jackhammer, he felt a rustling near his boots, and in the beam of his headlamp, he saw the pointed nose and tiny ears of a rat. He swept the light across the furry body, from the twitching whiskers to the black tail. Beady little eyes stared at him boldly as the rat inched closer and closer. A few months ago, the sight would have filled him with disgust. Tonight, he merely shrugged. He couldn't deny it—he was getting used to the graveyard. He was turning into a ghost himself. He closed his eyes, trying to shut out the depressing truth.

When he opened his eyes, he saw Willy squatting in the corner, leathery jowls puffing in and out with a hissing sound like worn-out bellows. Reiter watched as the old man turned his head, directing the light on his hard hat to a spot on the wall. Taking careful aim, Willy puckered his lips and spat out a shot of saliva. He seemed oddly fascinated by the tobacco-stained spittle as it found its mark and dribbled down the wall.

Reiter turned back to his work, struggling with the cumbersome jackhammer and its temperamental switch. Time and time again, it failed to start or started before he was ready, clashing with the unyielding rock as he tried to carve out a long, narrow hole. Willy waited for Reiter to finish so he could put a charge of dynamite in the cavity, but it was clear he had no interest in lending a hand. There was nothing but contempt in his eyes and he seemed to take a measure of satisfaction in seeing the younger man fail.

Reiter re-aligned the drill for the third time. "God damn hole," he muttered.

A bear-like hand clamped down on his shoulder, and he whirled around. He found himself inches away from Willy's blackened face

3

and was blasted by the stench of his breath hissing through the darkness. Rust-colored saliva dribbled over the stubble of his beard, and his few rotten teeth were so black they looked as if he'd been eating coal.

The grip on Reiter's shoulder tightened, and Willy jerked him even closer. "So, God damn hole is what you call this place?"

Reiter felt the cold sweat of fear pouring from his skin, and he tried to pull back. The grip turned into a vice, and a demonic look came over the old man's face. "If God was down here, you wouldn't need old Willy, would you?" He laughed and gave Reiter a shove.

"Leave me alone." Reiter turned back to the rock. This time the steel drill bit deep into the wall. A cloud of dust spiraled through the beam of the headlamp.

"You got lucky, boy," Willy yelled over the noise. "Maybe one of these days you'll learn how to do it right the first time. But I've seen it take years."

The jackhammer ground to a halt. "What makes you think I'm going to be down here that long?" Reiter said angrily, glancing towards the entrance to the shaft. "Sooner or later, I'll be out of this place."

"And how are you going to do that?" Willy scoffed. He hooked his thumbs together and fluttered his fingers as if they were wings. "Fly away? Like some crazy bird?"

Reiter stared his tormentor in the eyes. "I'm not sure how, but I'm getting out of here." He paused to wipe the black dust from his eyes. "I'm going to America."

Immediately, he regretted sharing his dream with Willy, wishing he could retract the words. He could remember the day he'd first thought about going to America, but he'd kept it a private dream, something he'd never mentioned to anyone.

Willy's hollow laughter filled the shaft, and the echo resounded in the darkness. "There you go again with your dreams. This time you're off to America." A shadow of disgust crossed his face.

"Where were you when they were dropping bombs on us?" His hand went to his side. "I still have shrapnel in my belly from those bastards." He spat a chunk of tobacco on the ground. With the back of his hand, he wiped away the stain on his chin. "Quit dreaming, boy," he snarled.

Reiter said nothing, and Willy rallied. "I've heard it all before—the complaints and threats of others just like you—dreamers who can't take it and want to get out. But they never leave." He pointed a finger at Reiter. "You're goin' nowhere, boy." It sounded like an order. "You're stuck here with old Willy," he added. "For the rest of your life."

A crackling noise in the ceiling turned their eyes to the timbers above them. Reiter stole a look at Willy, but if the old man was scared, he didn't show it. "Hasn't been a cave-in for years," he muttered. He sounded resigned, as if doomsday was only a matter of time. His sunken eyes were lifeless, and Reiter wondered if the old man really cared whether he lived or died.

"What are you staring at?" Willy's voice rose a pitch. "I've been in here all my life and so will you. Get used to it." A sense of sadness edged his voice. "We were born to live in these pits. No different than phantoms."

Reiter felt drained. "You're right," he said. "I feel like a phantoms down here, half dead and half alive." His shoulders drooped, and his voice softened. "Don't take it personal, old man," he said as he picked up the jackhammer, "but this phantom is different. This hole is not where I'm going to end up."

He was in his last year of medical school and sought work there, hoping to get some hands-on experience. He felt a measure of pride when, even as a student "extern", the nurses began calling him "Dr. Reiter." It reassured him that someday he would have his medical degree. Linda was a university student who had just been hired as a staff secretary. In another twist of fate, Reiter wound up doing physical examinations on all the new employees.

How could he forget the morning he walked into the cold, drab exam room? A young woman waited on the examining table, a thin sheet pulled over her naked body. He could see her eyes wander to the faded portraits of bygone administrators hanging in bulky frames on the walls. They were all proper grandfather-types with handlebar mustaches and old-fashioned suits. They must have seen a woman's body before, Reiter mused, but it was not hard to imagine a glint of lust in their eyes. The girl on the table looked vulnerable and embarrassed.

He tried to put her at ease with an air of cool, professional detachment. As he gave instructions to the nurse, he tried to sound matter-of-fact, make every move strictly routine. Like a mechanic raising the hood of a car, he folded back a corner of the sheet to begin the examination. His face betrayed no interest, but he took a mental note of the high cheekbones and deep dimples, her elusive dark eyes and raven hair. He felt, rather than saw, her inquisitive glance and struggled to dismiss the uncomfortable feeling it gave him.

For a moment, he thought he caught the fragrance of wild flowers in a high mountain meadow. He couldn't decide if it was perfume or her natural aroma, but it engulfed him. He tried hard to pull himself together, clinging to the routine he'd been taught: eyes, ears, nose, throat, and chest. Her frame was small and delicate. He noticed a small, pigmented spot on her lower spine. It was a Mongolian Spot, which was common to the North American Indians. That meant she must have some Indian blood, which accounted for the high cheekbones and black hair. But Caucasian features hinted at other genes as well. Latin perhaps, even Spanish. Not that any of it mattered. She was what she was, and for him it was more than enough.

He didn't fix his eyes on her directly as he examined her body. It had suddenly become too personal. He skimmed over her small, firm breasts. The skin was silky, and she had the concave abdomen and flat, narrow pelvis typical of Indian women. Her legs were long and slender and her feet, small and arched. It occurred to him that if the body was a reflection of the soul, hers must be sensitive and serene.

He asked her to sit up. He tapped her knee with the reflex hammer. No reaction. He tapped again. Still no response. Was she so different or had he become so distracted that he couldn't perform a simple reflex test? He felt his face redden and hoped she didn't notice. Was she tense, holding back? He finally shrugged and let it go. All in all, she was as healthy as anyone he had ever examined. And better looking.

As he percussed and palpated her body, he felt her shiver wherever his hand moved. He had trouble concentrating on the usual routine. "Open your mouth. Say 'Ah.' Breathe deep. Sit up, please. Now lie down." He went on and on.

When the exam was finally over, she looked at him.

"You may get dressed," he said, like a teacher dismissing a class. The examination had been thorough and professional; the mechanic closed the hood of the car. He picked up her chart and walked out.

The nurse turned to her. "Go down the hall to the doctor's office after you're dressed. He'll have your report," she said. "Second door on the left, honey."

The office door was open, and she slipped in. He was working on a chart, but looked up. For the first time their eyes met. "Everything is fine," he said, still impersonal, as if he couldn't care less, not knowing that destiny had already swept into their lives.

"May I go now?"

He nodded, handing her a piece of paper. "Don't forget to take this slip back to personnel." There was a slight hesitation in the way he said it. And then his voice rose a pitch, and he sounded less confident, more like a teenager. "Could we get together some time?"

A look of surprise was reflected in her eyes.

"How about dinner tonight?" he continued. "At the Beer Gardens?" He looked at his hands nervously. She was in her early twenties, probably from a sheltered background. He was being too impulsive.

She just stood there and looked at him, hugging herself. "Tonight I have to go to my aunt's," she blurted out before she turned and left the room.

His mind refused to follow what he was writing on the chart. Suddenly, he rose, his breath coming faster. He ignored the inquisitive glance of the nurse as he rushed to the door, intent on stopping the moment, afraid he'd never see her again.

He watched her slim, shapely legs and the fluid movements of her curves as she walked down the hall. He forced himself to let go of the image and stepped back to his desk. A voice echoed in the back of his brain: *That's not the end of it. I'll see you again. Never mind your aunt.*

"Is everything all right?" The nurse frowned and straightened her white uniform.

"Who's next?" he retorted and opened a folder.

***

That evening, he drove to the hills west of town. He followed a gravel road cutting through rows of neatly planted cornstalks. The soft shadows of the setting sun bathed moss-covered barns and sheds in burnished gold. Every hundred yards he'd stop the car and get out, wanting to touch the purple-blue twilight. An owl called softly in the distance, its low pitched "hu-it, hu-it" echoing through the early evening. And everywhere he looked, the face of the dark haired young woman stared back. He saw her in the rustling leaves, in the waving grass on the hillside, in the wisp of clouds scattered across the sky.

He kept repeating her name to himself slowly, tasting each syllable: Linda. He liked the sound of it. Though he tried to dismiss it, he felt a strange yearning, and with it a persistent belief that her face would somehow figure in his life.

Suddenly, waves of doubt rose from the back of his conscience. She was a patient who he had examined. How could he think of her in any other way? He knew he was straying from his professional side and felt like an intruder, gliding into her life on the pretense of being a doctor. Still, he couldn't get her out of his mind, so when he got back to town he called her. She didn't seem surprised.

He saw her the next evening and every evening after that, all summer long. They would meet after her work was done, and she often joined him on evening rounds through the hospital wards. He felt strangely calm when Linda was with him; somehow it eased the pain he felt when he checked on "patients" who would never leave this place. He remembered the lines of distress on her face when he took her through the antiseptic rooms the first time. "I've gone to the building where the children with Down's Syndrome live," she'd told him. "But I had no idea there were children born with problems like these."

The children with Down's Syndrome had a separate wing, and Linda made a habit of visiting them on her lunch hour. One evening when the two of them were seated at a table in the back of the Beer Garden, she talked about it. "I wish I could take that little boy, Timmy, home with me." Her voice cracked. "He's one of the Downs kids in Building C, and he's always so loving and sweet," she added, touching Reiter's hand. "Do you know he's almost six, and he's been in that ward every day of his life?" She paused and sighed. "I don't think he even knows that he has a father and mother."

He wanted to reassure her but he couldn't conceal his own sadness. "It's hard to imagine that anyone could leave a baby in that place and walk away as if it didn't exist," he agreed. Yet many Down's children ended up in institutions in those days.

The plight of the more severely disabled patients strapped in endless rows of beds along the walls of the hospital ward made him feel even more helpless. There was so little he could do for them. For the rest of his life he would remember the faces attached to those twisted bodies. A humble acceptance of fate was reflected in their eyes, as if they were merely dealing with a slight inconvenience.

Walking through the sour smelling rooms, he sometimes stopped to touch a grotesquely gnarled limb, repositioning it to prevent the painful bedsores that could fester with immobility. He checked swollen gums, aggravated by years of medications. The supervising physician had spent hours going over the effects and side effects of drugs with him, and sometimes Reiter made notes in the chart suggesting changes in dosages or treatments. He felt his chest swell with pride when his orders were approved and signed off by the medical staff. It made him feel he was almost a doctor.

Often, after visiting with his little patients, Reiter strolled with Linda through the sun-scorched hills surrounding the hospital. The depression he felt in the wards was such a contrast to the joy he felt with Linda that at times the change felt too abrupt and intense. That's when he would hold her tightly, not wanting to let go, reassuring himself that the gentle swells and curves of her body were not a mirage. How could the same God create such perfection and such deformity?

**

Interrupting his thoughts, his secretary's shrill voice rang over the intercom. "Mrs. Reiter is on line three." He picked up the receiver. "I've been thinking about you. I just tried to call."

"I know."

"How did you know?"

"Because I'm a wizard, remember?"

"Someone from London just called," he said, and he told her about the conversation with the journalist. His voice made it clear he was having second thoughts about the Englishman coming to Puertecitos.

"I wouldn't worry," she reassured him. "It's a long way from London to Puertecitos. When he finds out it's in the middle of nowhere, he'll probably stay home."

CHAPTER THREE

For the rest of the month, Reiter felt a growing apprehension about the upcoming trip to Puertecitos. Maybe the visit by the English journalist was rattling his mind, he reasoned, because it seemed that no matter how busy he was over the next few weeks, a feeling of uneasiness was always present. Another haunting thought kept surfacing: he wondered if he'd run into Consuelo.

For his wife and two children, spending the week in Baja was like a camping trip. They had to prepare short lists of food and supplies because cargo space was limited. On the day of their departure, Reiter and Linda spent the morning stowing canned goods, soda, jugs of water, blankets and bedding between the boxes of medicines that would be used for the monthly clinic he held with his friend Martine. Packing clothes was the easiest part; jeans, tee shirts and swimming suits were the only things they needed.

Shortly after noon, they left to pick up the children at school. They spotted them in the schoolyard. The boy looked more like his mother with the chiseled facial features typical of Native Americans. Robin, on the other hand, had the blond hair and blue eyes of her Tyrolean ancestors. They came running toward the car.

"What about Cobo's boat? Will he take me out?" Shane asked as they piled in the back seat.

"Hey, I want to go too," Robin insisted.

Reiter glanced at his wife. As far as he was concerned, it was fine. Shane was only eight and Robin six, but they were good swimmers, and they would be wearing life jackets. Besides, Cobo, the half-breed Seri fisherman who lived at the edge of town, would guard them as if they were his own. But Linda was always more wary when the kids went out in the boat, so he left it up to her.

"We'll see what the weather's like," she said.

The kids cheered—they knew that was a yes—and settled back for the drive to the airstrip.

18

Once in the plane they climbed out of the high desert and flew over the sprawling city of Los Angeles. Thousands of cars crawled along the six-lane freeways that snaked around the buildings below. The maze of intersections and overpasses looked like giant spider webs ensnaring the city. The children's faces were glued to the windows. "All those cars look like ants crawling around an anthill," Shane said.

"It looks to me like they're crawling pretty fast," Robin added as she turned towards her brother. "Don't you think they'd rather have wings?"

"I'm just glad we're up here," Reiter interjected as he picked up the microphone. "November fifty-two Delta. Cessna 210. Request climb to six thousand feet," he asked the controller, as if by flying higher they could escape the confusion below.

Linda squeezed his arm, and he breathed a sigh of relief. At times like this he was grateful that he'd learned to fly years ago. He'd seen it then only as a way to support himself through college and medical school. Like work in the coalmine, the job paid better than most, but he found that it not only helped pay for his medical education, it taught him to focus on the moment. In the air, there was no time for distractions, no time to mull things over—everything had to be quick and to the point. Flying and surgery had a lot in common. Both honed that part of him that strayed to the edges of life.

Flights to Baja had begun more than a decade ago while he was still in surgical training. One Sunday morning, he'd borrowed a plane to fly to Mexicali, a border city on the Baja Peninsula of Mexico. On the tarmac, someone pointed to a short bow-legged man climbing out of a plane. "That's Ciro Martinez. The guy can land an airplane on top of a cactus."

Reiter's curiosity got the better of him, and he followed Ciro to a nearby bar. Over a drink they started talking in a mixture of Italian and Spanish. Between margaritas and mariachis they were at the bar till midnight. A few weeks later, Ciro surprised him with a phone call. "How about flying a plane for me next Friday?"

"Where to?" Reiter asked, trying not to sound as pleased as he felt.

"San Francisquito. A little resort halfway down the gulf. Where the rich gringos go." He didn't wait for an answer. "They need supplies from Mexicali. Blankets, baskets, flour, beer, the usual things. The plane will be full, but you can always climb in through the window." He paused for a moment. "Two hundred and fifty pesos, hombre. That's what they'll pay." He cleared his throat. "Mucho dinero. What do you say?"

Reiter didn't have to think very long. Two hundred and fifty pesos sounded like a lot of money for a resident surgeon. "I'll do it, amigo," he said. "Did you say Friday?"

That summer, he ended up flying to Baja on several weekends, making deliveries to different resorts. Each trip went like clockwork until the last flight of the summer when he ran out of luck or good gas. He never found out which.

He was half way up the coast on his way back from San Francisquito when he was startled by a change in the sound of the engine. He leaned forward to listen more carefully, hoping he was imagining the banging noise. His eyes narrowed when he saw the temperature gauge rise, and he pulled back on the throttle. He felt a stab of fear in his chest as he watched the altimeter drop: 4000… 3500…3000 feet. When a streak of black oil shot across the windshield, he knew he had to act fast. Instinctively, he tightened his seat belt and scanned the coastline for a place to set down.

Steep cliffs lined the dark, angry sea, but he knew the area well enough to remember a horseshoe-shaped bay with a road of sorts down the center a few miles ahead. The minutes dragged by until he finally spotted it.

He straightened out the tail with a kick to the rudder. His hand shook as he reached for the levers to lower the landing gear and flaps.

With a mixture of relief and terror, he pushed the plane into a steep dive, keeping his eyes glued to the unforgiving terrain rising to meet him. In the now-silent cockpit, he could hear the swish of the air, and he murmured a fleeting prayer. He ignored the few makeshift huts scattered on either side of the rut-filled road, now less than twenty feet below him. And then, with a resounding thud he was down and stepped on the brakes. He skidded to a halt and breathed a sigh. Within minutes the inhabitants of the shacks rushed to his plane.

"You did a good job, hombre. Flying must be in your blood," someone said. "Welcome to Puertecitos."

***

In the years that followed, he often wondered if fate had intentionally plugged his fuel lines in order to lead him to Puertecitos Bay. The moment he landed, the mystifying stillness of the sun-baked canyons snaking their way to the sea had captured his heart. Through the rest of his surgical training and after he began his medical practice, Puertecitos and Baja became his second home. He instinctively loved its people, most of them a mixed breed of Spanish and Indian. The Indians on the coastlines were Seris who fished for a living. Their word was their bond, a bond sealed with the flick of an eyebrow or a nod of the head. But whether pure Indians or mixed blood Mexicans, the people of Baja were loyal and hard working, always living on the edge, close to the earth and the sea. They reminded him of the mountain people of his Tyrolean homeland, just a shade darker and shorter.

His soul seemed to be caught up in the nets of the Indians who chased the schools of fish and shrimp in the bountiful Sea of Cortez. They'd set up camp on the rocky shores at the edge of a canyon and fish for months. Then they'd disappear as if swallowed up by the sea.

Many times he'd return to a camp and find them gone, the wind rustling through the empty cardboard shacks, black buzzards

21

perching on the rocks. He could feel the misty shadows of the fishermen in the torn nets that sometimes hung on the ocotillo fences around the camp. He missed their silent smiles. At times he would climb into his airplane and search the canyons to the south for signs of them along the sandy beaches and the windswept shoreline.

If he spotted a new camp, he would swoop down like an eagle landing on a hard-packed strip of sand for a meal and a visit. If they'd been lucky, there would be fresh sea bass or tortuava boiling in rusty kettles.

Sometimes two or three of them didn't return from the sea. No need to ask why. Their widows sat in a special place in the camp, as though removed from tribal life. They had no reason to go down to the shore, no reason to wait for the return of the boats at the end of the day. They mended nets in dry-eyed silence while the other women prepared the meager meals. The social order didn't change; it had been so for centuries.

***

A sudden bump in the middle of a cloud put an end to his thoughts and he glanced at his watch. They'd been in the air an hour and a half and should have Puertecitos in sight. Looking down at the Baja shoreline, he scanned the coast for signs of the familiar fish camps. "Those are Seri camps down there," he called over his shoulder to the children as they peered out the window of the plane. "If we have time on Saturday, maybe Cobo can take us up the coast to get some fish."

The children clapped as the aircraft touched down in a spiral of dust. A rickety jeep drove up, and Reiter greeted its owner, Martine. While Linda and the children walked to the beach, Reiter and Martine unloaded the plane.

Martine was eighty-two with a weathered-barn ruggedness that spoke of decades in Baja. His eyes were blue-green, like the Sea of

Cortez, and were deep-set in a sun-scorched face. His ready smile showed off gold-capped teeth, reflecting the dazzling sun of this land. But there were times when the smile would freeze into a snarl without any warning, like the "chubasco", the fierce winds that came out of nowhere.

His American name was Marvin, though few people used it anymore. The story was told that he left his farm in Montana one Saturday night and showed up in Puertecitos the following Friday. Nobody seemed to know the exact year, and that seemed to suit him just fine. Over the years, he came to serve as judge, doctor, father or priest, depending on the need. The people of the town loved and respected him, and he seemed to know how to dispense the right dose of authority to keep things in balance.

His front porch, where he spent most of his time, had become the unofficial city hall of Puertecitos. At any time of day, a steady stream of people could be found coming and going on Martine's porch: Mexicans, Seri and Yaki Indians, tourists down for the weekend, and American expatriates who lived in the town and had little else to do. Some came to pick his brains and get advice; others came simply to break up their day. Martine stitched up cut fingers, set broken bones, worked on stalled cars, and patched punctured tires. Often he was even asked to settle arguments over property boundaries, bar bills, and more elaborate issues like fights between husbands and wives.

Reiter had been sitting on Martine's porch a few years ago, listening to stories and nursing a beer when suddenly Martine had changed the tone of the conversation. "I've been wanting to talk to you about something," he'd begun, looking at Reiter. "The word has gone out that we have a doctor here from time to time."

"Don't tell me the Mexican government is finally going to send a doctor?"

Martine didn't let him finish the sentence. "Not exactly. But you seem to be coming here pretty often now, and I know you've helped people with medical problems from time to time. So what I was thinking," and here Martine gave Reiter one of his gold-toothed smiles, "why not make it a regular thing? Once a month maybe. Even give it a name to make it official. Something like Clinica Day." His enthusiasm made it sound as if it was a foregone conclusion.

Before long, Clinica Day had become a regular event, and Martine was the one who kept it going. Tomorrow would be no different, Reiter reminded himself as they put the last bag in the jeep and drove to Martine's cluttered porch. After they'd unloaded the medical supplies, he clapped Martine on the back. "Good to be here, amigo. How about a cold one?"

The two of them settled on the saggy couch with their beer and talked about the preparations for the next day's clinic.

"There's another one with a hare-lip coming in tomorrow." Martine didn't sound too concerned. "Juanita, the mother, and her husband came in by panga last night."

"How old is this one?" he casually asked.

"Let me see…" Martine wrinkled his forehead. "Two, I think. I ran into them in Muleje last month," he went on. "The father is the sour kind. Doesn't like doctors as I recall."

They rambled on for a while about the people who might be coming to the clinic and then got into a discussion about Cobo and his help. Finally, they climbed back into Martine's jeep and drove the food and water up the hill to the Reiter's sprawling house.

When the children returned from the beach, they piled the driftwood they'd collected into the barbecue pit for a cookout. Blue curls of smoke rose from the glowing coals and gave off an acrid smell that mingled with the salty air from the bay. Linda put fresh shrimp on the grill while the children set the table on the patio. It was a treat to eat outdoors, and the family lingered over their meal until the desert sky was filled with stars.

"Where are all the stars when we're at home?" Robin wanted to know. Even at the ranch, the night sky was never so clear, and in the city one could never see stars in the sky. Reiter tried to explain the difference artificial lights and air pollution made in the atmosphere.

When she still looked puzzled, he decided he had a better answer. "It's the magic of Baja."

He was pleasantly tired when he and his wife went to bed later that night, but remembering the scheduled interview made him tense up. He felt a need to seek refuge from his thoughts and gently brushed the back of her neck with his lips. Compliantly, she bent her face forward. "I have a hunch the Englishman might show up this weekend," he whispered.

Slowly, she turned towards him. "What makes you so sure?" She placed the tip of a finger on his lips when he tried to answer. "Sh, Sh," she insisted with a smile, pulling him closer. "Tomorrow is another day." She reached behind her and turned off the light. "But tonight is tonight."

CHAPTER FOUR

They woke the next morning to the red and orange glow of the sun rising out of the Sea of Cortez. From his patio on the hill, Reiter gazed in all directions, letting his eyes wander along the russet canyons that flowed into the glittering waves of the sea. This morning the bay had turned into rivulets of sand, the low tide baring all the secrets of the sea. He could see imprints of the giant manta rays that had lain on the bottom during the night. And he watched seagulls tiptoeing over the sand in search of the elusive razorback crabs buried there in abundance. Perched on the rocks at the far end of the bay was the usual flock of pelicans. There was a familiar beat to their shrill chants.

Walking down the hill, he could see Martine was getting ready for Clinica Day. He was methodical in the way he prepared the long table on his porch. First, he swept off the empty beer bottles, blown-out tires, and the rest of the junk. Next, he lined up throat swabs, the flashlight, surgical pliers, sutures, syringes, and something that looked like a stethoscope from another era. Martine seemed to stretch out the ritual of setting up as long as he could. It was obvious that Clinica Day was his favorite day of the month.

Martine's one-room house, dwarfed by a shady porch, was a dusty collection of shelves crammed with bandages, casts, potions, and pills. He had to step over cardboard boxes just to get to his bed. "The health of the village is what counts," he always insisted. The few times that Reiter didn't show up, Clinica Day went on without him. At the last minute, Martine would pick an assistant. Usually, it was Cobo.

On Clinica Days, Martine didn't t allow for distractions. He made sure every second counted. Patiently, he plodded between his 'supply room' and the table outside, stopping to swat flies and cast curious glances at the people slowly gathering near the porch. The prospective patients sat quietly and just watched and waited for their turn. Cobo was in charge of ushering them in today.

The first patient he brought to the porch was the slender young mother from Muleje that Martine had talked about. She seemed uneasy, as if looking for someone; her sparkling dark eyes darted all over. Some of her waist-length black hair was tied back in a bun. She kept trying to still the unhappy toddler, embarrassed by its whimpering as she rocked it back and forth. When the crying wouldn't stop she got up and paced the floor. A lanky young man, almost hidden under a straw hat, leaned against a rusty car, keeping an eye on her. "My husband," she said when Cobo asked who he was.

Reiter tried to put her at ease. "Como estas?"

"Bien, gracias," she replied without taking her eyes off the child.

Jaime, the father, stared at the ground. "Leave the boy the way God made him. He'll never be like other children," he muttered.

"Jaime doesn't trust doctors," Martine explained. He calls them 'Matasanos'. You know what that means…'killers of the healthy'."

Still, the strange gap in the child's lip must have bothered Jaime, and according to his wife, he spent more and more time alone in his fishing boat at sea. Even when the fish were not running, he went out, probably thinking about his boy with the strange mouth. "Yes, Juanita, he looks like a fish," he told her one day.

Reiter could imagine what must have gone through Juanita's mind. She didn't want her child to look like a fish. "If your Espanto can fix it," she said to Martine, "why not?" So she and Jaime had come by boat from Muleje for Clinica Day. It had taken them a week. They stayed at the fish camp north of town while they waited for the doctor.

This morning, Juanita frowned as she watched Reiter lift the upper lip of her little boy with a wooden stick and inspect the inside of his mouth. "No te preocupes," he told her. "We can fix this." He made it sound easy. Then he turned to Martine. "It's a unilateral cleft lip. We'll have to send him up north."

People kept trickling to the porch, but Reiter couldn't get his mind off Juanita. He'd seen so many afflictions of man, but birth defects bothered him the most. He'd seen what they could do to a family. And they had more than their share down here. A combination of poor diet, poor hygiene, no prenatal care, intermarriage, and who knew what else.

The tense moments of each delivery back at University Hospital suddenly flooded through his mind. Most of the time it was a joyful event, but sometimes it seemed that everything went wrong. When he was still an intern, one of his first deliveries had been that way. He remembered the long and difficult labor with the young mother panting and crying in pain. Finally, the baby was delivered, and Reiter thought he'd pass out when he first saw the child. The baby had only one eye, and it was in the middle of the forehead. For a minute, he wanted to turn around and run. Then he took a deep breath and got hold of himself. Instinctively, he lowered the baby out of the mother's sight. The anesthesiologist understood right away and quickly sedated her. Reiter cut the umbilical cord and handed the child to a nurse. Then he shuddered. What could he tell this young mother? And what about the husband out in the waiting room? How could he explain this cruel twist of nature to him? It had been a devastating experience.

At least for Juanita's child there's hope, Reiter thought. Jaime won't have to stay out in his panga and think about his son with the strange mouth.

The next patient was Felipe, the son of a fisherman from the south end of town. He grinned as he held up his hands and spread his fingers wide apart. When Reiter first saw Felipe a year ago, his hands had looked like shovels, with the fingers webbed together. The hands had been a stark contrast to the fine, well-shaped nose and sensitive mouth of his handsome face.

Reiter had taken Felipe to his clinic in California where he made zigzag cuts between the webbed fingers of the club- like hands. The medical term for these incisions was 'z-plasties' because they looked like long 'Zees'. Then they'd grafted skin from under Felipe's arms to cover the raw flesh between the fingers.

During the time Felipe was away, his mother told Martine that she kept a candle burning before a picture of the Virgin of Guadalupe. Apparently, her husband was another one who didn't trust the 'matasano,' and he vowed he would never forgive his wife for letting the boy go with Reiter. Like Jaime, he probably thought of a fish when he looked at his son's hands. Maybe to him they looked like fins. "Good for moving through the water. He will make a good fisherman just the way he is," he told his wife.

After Felipe hands had healed, Reiter flew him back to Puertecitos. When Felipe held up his hands and spread his fingers apart, the look on the faces of his parents told a thousand stories. Tears trickled down his mother's cheeks. She made the sign of the cross. "Madre de Dios, un miraglo," she said. Felipe's father stared in disbelief, then opened his arms and embraced his boy.

Now, a year later, Reiter examined the young boy's hands, and he was glad they didn't look like fins anymore. Even Cobo was smiling.

The sun climbed higher and the stream of patients seemed to have no end. Martine kept order, calling each person by name if he knew it or her or making one up if he didn't. He'd nod at Cobo, who would usher them onto the porch. They would sit down, and first, Martine would attach a blood pressure cuff to their arm. From time to time he'd call out, "Silencio", to the others, as if to remind them that this was serious business. Like a colorful rainbow, the strange assembly of people hung over Martine's porch. For the very sick this was a place of hope; for the rest it was a refuge from daily toils and worries.

By mid afternoon, the patients stopped coming and a gentle breeze began to blow out of the canyon. "I think I'll head for the beach for a while." Reiter felt apologetic because Martine gave no sign of slowing down. He continued with his work, boiling instruments and putting supplies away.

"Watch for sharks," Martine said, flashing a toothy smile.

***

Reiter and his family got up early the next morning, armed themselves with shovels and buckets and headed to North Beach. As he sat with Linda at the edge of the wet sand, Reiter felt a familiar glow of contentment watching the children play in the tide pools. Shane's green eyes darted across the sand as he looked for telltale signs of buried clams. When he dug one up, he studied the intricate groves before adding it to the clam bucket. The wiry boy seemed to be a collection of bones in constant motion. He turned to his sister who was nearly as tall as he, her straw blond hair whipping across her delicate face. Holding an empty shell to her ear, Shane asked, "Can you hear the ocean in there?"

But the drone of a Piper approaching from the north interrupted Robin's answer. Shane dropped the shell and looked up. Reiter shaded his eyes from the sun and searched for the aircraft. He squinted when he caught a glimpse of Ciro's plane, remembering the call from London. "They made it," he groaned, turning to Linda. "Never underestimate the British."

Reaching for Linda's hand, he started walking toward the airstrip. The children, curious, were not far behind. A leather sombrero pulled down over his forehead shielded Reiter's eyes from the bright sun and a denim shirt and faded jeans hugged his lean frame. Linda's petite body was clad in a pale blue beach dress with burgundy buttons down the front, her black hair tied back in a bun. They watched the puff of dust as the plane touched down and then taxied toward the end of the runway. Ciro parked his plane next to Reiter's blue Cessna.

Gordon Townsend had brought his wife, Deborah, and a cameraman for the appointed interview. Reiter couldn't ignore the long, shapely legs of Deborah as she climbed out of the small plane onto the hot, dusty runway. A thin white dress hugged her curvaceous frame. There were no signs of perspiration on her dress, a sharp contrast to the sweat-stained shirts of the others in the plane.

She must know how to handle the heat, Reiter thought. When she extended her slender hand, he was aware that she held his own longer than necessary.

"It's a pleasure to meet you," she smiled. Before he had a chance to respond, she added, "You look younger than we expected." She turned to her husband. "Wouldn't you agree, dear?" She seemed to ignore the others as she cast her green eyes at Reiter. Finally, she spoke to Linda. "Indeed, it's so lovely to meet you," she added, her voice a shade cooler. "And are these beautiful children yours?"

Deborah appeared cool and unruffled, her make-up impeccable, her face serene. But looking more closely, Reiter detected a downward pull at the corners of her mouth that reminded him of bitterness and a slight puffiness under her eyes that spoke of late nights and too much gin.

Gordon Townsend and his cameraman, Allister McGregor, introduced themselves in crisp, British accents. Reiter studied their faces as well: Gordon, a Brit with a prominent nose and protruding jaw that seemed to fit the blustering spirit that was so evident in the phone call from London; thick, horn- rimmed glasses seemed to obscure his eyes and his true feelings; McGregor, the cameraman, was a bulky Scotsman whose hound-dog eyes gave the impression he hadn't slept well in years.

Instinctively, Reiter visualized what he could do with their faces. He could imagine sliding under their skin with his gloved hands and long scissors, cutting the layer of skin and freeing it from the muscle beneath, then gently draping it back and snipping off what was left over. He could give McGregor smooth eyelids and no jowls, Gordon a thin Roman nose, Deborah a new neck line with the corners of her mouth pointing up, the puffiness under her eyelids gone.

His thoughts were broken by a nudge at his arm. It was Deborah. "We're very glad to finally meet you," she repeated. "My husband was told it would be impossible to find you, that you keep to yourself. Is that why in Hollywood you're known as the Phantom?"

Reiter nodded absently, half-lost in his own thoughts. "I wouldn't know about that," he finally answered.

Linda seemed to read his mood and gave her husband a barely detectable smile. He picked up her understanding look and smiled back. She turned to Deborah. "Please, won't you have lunch with us at the cantina?"

Deborah hesitated and then nodded. She shot another look at Reiter as she started off down the beach with Linda and the children. Gordon and the cameraman trudged along with their equipment.

Reiter stayed to help Ciro tie down the plane. As they worked, Cobo ambled over to them, hands in his pockets. His unkempt black hair hung limply to his collar. His neck had as many wrinkles as the ripples of sand in the bay. But when he cocked back his head to sing, the ripples flattened out as if washed away by his words. Every part of him was wrinkled and worn, but he didn't seem old. There was no way of telling his age; he acted like a youngster at times, and then for no reason he'd slow down as if he'd lived a thousand years.

The shirt he wore was bleached by a lifetime of sweat, yet it didn't look soiled. Frayed sleeves hung loosely above arms that looked like sticks, and his fingers were spider-like, with thick knuckles. After years of scraping fish scales, permanent green-black stains rimmed his nails. Threadbare trousers hung from his frame, held in place by the rope he used as a belt. A string was tied around the cuff of each pant leg. When he was asked about it, he'd point to his ankles, "Why would anyone want scorpions or snakes crawling up his pants?"

Cobo had worked in the fish camps for most of his life. But for the last few years he often complained that the work was too hard and didn't pay very much. There was seldom enough money for a glass of tequila at the end of the day. And then one day he ran into some gringos in front of the cantina who asked him about fishing.

He got in their boat and took them out on the sea he knew so well. They ended up catching their limit. The next day he scrawled "Fishing Gide" on the tarp in front of his shack and everything changed. He had plenty of money to buy all the tequila he wanted.

Cobo eyed the television camera and the British crew with a suspicious frown. Though he offered to help with the luggage, there was a "Who-are- those-stuffy- windbags?" smirk written all over his face.

Trying to divert any unwelcome questions from Cobo, Reiter turned to Ciro. "You should probably leave in the morning when it's cooler, amigo." It was nearly one hundred degrees, and the air was too thin for a safe take-off on the short, bumpy airstrip. "Have dinner with us at the house tonight," he added.

"Si, Doctor. It's a good idea." Townsend had talked about flying back after the interview, but as a reasonable man, Reiter was sure he would listen to the pilot.

Ciro was small-boned and short, his craggy face divided by a bushy mustache that hung over his upper lip like a heavy curtain that had to be raised whenever he talked. In the many years they'd known each other, it didn't seem to Reiter that he'd aged or changed at all.

After the plane was secured, they walked to the cantina. Standing behind the bar handing out drinks to the thirsty travelers was Don Rafael, the man who had founded the village of Puertecitos. Everyone here called him 'El Patron.'

As a young fisherman, Don Rafael wandered along these shores before the Second World War. He often told Reiter the story of how he'd been fishing along the Baja coast when he first saw the little bay of Puertecitos. One look at the quiet cove with its lava-lined pools of mineral springs and he knew he'd found his home. Shortly after that he brought his family to the bay, claiming the homestead rights granted by the Mexican government. Homesteading was the only way the government could get people to settle this barren land that teemed with snakes and coyotes.

There was something regal about the way 'El Patron' held his head when he spoke, his erect posture, and his refined and courtly features. 'A true Spaniard', his daughters proudly proclaimed. His high forehead projected an air of wisdom and nobility, but his sparkling eyes gave away his true nature, gentle and accommodating. A permanent smile was his most outstanding feature. His presence lent an air of harmony to the village.

Don Rafael had convinced some of his fishermen friends to stay on and rent a lot from him. On occasion, because of a chubasco or because they didn't want to endure another life-threatening trip across the gulf, other fishermen took him up on his offer. Over the years, the fishermen were joined by 'Norte Americanos' who were attracted by the rugged nature and stoic solitude of the land, or who were trying to escape a shady past. All of them built shelters and shacks on Don Rafael's 'lotes'. The Indians and Mexicans put them together with driftwood and scrap lumber, while the Norte Americanos always managed to go for something a little fancier—cement pads and plywood panels hauled down from the north. Within a few years, a strange collection of shacks and well-built homes sprang up around the bay.

In time, Don Rafael built the 'cantina'—a bar, eatery, and office all in one. It became the recreational center of the village, where everyone went for music and fun. Don Rafael spent hours behind the bar, greeting residents and strangers, selling them beer and sodas. Endless stacks of papers stashed on rows of uneven shelves gave the place the air of a dusty old town hall. "Mi officina," he called it, and smiled. Rumpled bills and receipts and contracts were stuffed between bottles of beer and tequila. Only Don Rafael could make sense of the mess.

Reiter greeted Don Rafael and made his way to the table where his family and the English visitors were sitting. Gordon was talking about the run-in they had with the Mexican customs officials at the border. "You should have seen those blokes with their pearl-handled pistols," he said as he drew his hands to his hips. "Sitting there eating their meat pasties." His tone of voice left no doubt what he thought of the customs officers. "At first they ignored us. Finally they mumbled something in the most awful English about our passports. They insisted there was no way for us to cross into Mexico. They sounded pretty emphatic, didn't they?" He looked at McGregor and went on. " At that point I knew I had to impress upon them that I work in television." His voice got louder. "Yes, that does it every time. Mention television or newspapers and people pay attention."

"That didn't seem to impress them," McGregor chimed in. "They were still outright rude and left us in limbo."

Gordon gave him a disparaging glance. "It's true they didn't believe us at first, and they kept asking all sorts of questions. What kind of television crew would go to Puertecitos, they asked. Coyotes and snakes are the only things to film there.

"So I tried a different approach and told them about the interview with Dr. Reiter. You should have seen their faces light up. 'Why didn't you tell us that in the first place?' they said. They were all smiles after that and wouldn't stop apologizing." Gordon laughed and took a long drink.

Just then Rafael's niece, Carmencita, emerged from the kitchen with a huge platter. The rich smell of fried shrimp and tacos rose in the air. Carmencita set the platter on a long plywood table. She hummed as she swatted at the flies and hissed at a few seagulls perched at the end of the patio.

Gordon picked up a taco and studied it. "Just like the pasties that the Mexican officials were eating," he said and put it back down.

"That's called a taco," Ciro laughed. "I bet there's nothing that good where you come from."

Gordon ignored him and started telling stories about life in London and his feats as a television journalist. "Just last week I finished an interview with Richard Burton." He made it sound like a casual remark. "Richard Burton," he repeated, his voice rising when he noticed the others weren't paying attention. Finally, he gave up and turned to Deborah. "This place is no Puerto Vallarta."

"It most certainly isn't, and I'm beginning to wonder about your Phantom," she answered under her breath.

Reiter caught the end of their conversation and felt a surge of anger. In an effort to ignore it, he waved to a lanky man at the end of the bar. "Enrique, la musica, por favor."

It was clear that Enrique was the right man for the job. He brushed his thin mustache with the back of his hand and took his guitar off the wall. Closing his eyes, he cocked back his head and started to croon, "Gabino Berrera..." Almost sobbing, his voice faded and surged, rising steadily until it broke into a shattering cry.

A distant look came into Reiter's eyes, the look he had when his mind roamed the canyons and the shores and deserts around him. Mexican music always did that to him. The beautiful ballads about canyons and valleys and towns with at least one hero, sometimes two, fiercely entrenched in struggles against corrupt governments and unfaithful lovers. Reiter could feel himself drifting among the tall cacti in the shimmering heat of the sand or on the wind-swept shores at the foot of steep canyons. As he listened to the music, he let the ballad creep into his soul. If he closed his eyes he could see Enrique's hero, Berrera, galloping through the hills of Sonora, leading his people. A real 'hombre', a leader, a legend.

As Enrique sang, the sights and sounds of the cantina were only a faint rumble in a distant sky. Then suddenly, like unwelcome thunder, a loud voice with a crisp British accent startled Reiter out of his reverie.

"Where do you suppose we could do the interview? We need some background shots first."

Reiter didn't respond right away, and Gordon cleared his throat a few times, ready to ask once again. Then Reiter turned towards the bay. "Down there on the beach near the runway," he suggested. "That's where it all began."

Rudi Unterthiner

And one day, there on the beach, Reiter would take Consuelo, setting in motion dark and unforgiving events.

CHAPTER FIVE

Reiter and Linda waited at the cantina while the Englishmen set up their equipment. His doubts about the interview were growing. The non-distinct gray of the sky, in spite of a bright sun, cast a mystic pall over a day that would end up with many unsettled questions.

The place Gordon picked to film— next to a dilapidated shack at the far end of the beach—didn't make sense. "Old Larry isn't going to like having those people in his front yard," Reiter remarked to his wife. "I can imagine what he'll say."

Larry was like many of the Americans who had settled in Puertecitos over the years, never giving a reason for ending up here. He often bragged about his days as a big shot electrical contractor in Arizona, but he never mentioned the town. He would go on about the hundreds of workers he'd employed and the contracts he'd juggled, but not one word about why he left.

"I've got to see this," Reiter said. He got up and made his way to Larry's shack. Linda went in the opposite direction to get the children.

Gordon was making notes on a yellow pad. "Just make sure that shack doesn't get into the view," he said to McGregor. "Or that battered old car." He grimaced as he pointed to it.

McGregor eyed the car with the chipped paint flaking off the rusty metal and shrugged, "I know, I know," he sighed.

As if he overheard the remarks, Larry suddenly appeared in the doorway with a threatening scowl.

"I say, would you very much mind moving your jalopy?" McGregor asked, trying his best to sound congenial. "I'm afraid it could block my shot."

Larry glared at McGregor and paused to slap at a persistent mosquito on his neck. "What did you call my car?" he asked as he spit on the sand.

Townsend rushed over as if to try a different approach. "Look, sir," he said as he tugged at his collar. "We're doing a documentary here, a film for British television. We want to take some shots with Dr. Reiter on the beach." He hesitated when he noticed the "I don't give a damn" look on Larry's face. "It's just that we can't have your vehicle in the scene. I'm sure you can understand," he added.

Larry was known around Puertecitos for his sharp tongue, but for some reason he must have decided to let Townsend off the hook. He jumped into the car and drove to the other side of the shack. McGregor winced at the banging of the engine and the puffs of blue smoke from the exhaust. Larry slammed the door of the car. "I don't want no part of this bull shit," he grumbled as he stomped across his neighbor's yard.

The neighbor, Dave, nodded as if he agreed, but that was just his way of staying out of Larry's hair. Dave was a placid old man with grizzled gray whiskers and a baldhead. He had retired from a Jeep-Willys factory after twenty-seven years on the assembly line. He kept to himself—just he and the fifty cats he'd acquired down here. Fish heads were strewn about the shack and Dave spent a good part of each day feeding his cats or fishing for their food. The rest of the time he tinkered methodically with his rusty Jeep. It was as if he'd never left the assembly line.

Reiter glanced over and saw that Cobo had joined Larry and Dave, 'the cat man'. Behind them on the beach Consuelo was sunning herself, her soft curves molded into the white sand. His eyes lingered on the on the dark-haired woman who had been creeping regularly into his dreams. His eyes lingered oner long thighs, fleshy and inviting. He frowned, annoyed at himself and at the unmistakable heat rising from his loins. He was surprised at the effort it took to tear himself away.

Gordon and McGregor had arranged two canvas chairs in the sand. Seagulls and buzzards circled overhead as Reiter and Gordon took their seats and McGregor's camera began to whirr.

39

"So tell us, Dr. Reiter," Gordon finally began, "What's it like to work so intimately on famous and powerful people, to have their lives in your hands?" He lowered his voice. "Does that ever make you feel as if you're playing God?"

"I never thought of it that way. They're just patients to me. And I like working with my hands," Reiter added, eyeing his hands. They seemed rather ordinary, he thought. Not particularly pampered. The fingers were long and slender and there were prominent grooves in the palms. "Ever since I can remember I've felt my life would depend on my hands."

Gordon studied them too. "But those hands," he insisted, "have worked on famous people, haven't they?"

"They're just hands," Reiter shrugged. "Could belong to a carver or a miner. My grandfather worked in the mines." He glanced at Linda. "For a while I worked there myself."

"That's extraordinary. Yes, indeed extraordinary," Gordon commented. "Would you care to explain how a person could begin in a coal mine and end up as a plastic surgeon in Hollywood? " He smiled. "You must admit the leap from mining to medicine isn't exactly an everyday story. And all this in opposite parts of the globe." He paused for only a moment and straightened his jacket. "Do you mind telling us about it?"

Reiter crossed his legs and leaned back in his chair. "Towards the end of the war the Allies bombed the Brenner Pass where we lived. They were trying to blow up the railroad bridge. We spent hours in the air raid shelters …caves dug in the mountains. Many times we came out to find bomb craters in the fields, more wounded and dead." He looked down at the sand, then back at the camera. "It made me feel helpless and small. Maybe that's when I began to dream that I could someday use my hands…" His voice cracked slightly. "Use my hands to work on disfigured bodies."

"And what's all this about a coal mine?"

"It was just a way to make money. Work in the coal mines paid well."

"That still doesn't explain California and Hollywood," Gordon interrupted. "Did your family immigrate to the States after the war?"

Reiter had a pensive look. "No, I came alone...in nineteen fifty-seven. I didn't see my family again for twelve years."

Gordon paused for a moment and then raised his voice as if trying to clear up a misunderstanding. "This noble calling that brought you to America. What happened to it? You're not fixing disfigured bodies now. You're performing surgery—and correct me if I'm wrong—surgery for looks. For vanity, wouldn't you say?" When Reiter said nothing, Gordon glanced at McGregor and continued his barrage. "To me it looks like you've strayed from your true calling. Or do small breasts count as disfigurements?"

Reiter frowned. "I understand what you're driving at. And frankly, plastic surgery wasn't my first choice. I thought I'd become a neurosurgeon, operating on the brain, the nervous system."

He thought he detected a flicker of surprise in Gordon's eyes, as if he was disappointed there could be another explanation.

Reiter continued. "I tried it for a few months, but I found I wasn't cut out for work on hopeless cases...stroke victims, accidents, people always dying. Something in me was weak." He couldn't hide his embarrassment. "I couldn't cope with it. I couldn't face the coward in me."

Gordon's face lit up with a 'touché' type of grin as if he had uncovered a long-hidden secret. Or did he think he was dismantling a myth?

Suddenly McGregor interrupted them. "Can we hold it for just a minute? I'm running out of film. " He pulled a metal container out of a bag. "We'll be editing for years if we don't keep this on track," he warned.

Gordon lit another cigarette. "Why don't we take a short break?" he said.

***

While McGregor was loading the camera, Reiter made his way to the edge of the water and watched a pelican as it circled overhead and dive into the water, coming up with a fish in its oversized beak. Gordon's questions propelled him back to those harrowing nights in the Emergency Department of the sprawling University Hospital. He remembered the Sunday evening when fate shuffled the cards and changed the direction of his surgical training:

It had happened at the end of a twenty-four hour grind as a resident on the neurosurgical service. Every second had been grueling and he'd finally had a chance to collapse on the rollaway bed in the corner of the doctors' lounge. He hadn't been asleep long when the phone started ringing. It took a long time for him to come out of that sleep, to wake up and figure out where he was. He threw his feet on the floor and rubbed his face with both hands. Then he shook his head, trying to bring himself to the present. "What is it now?" he mumbled. Like a drunken old man he reached for the receiver. At first he missed it. The damn thing fell off the cradle and bounced on the floor. The shrill voice of a nurse sounded like a lost echo in some far away cavern. "Gun shot wound to the head."

He rubbed his tired eyes and flicked on the light. The sweet fragrance of blooming lilacs drifted in through the window and he found himself resigned to an uneasy state of mind, as if sensing an unusual twist in the order of things. He felt trapped in what had turned out to be a specialty at the outer edges of life, closer to death than life. Like in the coal mine. Lately he'd been more and more troubled by the never-ending head injuries, car accidents, bullet wounds and strokes that blundered in through the night. It seemed he was watching a parade of the remnants of life balancing on trenches of death.

Picking up the phone again, he heard the voice clearly. "There's a bad one out here. An attempted suicide. You'd better come quick."

"What about vital signs? " he snapped back.

But the nurse didn't allow him to dwell on that. "His head is blown off," she said flatly. "Well, most of it. He's still breathing."

In the corridor the dark blue uniforms of two policemen stood out against the white wall. The bright fluorescent lights high on the ceiling gave them a pasty, pale look, as if they'd come from the moon. Two nurses ran up to him as he reached the door. "An attempted suicide," one of them rattled on.

Blood oozed out of ragged pieces of bone and what was left of a skull. There was no face above the teeth. He thought he detected the hint of a smile in the curling lower lip that quivered among a few bloody teeth—a grotesque sort of grin that must have been on his face the instant before he pulled the trigger, blowing the other half of the smile up to the ceiling. A mass of red jelly oozed out of the hole where the brain had been. Reiter smelled singed flesh and it turned his stomach. For a minute it made him gag. Then he saw it again, a grimace on what was left of the face.

He sought refuge in his detached professional side as he put a stethoscope on the hairless chest, moving it like a pawn on a chessboard. The nurse looked on as if waiting for orders. But Reiter kept listening for a sign of life, a breath, a heartbeat, or the gurgling sounds of the bowels. He couldn't seem to find any sounds though he kept pushing the stethoscope around. He knew the chess game was lost; death was winning. But it wasn't going to win swiftly and mercifully. It would be slow and painful.

The man on the gurney suddenly took a few deep breaths, shaking wildly for a second or two. His convulsions startled Reiter, and he backed off, as if to get out of the way in case he might grab him. The nurses standing at the end of the gurney stared. One held up an I.V. bottle, like some last minute weapon.

"We won't need that," Reiter said, feeling defeated already.

The game went on for several hours while what was left of the man kept struggling, as if trying to get out of death's unyielding grip. Reiter found himself wondering if the man's soul had second thoughts after a fleeting glimpse of the other side. Perhaps it had decided to come back, hoping it wasn't too late. Or could it be that the body hadn't wanted to go along from the beginning? Who made the fateful decision, the body or the soul? Nothing about the game seemed fair, but it was already lost.

He glanced at the clock, grateful that the shift was over and he could leave. He was almost out the door when he heard the familiar whine of an ambulance as it approached the Emergency Room entrance. Probably another car accident, he remembered thinking.

He passed the paramedics wheeling in a gurney with a young boy on it. It must have been the feeble whimpering, the distant look and tears in the boy's eyes that made Reiter follow them. By the time he reached the bed in the corridor, nurses were already hooking up the monitoring machines, checking vital signs. An I.V. was started and pain medication injected into the tube.

The child's right arm and hand were wrapped in a bloodstained bandage that was strapped across his chest. "Let's take a quick look," Reiter said as he gently lifted the arm. "I won't hurt you. Honest. Believe me." There was almost a pleading tone in his voice.

"I know," the boy whimpered and turned his head the other way.

Reiter felt a strange warm surge through his body and an inner voice telling him what to do. It was almost a command: "Help this child." He knew he had to do something for the little boy, but he didn't know that this decision would affect the rest of his life.

With scissors he gently cut the bandage away. Layer by layer he peeled off the wet dressing that was wrapped around the little hand. When he got to the final layer he braced himself for the worst, but even then he wasn't prepared for what he saw. It took all his inner strength not to flinch, to appear matter-of-fact when he stared at the carnage.

Strings of glistening white tendons and sharp fragments of bone stuck out of ground up red pulp. The fingers hung backwards, attached to a few strands of flesh as if they didn't belong there. What was left of the thumb was stripped bare of flesh.

"It's okay, my friend. It's okay. We're going to fix this. Believe me, will you?" he said as he leaned over and patted the boy on the cheek. He didn't think he sounded that reassuring, but the boy licked the tears trickling down his cheek and flashed the hint of a smile.

Reiter's lip quivered and he placed the boy's hand over a basin near the bed. He poured a sterile solution of saline over it and began to gently cleanse the wound. The boy closed his eyes and seemed to drift off to sleep.

"His father was cutting grass," a paramedic explained. "He told us that when the mower stopped, he left it sitting there, thinking it just needed more gas. That's when the boy must have started fooling with the blades. There must have been a short somewhere because suddenly the motor started up again. You can see what happened after that."

"Let's get him to the operating room as soon as we can. And call Dr. Hansen," Reiter interrupted.

Dr. Hansen was the plastic surgeon on call. He was known as one of the best hand surgeons in the country.

Once in the operating room, Hansen showed him how to meticulously line up the splinters of bone and then drill pins into them to hold them in place. They kept checking the x-rays plastered to the lighted frames on the wall and spent hours matching vessels, nerves, tendons, painstakingly piecing them together with tiny stitches and wires. Reiter's eyes were glued on the puzzle before him and hardly noticed when Hansen stood up. "You can handle it now," Hansen said. "I'll be back."

Reiter glowed with pride, happy and content to be left in charge. With every tiny piece of the mosaic that he put in place, the little hand gradually gained some of its original shape. By the time Hansen slipped back into the operating room, Reiter had almost finished. It was late in the afternoon.

They placed the final stitches in the skin and slipped the hand into what looked like a tennis racket, with strings holding the fingers apart. They put cotton between the webs of the fingers and a loose bandage over it.

He felt the rush of adrenaline pounding in his temples. He knew there was hope. Hope for the child's hand and hope for him. That was the moment he decided to get out of neurosurgery. He would become a plastic surgeon and get out of the trenches of hopeless cases. Yet he knew he could make a difference in people's lives.

***

"Let's roll!" McGregor's voice snapped Reiter back to the present. He walked to the 'set' aware that he could never really share these experiences with others, certainly not with the journalist waiting for him. Still, he was taken aback by Gordon's next words, "So the next thing, as you say, you find yourself doing plastic surgery instead. Working on faces and bodies only for beauty. And making money." Gordon bit his lip and hesitated, but his journalistic instinct pressed on. "You can't deny the monetary rewards of your work. All those beautiful faces and bodies have made you millions."

Reiter's eyes flickered, and he shifted in his chair. Gordon ignored that and shot a brief look at McGregor. 'I hope you caught that on film' was what his look seemed to say. Or 'make sure that shows. I want every one to see the phantom squirming.' Without missing a beat, Gordon continued like a stubborn inquisitor. "It is a matter of public record that you earn a lot of money operating on people who have a craving for beauty." He glanced at his notebook. "It looks like you cost them a penny or two, doesn't it?"

Out of the corner of his eye, Reiter saw Linda get up from her chair. She walked behind him and put a hand on his shoulder, her eyes fixed on Gordon. "I think," she began as she brushed the hair out of her eyes, "I think," she repeated, "Some of your questions are misguided."

"I'm sorry, madam, but we can't use..." Gordon moved his hand across his throat as he looked at McGregor. "Cut," he commanded.

She glanced down at her husband and caught his appreciative look. It seemed to give her courage. "Let me make something clear," she insisted, taking a step towards Gordon. "My husband," she explained, " doesn't care about money. Never has. In fact, I'd be surprised if he has the faintest idea of his annual income." She paused and nodded towards her husband's clasped hands.

"I'm sorry, madam. Please, let me assure you," Gordon added hastily, "I'm not accusing your husband of being driven by money. All I'm trying to do is shed some light on the facts. For our viewers."

Linda continued, her voice soft, but with a note of determination. "You heard for yourself how he came to this country, by himself, without a penny, hardly speaking English." She cleared her throat as if to hold down her emotions. "He worked at dozens of jobs to put himself through school...as a janitor, a ski instructor, a bush pilot..."

Reiter became aware of the warmth of the Baja sun on his back as Linda's voice rose like the crest of a wave. "It's obvious you have no idea of the time he spends taking care of people down here. What do you think he earns here?" She looked over at the Mexican fishermen on the beach. "The truth is, a lot of the money he makes ends up in places like this."

On one of Dave's rickety chairs, Cobo sat next to Larry and Alfonso, the village carpenter. He spoke little English and probably couldn't tell what the argument was about, but his fist tightened around the shells he'd picked up, and he kept shifting his eyes from Townsend to Linda. Suddenly he threw the shells on the ground and headed straight toward Townsend.

Gordon's eyes widened. "Won't you sit down sir? Please?"

Cobo stopped and stood, hands on his hips, glaring at Townsend. "Is this man trying to insult you, Espanto?"

McGregor was frozen behind the camera, his mouth slightly open.

"No," Reiter said quickly. "He's just asking me about my work. Linda took it the wrong way, amigo."

"I'm not so sure about that," Linda said softly.

Reiter looked up into her face. "Believe me, it's fine," he said squeezing her hand.

"Yes, yes. All right, all right." Gordon said, trying to put an end to the intrusion. "Dr. Reiter, do you mind if we go on?"

For the rest of the interview, Gordon was more subdued, though he made repeated efforts to bring up the subject of celebrities. He tried every trick he knew to get some names from Reiter, but as the time slipped by, he seemed to lose his focus and eventually every one's attention.

Even McGregor didn't seem to be able to keep a sharp picture. He, who had caught celebrities through curtains and windows across London, seemed to have lost his touch in this sleepy little town under the bright Baja sun.

Reiter glanced over at the locals on the beach. He caught Cobo's attention with an expression that said he'd had enough of the interview.

Cobo got the hint. He got up again and walked over to Reiter, ignoring every one else. "What time are we leaving tomorrow? Remember you promised to take me to see my brother's place in Bahia Kino."

"Cut," Townsend shouted.

Rudi Unterthiner

CHAPTER SIX

Reiter breathed a long sigh of relief. He waited impatiently while
Mcgregor and Townsend gathered their equipment and then
made his way to the water's edge where his family waited. The rest of
the onlookers had dispersed. "Why don't we go out to the hot
baths?" he suggested. "It's been a long day."

Shane walked next to his father as they followed Linda and
Robin to the outcropping of lava rock on the point. At low tide, a
number of pools were exposed which grew warm as mineral water
bubbled into them through the sand.

"That guy sure asked a lot of questions," Shane said. "I didn't
know you were away from home so long. Oma must have been sad."

"Could you stay away from us so long?" Robin slowed down
and turned towards her father.

Reiter felt dryness in the back of his throat. "They weren't easy,
those days. I never had the money to go back home. But in my heart
I knew they understood."

The family stepped into the warm waters of the mineral baths.
Reiter settled at the edge of the pool and let his mind drift slowly
back through the years. Being away from his homeland had been
painful. The village at the foot of the Alps where he'd spent his youth
reminded him of a fairytale painting—cobblestone streets and faded
buildings that were a thousand years old, tidy farmhouses with stones
holding down the shingled roofs, and a foaming river meandering
through the narrow valley. Mountain meadows sprouted wild flowers
on the steep slopes rising from the valley floor. The only thing that
spoiled the painting was a massive beam painted with green and red
stripes that cut across the gravel road. It marked the border that tore
the region in two—on one side of the border the Alps were part of
Austria, on the other side, the same mountains belonged to the
Italian Republic. Yet the people on both sides of the border spoke
the same language, came from the same stock.

He'd heard stories from his grandmother how everything had changed at the end of World War I. Overnight there was a new border where victors had drawn a line through the landscape. "The peacemakers in Versailles didn't care about us," she often said with a note of sadness and dismay in her voice. "Thousands of people were herded down the road because they had the wrong blood—German or Italian, French or Jew—or they were from the wrong side of the border."

Another devastating war would be fought because of borders and blood. After the bombs of the Second World War stopped raining down and peace was declared, Reiter ran into an American soldier sitting by the side of the road, balancing a rifle across his knees. The man spoke a little broken Italian, and Reiter couldn't believe his ears when he started telling him about his home—Idaho or Iowa, he called it, Reiter couldn't be sure. But it was a place with no borders, the man told him, and nobody cared about bloodlines.

The soldier's words lit a fire in his mind that secretly smoldered, and over time became an obsession. He was determined to find out if such a place really existed. But first he had to get there. The thought consumed every moment of his day, though he kept it a secret, not daring to talk about it to his family or his friends in the village.

At every turn all he heard was 'no'. The 'no' of the clerk at the American Consulate was firm. "No visa is possible right now. The waiting list is long; it will take years for your name to come up".

One gloomy Monday night, when he felt himself sliding into a give-up type of mood, he decided there had to be another way. He would write a letter directly to the President of the United States and ask him for help. He knew it was a bizarre idea, but so was the idea of going to America alone. It took hours to compose a letter, writing and re-writing, then tearing up the paper and starting all over. He translated each word with the help of an old dictionary he'd dug up. Each word in that letter spelled out his determination.

Month after month he waited for an answer. After a while, he gave up hope and quit going out to meet the mailman. Finally, one rainy Saturday afternoon, the mailman surprised him. "Say, boy, are you still waiting for mail from America?" He sounded cold and official as he handed over a letter with the insignia of the United States on the envelope. "Is this what you've been waiting for?" he teased and walked off, as if he wasn't interested in the young man's response.

Reiter saw with a sinking heart that the letter wasn't from President Eisenhower. But it was from somebody important, John Foster Dulles. And under his name was written "Secretary of State".

He could hardly wait to see how Mr. Dulles would help him, and he hurried back to his room and opened the dictionary. But the letter didn't tell him anything new: It directed him to an American Consulate.

He began again. Every week he seemed to be taking a train to a different U.S. Consulate. He always had the letter with him, but it didn't prove to be an open door. He'd show it the clerks and pointed to Mr. Dulles's signature, but they just smiled and shook their heads. They'd seen a lot of form letters. The answer was still 'no.'

Then one day, he came across a balding American Consul who grabbed his hand instead of showing him the door. The man patted him on the back. "I admire your spunk," he gushed. "I like someone who won't take no for an answer." Reiter wasn't sure whom he was talking about, but the man pointed a finger at him. "You're doing things the American Way."

Reiter was inclined to tell him that it was no different from the way of his own people, but something stopped him. Then the man surprised him. "I have an idea. You could apply for a Fulbright Scholarship. You'd get a visa for sure, and they even pay for part of your plane fare and tuition to an American university." Reiter had to swallow the lump in his throat; he was too excited to speak.

He applied for the scholarship and two months later passed the qualifying examination. With the scholarship came a visa, all stamped, official and proper. Going to America was no longer a dream

The following year, he worked in the coalmine to save enough money for the fees the scholarship didn't cover. Before he left for America, he was given a lengthy list of requirements, and he had to be examined by a doctor, with laboratory examinations and a chest x-ray. He had no way of knowing the bomb he'd thrown into his dream when he left the chest x-ray behind.

It was his first time on an airplane, and he could feel his heart pounding as he strapped himself to a seat in the huge metal monster. The other passengers looked like they'd done this hundreds of times, and he felt out of place. He could hear the noise of the churning propellers next to his window. As the plane plowed through the night, he found himself fighting off recurring doubts: Maybe he'd be better off to stay at home like the rest of his friends. He asked himself over and over again if he had dared too much.

Every cell of his body tingled with excitement when the plane touched the runway at the sprawling Idyllwild Airport in New York City. But the stern look of the U.S. passport agent immediately dampened his spirit. The man had a wide-rimmed hat that reminded him of a sheriff in the Western movies. He had a large head with muscles bulging in his powerful neck. The insignia on his uniform read "Immigration Officer" and Reiter noticed how he puffed out his chest, as if to show how important he was. Reiter eyed the gun in the holster and the handcuffs sticking out from a pouch on his belt. Looking at the pockmarks on the officer's face and his angry expression, he had the sinking feeling he was staring at Willy from the mine.

The more he looked at the man, the more uncomfortable he felt. Reiter understood only a smattering of English, but the officer seemed to be swallowing his words in mid-sentence. It was impossible to follow the officer's directions.

He was grateful when a small-framed man in a rumpled blue jacket came through the door. The words "Air France" were written below the silver wings on his lapel. He was obviously there to translate, though his Italian was broken. "Do you know that you're illegal?" He spoke loudly, shaking his head. "Where is your chest x-ray? They won't let you in without one."

"But I had a chest x-ray taken. It was normal." Reiter's voice couldn't hide his dismay. "Nobody told me to bring it." He felt his heart pounding. Whatever it took, he reminded himself, he could not let go of his dream. That's when he noticed a large photograph on the wall behind the desk. He recognized the face of General Eisenhower, the President of the United States, who had asked his Secretary of State to send the letter. He seemed to be smiling at him.

"Messieur Reiter..." The man from Air France interrupted his thoughts. "I'm afraid nothing can be done." There was an air of finality in the way he spoke. He cleared his throat and glanced at his wristwatch. "The next flight to Paris leaves at ten in the morning." He gave Reiter a threatening look. "You'll have to be on it."

When morning finally arrived, a little light filtered through the only window in the tiny room where Reiter had spent the night. He climbed up on a bench to look out through the bars, but all he could see were a few barrack-like buildings surrounded by fog, not the towering spires of New York City that he'd seen in books. It all looked so gloomy.

Suddenly, there was a rustle at the door, and the immigration officer came in. All business, he handed Reiter some papers. The man wasn't chewing gum this time, just rambling something more about x-rays and Air France.

Reiter shuffled through the papers and was almost resigned to going back when his eyes caught a ray of sunshine streaming through the window. He thought he could hear birds outside, and he felt a new surge of hope.

They walked back to an office where the Air France officer waited. With him was a heavy-set lady with snow-white hair. "Good morning, signore," she said in a marked Italian accent. Reiter caught a whiff of cheap Italian cologne. He looked down at her thick ankles, wondering how they could fit in such narrow, high-heeled shoes. When she turned around, he also noticed that her flesh-colored nylons had a dark stripe in the back, as if dividing her plump legs would make them look smaller. Reiter sensed that she might be the one who could put an end to all this.

"Good morning, signore," she repeated. "I am from the Consulate of Italy." She turned to Reiter. "You've already been told that you must take the next flight back to Europe, haven't you?" She looked at his papers. "The Consulate always tries to solve problems for Italian citizens, but there's nothing I can do." She sounded almost pleased with herself.

Reiter felt his stomach churning. "Signora, why can't I have a chest x-ray right here in New York?" He wanted desperately to sound convincing. "I can pay for it," he added. Instinctively, he fingered the bundle of dollar bills wrapped in newspaper in his pocket.

She looked up from her folder in surprise.

"Yes, I'll pay for it,'" Reiter repeated. His voice was firm with a more determined tone.

The three officials huddled together, and he knew his fate hung on their decision. Finally the lady from the Italian Consulate turned to Reiter. "'The immigration officer will take you to a military hospital for a chest x-ray. It will cost you seven dollars." She closed her folder. "Consider this a most unusual exception." She handed Reiter some papers, and he signed them.

The next thing he knew, he was in a huge American car, just like in the movies. The sun was bright, and they drove down wide streets with rows of houses that all looked the same. When they entered the city, he finally saw the tall spires he'd dreamed about. He thought of his little town in the Alps, and he had to keep reminding himself that he wasn't still dreaming.

The chest x-ray they took was normal, and after it was paid for, he still had twenty-three dollars left, enough to get a bus ticket to the university where his scholarship waited.

CHAPTER SEVEN

Disk seemed to settle earlier than usual that evening. Reiter kept a wary eye on the three English visitors trudging up the steps to his house on the hill. He already regretted his suggestion that they spend the night. It might give Gordon a chance to ask more stupid questions.

The climb was steep, and they were clearly out of breath when they reached the landing just below the main house. Gordon turned to his wife, "Why would anyone live up here?"

"Only a phantom or someone hiding from the world," Deborah responded in a tone of disbelief.

Reiter and the children overheard the cutting remarks. "What's that supposed to mean?" Robin whispered to her father before he walked down the short flight of stairs to greet his guests.

"A jolly good workout," Townsend puffed. He turned to Reiter. "Your guests must fall asleep at the dinner table," he added with a tinge of irony in his voice.

Deborah gazed out over the town toward the bay. "My goodness, you most certainly are secluded up here," she said. She looked to the left of the landing where a separate room was perched precariously on the hillside. "Wasn't it a trifle daring to build a room up here?"

"That's our bedroom. You're not the first to wonder about it," Reiter came back. "I had to do a lot of convincing to make that room happen. It's been a few years. I was sitting with Martine when I looked up the hill and got this idea," Reiter went on. "I told him a bedroom up here would catch all the breeze. And I could see for miles around."

Linda had joined them on the landing. "Alfonso and the others thought my husband was crazy." She looked up at Reiter and smiled. "Everybody had something to say—the hillside was so steep or the boulders were too big. Martine said it would take years to carve into the hillside."

55

"What made you ignore them?" Gordon wanted to know.

"I'd heard about some guys who worked with stone over in Puerto Penasco, " Reiter said. "So one weekend we flew across the gulf and brought back three stonemasons. They brought their own sledgehammers and chisels. "Reminded me of the work...in the coal mines", he was going to say, but when he glanced at Gordon the words froze in his throat.

Linda must have sensed that Reiter didn't want to visit that subject again. She opened the entrance to the room and invited the guests to look inside. "They kept pounding for weeks," she said. "The children couldn't believe the ledge they carved into the hillside. Then they used the rock they'd hammered out to build the walls."

A wide window took up most of one wall. "On clear days, you must see all the way across the Sea of Cortez," Gordon commented.

Deborah ignored him. "This must be a great place to go to bed," she said with a sultry look at Reiter.

"What we like about it is that the bed is a piece of the hillside." Linda said, nodding toward the mattress on a rocky ledge.

As the evening wore on, the beer, tequila, and food softened the mood of the party. The family told a few more stories of life in Puertecitos—the characters who made up the town and the sense of community among these diverse peoples. Cobo brought his guitar and added his own brand of music.

Reiter tensed up when Gordon turned to Shane. "So you like coming to this place? I'm wondering what you do in Puertecitos all day?" He drew out the name of the town with just a hint of deprecation, but Shane was ready with an answer.

"For one thing, we go to school on the Saturday mornings we're down here." He pointed to a stucco building with a rusty tin roof sitting by itself between the town and the runway. He glanced at his sister before continuing, "My dad convinced the teacher to open the school on those Saturdays."

Robin seemed embarrassed that the conversation was suddenly centered on them. She blushed. "Yeah, Dad talked to the teacher and asked if we could go to class," she said. "We salute the Mexican flag and sing the national song in Spanish." Robin's shyness melted away for the moment. "I like it. I like the other kids."

A warm feeling of pride came over Reiter as he listened to his children. "I wasn't sure you'd forgive me for talking the teacher into opening the school an extra day." He looked playfully at the children. "It didn't exactly make me a hero with the rest of the kids," he added with a smile.

Gradually the mysterious phantom of Beverly Hills took on a new persona…Gordon and Deborah laughed at the anecdotes the children told, and they seemed amused by the contrasts in the family's life.

***

When the visitors finally left and his family had gone to bed, Reiter sat down on the bench outside the rock bedroom. It must have been the waves lapping on the beach far below that swept him into a dream.

He saw himself in the cockpit of a plane with Deborah Townsend in the right seat. She caressed his face with a feather-light touch, and then, with a smile, she leaned over him and unsnapped his seat belt. "Why don't you relax?" she whispered.

It was easy to comply. He switched on the autopilot and adjusted the controls to keep the plane level and steady. Then she touched the button that lowered his backrest. The seat reclined. "There," she said in a sultry voice, "Isn't that better?"

She leaned forward, and his eyes shot to her cleavage. "Have you ever seen such a view?" she asked and pushed out her chest.

He felt he was losing control of his senses. Deborah was turning him to jelly in less than a heartbeat. Like a powerful earthquake rolling through the desert, a deep rumble of lust rattled through his dream so real that he felt a warm surge of blood through his veins.

Next, her hands wandered under his shirt. He struggled for a moment to keep his mind from sliding down the dark side of his soul. He could feel himself perspiring, his chest heaving, and his hands trembling, caught up in the spell of the moment. Deborah unsnapped her bra, and her breasts tumbled out. He touched them, instinctively feeling for the outline of an implant.

He could see a look of pleasure in her eyes as she moistened her lips and gave him a tempting smile. But as she moved urgently towards him, her face, her hair, her body blurred into another image, another person. Suddenly the woman above him was Consuelo, the Mexican woman on the beach.

She bumped the control wheel hard enough to disengage the autopilot. The engine surged as the plane began to plunge, spiraling, twisting. They were thrown out of their seats and against the door as if a giant hand was pinning them down. He struggled to get out from under the naked body.

His heart was pounding, and he felt as if his eyes were being squeezed out of their sockets. He focused in horror on the blue-green waves of the Sea of Cortez coming closer and closer. Desperately, he reached for the power lever, but his hand felt like lead. He couldn't move. With all the might he could muster, he pushed himself off the door while he braced a foot against the floorboard. But there was no way to reach the yoke or push Consuelo away. The dial on the altimeter was spinning faster and faster—four thousand, three thousand, two thousand…"Stop it, stop it. Do something, you idiot," he screamed. But they kept spinning and dropping. He squeezed his eyes shut for the final few seconds before the sea would swallow them up.

Reiter bolted out of his dream out of breath and sat up straight. He was soaked with droplets of shame. He rubbed his eyes, waiting for the dream to fade away.

Walking into the bedroom, he looked down at his sleeping wife. To him, her beauty was like a gentle spring meandering down the mountain slope with hardly a ripple, while the woman in his dream was a roaring waterfall that swept his conscience away. But there were times when Linda too could turn into a torrent, sweeping over boulders with a force that tensed his nerves and then some. It was her contrasts that captivated him.

Still perspiring from the heat of the dream, he thought the words of Papillo, the Yaki Indian who lived at the fish camp. As they strolled on the beach one night, Papillo had pointed to the sky. "There are bad dreams up there," Papillo had mumbled. "I can feel them floating around." At the time, Reiter had ignored him, but tonight he remembered Papillo's insistence. "Haven't you ever seen sparks light up the sky? It happens when wild dreams collide. They burn up and light up the night like shooting stars."

Reiter frowned and hoped Papillo was wrong. He didn't want his dream of plunging into the sea with another woman floating out there, running into other wild dreams, sending sparks through the night.

Reiter would recall this dream in times to come. But it would be Consuelo and not Deborah who would occupy center stage.

CHAPTER EIGHT

The morning sun filtered through the window as Reiter tried to sort through the remnants of his dream. Looking out, he saw Ciro and the English journalists leaving the rented rooms behind the cantina. He couldn't ignore a tinge of lust that crept over him as his eyes followed Deborah on the path to the airstrip. She walked next to her husband, and Reiter blushed when he saw her turn and give him a parting wave. It was as if she shared his secret.

Linda walked up behind him, and he jumped. "I dreamed about you last night," she said, looking at him mischievously. When she saw the visitors below, she added, "Don't you think we ought to go down to say good-bye?"

At the airstrip, Reiter felt a pounding in his temples as he met Deborah's probing gaze. He kept turning to Cobo, trying to hide behind some airplane jargon. "You have to even out the weight. You never put it all in one place," he lectured as he and Cobo packed the cameras and bags. He was relieved when Ciro finally climbed into the cockpit and readied the airplane for take off. He was even more comforted when the airplane roared down the strip and disappeared in a trail of dust.

Reiter and Linda went back to the main part of their house where the children were just getting up. While their mother prepared breakfast, Shane and Robin scrubbed the remainder of the clams gathered the previous day. "We'd have a lot more clams if those nosey people hadn't come," the boy complained.

It was mid-morning when Reiter reluctantly started down the stairs for the airstrip. He'd almost forgotten his promise to take Cobo to Bahia Kino; he would have preferred a leisurely day with his family after yesterday's circus. But Cobo was already pacing restlessly near the plane, anxious to get started.

Bahia Kino was on the other side of the gulf, more than a hundred miles to the southeast. Before he crossed the open sea,

Reiter spiraled the plane up to nine thousand feet. It was a habit. If the engine failed, he knew he'd be high enough to glide to either shore. As they neared the mainland, sparkling white beaches unfolded beneath them lining the Sea of Cortez like a diamond-studded carpet.

Cobo kept to himself, and Reiter was curious to know what was on his mind. He studied the fisherman's lean face, etched and weathered. Hooded lids hung like drapes over deep-set eyes, and his brows were furrowed as if he was angry.

Finally, Cobo opened his eyes, shaking his head like an old man waking up from a nightmare. "I was just thinking about Roberto," he began. "My brother is a very good man. His heart attack was because of his wife. I know it." He nodded, as if agreeing with himself wholeheartedly. "He married a gringa, you know. You should have seen her when she showed up the first time in San Felipe." He slid his hands down his sides and wiggled. "Flaunting her curves and tempting all the boys on the beach. Roberto told me he'd found the love of his life." He sat up in the seat. "Three times." He waved three fingers in Reiter's face. "Three times she'd been married. What does that tell you? That no good gringa."

"Hold it a minute," Reiter demurred. "She might be no good, but not because she's a gringa." He frowned. "I'm an American citizen now. Some people might call me a gringo. What do you think about me?"

"I don't know about you," Cobo shot back. "You speak like us; you're crazy about mariachis. You could be one of us." His eyes narrowed. "But then I look at your skin, your hair, your face, and I have trouble. The pieces don't fit." A look of bewilderment crept over his face. "As if nature went wrong and mixed you up—outside a gringo, inside like us."

Reiter sighed. It was people like Cobo who made him feel he belonged more to Baja than anywhere else in America. "And what's wrong with that?" he asked. "Most people are mixed up. There's good and bad in all of us."

Cobo seemed troubled. An instinct told Reiter that he had something else on his mind, but he could only guess what it was. Was it the interview? Cobo had been acting strangely ever since.

Reiter attempted to reassure him, just in case his instinct was wrong. "Your brother will be okay," he said. But Cobo stayed gloomy and leaned his head against the window with a sour look on his face. Reiter decided to wait and let him brood. Whatever it was would come out soon enough. He knew Cobo that well.

Finally, Cobo turned to him with a steely look in his eyes. The next words were slow and deliberate. "Tell me one thing," he began, as he shot a questioning glance at Reiter. "You know the man from England you talked to on the beach? The one with the curvy wife like my brother's. The boys on the beach were sniffing around her too." Cobo paused. "I had no idea!" There was a condemning tone in his voice. "I thought you were a medico. Not someone who operates on people who aren't sick." He shot a disapproving look at Reiter. "The Seri medicine men help only the dying."

Reiter pulled back on the throttle and winced. The engine grew quiet, but Cobo gave him no time to reflect. "I heard the Englishman talk about your operations on beautiful breasts, bottoms, and whatever else makes a man's knees weak and clouds his mind." He shook his head from side to side. "Does that sound like a doctor?"

Reiter bristled. "Why do you think I come to Puertecitos?" He hoped that would end the discussion, but Cobo's voice rose again.

"I'll tell you again. I'm never sure about the real you. Gringo or Mexicano? You work on rich people who don't like themselves and want to change how God made them. And you make mucho, mucho dinero. That's when I said to myself, 'One minute my amigo is a mule but acts like a horse; the next minute he is a horse, but acts like a mule. He's supposed to be a doctor helping the sick, but he operates on people who don't need it. He acts like the best husband in the world but can't keep his eyes off the curvy women."

Reiter paled. Did Cobo see him gazing at Consuelo? And his questions about doing surgery on the healthy troubled him even more. Cobo would never understand that in Hollywood it was unhealthy to grow old. That a few wrinkles or a hint of jowls were like sudden death, and a weathered face with a story to tell wasn't something to be proud of. He sighed. Yet he was part of the charade. There was nothing he could say to change that. He looked over at Cobo and for a moment he thought he saw tears in the eyes of his friend. Disillusionment is a terrible thing.

After a while, Cobo reached over and put an arm around his shoulder. "It's okay, amigo. It's okay. You know I got a big mouth. You're not the only one who does crazy things."

Reiter nodded as he lined up the aircraft with the short runway he saw in the distance.

CHAPTER NINE

Cobo hopped out when they landed in Bahia Kino. "Thanks, amigo. I'll get a ride back on a shrimp boat."

Reiter taxied to the fuel pump to fill up for tomorrow's flight to California. They told him they'd just drained the tank because the fuel had gone bad. That meant he'd have to fly to San Carlos Bay, eighty miles south. He attempted to radio the intercom in Puertecitos to tell them he'd be late, but all he heard was static and worried chatter from far-away shrimp boats.

Back in the air, he began to sift through yesterday's interview and Cobo's reaction. His friends in Puertecitos had always known him as a simple medico. Now that his work in Beverly Hills was out in the open, maybe they'd all look at him like Cobo did, wondering what kind of doctor he really was. Until now he'd been able to keep his lives separate, but Gordon's probing had ended that. Maybe the interview in Baja would change the way people in Beverly Hills looked at him too. Remaining a phantom might have been easier.

Suddenly, all thoughts were torn from his mind by the sharp bucking of the plane as a gust of wind slammed into it. He drew in his breath, and every muscle in his body coiled into a spring. He felt the blood drain from his face. He knew he'd struck a "chubasco"—the Spanish name for the fierce winds that came up in seconds out of nowhere. "Only when the gods are furious and ready to kill," one of them told him. The gusts pounded the plane like ten thousand fists, and he tried to ignore the creaking sound in the wings, hoping it wasn't the metal buckling. He strained his eyes to focus on gauges and dials that seemed to have gone wild as they shook in the dashboard. The only thing that was certain was that the airspeed had dropped. The plane was thrown up and down, and he was getting nowhere. He'd have to land and wait out the storm.

He thought of his family waiting for him, and with a hoarse voice he spoke into the mike. "Mazatlan Center, this is Reiter. I'm sixty miles north of San Carlos Bay. I've hit a chubasco. I'm afraid it'll blow me over to Baja. I have a message for Commandante Calmira at the Mexicali tower."

It seemed to take forever for the garbled answer to blare through the radio. "Espanto, is that you?" There was a mixture of dismay and surprise in the controller's voice.

Reiter tried to reply before the plane was struck by another powerful fist that ripped the words from his throat. The right wing snapped up in the air, and he struggled with the rudder to kick it back down. "Whoa, Madre santissima," he hissed into the mike. "Tell Calmira to radio Puertecitos," he added when he was level again. "I can't get back today."

The palms of his hands felt clammy. He looked at the churning waves and felt being blown sideways across the Sea of Cortez. He took a deep breath, tightened his seat belt, and searched the horizon. To the right he saw a place he knew, Calamajue Canyon. Its steep cliffs cut to the shore like a funnel, and in the wide part of the funnel was a dusty road. He had to land there.

The canyon lay in a southwesterly direction, and the wind was out of the southeast. That meant strong crosswinds. He lined up the craft, lifting its nose to kill the airspeed. His eyes were glued on the road and on the tall eucalyptus trees lining the north side of the road. The branches like menacing fingers reached up in the sky, ready to grab him if he came within reach. The entire landscape seemed angry and forbidding.

He banked steeply toward the canyon on final approach. "Constant rate of closure," the flight instructor's words of years past shot through his mind. He pushed the plane into a steep dive, fixed on the spot where the road widened onto a white sandy beach. "No flaps," he admonished himself. "Go for the road and hug it." He pushed on a lever, and the landing gear ground down. His heart pounded as he fought the plane's pitching and yawing.

At the last second, he pulled back on the throttle, easing the plane upward to bleed off more airspeed before pushing down the nose. He heard the wheels, like giant buzz saws, cut through the ruts in the road. Then he stomped hard on the brakes, bringing the plane to a stop. Out of the corner of his eye, he spotted several small children running toward the plane. He instantly shut down the engine.

Releasing his harness, he made a cursory sign of the cross and sighed with relief as he climbed out of the plane. He let his hand glide over the rivets on the edge of the wing as if he could thank them for not coming apart. He shot an admiring glance at the sleek plane and headed toward the children. "Hey, amigos!" His voice was drowned out by the howling wind.

One of the little boys tugged on Reiter's sleeve. "Alicia, Alicia," he said pointing to some tarpaper shacks tucked between some ocotillo shrubs.

Through the blowing dust, Reiter could barely make out the cluster of shacks. A figure silhouetted against the darkening sky hurried towards them. Reiter recognized Chaparito, one of his fishermen friends. He was a small, wiry man with a deeply lined, sun-scorched face.

"Madre Santissima, this is miracle," Chaparito shouted, waving his hands. "Where did you come from? God must have sent you." He caught his breath. "Alicia, my daughter, is having a baby. She's been in pain for two days." He paused and shot a pleading look at Reiter. "She looks like she's ready to explode. I think the baby will tear her apart."

They held up their arms, trying to shield their faces from the blowing sand that felt like millions of needles flying through the air. "Help me tie down the airplane," Reiter shouted over the roar. "I'll get my medical bag."

They looped a long rope through the metal hooks under each wing, and then tied it around several boulders. Once the plane was secured, Reiter took a small bag from the back seat and hurried with Chaparito toward the cluster of shacks.

At the fish camp, a ring of ocotillos bushes broke the force of the wind and offered welcome protection. The ocotillo was a wonderful plant, surviving with scarcely any water and growing in stubborn abundance in these barren lands. When the Indians made camp, they would chop off a few spiny branches and stick them in the ground. Almost overnight the cuttings would take root, providing shelter and shade.

In the middle of the circle of shacks, he saw the flickering flames of a fire. Several men and women huddled together on the leeward side of the fire pit, trying to catch some warmth. A large pot hung over the flames, and Reiter caught the sweet smell of manzanilla wood mixed with the aroma of hot turtle stew. He recognized some of the fishermen and quickly clasped their arms before following Chaparito into one of the shacks. Sheets of plywood were nailed to sturdy manzanilla trees and formed the crude frame of the hut. Several pieces of tarp had been wrapped around each corner to keep out the wind. A rusty piece of corrugated tin was strapped down as a roof.

As he pushed his way in, Reiter saw a makeshift bed of plywood on one side of the shack. During the day it was probably used as a table. A young woman with an enormous belly lay on a rumpled sheet. The cotton shift she wore exposed her long cinnamon-colored legs. Her feet were highly arched with well-aligned toes. Peach-like down covered her limbs. Her large, dark nipples seemed vaguely familiar, a bit like the small-framed woman he'd examined and married a long time ago. He noted the high cheekbones of a face framed by jet-black hair. Her deep-set eyes reflected a mixture of fear and determination. She whimpered between bouts of panting. "Ayudame, Ayudame." She looked to Chaparito.

"Es Espanto, el medico," Chaparito reassured her. "I think you know him," he added, pushing a stray strand of hair gently off her forehead.

Alicia nodded with the faint hint of a smile. Once again, Reiter noted her striking dark eyes. He thought he detected a glimmer of hope.

An oil lamp stood on a fish crate next to the bed. Its flickering yellow light seemed to soften the tension in the room. He listened to the sound of the wind as it swooped around the shack on its way to the sea, rattling the walls as if intent on ripping off the roof.

"Alicia's husband, Juan, is away at sea. He was to bring the midwife back with him," Chaparito explained. "Nobody expected the child for at least one more month." A wave of sorrow passed over his face, and Reiter was reminded that Chaparito's wife had died in childbirth when Alicia was born.

Reiter nodded and approached the girl. "Alicia, everything is going to be fine. Don't worry," he said in Spanish as he gently placed his hand on her belly. It was warm and felt like stretched silk. He tried to time the contractions and gauge the baby's position by feeling for its spine. He thought he felt it on the right side of her belly and followed it to the outline of the head suspended in the lower part of the pelvis. He wasn't sure whether the baby's face was turned upward or not. If it was turned upward, it could be a problem. The birth canal could be torn during delivery or the baby could get stuck there, requiring a Cesarean delivery. He shuddered as every possible outcome rushed through his mind. He knew that Cesarean sections had been done in primitive places, but he was no Dr. Schweitzer, and without anesthesia and the proper equipment, there was a good chance she'd bleed to death.

A dozen questions popped into his mind. It had been more than fifteen years since he'd delivered a baby. Even then, he'd only been an intern at the University Hospital, and there was always someone more experienced to call on. The oil lamp flickered and seemed to bring everything into focus. He had to help; they were depending on him.

Alicia arched in a new contraction. "Ayudame!" she cried. Her dark eyes reminded him of a frightened doe.

"Push, Alicia," Reiter admonished. "Breathe and push." He turned towards Chaparito. "Give me a little more light, amigo," he said.

Chaparito produced another oil lamp. With trembling hands he lit the short wick.

Reiter felt a rush of adrenaline as he planned his next move. He hoped his concern didn't show in his face. From his medical bag he took out a green bundle and unwrapped a few surgical instruments. One by one, he placed them on the towel he'd spread over a fish crate: syringes, scalpels, needle holders, forceps, scissors, sutures, and several ampoules of local anesthetic. The silver instruments sparkled in the yellow glow of the flickering oil lamp, and for a moment, he wondered if he'd wandered onto another planet millions of light years away.

Quickly, he took out a bag of intravenous solution and hung it on a rusty nail, just in case he might need it. Another gust of wind pounded the shack, and the plastic bag began to sway. He looked at Alicia and silently marveled at the incongruity of it all—high-tech solutions hanging on a rusty nail, shiny surgical instruments spread out on a fish crate in a rickety shack that felt like it might be blown into the sea. The beginning of life and the destructive forces of death were about to collide. It took all his power to quell the fear rising in his chest.

Chaparito stared at the syringes and made the sign of the cross. "I'm going out for some air," he said.

Reiter's face was lined with concern as he reached for the stethoscope. "Hey, Chaparito, wait a minute," he said, with the ring of an order. He didn't want him to leave. He needed him and so did Alicia. Chaparito turned around. "Hold this moist towel on her forehead," Reiter suggested, trying to put him at ease. "It'll make her feel better."

He adjusted the stethoscope to hear the baby's heartbeat. He thought it sounded steady. With his gloved hand he reached in the birth canal and felt the stretched opening of the cervix. Next he took the bottle of anesthetic and drew it into a large syringe. He began to inject the soggy tissue around the bulging vagina, side-to-side, top to bottom. Next, he probed the skin on the inner side of the buttock. He knew that the nerves he needed to inject had to be there, and it annoyed him that he couldn't locate the spot. He bit his lower lip, trying to remember where the nerves curved around the deep bone in the groin.

Suddenly it came to him. The name of the bone was *ischial tuberosity*. The nerves crossed in front of it on the way to the vagina. Gently, he slid the middle and index finger of his left hand along the side of the birth canal. With the other hand, he eased the syringe through skin and muscle, aiming for the nerve next to the bone. He tried very hard to keep his face impassive in case Alicia was looking. He waited and prayed. He remembered hearing that the Seris boiled bundles of kelp to put on the vaginal tissue. It relieved the swelling and eased the pain. He kept that in mind in case his syringe missed the nerve.

He stole a quick glance at Alicia. She had stopped writhing. Her expression was suddenly peaceful. The lips that had quivered with each wave of pain had stilled. Alicia closed her eyes as if it were time for a nap, tears sliding from under her thick, black lashes. He sighed with relief. The needle must have found the right spot. He smiled to himself.

A thatch of black hair covered by taut membrane appeared way up in the birth canal. Trying to suppress the tremor in his hands, he used the forceps to grasp the glistening birth sac. Pulling it away from the head, he stabbed it with the tip of his scissors. Instantly, a yellowish fluid gushed out and splashed on the sandy floor in front of his feet.

Out of the corner of his eye, he caught a glimpse of Chaparito with a remnant of sailcloth in his hand. Without looking at Alicia, he laid the tarp near Reiter's feet.

"To keep things limpio, clean," he insisted, as if excusing himself.

Alicia began taking deeper breaths and pushing harder with every contraction. The birth canal bulged with the soft, downy triangle of the little scalp. But even though Alicia was pushing hard, the head didn't seem to budge. The skin over the pelvic muscles seemed stretched to the limit, and he knew she couldn't push harder.

"Ayudame," she implored.

Trying to hold on to his composure, he checked Alicia's blood pressure and pulse again. He looked somber as he moved the stethoscope on her heaving belly, trying to catch the baby's heartbeat. His face was lined with concern. Again he made a quick list of the worst possibilities: Was the cord wrapped around the neck? Was Alicia's pelvis too narrow? Was the baby's head too large or turned the wrong way?

Quickly, he placed two fingers into the floor of the birth canal, and with the other hand he guided the shanks of his scissors downward and sideways. He snipped through the stretched flesh and the vaginal opening suddenly widened and a little head with black shiny hair appeared. The small, wrinkled face was looking downward in position for a perfectly normal delivery. He could have sworn it had been the other way around. Had the baby turned on its own? He marveled at how nature had taken over.

Reiter slid the palm of his right hand into the stretched vagina and under the baby's face, his fingers around the chin. He placed his other hand at the back of the scalp, tugging gently, easing the little head out; the little chest followed and then the arms and legs. Finally, the whole body slid into his hands like a slippery eel. A shrill cry pierced the sudden still of pre-dawn. A wet, dark-haired little girl brought new life into life. The trip had been rough.

It was ironic that life had to begin with such a difficult journey, he thought to himself. There was a mystical feeling in the air, and he thought of the gusting headwinds that had forced him to land here. The storm had been part of the greater order of things.

He held the baby lower than the table to allow the blood in the afterbirth to siphon through the umbilical cord into the baby. He handed the now squealing baby to Chaparito while he clamped the cord, then cut and tied it with a suture. The little girl was severed from her mother. Now she was her own person. Forever.

He took back the baby and held her up by the tiny ankles. He studied the face, wrinkled and wet. Her features were strong and determined, as if she already knew what she wanted. He went on to check the baby's chest, the hands, the feet, and every detail. She was perfect. He was relieved.

Birth defects were the one thing he dreaded about every delivery. During his surgical training, he'd worked on many of them: cleft palates, cleft lips, webbed fingers, openings in the spine with nerves exposed. They were tragedies he wasn't sure he could face on a personal level. Suspiciously, he glanced at Alicia and Chaparito. Had they picked up the hesitation in his eyes? Did they have any idea how frightened he'd been?

Gently, he placed the baby in Alicia's arms. Tears silently trickled down her cheeks. She beamed at the child in her arms. "Aparace Juan," she said. "She looks like her father." She smiled. "And like you," Chaparito added. Alicia traced each tiny hand, each toe with the tips of her fingers before putting the baby tenderly to her breast.

Reiter started kneading Alicia's now flaccid belly, hoping that the placenta, or afterbirth, would come out all in one piece so there would be no blood loss. This was always a tense moment at every delivery. Gently, he tugged on the cord while he kept massaging her tummy. When the afterbirth slid out all in one piece, he sighed with relief.

"A little more light here," Reiter said, looking at Chaparito, who picked up the old oil lamp and held it even higher above Alicia's head. He bent over slightly, turning his back to give her all the privacy she deserved.

Next Reiter sewed up the incision—the episiotomy—he had made. The silver needle slipped in and out of the swollen tissue. For him, this was the easiest part of the procedure. First, he stitched the muscle together, then the slippery lining and finally the skin. It was a perfect cosmetic closure.

He packed his instruments into the brown leather bag and stepped outside. Everything was suddenly quiet in these hours before dawn. With no more howling wind, the ocean was flat and still. Just minutes before, nature had defied the struggle for new life with merciless gusts of wind trying to blow down the shack. Now everything was quiet. The battle between life and death had ended

The few men and women still around the manzanilla fire watched him in silence. Some of them nodded and smiled. Reiter's head was clear once again, and he walked toward the airplane as if a great burden had been lifted. He leaned against the wing and took a cold beer from the cooler. It had been a long night, but a good one, he thought, yawning. Then he cracked open the beer and took a gulp before lying down on the coarse white sand to sleep. They all left him alone, but they watched him from a distance.

A few hours later, the red sun rose above the horizon. He scanned the immense, rose-tinged Baja sky and whispered, "Thanks, God. But please, never again."

CHAPTER TEN

The air was calm, and there was not a ripple in the sea by the time he landed in Puertecitos. The flight seemed to take only minutes, as if time had spilled over a dam. He saw Linda rush up to the plane, lines of worry etched on her face. "I hardly slept last night," she said. "We did get your message, but I still worried."

"Didn't I tell you Dad was okay?" Shane sounded like a grown-up.

"I forget our Phantom has nine lives." Linda smiled, tousling her son's hair.

They stopped for fuel in San Felipe, and then Linda curled up in the back seat and slept. The boy sat in the left seat and pretended to be his father's co-pilot as they flew on to California.

From thirty miles out they saw the jagged skyline of Los Angeles poking through the dirty, gray mist. Further in the distance Reiter could glimpse the mansions nestled in the meticulous landscape of Beverly Hills. There was something unique about the town below, his workplace. He wondered if he'd ever fit in with all that glitz and glamour. It reminded him of sleeping in a bed with fancy pillows, but with a lumpy mattress and hidden springs that kept poking his backside. No matter how he twisted and turned, the city never felt right.

He searched the high-rises for the building where he had his clinic. He thought he could see it at the west end of Sunset Boulevard. His gaze followed the neatly trimmed trees lining the boulevard like rows of uniformed soldiers. "Did you ever notice that even the dog's poop is in exactly the same spot?" he remarked to his wife.

"That's only because of their medically supervised diets," she answered with a smile. The well-groomed city canines were certainly different from the mutts and the mongrels of Baja that didn't know about leashes and diets, free to do whatever they wanted at the spur of the moment.

Eyeing a sprawling villa on the hillside, Reiter thought of the party he'd gone to a few weeks before, on one of those nights when he should have stayed at the ranch. He remembered the tightness in the back of his neck when he walked through the door into the crowded room. The air reeked of expensive cologne, and everyone was hugging and kissing everyone else. Out of nowhere, an elderly lady in a fire-red pantsuit had approached him. Her blue-black hair was piled high on her head. "I love you," she said planting a kiss on his cheek. He tried to think who she was, but before he could say a word she was gone, hugging the next person. "I love you," she said again, as if she'd run into her best friend. "I love you too," the new friend had chirped before she turned to kiss another passing stranger.

Suddenly, the voice of the air traffic center shook him out of his reverie. "Turn right 0-90 degrees," he was ordered. Beverly Hills faded behind him. In a few minutes, he and his family would be landing at the ranch.

***

During the next three weeks, Reiter's mind often drifted back to the night in Calamajue Canyon. He couldn't stop thinking about the hours of Alicia's labor. What if he'd missed the nerve when he gave the anesthetic? What if the afterbirth hadn't separated, and Alicia had bled to death? He shuddered thinking of all the things that could have gone awry.

He reminded himself to take down vaccines for the baby's inoculations, and he pulled out his pediatric books from medical school to check on the dosages. He was anxious for the next Clinica Day when he could make sure mother and daughter were okay. His wife seemed to sense his concern as she tucked some tiny pink pajamas for the baby in his medical bag. "I think these will be about the right size," she said.

The day before he was to leave for Puertecitos, Reiter rose earlier than usual and stepped out on the lawn. A gentle wind blew

75

through the dawn and rustled the bushes surrounding the house. The rising sun cast a soft glow over the desert, and he savored the stillness of the morning. Lonely yucca trees stood silhouetted against a purple sky, the muted colors blending into the bloom of a new day. It was so different from that stormy night in Calamejue Canyon. But even then, morning had brought the sun, diffusing soft shadows across the sea as if reassuring him that everything would be okay.

From the house, he could hear the other sounds of morning. Linda was waking the children, urging them to get ready for school. He understood their reluctance because he felt it too. It was time for him to leave. He had surgery scheduled.

The sight of his wife walking out on the patio perked up his spirits. He smiled at her. It was amazing, he thought, that with all the crazy things he'd done in life, he'd managed to pick such a partner. This morning, like every day he saw her, he was overcome by a sense of wonder. Not even the most beautiful love song could explain how he felt. It wasn't merely her looks: the petite body, her deep-set, dark eyes, or her warm smile. There was something mysterious about her that went much, much deeper. She was the gentle wind that cooled down his wild side.

As the years went by, it seemed he couldn't get enough of looking at her. Lately, he even liked the fine prints of time that he'd started to notice on her face, the beginning of crows' feet at the side of her eyes, the fine lines that were beginning to cut across her forehead. He loved the marks of trust, which seemed to get deeper whenever she smiled. They all reminded him of the road they'd traveled together, not always smooth and well planned, but luckily her map of time didn't show all the detours.

"You look troubled. What's on your mind?" she asked him.

"I've been thinking about Cobo." He closed his eyes as if he didn't like to remember. "What he said was that he'd never heard of a doctor whose patients aren't sick. He thinks what I do here has nothing to do with being a doctor. He seemed disappointed in me."

She shook her head. "It's hard to believe that you let someone like Cobo throw you off balance after all the years you've been taking care of people like him." She put a hand on his arm. "Come on, Doctor, you've got to believe in yourself."

He leaned against the wall by the pool and looked at her. "It's still hard for me—how he sees all this." His voice was sad. "For one thing, I'm doing a facelift today."

"Maybe this isn't the life you want. Have you thought about that?" She turned towards him. "Flying to Beverly Hills, doing cosmetic surgery for famous people. But it doesn't change the fact that in the end, all you're doing is taking care of people."

He put the coffee down. "What matters is that you believe in me." He sounded relieved as he kissed her good-bye. Without lingering, he climbed into the jeep. As he drove out to the airstrip at the far end of the ranch, he remembered the day they'd talked about building it. Together they'd spent days combing every inch of the ranch, making sketches of the way the winds bent the trees and bushes. In the end, he'd known where the runway should be.

This morning, like most mornings, there was a steady wind from the south. He turned the ignition and heard the engine purr, primed and ready. It ran smoothly and steadily as he accelerated. At the end of the runway, the aircraft lifted off the ground. He cast a last look at the ranch house before heading west over the mountains. Then he contacted air traffic control. The earlier weather forecast had predicted rain in the Los Angeles Basin, but right now the sky was clear, so he headed toward the skyscrapers in the distance. Santa Monica airport was just a few miles beyond them.

They cleared him to land behind a twin engine Beechcraft, and he touched down. He taxied to his spot at the far end of the tarmac and spotted Brian, his driver, pulling the car up in front of the tie-down. Brian was a big man with broad, stubby hands and a solid frame. He was bald now, but his friendly eyes and a broad grin still made him look younger than his years. In many ways, he was more like a good friend than an employee.

The two of them had met several years ago at a small airport in the high desert. Reiter had always sought out other pilots, and one of them told him about a new helicopter instructor. His name was Brian.

"Have you ever thought about flying one of those things?" Brian had asked when he saw Reiter eyeing the helicopter on the tarmac. "Why don't you let me teach you?" he added.

Reiter gave him a quizzical look. "Okay," he said. Without taking his eyes off the machine, he casually added, "I'll give it a try."

"When?" Brian asked with a look of surprise.

"How about now?" the answer shot back.

It wasn't long before Brian was on his payroll. His accountant had screamed, "Why do we need a helicopter pilot? I can see it now…next you'll want an astronaut. Maybe you'll decide to go to the moon!"

But Reiter prevailed, though the 'job description' the cranky accountant demanded was hard to define. Brian 'filled in' in a myriad of ways, from giving him helicopter lessons, to flying patients and friends around, to helping with office administration, and driving through city traffic. Wherever and whenever he was needed, Brian was there. Most importantly, Reiter knew that Brian was a loyal friend.

As they drove to the office, Brian did his best to hit all the green lights along San Vincente Boulevard. He knew Reiter didn't like this part of his commute. Finally, they pulled into the parking lot of the medical building on Sunset Boulevard, and Brian handed him a schedule. "You've got a facelift, some rechecks, and six new patients." He always waited until the last minute to give Reiter the details. It seemed to put him in a more relaxed mood.

The elevator took him to his elegantly furnished clinic where nurses and assistants were waiting. He made his way down the hall to his paneled office, glanced at the schedule again and changed into operating greens.

"Let's do it, amigo," he said to the anesthesiologist as he walked into the operating room. They would be doing a routine facelift, a procedure he'd done so many times it was almost second nature to him. The surgery, from the first incision to the last suture, would take a little more than two hours.

When it was over, he got up from the stool. "Thank you all," he said, and walked back to his office. He felt content for the moment, but somehow there was emptiness in this ritzy world where he tampered with beauty. He felt the need for his other world, to hear Linda's voice, to know about the children and the Chapparral. He called the ranch. The phone rang for a long time; finally he left a message. "Hope everything's okay. I'll be home by seven."

He hung up the phone as an assistant walked in. "Mrs. Grant is here," she said, giving him a chart. Reiter needed a moment to place this patient. He'd first seen her three weeks ago. She'd wanted a facelift immediately, and there was something disturbing in her insistence. He didn't like to be rushed. For that reason he tried not to do more than one facelift a day. Because the waiting list was growing, he was under pressure from his staff to change his policy, but assembly-line surgery wasn't for him.

Despite his training in a wide range of plastic and reconstructive surgery, a lot of his work focused on cosmetic surgery. He hadn't planned it that way. His thoughts went back to the child with the injured hand and how that experience that changed the direction of his life.

He managed to get a training position for the required residency in general surgery. During those years, he learned how to operate on hernias, stomachs, bladders, and lungs. They even let him graft those life-saving veins from the leg to by-pass the clogged arteries to the heart. But he never strayed from what he'd dreamed of when he worked on the small hand. His mind was set on training in plastic and reconstructive surgery. At that time, there were only fifty residency positions in the country, and he knew it would mean another two to three years of training.

He started writing letters, filling out long forms outlining the procedures he'd done, and arranging for certificates of qualification. During that time, he learned a lot about Dr. Young, chief of one of the best training programs in the world. Dr. Young was one of the founders of the American Board of Plastic Surgery and had trained many well-known plastic surgeons. Reiter's dream to train with the man turned into an obsession. He applied for his program, and for months, he waited each day for the mailman, hoping he would bring a letter of acceptance.

The balding letter carrier seemed to sense his anxiety. "Be patient, young man," he cautioned. "What's meant to be, the post man will bring." Reiter grew to like the man, but it wasn't enough, the letter never came.

Then one day, he saw Dr. Young's name on a roster of speakers at a plastic surgery conference in San Francisco, and he made up his mind to attend. Maybe destiny would give him a chance to confront the famous doctor.

At the conference, Reiter kept his eye on the portly man with neatly combed hair and patrician features sitting in the front row. He seemed to be listening somberly to the other speakers on the program. Finally, when Dr. Young got up to leave, Reiter followed him as he made his way to the bank of elevators. Dr. Young was already in the elevator when he caught up with him. He felt a thump in his chest when the doors began to close in front of his face.

There was a startled look on Dr. Young's benevolent face. Reiter fought a wave of panic, but didn't have the courage to push the elevator button. Young must have done it for him because the doors slid open with a welcoming hum.

Reiter stepped in. They were alone in the elevator. "Thank you. Thank you, sir," he said, aware of the sudden flush in his face.

"What floor, young man?" the doctor asked with a fleeting smile.

Reiter shot a quick look at the embossed panel with shiny buttons and saw the red light on number twenty. It was the top floor of the hotel. "The twentieth," he quickly came back, not believing he'd said it.

The doors closed with an ominous click. Dr. Young's eyes narrowed as he read Reiter's nametag. He must have wondered what a surgical resident would be doing in an expensive suite on the top floor.

Reiter felt like he needed more air, but the words came tumbling out before he could take his next breath. "Dr. Young, my name is Paul Reiter. I applied to your program. I want to be your resident surgeon." Dr. Young listened attentively. "Would you give me a chance?" Reiter asked.

The elevator rose and halted on four different floors. No one else got on.

Dr. Young's square jaw jutted forward. "The problem is, you see," he began as his chubby hand tightened on his leather folder, "we have another hundred surgeons like you." He paused as if to let that fact sink in. "For this one position." He must have noticed Reiter's lips quiver. "I think we need to determine what makes you better. More qualified, I mean."

This sounds familiar, Reiter thought. He'd heard the same thing when he applied to medical school and faced the skeptical members of the Admission Committee. He'd heard it from the immigration officers when he landed in this country. But this time the answer came easy, even though his face turned crimson when he spoke. "Dr. Young, I'm not sure. I can't tell you that I'm better than the rest." The elevator stopped on the twentieth floor. "All I can promise you is that I won't leave a stone unturned to make sure you'll never regret it." He looked him in the eyes. "I'll do everything I can to make you proud."

Dr. Young's voice softened. "Let's talk for a moment," he said and pointed toward a teak door with the relief of a golden eagle on it. "Won't you come in?"

**

The following year, Reiter began the program with Dr. Young. During the years of training, Young began to turn more and more cosmetic surgery cases over to Reiter while he concentrated on the reconstructive operations in his practice. Maybe he felt it was easier to let his young trainee fret with the surgery for beauty's sake while he stuck to the more noble pursuit of reconstruction. Reiter ended up doing many facelifts while still a resident surgeon.

He remembered Dr. Young, with his puffy cheeks and hypnotic gray eyes, shuffling into the operating room before the anesthesia was given. His patients always showered him with grateful looks and glowing words, proud to be under the knife of such a master. Dr. Young would beam and pat their heads like a loving father. And the moment the patient was asleep, he'd tap Reiter on the shoulder. "Have at it, young man."

For a number of reasons, after he finished training and had established his own practice, Reiter found himself doing less and less reconstructive surgery and more and more surgery to smooth wrinkles and eliminate jowls. There was no question that in Beverly Hills, he'd strayed into a fairyland of vanity and the search for perfection.

The next patient—Mrs. Grant, interrupted his thoughts.

"Doctor, make me beautiful," she said as she sat down. She paused long enough for him to lift his eyebrows. "Beautiful again," she repeated. It sounded more like a command. "There were times when men stopped and stared at me. I want you to give me back those days. I want jealous wives to glare at me like they once did. I want to be myself again. A young Harriet Grant."

For a moment, Reiter thought she sounded more like a poet than a patient. But when he looked in her eyes, he was sure he could see a sad story there. For her, springtime was gone, and summer had never really come. Autumn was here with winter just around the corner.

Over the years, he'd heard so many demands for fresh, baby-smooth faces, velvet skin and eyes with no hooded lids or puffy bags beneath. Some wanted surgery to keep husbands from straying, or to catch a new one; some needed to keep jobs meant for the young. Sometimes, it was a desperate attempt to ease the lonely pain of widowhood that had marked the face with lines of mourning. He'd heard it all, and there were times when he felt backed into a corner by this never-ending quest for beauty, this obsessive search for eternal youth. And at those times, as he explained to Linda, he felt he had to perform just to get out of the corner. He was expected to remove the wrinkles of sorrow, the jowls of discontent, and somehow stop the merciless clock that kept etching deeper lines with each passing year.

But the ravages of time often didn't stop at the face. After a facelift, for many the body suddenly seemed too old—bulges at the waist, breasts that were sagging, and thighs that had lost their tone. Didn't they know that a tight, firm face could look unnatural on a shriveled old body? There had to be a balance. It seemed that few were willing to walk into the evening shadows of life with lines etched on the face or the laugh lines around the eyes that grandchildren adore.

As if reading his mind, Mrs. Grant gave him a defiant look. "I've already seen other plastic surgeons. Dr. Sporks told me I'm a perfect candidate and that there was no doubt he could give me back my looks." A frown crossed her face. She seemed to be annoyed with him; she spoke quickly, as if determined to sweep any doubt from his mind.

Suddenly the torrent of words came to a halt. He was glad for the reprieve. He leaned back and collected his thoughts. Their eyes met. "It means a lot to me, Dr. Reiter. I really want this facelift," she pleaded. "In my soul, I'm seventeen. Who wants to look in the mirror and see a worn-out stranger? I want the best facelift anyone's ever had. And you're the man to do it."

He sent her to the scheduling secretary in the front office.

Reiter walked into the next exam room. Jeff Clancy was studying his face in a mirror. After twenty years as a television and screen star he still had the same boyish charm and disarming smile. His fans must feel that he didn't age; they couldn't know of the surgery that had erased telltale lines and kept his famous jaw line taut and square.

"What's up, Jeff?" Reiter asked as he entered.

Jeff turned slowly around. "I hate to admit it, but you're a genius," he said with a flair, as if the cameras were rolling. "What I like best is that no one has noticed I've had anything done." He glanced in the mirror sideways. "Just today my director, who's known me for years, said that my vacation had done wonders for me." There was a mischievous look in his eyes. "I've fooled everyone."

***

At last the day ended and Reiter was ready to go back to his other world, away from the city. Brian drove him back to the airport. The air was clean after the brief rain, and even the traffic seemed to flow more smoothly. Soon he would be above it all.

"I'll ask for an instrument departure until I break through the clouds," he told Brian as they parked near the plane. "It'll make it easier."

Carefully, Reiter undid some screws and lifted the inspection lid off the engine. Both awe and respect were reflected in his eyes as he studied the intricate machine. He had never been able to take these coils and lifeless valves for granted because in the end they gave him the freedom to soar through the skies whenever he wanted. How could he see them as just a collection of steel without something of a soul? Brian watched Reiter's fingers wander along the jumble of hoses, touching the long, shiny wires as he inspected them.

Out of the corner of his eye, Reiter saw Brian shaking his head, as if he wanted to protest. "You know damn well that I checked every inch of this plane earlier this afternoon," Brian finally blurted out. The annoyance on his face didn't escape Reiter.

"Haven't you ever felt like paying your respects to a fussy old lady?" Reiter winked. "In my book you're still the best," he added, and without waiting for a reply, he bounded up the steps and pulled up the door behind him. He peeked out at Brian through the drops of rain that still clung to the windshield. Brian was smiling now with a wide, easy smile.

The control tower gave him clearance, and he taxied the plane to the runway for lifted off. The 'ceiling' was barely twenty five hundred feet, and the need to get above it made the few minutes of darkness seem longer. With a critical eye, he scanned the instruments in the cockpit. Suddenly, he broke out of the clouds. He loved the stillness of the sky as he banked the aircraft toward the southeast. The cloud cover cut him off from the city below and drifted like a moving canvas. He was back in his other world. Free again, the freedom he lived for.

"I'm going on visual," he advised the controller as he soared over Los Angeles toward his desert home. In just a few moments, the city was behind him, and he was swallowed up by the solitude of the landscape to the east, sweeping over the hills toward the high desert. It always seemed a miracle what half an hour could do.

As he relaxed with his family that night, he couldn't dismiss the uneasy connection he felt with the world he'd left behind hours earlier. It was second nature to pick up the phone and call the clinic, as though confronting the memory of a troubled love. The nurse assured him that his patient was fine, but in the end, not even an airplane could separate him from the world of his work.

***

That night he had another strange dream. He dreamed he was on a shrimp boat on the Sea of Cortez, lost in a storm, panicky, unable to find the harbor. It was dark and cold. The angry sea pounded his ship, bouncing it on frothy waves intent on taking his life. He tried to get into an old coat to fend off the cold, but no matter how he tried, he could only manage to slip into one arm. He struggled with the other arm. Why couldn't he put that arm in the sleeve? Was his body split in two? Were his face and his soul miles apart, one part floating in the dark water, the other part floating through a sunny sky, evenly divided between life and death? Would he always feel like Phantom?

Music drifted up from the distant waves. His youth flashed by in an instant. He saw a familiar band marching on the water, striding through the surging waves wearing green Tyrolean hats with the brims turned up on one side, white feathers flapping in the stiff wind, shiny red jackets over brown vests with silver buttons and leather pants that ended below the knees, worn only by the mountain men of the Alps.

Reiter tossed in his sleep as the musicians seemed to skim across the water—not to a somber Tyrolean march, but with the strange, guttural whoops and drum beats of the Baja Indians. And as the band of musicians drew closer, he saw small dark faces with long black hair and shells in their ears. This marching band was made up of Indians. He tried to make some sense of it, but couldn't. Baja Indians in Tyrolean attire.

The next morning, when he climbed out of bed, Reiter found Linda and the children already at the breakfast table. "Good morning," he said and brushed his lips across Linda's cheek. He sat down between the children while Linda handed him a cup of coffee.

"Why were you so restless all night?" she asked. "What on earth were you dreaming?"

As he related the dream, he tried to make sense of it. "That's the third time I've dreamed about Tyroleans and Indians. Maybe the dream's telling me that my life is too disjointed; I'm always going from one world to the other. Don't you wonder sometimes whether you married a nut?"

She smiled. "No, I didn't marry a nut. I married a man with more contrasts than most. And I happen to love it."

He looked at her with gratitude. "And you don't mind that tomorrow the contrast goes on? It's the end of the month. Clinica Day. I'll be leaving for Puertecitos after work."

CHAPTER ELEVEN

The next morning Reiter sensed a vague uneasiness as he worked in his clinic. The fact that he couldn't explain it only kept him more on edge. He knew he'd have to leave early to get to Puertecitos before dark, but he suppressed the urge to hurry as he examined his patients.

In his mind, he could see Martine and the other Puertecitos friends preparing for a busy Clinica Day. He could picture Cobo sweeping Martine's porch while Martine took stock of the supplies and medicine on the cluttered shelves. What he couldn't know were the other events of that morning. Pablo, Don Rafael's rent collector, had already started out on his monthly rounds with a long list of delinquent renters to call on.

With a worn attaché case in one hand and a fly swatter in the other, he began combing through the village. People could hear him arguing with himself as he limped along the dusty street and stopped every once in a while to nurse the gout in his inflamed toe. Then something on Martine's porch seemed to catch his attention.

"What the hell's going on over there?" he muttered as he saw Hector's battered old water truck grinding to a halt in front of Martine's porch. Its noisy motor kept coughing like an old man out of breath. Something wasn't right. Everyone knew that Martine would rather die of thirst than buy water from Hector. Not because he charged two centavos a gallon, but because Martine was his own man. "A man should get his own water, like his own woman. And he shouldn't have to pay for either," he believed.

On the second Friday of every month, Martine would load up his jeep with big plastic drums and head for the well eight miles north of town. He'd tinker around and fill the containers patiently, one at a time. Then he'd drive back and pump the water into a storage tank, la pila, on the hill behind his house. "I'd never depend on that drunken jackass, Hector," he'd said to Reiter. "Hell, I've got my own private spring." He'd waved a hand towards the 'pila' on the hill.

87

Pablo didn't take his eyes off the water truck in front of Martine's porch as he made his way straight to the place. Hector was already on the porch by the time he got there, handing what looked like a small bundle of soiled blankets to Martine. "Audame. Audame. Mi hijito esta muy malo," he pleaded. "Help me. My little boy is very sick." He cast his eyes at the bundle. "Yesterday he played and laughed around the truck all day. But when he got up this morning I knew something was wrong. He shivered like he was freezing to death." Hector spoke in staccato bursts that reflected his pain. "I wanted to take him to the medico in San Felipe, but it takes hours to get there," he added, his voice strained and trembling.

Martine shot a quick look at the boy and turned to Cobo who was standing at the edge of the porch. "Tell Rafael to radio the commandante in Mexicali. He has a phone and can get a message to Reiter." As he spoke, he placed the limp child on the table. "He'll be coming down tomorrow for Clinica Day," he added. "See if he can get here earlier." Cobo hurried off.

"The body feels cold," Martine muttered. He grabbed the tiny wrist and felt for a pulse and placed his ear on the little chest. "I can't hear a thing," he said, his face troubled and pale. He picked up a flashlight and checked the child's eyes. Finally he moved a stethoscope over the limp body. He looked bewildered, trying to catch a heartbeat. There was no heartbeat, no breath. He turned to Pablo with a look of despair and seemed to be groping for words.

Martine's deep lined expression made it clear that he had a hard time dealing with the irony that death could be found on the same porch where so many people had been helped. It must have seemed too swift and cruel to him, but in this harsh land at the edge of the sea, with its hot days and cold nights, life was fragile.

The lines in Martine's face softened with compassion as he pulled the blanket over the lifeless body and turned to Hector. "This is the time to be strong, Hector. The boy is alive no more," he said quietly. "The boy's gone. We must let him go with dignity, your son."

He placed a hand on Hector's arm. "I'm sorry," he said, shaking his head. "Very, very sorry."

Hector stared mutely at the lifeless bundle. Then, an inner strength that was part of his Indian heritage seemed to assert itself. Survival had never been easy for the Yaki people. But in their culture, death was merely an earthly event. It wasn't final. There was more to life than a body. They called it "ktoa", the soul. In his mind his boy was alive somewhere, his ktoa hovering in the sky.

The waterman straightened his shoulders and stood taller. Then he tenderly picked up the bundle and placed it on the worn seat of the truck. He turned the key, and the old engine groaned. His eyes stayed riveted on the child for a long, silent moment. He would follow the ways of his ancestors, making a resting place for his son atop the bushes, in the sun and the wind, not in the bowels of the earth. That way it would be easier for his ktoa to rise. As he started to drive away, tears trickled down his face.

Pablo rushed toward the truck, wanting to say something. Martine reached for his arm. "Let him go," he said softly. "He'll find a place for the boy out there in the desert." He tightened his grip on the arm. "Just let him go," he insisted.

Pablo looked somber. "All right, all right," he said. Gloom hung in the air like a flock of hovering buzzards. The child's death had cast a pall over everything. Even the sun, which had shone so brightly early in the morning, looked dull.

Cobo, dashing back from the cantina, startled them. "Martine," he panted. "We got through to Mexicali."

Martine sighed. "Okay, Cobo. Thanks," he said without looking up. "But it's too late. There's nothing anyone can do." There was a mixture of sadness and disappointment in his gravely voice.

***

In the Beverly Hills office, Reiter's kept thinking of Puertecitos. He had to keep reining in that side of him—the one that longed for

89

Baja, that sat on Martine's front porch with Cobo and Alfonso, and that roamed the fish camps and the wind-swept shores. He could hear voices in the back of his head: "We need you down here." It was Cobo. "It's Clinica Day. There are lots of sick children waiting. And mothers," Martine seemed to be saying.

The nurse opened the door to the exam room. "Mrs. Myers is waiting," he said. The bleached blond in the examining chair beamed. "I can't believe it. You've taken twenty years off. You should see my husband gawking." She giggled. "He's paying attention to me, like back in the old days."

"It's been three months since your surgery, Mrs. Myers," Reiter said as he studied her chart. He noticed that she was sixty years old. "You've healed very well." He inspected the barely visible scar in front of her ear.

He must have sounded as if this was her final visit because she didn't hesitate a minute. "When can I see you again?" she wanted to know. "I've been thinking we could talk about my sagging breasts. I'm going to be a grandmother. I don't want to look like one."

His secretary caught him as he was leaving the exam room. "There's a phone call from Mexico. I can't understand what they're saying."

He picked up the phone and heard Calmira on the other end. "Espanto, I had a message from Puertecitos. They need you today."

***

"Nancy," he said as he grabbed his jacket. "Have Barbara see the last two rechecks. I have to get going."

He hurried to the Santa Monica airport and went through the routine pre-flight inspection as quickly as he could. When he taxied to the end of the runway to the take-off position, he could see the dark fog billowing at the other end. He checked his seat belt, tapping a finger impatiently on the dashboard as he waited for clearance to take off. There were three airplanes ahead of him. He heard the deep voice of the controller. "You're number four for take-off." Taking a quick look at the clock in the center of the control wheel, he noted it was already two forty-five. Quickly, he copied down the departure instructions and waited. He finally heard the welcome words, "You're cleared for take-off."

The plane roared down the runway, and in seconds he was in the middle of the fog bank. Instinctively, his eyes scanned the instrument panel to make sure he would climb straight and level. He noted that everything was normal and found it ironic that his life depended on a few shiny gauges. "You're cleared to four thousand. Maintain one eighty degrees and advise when you're clear of the clouds." The calming voice of the controller came over the speaker.

"Roger on-eighty degrees. Will advise," he replied calmly. It seemed to take forever before he broke out into a clear blue sky. "54Mike is clear at 5,400 feet," he spoke into his headset. Suddenly, he was overcome by a welcome feeling of relief. It was the same feeling he had years ago when the rickety elevator brought him out of the mine back into daylight. It was as if he'd reached the world where he belonged. It felt the same today.

He reached up and flipped down a leather visor. A black and white photograph of his wife fell out. When he looked at her face and the dimples in her smile, a stab of guilt overcame him. They'd made love that morning and even while basking in the after-glow of passion, he'd let his mind wander to Puertecitos, wondering if Consuelo would be there. He was surprised how easy it was to love and lie at the same time.

He'd caressed her face, relieved that she couldn't read his mind. If she could have, she wouldn't have looked up with flushed cheeks and the remnants of lust on her face to whisper, "I love you, Paul."

The sudden appearance of jagged mountains that seemed to spring from the desert interrupted his thoughts, and he tucked the photo back in the visor. Reaching for the microphone, he dialed in the frequency of the control tower in Mexicali: 119.2. He knew it by heart.

"Request permission to over-fly Mexicali. Direct to Puertecitos." Reiter spoke in the flat Mexican dialect of the north.

"Un momento." The controller sounded startled. *He must be new*, Reiter thought. He could picture him sitting up straighter in his chair and shaking his head. Private planes bound for Mexico all had to land in Mexicali for visas and aircraft permits. It was standard procedure. But Reiter and the commandante, Mauricio Calmira, had an unspoken agreement about over-flying the border. Calmira knew that Reiter would never tell anyone about his long-standing routine of over-flying the airport of entry. "If something should happen to me down here, you know what to tell them. Just say the crazy gringo forgot to land." Reiter had said more than once.

Reiter was a few miles from the airport when the scratchy voice from the tower came over the radio again. "Senor, Commandante Calmira's nephew was bitten by a dog." He heard the controller take a deep breath. "The boy is here at the airport," he added.

Reiter bristled. But he banked the plane and headed toward the runway. On final approach he lifted the nose of the plane and lowered the landing gear. Recognizing his friends as he taxied to the main terminal, he opened the window and waved. As if on cue, he jumped out of the plane and the embracing and backslapping began. Ramon, Chewi, and Hannibal...like a big family, they hurried with him through the terminal to the Commandante's office.

It was a disorderly place, stacked with papers and parts of old radio equipment. In the corner behind a scratched metal desk sat Mauricio Calmira, a somber look on his face. He held a little boy in his arms. "Pepito is my nephew. A dog bit him," he said, looking down at the child. "I asked them to bring him here. I knew you were on your way."

Reiter took one look at the little boy and immediately recognized a genetic condition called hypertelorism. Although he was used to facial deformities, it was always a shock when he saw one. The little boy's eyes were spaced very far apart, not near the nose but closer to the temples. He reminded Reiter of a giant frog with bug-eyes sticking out from the sides of his skull. The corners of his mouth were turned down, and he whimpered as he stared at Reiter. Calmira held a bloodstained cloth against Pepito's mouth.

Reiter knew immediately that the teary-eyed woman twisting the rosary beads in her hands was Pepito's mother. "That nasty dog bit him," she said with a catch in her voice. Deep lines of fear were drawn on her face, her mouth set in a firm resolve as if she was ready to fight any demon that might harm her Pepito. She had the look of an anxious Madonna that Reiter had seen before on frightened mothers.

"That damn dog of Nacho's," Calmira spoke up. "I've seen it play with the other children, but the only one he ever growls at is Pepito." He put a hand on Pepito's shoulder. "We should have known…" he added and shot a guilty look at his sister.

Pepito's mother nodded. "I told him to stay away from that dog," she sighed. "But he wants to be like the other children."

"I only wanted to pet him." The cloth over Pepito's mouth muffled his voice.

Reiter couldn't help thinking that if seeing Pepito was hard for him— a doctor who was used to birth defects and deformities—he could hardly blame the dog for being frightened. He could picture the dog circling the children, keeping an eye on what must have looked like a big bullfrog. Frogs snapped at insects; maybe the bullfrog would snap at him. And so, when the "bullfrog" went to pet him, the dog snapped first.

Turning to the boy, Reiter gently removed the piece of cloth from the lip. There were teeth marks and some haphazard stitches around Pepito's lower lip. He knew the lip could be repaired, but something within him wanted to do more for the boy.

He'd assisted his mentor, Dr. Young, at the University Hospital when a visiting French surgeon operated on a child with a face just like Pepito's. He'd never forget the churning in his stomach when the first incision was made across the child's forehead. The neurosurgeon had nodded to him, and Reiter had peeled back the scalp. Then Dr. Young used a blue pen to mark the places in the middle and sides of the forehead where the bone would be cut.

"We'll stay on either side of the cribiform plate," Dr. Young had explained and handed Reiter a Stryker saw. Reiter winced at the whining of the blade as it ate its way into the bone, and he narrowed his eyes to keep out the fine bone dust that rose from the blade. After they'd removed pieces of bone and realigned the skull, they wired the fragments into place. Then the scalp was replaced and sewn back down. The eye sockets were now closer together, and the child looked more normal.

He could remember the feeling of relief and pride that had flushed his cheeks at the end of the surgery. No facelift left him feeling like that. It was different than operating on someone like Mrs. Myers. Many times, his work left him feeling empty, as if his accomplishment lacked a real sense of purpose.

Pepito's whimpering put a halt to Reiter's reminiscing, but not before he'd promised himself to take the boy to the University Hospital as soon as he could. Maybe they could make Pepito look normal someday. For now, he had to deal with the dog bite.

He turned to Pepito's mother and reassured her that the doctor at the public hospital had done a good job. It looked like he'd cleansed the wound and put in some stitches. "Just keep wet compresses on the wound," he told her. "Make sure you boil the water first." Sitting down at the Commandante's desk he wrote out a prescription for penicillin. "Take this to Flaco at the Farmacia Sagrado Corazon. And bring Pepito to Puertecitos next month. On Clinica Day," he added. "We'll see then if his lip needs more surgery. He's going to be okay."

Remembering the call from Puertecitos, he turned to Calmira. "I'd better get going."

He hurried to say good-bye without the usual the bear hugs and backslaps. Taxiing down the runway, Reiter cinched up his seat belt and kept his eyes fixed to the south. He figured that with a good tailwind he could reach Puertecitos in less than an hour.

He scanned the barren hills below. They looked like craggy old hands, strong and wrinkled, gripping the shoreline. In the faint light of dusk, he had the feeling he was flying over Mars. He switched the dials of his radio to the Mazatlan Center some three hundred miles southeast. Located on the other side the Gulf, the Center controlled all the traffic to and from the Mexican mainland. Instantly, the radio came alive with the distant chatter of controllers and airline pilots. He imagined the passengers in the big jets, slumbering peacefully as they hurled through the night to their destinations.

The cozy feel of the cockpit was enhanced by the amber reflection of the instrument panel. Reiter squinted at a cluster of lights sparkling in the dusk. It was San Felipe, the first fishing village on the eastern shores of the Sea of Cortez. In the distance, rising out of the sea, he could make out the two familiar buttes that guarded the northern part of town. Keeping to the left of them would keep him slightly off shore.

The scattered lights of fishing camps peppered the beach. In his mind, he could picture the Seri fishermen sitting around boiling pots of fish stew, talking of their day on the sea. There was something within him that needed to be with these people. Instinctively, he began a gradual descent, as if to get closer, to breathe the smoke from their fires or to hear the mariachis in the seaside cantinas.

He could see the flashing red lights of the Corona Bar at the north end of town. Just a few months ago, he'd been sitting in the smoke-filled bar with his fishermen friends. They'd told him again about the colored crows they'd seen—large black birds with red, green and blue markings on the tips of their feathers. He'd turned toward Alfonso at the far end of the bar. "Have you seen the colored crows?" he'd asked with a twist of sarcasm.

Alfonso shot a look at the Seris and shrugged. "Yes, I've seen them," he shot back. "They land on our pangas. They bring good luck," he added. "Too bad that they stay away from the north end of town. Have you ever wondered why that's where everything dies? Everything bad happens on the north side of San Felipe."

Alfonso's eyes had widened as if talking about death scared him. "Think about it," he'd pressed on. "The camposanto is in the north part of town, and that's where Raul makes his caskets. The butcher shop is there, with dark places in the back where Jaime slaughters the cows and the goats and where he wrings the necks of turkeys and chickens."

"I never thought about it," Reiter admitted, furrowing his brow.

Alfonso went on. "That's where Chana's brother hung himself and where the chupacabra hangs out. It's where they chop the flippers off the turtles and carve meat out of the shells, and where they cut up the fish they bring in?" Alfonso paused for a minute to swat a moth that kept circling the candle. "And they hold the cockfights in the north part of town. You've been to the Palenque yourself."

Reiter remembered going to the cockfights, sitting in the bleachers, his eyes glued to the arena where the colorful roosters strutted. For hours, he'd watched the stringy handlers with their big sombreros hissing at the birds. They all had different tasks. The ones who kept the birds in the cages were Tapaderos. There were also feeders, trainers, and the ones who sharpened the knives in the velvet-lined boxes. One of the elders would usually hold the rooster in the crook of his elbow while he strapped a knife to its leg with a long, leather thong. He would whisper to the bird, brushing his lips across its beak and stroking its back. Someone else was in charge of collecting the bets. "For the green or the red?" he'd ask and give the gambler a tag that corresponded to one of the birds. In the background a group of mariachis with their silver studded jackets blared lively music. Their songs were mostly about death.

The roosters kept fighting until one of them stumbled in a puddle of blood and fluttered its wings in a primordial quest to survive. The handler would take it aside and try to blow life into it, as if imploring it not to give up. Then he strapped new knives to its legs.

Often he made the sign of the cross, seeming to pray first. At the end of the fight, the bird that was killed was picked up ceremoniously and with dignity carried away. The winner was placed back in its cage, to fight and die another day.

When the evening ended and the winning tickets were paid off, Reiter had never seen the losers get angry. The Palenque taught him a lot about these people. The ongoing killing seemed to have a mysterious effect on the crowd. He saw their eyes come alive as they watched the birds being stabbed. He'd studied the crowd and wondered why the cruel death didn't show in their faces. The only thing he saw was a mixture of passion, pain, love, the emotions of souls who expected little from life.

They made it clear they weren't afraid of death. They lived on the edge every day with cockfights, chubascos, earthquakes, sharks, pumas, and poisonous snakes. He thought of the miners he'd known so long ago, who also lived close to death, never knowing if they would come out of the tomb of the mine. Perhaps miners and Mexican peasants were less afraid of death because it was always so near.

He, for one, had decided to live. That's why he got out of the mines, and that's why tonight he felt like shouting at the top of his voice, "I'm going to live, Alfonso."

***

Up ahead, he could see a few scattered lights around the horseshoe bay. He was getting close to Puertecitos. He'd taken a big chance flying on from Mexicali, but they must have been desperate to call him, and he was determined to help, whatever the need. He had to tear himself loose from his thoughts and focus on landing.

He remembered when he and his amigos had talked about landing after dark. He hoped they were remembering it too. They'd been sitting on Martine's porch when they heard a plane overhead. It was dark and the plane seemed to be flying too low. Everyone had looked up. "I hope he's not going to try landing here tonight," Martine had remarked with a worried note in his voice.

"Nobody can land here at night," Cobo agreed. "Never."

That's when Reiter spoke up. "I wouldn't say 'never'. What if someone is dying?" As if to make that point, he had cleared off the table and placed a flickering candle at one end. With his hand, he wandered along an imaginary line. "Let's say this is the runway ending at North Beach." He put a second candle at the opposite end. "If cars parked at either end of the runway and turned on their headlights, a pilot overhead could see where the landing strip begins and ends." He'd pursed his lips as if he was thinking it over. "Yes, yes. I'm sure it would work in a pinch," he concluded.

Tonight he hoped that each of them at that table remembered the "pinch" they had talked about.

CHAPTER TWELVE

Two thousand feet below the plane, Martine was making his way to the cantina. He had to pass by Papillo, who sat leaning against his rock, his jowls drooping like a cantankerous walrus. Martine was halfway through the door of the cantina when he suddenly turned around. "Papillo, una cervesa?" he asked. It sounded like an afterthought. Martine knew how to handle Papillo. He never pressed for an answer. Papillo's answer was his response; he'd come along or he wouldn't. It was the way of the Yaki.

Papillo gave no clue that he had seen Martine go by or that he'd heard anything. He slid off the rock and brushed his hair out of his face. Then he waddled into the cantina, swatting at the swarms of flies around him. He placed his elbows on the bar next to Martine. They had a beer together, but found no reason to talk. Their thoughts could only have been with Hector, the waterman, fending off the vultures from his dead son. They knew he was preparing a resting place in the dry chaparral, cutting branches of ocotillo and fashioning a tiny bed in the bushes. He would gently place the small body on the bier. With trembling hands, he would close the boy's eyelids, scanning the skies and watching for birds circling above. Finally, he would stoop down and grab a handful of dirt to sprinkle over the body as he cried out in his pain. He would be humming Cobo's favorite tune, *A Fistful of Sand.*

Martine looked down at Papillo's broad hands that looked more like shovels. Papillo could break huge chunks of driftwood with his bare hands, or they could turn into powerful weapons. But tonight they were still, gently cradling the beer bottle, as he peered into it. Maybe he was searching for an answer, wondering what in Hector's past had cost him the life of his son. "Donde esta el Espanto?" Papillo kept asking as he looked at Martine.

There was no answer, and they each seemed to drift back into their own thoughts. When Pablo walked up, they barely nodded. Pablo must have heard Papillo's question because he was ready with his own answer. "What do you mean? Where is the Phantom?" he mocked. "Do you think Reiter could have made a difference? Come on! The kid ran out of time; it's as simple as that." He looked sideways at Martine and wiped his nose with the back of his hand. "Hell, the boy's dead. And here you are looking for some pie in the sky that could change it."

Martine didn't reply, and Pablo kept talking. "Anyway, for all we know, the Phantom's a phony," he insisted. "How do you know what he's up to?" He paused and stamped a cockroach that ran by his foot. "Yes, I know we heard the Englishman's television bullshit about his being a big shot surgeon, but we weren't privy to it. I've never seen it." He shot a questioning look at Martine. "Neither have you," he added.

Martine cleared his throat as if ready to back up his friend, but he said nothing. Pablo's eyes bore down on him and his voice rose a pitch. "Come on, man, people have been fooled before. All we know is he flies down here and takes care of some of these folks." He wrinkled his nose and became more emphatic. "But something smells fishy. It doesn't make sense. Why would a surgeon from Hollywood bother with this god-forsaken place to begin with?" Martine looked away. "And now you expect him to raise the dead."

Martine's eyes narrowed in a disapproving scowl, and he turned towards Pablo. "Why don't you shut up?" he exploded. "Reiter is no phony. You've seen him work here. He's sewed up enough wounds and set enough broken bones to fill a hospital ward." He shook his head. "And you call him a phony?" A flicker of disappointment mingled with anger flashed across his face.

Pablo tried to placate him. "I didn't mean it that way, amigo. You're over-reacting. Have another beer."

Just then, Cobo showed up with Alfonso and the rest.

In Puertecitos, daylight usually lingered like the weak flame of a candle that had run out of wax. But today, as the group of friends gathered in the cantina, the light was snuffed out suddenly, and darkness caught them by surprise. Except for the shimmer of the moon, it was black in Puertecitos, as if an impatient hand had pulled a curtain across the deep purple sky and told them, "That's enough for this sad day."

The men hunched their shoulders. Nobody said much, not even Pablo, but they listened. There was a chilly stillness in the air, and they could hear the raspy cry of buzzards and the sound of bat wings cutting through the stale night. From out on the point, the haunting sound of a lonely guitar drifted across the bay, a mournful tune about pain, about love and death.

They knew who was singing out there. It could only be Beto, the Seri fisherman, who had stumbled off a shrimp boat a few months before, too sick to go on. He'd dug out a shelter beneath a big boulder at the far edge of the bay at a place they called 'the point'. After a few days, he seemed to get better and started venturing into town clutching a beat-up guitar under his arm. He walked carefully, as if testing the ground like a sailor trying to get a grip on a slippery deck. No one was sure why his legs seemed so unsteady, his feet feeling for the ground with each step he took. Was he drunk? Or was it a limp, one leg lagging behind the other? Nobody knew and everyone wondered.

Most of the time, Beto's songs were drowned in tequila and sorrow, and no one bothered to understand what he was trying to say. But tonight it was different. There was so much pain in each word, the agony of a man whose every breath was a plea for his love to come back. "I'll find you, my love, wherever you are, somehow, someday." His voice rose to a high-pitched howl begging, imploring. "I know you are out there, and I know you can hear me," he sang. "Till then, my love, I will keep waiting, crying for you, searching the stormy sea of my soul and the rugged shores of my mind. I'll never give up." His voice trailed off, but his fingers kept strumming the chords as if he could pluck the barbed thorns from his heart.

Everyone at the table winced with pain as if each word was a whip that tore into their hearts, as if they'd each lost a love they couldn't forget. They tried not to look at one another, their faces like ghosts in the darkness. "He's sure hitting those notes tonight," Pablo finally said, hoping to break the silence.

Behind the cantina, the generator coughed a few times and then sputtered. Finally, the motor turned over with a clatter, and in the flickering lights, the faces in the cantina came to life.

Suddenly, they heard the sound of an airplane. Looking up, they saw the flashing lights of Reiter's plane. "It's got to be Reiter," Martine said. "Do you remember where the cars need to be?"

"We're on our way," Pablo shot back as everyone scattered.

***

Looking down, Reiter could see headlights moving along the ground and stopping exactly where he'd put the candles on the table that night. He sighed with relief and headed for the lights near Larry's shack. Quickly he made the sign of the cross, more out of habit than as a fervent believer. When he felt the familiar thud of the wheels grabbing the ground, he steered his craft straight toward the set of lights to the north. The plane slowed at the end of the runway, and he made a wide arc to turn around. By the time he taxied to the south end, a large group had gathered.

Reiter jumped out of the plane, greeting his friends, Mexicans, gringos, and Indians alike, with embraces and backslaps. Their response was subdued, different, and Reiter sensed that his arrival was too late. Had someone died or been wounded? Why didn't they talk? The questions flooded his mind and furrows of worry lined his face when he looked at Martine.

Martine solved the puzzle. "Hector's boy died today," he whispered. "I could tell it was bad when I saw him this morning. I had Cobo radio Mexicali to see if you could get here." The words seemed to catch in his throat, and he avoided looking at Reiter. "Before I could do anything, the kid died. Right there on my table."

Reiter listened in silence, knowing perfectly well there probably wasn't a thing he could have done. It was ironic that he'd thought about death on the flight down. It was true; the people here faced it so often. There was nothing he could say, and he motioned towards the cantina. Martine nodded, and they headed in that direction. Reiter couldn't dismiss the feelings of guilt that hung between them. "There are many times, amigo, when a doctor faces death," he began, in an effort to reassure Martine, and maybe himself. "You have to be detached, keep your emotions separate from your work. After you've done all you can do, you have to let go." But as he said it, there was a dubious frown on his face, for he knew the words didn't help Martine, and the truth was he couldn't detach himself from patients either. *Isn't that why you went into plastic surgery in the first place?* he asked himself. *Isn't that why you ended up in a specialty where you don't have to face death every day?*

"It sounds like by the time Hector brought the boy you couldn't have done much for him." He turned to Martine. "And neither could I. Even if I'd been here." They stopped for a moment. "But it's never easy to lose a patient."

They entered the cantina. It seemed different tonight, even though Don Rafael was behind the bar as always. The usual smile on his face wasn't there, and his eyes betrayed sadness. When he saw Reiter and Martine, he stirred for a moment in a feeble attempt to break out of his gloom. There was a sense of relief in his brief smile. "Bienvenidos, amigos. Welcome, friends," he said. "I'm glad to see you." Then he started passing out the cold beer.

Martine seemed to want to change the atmosphere, and he lifted the bottle Don Rafael handed him. "Salud, Don Rafael. Why don't we have a fiesta tonight?" he suggested. "An old Tyrolean wake is good for the soul, even in Mexico."

CHAPTER THIRTEEN

The somber mood hanging over the town began to lift like a lingering fog that had dampened the spirit. The lights in the cantina burned brightly, inviting everyone in the village to join in the wake. Fishermen started coming out of their shacks and heading for the smoke-filled cantina.

Martine and Reiter heard someone arguing on the patio behind the cantina. They walked towards the voices, and Reiter caught his breath when he saw it was Consuelo and her husband, Pedro. Consuelo's breathtaking good looks were in stark contrast to her rather ordinary-looking husband. Pedro's father, Capi, had told Reiter that theirs had been a whirlwind courtship. And that's what Consuelo was, a whirlwind. She'd swept Pedro off his feet the way she did everything, like a chubasco that came out of nowhere, unpredictable and forceful.

The couple was still childless after six years of marriage, and the gossiping tongues had concocted all sorts of stories as to why. Martine had wondered out loud if Consuelo was just one of those types with no time for children. "Seems to me all she ever does is fuss with her hair and paint up her face," he'd quipped.

Pedro sat on a wall along the edge of the patio, looking up at Consuelo as she stood in front of him, her hands on her hips. He seemed oblivious to the onlookers as she bore down on him. "What kind of man are you?" she shrieked. "Sterile or something?" She tilted her head to one side as if she was questioning an idiot.

Martine and Reiter looked at each other. "This woman knows how to hit where it hurts," Martine remarked.

Consuelo took a step closer. "You're like one of those bushes out there." She pointed to some bushes in the desert. "The ones without seeds. They just wave in the wind." Her voice was sarcastic. "In the end they wither away."

"That's not true!" Pedro shot back. "What about you? You're an only child. I have six brothers and sisters, remember? What does that tell you?"

Consuelo turned her back on him and smoothed her long hair with delicate fingers. In the yellow light, she reapplied her make-up with an expert touch and dropped the compact back in her pocket. She took her time, and Reiter thought he detected the hint of a smile on her face. Then she took a small blue flask from her skirt pocket and sprayed her shoulders with perfume.

"Vamonos a la cantina," Pedro finally said, as if he was hoping that this was the end of their fight. He looked as if he knew from experience that their fights never led anywhere. He followed his wife into the cantina.

Reiter and Martine went back to the bar without looking at the young couple again. The argument had embarrassed them. "You know," Martine said, trying to change the subject, "When I first heard your plane I was afraid you didn't get the second message about the emergency." He didn't try to mask his concern. "I didn't like the idea of you flying down here at night, especially when the boy was already dead."

The music started up, and Reiter nodded. There wasn't much he could say. By any standard the night landing was crazy, and he wouldn't want to try it again. He shrugged, lifted his beer, and smiled at his friend. "It all worked out in the end, amigo," he tried to reassure him. He lifted his beer. "Salud. Here's to Puertecitos."

Martine flashed his gold-capped teeth. "Salud, Espanto," he replied and turned to Don Rafael behind the counter.

Reiter had a feeling that someone was staring at him from the other side of the room. He turned around, scanning the noisy crowd. His eyes stopped at Consuelo. Her brown eyes, sultry and pensive, bore into him, ignoring her husband who had joined the band. In her look, Reiter sensed a primitive need that unsettled him. He tried to look away, but he was riveted.

Without taking her eyes off him, Consuelo moved toward the long bench by the window. She seemed to be consumed by some mysterious thoughts, and for a minute, he detected a blush on her cheeks. Then she sat down and crossed her legs, as if hiding her guilt.

His slender fingers caressed his cigar, and she smiled knowingly.

On the other side of the room, Pedro was tuning his electric guitar, his short stubby, fingers adjusting the strings. Everything about him—his weak chin, his bulging neck, and his flat nose—didn't seem to fit his small, round face. Only his ears were large and floppy, the left one sticking out more than the right. Clumsily, he picked up at his guitar and strummed a few chords. He cast a fleeting look at his wife, hoping for some reassurance, but he couldn't make contact. Consuelo was looking in the other direction.

Consuelo sighed when Reiter returned her gaze. Gently, she brushed back a long strand of hair from her forehead. There was no doubt this man had stirred a long-hidden passion in her. Maybe the passion it took to make babies.

Reiter thought of Consuelo on the beach, sunning herself in front of the cantina. He always pretended not to notice, but still she haunted his dreams. He'd always thought of himself as strong when it came to women, but with this woman, the winds of temptation had begun to rattle his resolve.

Tonight, those winds began to blow again as his eyes met Consuelo's. He felt he could read her intimate thoughts and that they left no doubt what she wanted. She smiled for a moment, and blushed. He turned around to get out of the wind, ashamed. He wondered once again about his soul, and whether it showed in his face.

Throughout the evening, Consuelo's persistent gaze had an unsettling effect on him. Though he did his best to ignore her, he couldn't help but be drawn to those dark eyes. He looked past her and tried to focus on the band, but he found it impossible to stay with the music. She got up and made her way to her husband. A sensuous smile crossed her face as she snuggled up to him. Reiter felt his jaw tighten; he knew he was jealous. He puffed on his cigar as if denying how he felt and watched the smoke rings float to the ceiling. She flashed her teeth; it didn't look like a smile. A shadow of annoyance flickered over her face. And it didn't escape him. An undercurrent of anger seemed to be floating towards him. She was not the type to be slighted.

The musicians in the cantina broke into a song about the harsh life of these lands, about the craggy canyons feeding into the stormy sea that brought him back to the moment. The words of the song made him ponder. "Mexico lindo y querido. Que me entierran en esta terra, de hombres y caballos, praderas sin flores, tierra de magellales…My beautiful and dear Mexico…Let me be buried here with horses and men, in flowerless meadows, among the tall cacti." The music struck a chord in everyone's heart. It was a raw and open song of love for this land, and their faces reflected their connection to it.

It was quiet for a moment, as each person seemed lost in thoughts of the waterman and his dead son. It was their way of praying for his comfort. Life would go on, even for the waterman. His boy was resting now, and Simon's song made that clear. "Among tall cacti, with horses and men."

***

Hours later, the music finally ground to a halt. Gradually, everyone left the smoky cantina and filtered into the silence of the night. Even though the winds had died down, Reiter walked to the plane to tighten the ropes and secure it.

The stars had faded, and there was an eerie feeling in the darkness. He found himself drawn to the beach, as if pulled by a powerful magnet. As he got closer, he heard what sounded like the shriek of a bird coming from the water. He turned his head, and heard it again, but this time it sounded more like the feeble cry of a child. He flicked on his flashlight and aimed it in the direction of the

107

sound. Something was moving at the edge of the water. He hesitated for a moment, afraid that he might be intruding.

In the beam of the flashlight, he could see the long dark hair and then the slender arms of a woman. She was lying with her face on her arms in the sand, her legs in the water. She looked up in alarm when the flashlight beam hit her and instantly stopped sobbing. "Go away," she cried angrily. "Will you please just go away?"

He felt his heart race faster. It was Consuelo.

She pushed herself off the sand and stood up. "What are you doing here? Leave me alone," she pleaded, making every effort to sound in control.

Reiter still hadn't said a word. He didn't even try. He could see the tears sparkling in her eyes. Her soaked nightgown clung to her breasts and hugged her shapely thighs. He felt an electric current travel from his brain to his groin. And the magnet kept pulling.

The next thing he knew, he was holding her, wet and luscious, in his arms.

It all felt surprisingly familiar—the curves and swells of her body. The feeblest attempt to think this over was swept away by the moment, any remnant of conscience washed out to sea. He didn't know who made the first move, but suddenly their tongues touched, and their bodies locked. Prisoners of pleasure, they collapsed in the sand.

***

When he woke up late the next morning, he was spread-eagled on the terra-cotta tiles of his bedroom floor. The windows were wide open, and the rays of daylight warmed his senses. He tried to remember how he'd gotten back to the house. Had a giant wave swept him from the beach, up the hill, and dumped him on the floor like a piece of driftwood? Or had he turned into a seagull during the night and simply flown up from the bay? His clothes still had the salty smell of the sea, and they were caked with black sand from the beach. He felt for the buttons of his shirt and found only torn holes, as if he'd ripped off his clothes in a hurry. His hair was full of coarse sand, disheveled and damp. He turned over, crossed his arms, and lay face down on the tiles.

Eventually, he made a feeble attempt to lift his head but plopped it back down when he was blinded by the sunlight. How could he make sense of what happened? Was it that damn tequila at the cantina, that powerful stuff that Cobo brought from Sonora? "This stuff is a keeler. You'll see what it does," Cobo had laughed. But Reiter had been stupid enough to drink it.

In a daze, he walked down the stairs and headed north on the road toward Speedy's. There was not a ripple of wind across the hazy sky. He heard the sea gulls in the distance, but avoided looking at the beach. With his hands in his pockets, his leather hat low on his brow, he moved like one in a dream as he skirted the town. He stopped twice, not sure where he was going. He picked up a pebble and rolled it around the palm of his hand as if to flatten it, and then he tossed it towards the sea.

That's when he knew where he was headed. He wanted to talk to Beto, the limping fisherman with the beat up guitar who sang every night about pain and love. Maybe Beto had also gone through a night that his conscience refused to accept; maybe he too had betrayed love. His music suggested it.

From a distance, Reiter could see Beto propped against the boulder that jutted out from his shelter. His chiseled face looked out to the quiet sea, as if searching for something.

"Buenos dias," Reiter said, hunching down and clasping his hands in front of him. A flock of pelicans perched on the boulders. Their chatter made him forget for a second why he'd come.

"Que paso, Espanto?" Beto asked without taking his eyes off the water.

Reiter sat down and turned towards Beto. "I need to know, what is it that makes you crazy with pain for your woman? The one you sing to night after night?"

Beto arched his eyebrows in surprise and hunched his shoulders as if trying to fend off Reiter's strange question. "Why do you want to know?"

"Because I'm hurting too. For the woman I love. And someone once told me it hurts less if someone hurts with you. It's supposed to make it easier."

Beto said nothing for a while. Then he turned towards Reiter. "That depends on why you're hurting." He spoke deliberately, like he knew what he was talking about. "How can you share pain if the reason is different?" Reiter grew pensive, and Beto went on. "My woman disappeared in a storm. Years ago, I was crazy and chased a school of fish across the sea. A chubasco came up during the night, and our boat was pounded to bits. I was washed up on shore, but they never found her."

Beto's voice slowed, and he picked up his guitar. "But that doesn't mean she's gone," he said more quietly. "I can feel her out there, and there are nights when I can hear her, too. So I keep singing to her and plucking the strings of my heart. I know she loves me, and I'll never give up trying to reach her. Never."

Suddenly, Reiter felt himself turn red with shame. He shouldn't have bothered Beto; the reasons for their pain were not the same.

He started to get up, but Beto stopped him, as if he'd read his mind. "Don't despair, amigo, don't give up," he said. "Whatever it is, even if you think you've destroyed your love, do what I never could do." He looked at his bony fingers with the scarred, brown flesh and stubby nails. "Write to her. Write her letters every day, even if she never comes back. I never learned how to write, so I do the next best thing, I play my guitar." He looked at Reiter. "You must keep trying to reach her, one way or the other."

Reiter held back his tears and slowly got up. "I'll do that. Yes, I'll write her a letter."

As he headed back up to his house, he heard the sound of Beto's guitar and his heart breaking cry: "I'll never stop looking. Someday you'll be back. Someday we'll be together again. "

Rudi Unterthiner

CHAPTER FOURTEEN

Reiter climbed the stairs and looked down at the bay. The sea was calm and dark and green, like at the end of a storm. But a black cluster of clouds on the horizon looked like a warning. Linda and the children were driving down, and he would have to face her. He paused on the landing, trying to ignore the sudden chill that ran down his back. Reaching for the railing of his innermost strength, he made his way to the kitchen. He sat down at the table and picked up a pen:

"My darling," he began, trying to stop his hand from trembling. *"Do you have any idea what it is to tell the most precious person on earth that for a fleeting moment you lost your soul? That all it took was the flicker of an eyelid, and a powerful gust to blow it away and whirl it through light years of darkness? I don't want to remember what happened last night. What I want to believe is that I could never be unfaithful to you."*

His heart sunk with the last sentence.

"But what I must face for the rest of my life is that something did happen—that in a second of wavering, my soul lost its center, like an atom that unleashes it might as it splits. I swear I can't remember how or why. But a dark part of me burst into flame and went hurtling through time, coming back to earth only when it had burned itself out.

I'd like to sweep it all out of my life. But our love is such that I can't keep even the thought of betrayal from you. The only thing I can do is to bring it to light, so that both our hearts can decide. I know I'm walking on the edge. Perhaps I'll be snuffing out our candle forever, but in my heart I have to believe that only truth will keep it burning.

I'm convinced that out love is not an every-day kind of love, my darling. It's like a comet that streaks through the sky once in a hundred years and is seen by a few lucky souls. Do you remember how and where it all started? Was ours only a chance meeting? I don't believe so. Only those who see the comet know when the time is right to leap into that magic stream and let it sweep them away.

Forgive me for what happened. Forgive me for being weak. Forgive me for wishing that it were all a dream. In the end, whatever you decide, you will always be the best part of me.

111

I love you always, Paul."

He stood up, folded the letter and tucked it in the back pocket of his jeans. He knew he should give it to Linda as soon as he saw her. He sat by the window watching as the ebbing tide emptied the bay.

As the morning wore on, an eerie craving to be alone overcame him, as if he needed to prepare for another dreadful night. He sat on the low wall that encircled the patio, his feet dangling over the edge. He blanked out the life of the village below as if it didn't exist.

A figure in the distance made him wonder whether he was dreaming again. But it was no mirage out there on the point. From the limp and the unsteady gait, he knew it was Beto. Though it was hard to be sure, it looked as if something was strapped to his back. It must be his guitar, he thought, for that was the only thing he owned. Reiter strained his eyes and watched him struggle over the rocks until he finally reached the top of the boulder behind his shelter.

Reiter could hear the faint, drawn-out sounds of the guitar rising towards him on the incoming breeze. Beto must be pulling its thick strings with all the might his crooked fingers could muster, he thought, because when they snapped back, one after the other, the vibrating echo spread over the bay and up the hill. With every note Reiter felt his own heartstrings surge with hope, only to plunge back in despair when Beto's fingers let go of the string.

***

He heard a car laboring up the hill, and knew with dread that it was bringing Linda and the children. By the time she walked in the door, his face must have spoken for him. He'd showered and cleaned up, but all the water in the world couldn't wipe away his blood-shot eyes and puffy lids or the deep lines cutting across his face.

"Paul," she said, her eyes widening, "you look terrible. Are you okay?"

"Yes, yes," he answered as he reached out and pulled her toward him. He held her in his arms and avoided looking directly at her. "I'm glad you're here," he said brushing her cheek with his lips. The slight, accepting flutter of her eyelids and the familiar way she let herself melt in his arms assured him that she had no suspicions. He kissed her again, on the forehead this time. "I'm glad, really glad to see you," he said. "You must have left real early," he added.

She leaned back and gave him a curious frown.

"Can we go down to the beach?" The children broke in suddenly.

Reiter breathed a sigh of relief. "Why not?" He stole a look at his wife. "The water's calm," he added more for his own benefit than hers.

Linda smiled. "Let me grab my swim suit." She headed toward the bedroom below.

Reiter frowned, and he placed his hand over his back pocket, as if to make sure the letter didn't show. Perhaps it should stay hidden, like his guilt. *Why tell her*, he asked himself. *What's the point?* After all, he still wasn't sure he hadn't dreamed it all up. Maybe his imagination had run away. For a moment he sought refuge by believing that lie.

He felt as if a fire was raging through his conscience, and it took all his mental strength to keep it at bay. They walked down the hill to join the children looking for shells on the beach, and he was grateful for the diversion. While she was with them, he could gather his courage and confront the unrelenting demons that gnawed at his soul. Praying that she'd overlooked the pearls of sweat on his forehead, he took off his leather hat and wiped the soaked headband.

He changed into his swimsuit in the men's room of the cantina. Once he got to the stretch of beach where the children were playing, he folded his jeans and put them on the sand to use as a pillow. When he stretched out and placed his head on the jeans, he heard a rustling noise from the folded letter in the pocket. Immediately, he bolted upright. Trying to appear casual, he mumbled something about taking a dip and waded into the water. Perhaps the cool waves would put out the fire.

He waded out until the water was waist high before he tilted back, plunging his head in the salty waves. When he lifted it out, he could see his wife standing at the water's edge smiling at the children. That's when he knew the fire would keep burning. He couldn't live with a secret that would eventually consume him. There was no way out. He would have to tell her.

A swarm of seagulls dove into the calm waters behind him and began to feast on a school of fish below the surface. His legs felt heavy as he plowed through the sea.

***

The sun had dipped below the horizon as he sat at the kitchen table waiting for Linda to put the children to bed. A noisy fly buzzed along the wall of the room carefully skirting the down draft of the squeaky fan on the ceiling. Reiter rested his chin in one hand and followed his finger as it tapped an invisible keyboard on the table before him. His conscience bumped into the earlier decision to give her the letter, and his heart pounded in his chest. The day had been pleasant despite the gnawing sense of guilt, and he didn't want to end it by throwing a bomb into her life. After all, whatever happened on the beach, nobody would ever have to know. The only one who knew for sure was Consuelo, and she'd never tell. They could take the whole thing to their graves. Better to take a shower, get out a bottle of chilled wine, and pretend nothing had changed.

Once out of the shower, he put on some clean clothes and went to the refrigerator for a bottle of wine. As he walked through the house, he caught sight of Linda picking up the clothes he'd foolishly left on the bathroom floor. She picked up his tee shirt and shook sand out of the frayed jeans. His heart stopped as the paper in the pocket fluttered to the floor. Picking it up, she began to read the letter that was addressed to her.

His breath caught in his throat. There was no way to get the letter away from her. He groaned and continued walking to the patio. He leaned against the wall, standing on one leg with the other bent up behind him, arms crossed over his chest. It seemed to take forever, but he knew she was the meticulous kind, that she wouldn't skim over his words. The blood was pulsing in his temples, and his palms were wet by the time she stood in the doorway, the letter in her hand.

Though her hands trembled, she seemed very calm. "We have to talk," she began. There was not a clue in her voice as to what was going on in her mind. Reiter had a hard time maintaining his own composure.

"Yes," he replied. It sounded as if he was inviting her to a candlelight dinner. They sat down on the old couch as they'd done hundreds of times, but this time it felt awkward. A gentle breeze blew through their hair. Slowly, pain, confusion, disappointment, anger appeared on her face, one after the other, like different landscapes under fast-changing skies. But her dark eyes remained frozen in a far-away look like an almost tame deer that had suddenly been shot by someone it had come to trust.

He turned towards her. "I don't know what to say," Reiter probed, trying to loosen the crust that seemed to be hiding her thoughts. "You know how I feel. I could never think of a life without you." He bit his lower lip. "To tell you the truth, I don't know what to do." There was panic in his voice. "What choices do we have? Divorce? Just the thought makes me shudder. And yet maybe it would be the quickest solution, the easiest way out for you. Or we could pray for a miracle and stick to the thought that it was a bad dream. That would be the easiest way for me."

He stared at the floor. "I know it's hard to believe, but the thing is, I swear, I'm not sure what happened." His eyes were fixed on her, pleading "If it happened, I mean let's say it did happen, the real question is, could you ever forgive me?" He sounded to himself humble and small. "I don't mean forget, but forgive."

She listened as she studied her slender fingers clasped on her lap. "I don't know what to tell you. I really don't have an answer now." She still didn't sound angry or bitter, or that she was ready to throw in the towel, but there was a prickly side to her voice that he decided was pain. "I can't believe this is happening," she added, shaking her head.

A flock of crows swept by the porch and flew up the hill. Their screeches intruded into their thoughts. "You're absolutely right...you can't expect me to forgive you just by asking." A flash of regret flicked over her face. "Just like that," she sighed. "First you betray me, trample on the most precious thing in the world, our love. The next thing you try to hide it all behind some far-out story about whether it actually happened or not." She wiped at her moist eyes with the back of her hand. "Why?" She stared at him. "Why can't you at least be honest? What's the point in hiding the truth?"

"Linda, I tried to..." His voice trembled.

She cut him short. "If I hadn't found the letter, Paul, would you have ever given it to me?" Her voice was adamant. "Could you have gone on as if this had never happened?"

"You're right. I'm a coward. I never would have told you."

"Well, at least at one point your, conscience made you write the letter. I guess that counts for something." She let the letter fall from her hand. "But it really angers me that I had to find out accidentally."

Desperately, he scanned his brain for an excuse. There was none. "Look," he sighed. "Why don't we take some time out? I know you've got a lot to think about. You need some time." His voice lowered. "I swear I'll respect that. Why don't I get out of your life until you have a chance to make up your mind? I'll go back to California and stay at the office in Beverly Hills. You and the children could take a trip somewhere...go spend time with your folks."

"No, I want to leave my folks out of this. I don't think it would be right to get them involved. I'm their daughter; they'd have to take my side. No, the decision is mine, and I want to make it alone."

He felt a measure of pride. "I love you, Linda. You know that."

116

She cut him off. "Well, I have to wonder about that. But you're right about one thing...I need to be alone," she said. "I'm going down to bed. Please don't follow me."

He felt like a thousand snakes were crawling around in his stomach. "Okay," he replied. "Okay, I understand."

"I doubt you do. You want it to be easy. But once a person forgives, it should be like it never happened, and I'm not sure I'm up to that. I'm not super-human, you know." She pushed the hair off her forehead and shook her head tiredly. "To tell you the truth, I'm not sure I'm anything right now. I'm just empty inside."

He tried to say something, but she held up her hand. "I'm not through yet," she insisted. "There's no need to get the children upset or for their lives to change. I'm going to stay here with them for a couple of weeks as we'd planned." She sounded firm. "Later, after we're home, I'll call you. Maybe I'll know by then what we have to do." She turned away.

He held back his tears. "I guess that's best for now. I'll fly out in the morning. Tell the children I have an emergency or an important meeting or something. Just don't try to make any major decisions right now."

She nodded and headed for the bedroom.

He spent the night slumped over the table, his head resting on his arms. At sunrise, he walked out to the porch and looked out over the village still tucked under a blanket of dark blue. In the morning chill, he hugged himself for warmth and hurried down the steps on his way to the airplane. By the time he got to Martine's house there were black clouds rolling in from the bay. If he was superstitious, it was a sign of big trouble ahead.

Suddenly a fierce wind screamed out of the canyon behind him with a roar, almost knocking him over. Instinctively, Reiter quickened his pace, turning away from the wind and shielding his face with his arms. It sounded like Willy was shouting at him from the coalmine. "Fool...Fool...Fool!" He knew his guilt was playing tricks with his mind. Was he going insane? He covered his ears until he reached the airplane.

The plane itself seemed to be straining, trying to break the chains that held it, as the gusts grew stronger by the minute. Reiter struggled to undo the tie-downs and remove the chocks under the wheels. Then he climbed in and bolted the door.

As he often did, he began talking aloud, as if he had an experienced co-pilot by his side. "You can be sure you're in for a rough one today, hombre." He cinched the shoulder harness and seat belt tightly. The eerie sound of the wind was like a thousand coyotes hunched down on the hills, raising their snouts, all howling together. Not the usual laughter-like howl, but a blood curling scream as if they knew they were dying. Reiter had to force himself to sit still long enough to let the engine warm up as he pushed on the brakes to keep the plane from rolling.

Instinctively, he cast a quick look up the hill at his house. He was sure he caught the silhouette of a slender figure in the window. *You're letting your imagination run away*, he said to himself. But he couldn't help looking up one more time. He shook his head and rubbed the dust out of his eyes.

That's when he pushed the throttle and took his feet off the brakes. The house disappeared behind a puff of gray dust. The airplane shuddered, as if reluctant to fly. It careened down the runway, kicking up gravel and leaping into the air as he struggled to level the wings and to keep the nose from pitching all over the sky. His hand grabbed at the seat belt, praying it wouldn't tear loose. When he thought he heard the sound of metal buckling, he was gripped by a wave of fear that the plane would come apart.

As if finding someone to blame would ease the rough ride, he instinctively searched for a scapegoat. First, he blamed Cobo's killer tequila. The plane almost flipped over. He decided to put the blame on Consuelo. He remembered her words before he'd taken her in his arms. "I can't live like this." She'd trembled then and leaned her head on his chest. "You have to help me." Her voice had turned into a magic whisper, and his mind had stopped working.

Come on, hombre, now you're really reaching low. Blaming a lonely woman. Taking advantage of her neediness. He glanced at his reflection in the windshield and saw it fogging up with guilt.

Looking up at the picture of his wife on the visor, he could almost hear her words, calm and matter-of fact-like over the storm. "You're the only one who knows the answer." He flipped up the visor and continued north, leaving the storms of Baja behind.

CHAPTER FIFTEEN

The storm didn't let up as he flew a straight line north to the Chaparral. He scanned the horizon, searching for the familiar runway at the far end of his ranch. When he finally spotted it in a bowl of gray dust, he swallowed the bitter taste in the back of his throat. Quickly, he pulled the control wheel back and lowered the landing gear. The aircraft slowed down, and he readied himself for a bumpy approach. The muscles in his neck felt like taut ropes, and he tried to dismiss a heavy feeling in his chest. He knew this could be the last time he'd land here. Gusts of wind whipped across the runway, and it took all his concentration to keep the wings level. In all the times he'd landed here, he could never remember such a treacherous crosswind. There was little doubt in his mind that it was another sinister omen.

When he entered the house, he felt cold and unwelcome. He walked through the rooms and felt like an intruder who didn't belong. Even the faint smell of Linda's familiar fragrance eluded him. He headed for their bedroom and removed a few clothes from his dresser, piling them haphazardly into a suitcase. In the bathroom, he let his hand linger for a moment on the nightgown hanging on the door. It was his favorite— lavender with dark blue buttons up the front. He lifted it slowly and brushed it with his lips. Replacing it on the hook, he steadied himself against the doorframe with the flat of his hand.

He fought back his tears and a flash of anger. He tried to shift the facts around in his conscience to rationalize what he'd done. After all, he hadn't killed anyone. Things like this happen every day, and life goes on. It was that stupid letter, he decided. Why couldn't he have kept the whole mess to himself? He flattened the palms of his hands against the doorframe as if he could push the last two days out of his life.

Tearing himself loose, he wandered to the children's wing of the house. He entered his daughter's room and gently slid a hand across the pink quilt on the bed. He picked up a fluffy slipper and held it close as he listened to the ticking of her Mickey Mouse clock. In his son's room he smiled at the paper airplane and toy soldiers strewn on the floor. *They were such wonderful children,* he thought to himself, *considerate and gentle.* They didn't deserve to have their world turned upside down.

He sighed as he walked out to the pool and heard the whine of the winds blowing through the fronds of the palm trees. Then he stared out into the desert and saw the horses huddled against each other on the lee side of some bushes. He shivered at the thought that he didn't belong here anymore, that he'd betrayed everything he lived for.

By afternoon, he'd moved into the private suite he kept behind his office in Beverly Hills. It was used on the nights when he and Linda were in the city late or when he had a difficult case and wanted to stay near the patient. Sadly he realized it would be his home now.

A plate glass window overlooked the city; behind it stood a mahogany bed. An antique mirror in a massive frame hung on the opposite wall. He avoided looking in the mirror, for he couldn't bear the lines of guilt and deceit that had begun to creep across his face.

He told his staff that his family was on vacation, though he'd gulped when he said it. He tried not to show how much he was hurting, that he was feeling more like a shell than a man. Without his family, he found himself wandering aimlessly through the days and dreading the restless nights. Besides doing the scheduled surgeries and the follow-up care, he kept mostly to himself. The days were bearable because he knew they would end. Work was a relief, but when it ended, he felt as if he was lost in a desert, counting the minutes of the night like grains of sand.

He actually welcomed the distraction when Jeff Clancy called to invite him to one of his parties and agreed to attend even before Jeff added, "I'm giving it in honor of Betty Love. She's getting some kind of award from the Academy."

Reiter had to admit that besides needing a reprieve from the lonely nights, he still had a child-like curiosity about Betty Love. He added up the years that had passed since he'd first seen her on the screen in 1949 or '50, a few years after World War II.

In the alpine village where he lived, there had been an unsettled period of disbelief after the bombs finally stopped raining down. It seemed to take a long time for everyone to get over the collective habit of staring into the sky, expecting to hear at any moment the far away drone of airplanes followed by sirens and shouts on the street to run for the air raid shelters carved into the hillside. The suddenly silent nights seemed out of place, and for months people still covered their windowpanes with blankets in the evening.

The months passed, and the planes didn't return. People became more at ease. They started showing films in the granite-block theater at the edge of town. Someone had even decided it would be all right to watch American movies again.

Reiter remembered the night he'd gone to his first movie. The first flakes of winter had put an end to a short autumn, dusting the piles of shriveled leaves with white. It was a lucky evening—the electricity was on and the projector was working. Everyone sat in the theater waiting for the projectionist, a soldier who had returned from the front with only one arm and a patch on one eye, to start the movie. He was having problems threading the film through the sprockets with his steel hook. "Silence," he kept shouting, even though the only sounds were the barks of dry coughs. Puffs of white breath rose into the ice-cold air of the theater.

Even with German subtitles, it had been hard for Reiter to grasp the meaning of the hollow-sounding voices and the blurred images that moved across the wrinkled sheet that served as a screen. But after a while, the only image that mattered had been the face of Betty Love, a face that flooded his innocent mind with millions of questions.

Above her prominent cheekbones, almond-shaped eyes slanted upward and outward, warm and exotic. Like a restless sea, the color of those eyes seemed to change every second, drawing him in and tossing his imagination around. A long, smooth neck, with a delicate chin made her look like a drawing of an ancient Greek goddess. He could remember the dimples and gentle curves around her mouth and how a glimpse of her generous breasts had sprinkled his dreams with the first stirrings of lust. While his eyes were glued to the screen something changed in him, like the beginning of spring giving life to a seed. It had frightened him at first, but the next time he saw her in a movie he was more at ease, almost proud of himself. In the dawn of his manhood, she was a goddess.

***

Seeing Betty Love at Jeff's party, Reiter was surprised that those famous eyes seemed clouded with apprehension as she walked through the crowd. He couldn't understand the air of uncertainty around her. In between moments of hesitation, she would bubble, "Hello, darling, I love you, thank you, dear," to one person after another, the words running into each other. From time to time she raised a hand like a queen imparting a blessing. The crowd responded with whispers and sighs.

He watched as she hugged people at random, wondering if she really remembered who everyone was. Her husband stayed close by her side, his movements studied, always nodding and smiling like a disjointed marionette. It was painfully clear who was pulling the strings.

Reiter stood back from the crowd, leaning against a bay window that overlooked the city. The same lights that he could see from his clinic's apartment twinkled below him. He felt awkward once again, unsure how he fit in—especially now, when he was drifting, alone, without his wife and children to anchor him. *I've never been sophisticated enough for this town,* he thought. *Maybe that's what sets me apart and makes me a phantom.*

Suddenly, out of the corner of his eye he saw Betty Love heading right for him. There was a new gleam in her eye, all hesitation gone.

"So you are the famous Dr. Reiter," she gushed in a raspy voice. "I've heard so much about you, and I've seen a lot of your work." He instantly froze, wondering if he was the next stranger to be hugged. "Gordon Townsend," she added in a whisper, "the journalist from Great Britain, has told me a lot about you." The way she said Gordon's name, drawing out the syllables with a deep hollow sound, aroused his curiosity. Somehow it didn't sound like he was a casual acquaintance.

"I admire your discretion, even though I know Gordon doesn't appreciate it."

Reiter shot a quick glance at Betty's husband. He was sure he hadn't heard the conversation, but he felt embarrassed for him just the same.

She stepped closer. It took only a moment to shatter the illusion of his boyhood. She was no longer a goddess.

"It's a pleasure to meet you," he finally managed to say as he took her extended hand. It felt clammy and cold. The cameras clicked, and he blinked in the flashing lights.

She took a glass of champagne from a passing tray and handed it to him. "Why don't you join me for a moment?" she asked in a way that made it clear it would be hard to say no. Without waiting for his answer, she nodded toward a couch in a corner.

Though she wasn't a goddess, she was still a beautiful woman, Reiter decided, studying her closer. She would have to be in her late sixties, with a facelift or two behind her. He noticed an unnatural tightness along the lower edge of her jaw. Her cheeks were smooth and shiny while the skin of her neck was loose and wrinkled. The famous dimples weren't there anymore, and her smile seemed taut and strained. Her eyes were rounder than he remembered, and the lower lids appeared to be pulled down a little. The outer corners of the eyes pointed down too, giving her a sad look even when she smiled.

He was annoyed at himself for automatically slipping into the nasty habit of criticizing another surgeon's work. He'd promised himself many times not to do it. But it was hard to avoid. It had become a game to take people's features apart and put them back together, playing with faces as if they were merely puzzles for a surgeon to assemble.

As if aware of his scrutinizing stare, Betty Love instinctively brushed wisps of her hair in front of her ears. It was obvious that she wanted to hide the telltale scars.

"Yes, Doctor. Everyone knows about your work," she repeated, jolting him out of his reverie. "I'm told you're the best."

"Thank you," he said, feeling uncomfortable. He wasn't sure she was serious.

"Could we meet in private sometime? I'd like to ask you some questions," she whispered.

Before he could answer, Jeff Clancy came up from behind and clapped a hand on his shoulder. "Didn't I always tell you, Betty, that the Phantom," he winked at Reiter, "I mean the doctor, is a gentleman? I'm proud to call him my friend," he added, his hand tightening on Reiter.

Betty's face lit up. Before she could answer the cameras started flashing again. Reiter squinted. Now he knew how an animal in a zoo felt with people staring and throwing peanuts.

***

Betty Love's agent called the next day to make an appointment for the following week. At Reiter's suggestion, she and her husband arrived before office hours in order to ensure her privacy. She wore a crimson hat with the wide brim turned down. Dark glasses hid her green eyes. Her husband, similarly camouflaged, followed her into Reiter's office. In the hushed, private setting, she seemed at ease.

At times like this, Reiter became acutely aware of his humble beginnings. He was a descendant of people who made their living with their hands in the mines and the fields. It was highly improbable that he could be sitting here with the goddess of his youth. Even more improbable that he was somehow in charge of her appearance. It was an ironic reversal of roles, and he wasn't sure how to handle it. He decided to let her do the talking

"I want you to know how glad I am to be here," she began. "You're the best. Everyone says so."

"Thank you," he managed to say. *Don't let it go to your head, hombre,* he tried to remind himself. *She's probably told the same thing to dozens of others.*

"I don't have to tell you, my life isn't easy," she continued. "So many people to please all over the globe...my public. It's no wonder that all the stress and pressure has taken its toll. I'm starting to look older."

She admitted to having had two facelifts already. "I don't think I really needed them to begin with, and they weren't done well. Look at my hairline," she said as she pulled back the hair above her ear. There was a bald spot going high into her temples, ending up in the scar she'd tried to hide the night before. "Last week I was doing a scene, and we had to keep shooting it over and over. They used tons of hairspray but the wind kept blowing my hair back, and here were these scars. You should have seen the cameraman's eyes." She stopped to take a deep breath. "I know you can help me."

Reiter just sat there tapping the end of a pencil, trying not to be too obvious as he studied the scars. It looked like a chord was pulling her cheek unevenly, causing an unsightly crease under the jaw line. "It's not so bad," he lied. "Most people wouldn't notice."

"It looks bad to me," she insisted. "And you can help me like you've helped so many of my friends. They say your work is like magic."

He bristled. It was this obsession with perfection that made him so uneasy. His eyes drifted to the crow carved from ironwood that one of the Seris had given him. It usually gave him a measure of comfort. But not today. Her unyielding conviction that he was supposed to work magic was unsettling. Apparently, it didn't occur to her that he was only human.

They seemed to be on different wavelengths. He liked to feel close to his patients but he couldn't make a connection with her. Betty Love was elusive. Or was he?

She leaned back in the chair as if sensing his hesitation. An expression of annoyance flashed across her face. "Dear," she said, turning to her husband, "why don't you hand me the photographs?"

Her husband pulled a thick manila folder from his attaché case. She reached for it and pulled out a stack of photographs. With a slight tremor, she began placing them on Reiter's desk, one after the other. Reiter noticed that many of the photos had an aged, yellow tint to them. They depicted the goddess he remembered from the hometown movie theater. "That's me. That's the real Betty Love," she exclaimed, picking up her portrait as a starlet.

She couldn't disguise her annoyance when he didn't respond. Turning to shuffle through the photographs, she shot a look at her husband. Where is the one from the set last year?" she demanded. "The one with the wind blowing through my hair?" She gave him an exasperated look.

"Here it is," she finally said. "Just look at this. It doesn't look like me at all. Does it? Look at those scars …"

Maybe the best thing was to be open. "Miss Love, I can try to improve the scars, but something tells me I can't give you what you really want."

"Well, I believe you can." She sounded adamant. "Let me give you a deposit," she said, as if that would convince him.

"Why not give this some more thought? Have you and your husband discussed this?" Reiter responded.

The husband's eyes lit up when he heard that. "It's fine with me, whatever she does," he said. He turned to his wife. "Whatever you decide."

She ignored him.

"There are other surgeons in this line of work," Reiter interjected. "Maybe you should get another opinion."

"But I've already decided." Her eyes flashed. "On you."

Reiter realized there was no point in more discussion. He pressed a button, and a nurse came into the room. She was young and pretty with a fresh, honest face. "Nancy, will you escort Miss Love to Miss Hopkins for scheduling?"

Betty Love smiled. "Thank you, doctor. By the way, why does Jeff Clancy insist on calling you the Phantom? Why such a strange nickname?"

"I'm not sure," he answered. "You'll have to ask him."

As Betty Love and her husband left the room, he remembered Gordon Townsend's remark that vanity was very expensive. He worried what Cobo and his friends in Puertecitos would think. He thought of the Seris and the way they did business, measuring the value of their work by how much sweat it produced. He had to admit there wasn't much sweat in a facelift. Or much magic either.

CHAPTER SIXTEEN

The days leading up to Betty Love's surgery went by more quickly than he expected. But he could not dismiss the discomforting thought that agreeing to do it had been a mistake. He could never make her look like the young heroine who had floated through his dreams thirty years ago. But he was sure that's what she expected. He'd operated on famous people before, but this was different, more personal somehow. With Linda gone, he had no one to talk to about it. He missed her support and input that, like a steady rudder, kept him on course.

On the day of her surgery, Betty Love arrived promptly at seven a.m., her husband in tow. While the staff was getting her ready, one of the nurses came to his office. "Mr. Love would like to have a word with you," she said.

Reiter glanced at the nurse with a look of surprise and didn't try to hide his displeasure. "He's had plenty of time for that. Why now?" he snapped.

"I'll tell him it's not possible," the nurse replied. She knew that before surgery Reiter coveted his time alone. He needed these minutes to center himself, to ponder his next moves.

His first reaction to this intrusion was to make an excuse. Instead he answered reluctantly, "Show him in."

Mr. Love walked in, his face surprisingly serene, the slave-like slump in his shoulders gone for the moment. He seemed more confident as he stood there alone in the office. He puffed out his chest and laid his pink glasses aside. But the look in Reiter's eyes seemed to unsettle him, and he put the glasses back on. "Dr. Reiter," Mr. Love began slowly as he looked at the floor. "What I'm here to tell you is that you'd better make sure this is the best job you've ever done." He halted and straightened his tie. When Reiter didn't react he went on, "Remember, my wife is revered around the world." When he reached the end of the sentence, his voice faltered.

"Mr. Love, I can only promise you I'll do my best," Reiter responded as kindly as he could. He regretted his earlier annoyance and besides, he felt sorry for the man. The way Betty's eyes lit up at the mention of Gordon Townsend's name had to mean something. He couldn't get over the feeling that Mr. Love had also been deceived by someone he loved and trusted.

"That's my commitment. Everyone gets that promise, whether it's the Queen of England or the poorest fisherman's wife in Baja. Or my own wife," he added, thinking of Linda. He felt himself blush.

Mr. Love blinked and, as if correcting a mistake, he made an attempt to agree. "Yes, of course," he almost whispered. He looked down at his pointed shoes again.

Reiter sensed an unspoken sorrow in the other man's voice, and he wished he could ease his pain. "I really put my heart into each one of these operations," he said, hoping his concern would help.

But his words didn't seem to put the man at ease. Love's momentary self-assurance was gone, melted like a heap of snow in the April sun. Stiffly, he made his way to the door, as if the conference was over, and he'd been dismissed. Back in the hall, he asked to see his wife. She was already in the operating suite so he spoke to her from the doorway. "I'll be waiting here, dear. I won't leave you."

Betty Love didn't seem to appreciate his concern. "Just sit down and be quiet. I know you're here."

The nurses snickered and didn't hide their contempt. "He's husband number five," one of them whispered.

"But he's the only one who goes by her name," the other one replied, lowering her voice. "Wasn't he her butler or something?"

Mr. Love's face reddened as he turned away. His mouth quivered as if he was ready to answer them, but no sound came out, and he hurried on. Back in the plush waiting room, he sat down and adjusted his tie once again.

In the operating room, the first thing Reiter did was to plan where to place the incisions in Betty Love's face. It was the soft line sweeping down her cheek when she smiled that in his youth had sparked so many dreams. And it was precisely that line, pulled upwards and sideways, tethered down like a rope to the scar underneath, that was his concern now. The skin of her face was stretched tight towards her ear; above it in the temple area, he could see the bald spot she complained about. With a blue marking pen, he drew a line where he planned to make the new incisions.

Holding the scalpel like a pen, he followed the blue marking from the top of the temple, curving down almost inside the ear to the ear lobe and then behind it into the scalp, ending up at the nape of the neck. The assistant blotted the drops of blood, red and bright, that seeped from the wound. Then, with double skin hooks he lifted the edge of the skin and used a pair of long scissors to free it from the tissue beneath. There was a gristle-like feel to the deeper layer that he knew was scarring from the previous facelifts. It made the dissection bloodier and more tedious.

As always, he refrained from grasping the small blood vessels in the muscle below and burning them to stop the bleeding. It was called *cautery* in medical terms. The sizzling sound when the tissue burned had always bothered him, and he didn't like the smell of singed flesh in the room. From experience, he had also found that controlling a bleeding blood vessel by burning it was many times only a temporary solution, blocking one route and forcing the blood to find another way. Eventually there would be even more oozing from the blood vessels nearby. Over time he had come to believe that nature's way of clotting was the best. Doctors called it *'internal clotting system'*, waiting for the blood to clot on its own. It took a little longer, but he knew it worked best. Only when the natural clotting mechanism didn't take over, usually because of liver problems, did he resort to cauterizing. Betty Love's blood clotted just fine.

He studied the shanks of the scissors in the beam of his headlamp and with the fingertip of his other hand he gently probed the cheek, keeping the scissors at the right depth as he advanced them toward the laugh line on the cheek. When he got there, he cut through the scar underneath, and the laugh line was free. Once again, he waited for the clotting to take place by putting gentle pressure on the area.

Next, he lifted the tissue just in front of the bald spot above the ear with yet a smaller skin hook. With finer scissors he started cutting backwards, under the scalp. He was determined to avoid damaging the hair follicles, small, glistening bulbs deep in the scalp, by making sure he stayed underneath them. It was obvious that the bulb-like follicles had been destroyed during her other surgeries, and that was why she ended up without any hair in the temple area. When the hair-bearing skin behind the bald spot was finally all freed, he grasped its edge and slid it forward to where her natural hairline had been. He sutured it down. He did the same with the opposite edge of the wound, draping the skin back over her cheek first.

Without looking up, he blotted the side of the face as he inspected it carefully. The glint of satisfaction in his eye didn't escape his assistant. "She looks wonderful," she said, and he nodded. He turned her head gently to the opposite side while holding on to the anesthesia tube that came out of her mouth. He started the same process all over again. Meticulously, he separated the outer layers from the muscle below, making a point to adjust the direction of the pull to match the curve of her smile. He was determined that it wouldn't look tight.

There was an area at the lowest point of the smile line that proved particularly difficult to cut through. He leaned sideways and re-adjusted his headlight to study the bothersome spot. It felt like gristle, hard and shiny, running in a band down to the edge of her jaw. Patiently, he kept advancing the blades of his scissors as his headlight searched the tunnels he was creating beneath the skin.

For a few critical seconds, his mind went to Linda, something he'd been trying to avoid. He knew he had to dismiss the sadness welling up in his chest as he tried to stay focused on the surgery. There was not a doubt in his mind that Linda's anguish and disappointment were as great as the pain he'd seen in Mr. Love's eyes this morning. His lips quivered, and he was glad that his mask hid his face.

Turning back to his work, he suddenly noticed a spurt of blood coming from the depths of the face. In seconds, it became a puddle that grew bigger and bigger. Frantically, he repositioned his headlamp so the light could focus on the spot. His eyes narrowed at the red spurt pumping away. He grasped for the suction device the assistant handed him and held it near the bleeding vessel. But the bright blood kept spurting out as fast as he could suction it away.

He had to stop the bleeding somehow, and he shot an inquisitive look at the anesthesiologist. He didn't seem too concerned, and that gave him courage. Placing several sponges on the troublesome spot, he applied pressure, even though he knew that probably wouldn't stop bleeding from an artery. His mind raced through the other options, fully aware that the vessel he'd accidentally cut was one that came up from the neck and wrapped around the lower edge of the jawbone. It lay next to a motor branch of the facial nerve that controls the movement of the mouth. He felt the perspiration staining the hat on his forehead as he envisioned Betty Love with the side of her mouth drooping, unable to smile her famous smile. He fought back a wave of panic and knew he was turning pale.

Carefully, he removed the blood-soaked sponges, hoping, praying that the bleeding had miraculously stopped. When he removed the last one, for a second the area looked dry, but then the red gush started again. He reached for a hemostat on the surgical tray while with the other hand he kept suctioning the puddle of blood. Pointing the tip of the suction devise to the spot where the stubborn bleeder was spurting, he made several attempts to grab it with the hemostat. The annoying hiss of the anesthesia machine was the only sound in the room. Finally, he found the vessel and heard the click of the hemostat as the steel clamped down. When he sighed with relief, so did everyone else around the table.

He ignored the cheerful, "You've got it, Dr. Reiter," one of his assistants offered and hoped that he hadn't grabbed the facial nerve as well. Cold perspiration ran down the back of his neck as he pondered the next step: He could eventually release the vessel and hope that a clot had formed or he could use a suture to tie off the bleeder. He could also burn the cut end of the vessel with a burst of electric current from the cautery machine.

He opted for the first choice and gently opened the jaws of the hemostat. But the stubborn bleeder kept pumping. Grasping it again he asked for the cautery. He cautiously placed the tip near the hemostat and pressed the button that released a burst of current. He heard a hiss and smelled singed flesh in the wound. A tiny column of smoke rose from the vessel; he winced as the side of her lip twitched for a second. He felt a pounding in his temple, and his throat became dry. Once again, he ignored the encouraging assistant. "I'm sure it's okay," she remarked.

Some time later when the surgery was complete, he peeled off his gloves and walked to the door. He kept trying to ignore the frightening thought that kept hounding him, the fear that when he'd nicked the artery he'd also cut the motor nerve or that he'd burned it when he used the cautery. The bleeding had stopped, but if there was nerve damage it could be permanent. As he walked past the scrub sinks, he glanced at the mirror above and caught the new lines of worry in his face. He had to face Mr. Love.

He made his way to the waiting room. "Mr. Love, everything seems fine. Your wife will be in the recovery room soon." Reiter sounded more encouraging than he felt.

Mr. Love straightened his shoulders and seemed to grow a little taller. "Thank you," he said, and he attempted the beginning of a smile.

CHAPTER SEVENTEEN

Throughout the night, Reiter juggled the worst scenarios he could think of. What had he done to the nerve in Betty's face? He turned, tried to reposition himself, shifting on what seemed a pile of hot coals, but sleep wouldn't come.

"Mr. Love, everything seems fine." He'd lied. The truth would have been harder to say, "Mr. Love, everything didn't go fine. Your wife's face may never be the same again." But he'd kept it to himself.

He could still hear Betty Love as she sat across from him. "Your work is like magic."

Her husband's words kept sifting through his sleepy brain. "What I want to tell you is that you'd better make sure this is the best you've ever done. Remember, she's revered around the world." The blood pounded in Reiter's temples.

"I'll do my best...the Queen of England or the poorest fisherman's wife, or my own wife...." His own words rang through the darkness, steady and clear. How could he have been so arrogant? He winced with every tick of the clock on the wall. He pulled down the window shades, trying to block out the lights and the sounds of the city. He lost count of the times he got out of bed and walked to the recovery room. The nurse must have sensed what was going through his mind, and, as if to disguise her own concern, she smiled and changed the ice bags on Betty Love's face.

Mrs. Love slept peacefully. He studied her face, wrapped in the bulky white dressing, and froze at the thought of her lip drooping on one side. All the shiny dials on machines that traced her vital signs were in order, and he sought consolation in that. He went back to his room and finally fell asleep.

A persistent knock on the door tore him out of a dream and into a dreary morning. "I'll be there in a minute," he responded as he slid out of bed. The raindrops pelting against the window seemed an appropriate reminder of the state he was in. The scream of a police siren in the distance only underscored it. He stumbled around in his mind, searching for a way to explain what had happened during the operation.

Maybe there's nothing to worry about, he dared to hope as the hot shower washed the sleep out of his blood-shot eyes. It could just be that some of the local anesthetic he'd injected had seeped into the nerve, he reasoned. It had happened before, and by morning usually the effect had worn off. He clung to the possibility as he headed toward the recovery room.

As usual, the nurse had removed the dressing by the time he got there. Betty Love was reclining in the examining chair, her white-blond hair combed back from her face. The overhead lights gave her face an alabaster, almost waxy appearance. But she looked peaceful and rested. There was not a hint of a problem until she opened her mouth. "Good morning" she said and attempted a smile.

Reiter froze when he saw that Betty Love's lower lip refused to move, as if it were detached from the rest of her face. He hoped she didn't notice the color draining from his face.

"Everything is fine," he started to say as he reached for a Q-tip and began to gently clean the incisions running in front of her ears like a miniature zipper. But the words froze in the back of his throat. *Everything is not fine, you liar*, he argued with himself. *Why don't you tell her the truth? Face it, hombre, give up the self-righteous veneer you try to hide behind. Remember Consuelo. You made a mistake. You're more than capable of doing the wrong thing.* He cursed that moment during surgery when his mind had wandered…those few seconds when he'd let emotions overwhelm him. Not so different from that night on the beach.

Betty Love picked up a mirror and held it in front of her face. "Marvelous," she said, in a low, sultry voice. He realized that she wasn't looking in the mirror when she spoke and that she hadn't yet seen the problem. "It's simply marvelous." She tilted her head sideways. "I'll be able to wear my hair up again. Even the fine wrinkles around my eyes are gone." She put down the mirror, and her blue eyes sparkled. She looked at him as if he were a god.

136

He was uncomfortable with her blind trust that seemed to ignore the frozen area of her lip, but he also knew that he had to level with her. He owed her that much.

"I ran into a stubborn blood vessel in the lower part of your lip. It wasn't easy to stop the bleeding." He tried to sound calm and kept focusing on the sterile Q-tip he used to brush antibiotic ointment along the incisions. "There's a slight weakness there when you speak," he went on. "It may take a while before the movement comes back." He heard himself say this as if he were giving her a weather forecast.

"All I can say is you did a beautiful job, Doctor," she insisted and gave him another lopsided smile.

He felt a stab in his chest and shoved his trembling hands into the pocket of his white coat. "Let's put a dressing back on," he said, turning to the nurse. He tried to appear in control and was grateful that she had no idea that he felt as if his insides were on fire.

***

Over the next several weeks, he saw Betty Love every day. Every visit turned into a ritual of hope, always ending in disappointment. The right side of her lip refused to move.

A long limousine would bring her and her husband to the clinic each morning. She would hold her husband's hand and flash an uneven smile every time she entered the exam room. By the end of the first week, he knew what she was going to say before she spoke: "Doctor, believe me, everything is going to be fine." His admiration for her grew. She was becoming once more the goddess that he'd known in his youth.

Late one afternoon, his secretary told him Mrs. Love was on the phone. His grip on the receiver tightened, desperate for good news.

"Good afternoon, Doctor." Her voice sounded subdued. "My husband has an urgent appointment tomorrow morning. I'd rather not come in without him." She hesitated a moment and lowered her voice as if sharing a secret. "We've grown so much closer, Edmund and I. He's been so supportive."

Reiter hoped he was only imagining the lisp that seemed even more evident over the phone.

"Is it absolutely necessary to see me tomorrow?" she asked.

"Yes, I'd like to," Reiter responded. "Maybe I could come by the house later in the afternoon."

"That would be lovely," she agreed and gave him directions.

***

As Brian drove him up to the guarded gates, he eyed suspiciously the cameras behind the hedges and on top of the walls near the entrance. The grounds were immaculate, and he had the impression that the place wasn't meant for every-day life. There was no sign of life, not a chirp of a bird or the hum of a cricket. The neatly cut bushes and rows of colorful flowers fit in precisely, as if the multicolored brush of a painter had put them on canvas.

It seemed to take forever before they got to the doorsteps of the mansion. A pudgy butler with a razor-thin mustache stood beside the massive steel door as if he'd been pasted there. He greeted Reiter in a low, raspy voice. "Please come in, Doctor. We are expecting you," he said.

Reiter followed him down long halls with white tile floors. Marble statues of naked women stood in lighted nooks, staring down at him. He avoided their gaze. The hall had oval-shaped windows of green and purple glass that reminded him of a temple of the occult. Finally, they stopped in front of a tall double-door, the entrance to Betty Love's private domain. The butler turned around and gave Reiter one last glance, as if to make sure he was presentable, then cocked his head toward the door and left.

Reiter knocked gently.

A voice rang out, "Won't you come in?"

The king-sized bed that dominated the room had a mirrored headboard between two beveled Greek columns. Betty Love's small frame seemed lost amid fluffy pillows and billowing, embroidered comforters. Bright-colored paintings covered the walls: women with long breasts on their backs and pudgy noses on their chests, a man with a penis on a fiery forehead and beady eyes right below it, landscapes with trees that grew down from a black sky, and open-mouthed frogs without limbs.

Mr. Love was leaning over his wife's bed, tenderly brushing his lips against her forehead. He acted as if Reiter wasn't there. "I love you, my darling."

Reiter blushed when he saw Betty Love's lips part ever so slightly. "Even with my crooked mouth?"

"Even if you had one eye in the middle of your forehead." With his finger he traced a line down the bridge of her nose to her chin. His voice turned to a whisper. "It's not your face I love, Betty. It's your soul." He lowered his eyes. "That's right, Betty. And that will never change."

Tears trickled down her face. She reached up and touched his cheek. "No one has every said that to me before." Her lips quivered, more on one side than the other. "I've been a fool all these years, Edmund." She dabbed at her eyes. "Can you forgive me?"

Reiter felt like an intruder. He cleared his throat to remind them he was in the room.

Edmund backed away, and Reiter stepped up to the bed. He studied Betty's face and thought he detected a slight movement in her lower lip. He felt a pounding in his chest. He took another look, and for the first time in weeks he had reason to hope. *Could Edward's devotion have had a mysterious effect on the injured,* he wondered.

When Reiter left the mansion, Brian drove him back to his lonely prison on the sixth floor. Maybe there's hope for me too, he thought before falling asleep.

CHAPTER EIGHTEEN

The next morning, he opened the shutters and was momentarily blinded by the golden rays of the sun dancing across the horizon of Beverly Hills. He sighed with relief as he closed Betty Love's chart. For the past weeks it had been opened every day. As if to put it all behind him for the moment, he slid the chart between some other files and slammed the drawer. He was glad it was the end of the month. He'd missed the last Clinica Day because of Betty's problem, and he was eager to get back on schedule.

On Friday morning, he was in the air. He landed in Puertecitos early, but Cobo was waiting for him. "Buenas dias, Espanto," Cobo said and helped push the plane to the cement pad and tie it down. He seemed unusually quiet, as if already caught in the web of the upcoming day. Reiter couldn't help glancing up the hill at his house perched above the town. It looked as forlorn and lonely as he felt.

There were a lot of people on Martine's porch. Some of them had been waiting for hours. Reiter tried to keep things in perspective and put the problems of the patients ahead of his personal ordeal. But perhaps his own pain made him more sensitive, and he was drawn to a stringy, unkempt man at the edge of the crowd. He held a frayed sombrero in his hands, and the soiled shirt that hung loosely over his bony chest looked as if it had been spattered by salt water and fish blood for years.

The man stood out from the rest because he didn't seem sick himself. He paced back and forth, as if ready to jump out of his skin. He kept edging towards the porch, but seemed hesitant to intrude, turning back repeatedly at the last minute. Finally, he got close enough to blurt out, "Por favor. I have to see el medico!" Then he stared at the ground as if he felt ashamed about his clumsy insistence.

Martine frowned. "Why not wait your turn with the others?" he admonished with an impatient wave of his hand. The man didn't look like he was ready to collapse, and Martine was a man who didn't like to stray from his routine.

Obviously dejected, the man wandered back to sit with the rest. They eyed him in silence. There was something about the man that evoked a feeling of pity in Reiter. Perhaps it was his own pain that made him more aware of the troubles of others. Or maybe, he thought ruefully, it was just a self-serving wish to be loved by somebody, anybody, that prompted him to whisper to Martine, "Why don't you see what's wrong with the guy?" Martine called the man over.

The fisherman looked gratefully at Martine and walked up to Reiter. "Buenos dias," he said. "My name is Nacho. I am from the fish camp," he stammered and took off his dusty sombrero as he lowered his eyes. "The one north of town."

"What can I do for you, hombre?" Reiter asked, placing a reassuring hand on his shoulder.

"I have a problem, medico." That's all he could say. Then he took a deep breath and tried once again. "Medico, por favor."

Whatever it was, Reiter realized it must be something serious. "Sientete, Nacho," he said. "Let's have a cerveza. Then we can talk."

Nacho shook his head, casting a curious look at Reiter. Then he twisted the brim of the sombrero with his callused fingers. He seemed lost. "Could you come out to our fish camp?" He pointed north with his hat. "Ten kilometers that way."

Reiter remembered that fish camp. He'd spotted a lot of pangas pulled up on the beach north of Speedy's when he'd flown in. "I know where it is." He looked at his watch, "I can be there in an hour or two."

Nacho put his sombrero back on. "Gracias, gracias, medico," he mumbled. Then he was gone.

Later that day, as they bounced down the winding road to the fish camp, Martine and Reiter were strangely quiet, each lost in thought, like two nervous spinsters on the way to a dance. Reiter had instinctively liked Nacho, but there was also something mysterious about him. Whatever it was, it intrigued him.

For his part, Martine had sensed that Reiter was troubled about something. "What's the matter with you?" he finally asked.

Reiter had been on the verge of sharing his burden with Martine several times, but he'd also promised himself not to lean on his friends. He would handle his problem alone without bothering anyone else. Perhaps the real reason was that a confession would be too humiliating. Maybe he wanted to hang on to his image. "Nothing's wrong, amigo. I was just thinking about this Nacho. There's something he isn't telling us, but I don't think his secret is a gold mine."

They turned off the road into the fish camp. There wasn't much going on in the settlement…the men must have gone out to fish in their pangas. Black buzzards circled overhead. The stench of rotting fish heads hit them before they climbed out of the truck. They brushed away the swarming flies as they walked.

Nacho must have been waiting and watching because he hurried over right away. A withered old man with a hunchback followed closely behind, his hawk-like nose perched above a bushy white mustache. "Es Juan, mi padre. This is my father," Nacho explained.

They led their two visitors around a clutch of ocotillo bushes and down a steep incline to a tiny shack nestled in a sheltered nook at the edge of the camp. It seemed hidden away, as though it held dark secrets. It looked as if it had just been thrown together today; the palm fronds were still a deep green.

A slender young woman stood at the entrance to the shack. She had an oval face with sharply defined cheekbones and rust-colored skin that seemed to blend in with the earth. Her neatly combed hair, with streaks of copper-brown, shone in the afternoon sun. Circles of pain lurked around her dark eyes. "Buenos dias. Nuestro hijo, Jorge, l'espera. Our son, Jorge, is waiting." She nodded.

"Maria es mi esposa, Maria is my wife," Nacho said and gestured towards the young woman.

The hunchbacked old man walked to the door like a domesticated ox. His eyes were fixed on the strangers. Then he stepped aside. ""Passale, come in," he said.

The tiny shack was dark, bare, and oppressive. They waited for their eyes to adjust to the dark. The stillness was eerie. A stench of decaying flesh filled the air. And then they saw him, a shadow in the murky light.

"Jorge, our son," Nacho said with a note of sad pride. He stepped over to a hole in the tarpaper wall and ripped off the piece of cardboard taped over it. The sunshine shot through the opening and reflected Jorge's shadow against the wall. The boy stepped out of his shadow and a beam of sunlight hit his face.

But there was no face, only a hole where the nose had been, with blobs of rotten flesh molded around it. The rest was a contorted bundle of scars with the upper lip twisted around the upper teeth like a rope. The lower lip was pulled down towards the chin, exposing the gums. The skin below the lip was like wrinkled parchment, freezing muscles and movement forever in a lifeless grimace. The boy's dark eyes blazed in their deep sockets like flickering flames from the bottom of a pit. They were the only part of the face with any expression. Any pain or joy had to come through them.

"A tank of butane exploded in his face." It was Jorge's mother who spoke. She paused as if to gather strength. "He screamed for weeks and weeks," the mother continued, trying to suppress a sob. "He never got better. After that things changed. The other children made fun of him. It has all been a nightmare." She looked toward her husband as if she was pleading with him to help her explain.

"Auda mi hijo, doctor. Help my son, Doctor," Nacho begged, tears welling up in his eyes. "So he can go to school again like the rest of the boys. That's all I ask."

The boy glanced at his father and mother, as if asking forgiveness for the way he looked. Then he turned slowly and looked at the strangers. "Buenos dias, Senores." His voice sounded high pitched in the dark.

They could almost touch the gloom in the shack. Reiter felt the heartbreak of the moment, but his mind wandered, knowing what they wanted of him, not sure he could give it. Instinctively, he looked around, as if searching for an opening, a way to get out. He wanted to vanish. He hesitated and felt a knot in his throat.

And then he got a grip on himself. Stepping up to Jorge, he took his hand. It felt small and trusting. "We're going to work together, amigo." He paused, overcome by the moment. "It may take a while. But I know we can do it."

Jorge didn't answer. He put his hands on what was left of his face and wept.

CHAPTER NINETEEN

As they drove back to Puertecitos, Reiter had the strange sensation he was being followed as he climbed the stairs toward his empty house. He stopped several times to catch his breath and look over his shoulder. He decided his imagination was running away from him when he heard the sound of footsteps again. "Will you help me?" It was Jorge's sad voice in the darkness. He tried to ignore it and continued on his way to the bedroom.

He sat down near the window and stared in the direction of the fish camp, overwhelmed by the promise he'd made to Jorge. He'd had no choice but to give him hope. Everyone needed hope. Perhaps that's why his mind shot back many years to the most hopeless place he'd ever known. It was known as Ward D at the State Hospital in Montana. He remembered those children who truly had no hope and no one who could help them.

He'd worked at the State Hospital the summer he met Linda, but Ward D was one place he wouldn't take her when he made rounds. 'Ward D.' D for Devil, as if he'd named it for himself. The most hopeless cases were hidden there, severely handicapped children who were thought beyond help.

Its chipped plaster walls and filthy windows gave Ward D an air of neglect. The building was hidden at the eastern-most corner of the hospital complex where the sun couldn't reach it. Tall oak trees with gnarled trunks cast permanent shadows over the grounds, making the building a perfect place for the outcasts. Brazen crows perched on the branches, their chatter drowning out the wails coming from the building. The complex looked abandoned except for the crows and an occasional male nurse who wandered in and out.

Reiter remembered the first time he'd gone there. He'd been asked to help a dentist who came to the hospital twice a month. His heart had pounded as he'd made his way to the building. Peering through the tiny window in the steel door, he could see water-stained paint peeling off the walls. The row of windows near the ceiling looked as if they hadn't been opened in years.

When he stepped inside, the fetid air and stench of human waste stung his nostrils. He gazed in disbelief at the wretched collection of children in the room, and for a minute he hoped he was having a bad dream—a nightmare about a dark forest with twisted limbs attached to writhing trunks with blank faces and flickering eyes. But it wasn't a dream. He heard strange moans that sounded as if demons were laughing. *No wonder they keep the place hidden away,* he thought. *This kind of hell was not meant to be seen.*

Some of the children were chained to the wall, shackles of leather around their wrists. Other patients seemed frozen in place, staring into space, oblivious to buzzing flies and the screams of the others.

A male nurse with a sour expression and a fresh crew cut walked up behind him. "We're waiting for Dr. Toose," he said. "How about sitting here for a minute?" He pointed to a bench by the door. "I have to get them ready." He might as well have told him to shut up and stay out of the way.

Reiter watched in disbelief as the nurse turned on a water hose and started spraying the cowering children. Some of them held up their hands and howled in gestures of surrender, begging for mercy, while others just crouched down, trying to shield themselves from the ice-cold blast. They were all naked, covered with waste, dried bits of food and something slimy that could only be vomit. As the water splashed over them, it trickled onto the rough cement toward a drain in the middle of the floor. The grate had been removed, and it looked like a gaping wound in the floor.

Finally, Dr. Toose came through the door. He had a long, bony face that made Reiter think of a horse. Sparse eyebrows crossed a prominent brow, and other than a rim of fuzzy hair, he was bald. His spider-like hands seemed tailor-made for the work he did, poking shiny tools into pried-open mouths. As if on cue, one of the male nurses grabbed the first patient, a wide-eyed girl who instinctively held up her hands and tried to back away. Her skin was stretched so taut over knobby joints that Reiter thought it was ready to tear apart. She reminded him of a gargoyle, with matted red hair plastered on her forehead.

The nurse held on to her hand and snapped the shackle off her wrist. Then he rubbed a spot on her arm with a swab and plunged in a syringe that he'd held at the ready. It must have been a strong tranquilizer because she instantly became limp and silent. Her glassy eyes stared at the walls before her head dropped to her chest. "I think she's ready, Doctor Tooth," the attendant said.

"Stop calling me Dr. Tooth," the dentist insisted. "How often have I told you it's pronounced with an S and not a TH?" he snapped. "Hold her down, you hear?" he ordered without a hint of compassion in his voice.

Dr. Toose slipped a rubber wedge in the corner of the girl's mouth. She gagged a few times, and her eyes filled with terror. Then he reached into his bag and pulled out a pair of dental pliers. Without saying a word, he applied them to what must have been the troublesome tooth. "Hold her steady, fellows. Real steady," he said as he rocked the handle of the pliers. There was a cracking sound when the tooth was finally wrenched out. He held it up for all to see, a gleam of triumph in his eyes.

Tears streamed down the girl's cheeks, her sobs muffled by the rubber device still in her mouth. The nurse's eyes were fixed on the tooth, and he nodded. "She won't be biting for a while."

Reiter wanted to speak up, but he knew it was useless. He surveyed the room. *If there's a hell on this earth*, he thought to himself, *this is it*. A hell made by man. He felt discouraged and helpless, but he was determined to do something. The first thing that came to his mind was to go to Dr. Gage, the hospital administrator. Maybe Gage could do something.

Reiter liked Dr. Gage from the first day they met. Edwin Gage was a short, stocky man with a gentle smile. He'd been in Public Health most of his life. His thin gray hair was neatly combed back, and his deep-set eyes glowed with good intentions. For Reiter, spending time in Dr. Gage's office was always special. They talked about all sorts of things: about life and death, health and disease, and things that had nothing to do with their work in the hospital. Their lengthy talks always filled him with fresh ideas and never failed to rekindle his spirit.

He rushed to the Administration Building and when he reached Dr. Gage's office, he burst in after barely knocking. Dr. Gage didn't act surprised as he looked up from his desk. He leaned back in his swivel chair and slowly took off his glasses. "What's up, young man?" He almost sounded as if he'd been expecting him.

"I need to tell you about the patients in Ward D." Reiter paused, not wanting to sound impulsive. "Why are they treated like that? Worse than animals." There was almost an accusatory tone in his voice. "Have you ever been over there?"

Gage stroked his chin, as if searching for words. "I know exactly what you're talking about." Reiter detected the sadness in his voice. "But there's only so much we can do. The budget is tight, and we can't hire the number of people we need." He looked directly at Reiter. "But more than that, it's not easy to find staff to work there very long. You can't even stand it for an hour."

Gage got up from his desk and looked in the direction of the cluster of trees hiding Ward D. "I hate to agree it is hell for those youngsters over there. A waiting game till they die." Gage shrugged. "At times, you find hell here on earth. Those patients have it a little better than hell if you remember it's not forever."

As if he knew his explanations weren't enough, Dr. Gage attempted a weak smile. "Do me a favor," he said. "The next time you go in there, just show them you aren't afraid to care. Even those poor children can understand the meaning of love. I know that in the long run, you'll be a better doctor for it." He bore down on Reiter. "Or isn't that what you want?"

Reiter's eyes wandered to the window behind Gage where the rolling hills were framed in the afternoon sun. He thought he caught a glimpse of Linda walking across the grounds. It was her love that made him a better doctor and a better man. Maybe he could go back into that place and, like Gage said, "Make their hell a little easier."

"Thank you, Doctor Gage. I think I understand," he said and left the office. He couldn't get the girl in Ward D off his mind. He bit his lip at the thought of the pain she must be feeling. He turned in the direction of the infamous ward.

Once again he looked through the small window in the door. The red-haired girl was still writhing on the floor. He knocked, and the startled male nurse let him in. "I just want to look at the patient for a moment," Reiter said. It was even an effort to speak calmly, and he felt himself choking up.

"Don't touch her, man, whatever you do," the nurse warned him. "The next thing, she'll bite you too."

Reiter ignored him and walked over to the girl. She was lying on a mat with her knees drawn up to her chest, rocking back and forth and sobbing silently. Her unshackled hand was under her cheek, and a trickle of blood mixed with tears ran down the side of her chin. She was in pain. He fought back his own tears. Gage's words kept rattling his mind: "It's a waiting game till they die. A little better than hell."

Reiter crouched down and patted her shoulder as he looked into her sunken eyes and studied her features. Her eyes spoke of despair, and her mouth was turned down at the corners. He could almost hear the desperate cry of her soul, "Put me out of this misery."

He asked for a syringe of pain medication and without a word, injected it in her arm. Gently, he kneaded her shoulders, and her sobbing gradually ceased; the corners of her mouth turned up just a little. Whatever he did must have surprised her. How would she know about tenderness, about caring? It wasn't part of her world.

Then he noticed an angry-looking sore on the girl's left wrist where the shackle had been. Carefully, he cleansed the red and rotting flesh around the wound and applied some antibiotic salve with a thick dressing. The girl closed her eyes and sighed.

"I don't want you to put this on her wrist till the sore has healed," he told the nurse, pointing to the shackle in his hands.

The nurse shrugged his shoulders. "You should know we can't do that. She almost broke a man's jaw a little while back," he muttered in a way that left no room for discussion. He picked up the manacle and clamped it back on the bandaged wrist.

Reiter tried to ignore him. With a tissue he wiped away the blood trickling down her chin. And the girl gave him the look of a grateful dog. He wasn't sure if he detected a ray of hope in the dark eyes that were locked on him. The only thing he could do was to stay there with his hand on her shoulder.

The rest of the patients were quiet and looked at each other as if they were confused about what was happening. He could feel her relax. He lifted his eyes and looked around. The rest of them were staring at him. Was he just dreaming or was there a breeze sweeping through the stench?

Slowly, he got up and made his way to the door. The nurse-attendant followed him and whispered in his ear, "Don't let it get to you. They don't really feel a thing. They don't know about pain and forget real quick."

A few minutes later, he was back in his room. It was a neat, clean place with a comfortable bed and a desk in one corner. Bright sunshine streamed through the open window. He lay down on the bed and buried his head in the pillow. He felt his anger turn to sorrow, and he sobbed.

***

Ward D, hidden beneath the twisted oaks or Jorge's shack at the bottom of the ravine of the fish camp…neither place was meant to be seen. It was as if the world wanted to wish them away, pretend they didn't exist.

He was disturbed that he'd flirted with the idea of bolting out of Jorge's shack that afternoon. He wondered if the isolation from his family and his fear of seeing Consuelo again were turning him into a recluse both in Baja and in Beverly Hills. He felt reluctant to reach out to other people. And that was not like him.

Suddenly, he felt the need to talk to Beto. Though it was getting late, he flew down the stairs and hurried out to the point. Beto was hunkered down in front of his shelter, staring out at the waves.

"My life is turning into a living hell," Reiter began. "My wife hasn't come back, and I'm going out of my mind. All I do is walk around like a dead man. I want to hide from the world. How can I make all this go away?" Reiter pleaded.

Beto studied the angry sea. "Nobody can wish a storm away. Only the clouds and the winds can put an end to it. If you fight it, you end up unleashing more fury," Beto admonished him. "Why don't you stop trying to end the storm and just steady the boat, hang on to the rigging and think of someone who's got it worse. There are people about to drown in waves bigger than yours."

Reiter frowned. How could Beto know about Jorge?

Listen to me." Beto sounded emphatic. "No more fighting the winds. It's time to let go." Beto warned him, "Stop trying to control the people you care for, the people you love." He paused and turned to Reiter. "It will only torture their spirit and chase them away."

"Put into your head that your woman is gone," Beto said as Reiter drew near. "And there is nothing you can do about it," he added. "But even if she never comes back, a part of her will never leave your heart."

Reiter nodded. *Yes,* he told himself, *Beto's right. Get rid of the obsession that you can control her spirit, wherever she is. You promised to let her have her way, but keep insisting on your own. Didn't you make a pact to give her time to think it all over? In the end, like Beto says, there's nothing you can do about it anyway. Let go, hombre! Think of someone else. Think of Jorge, and the storm he and his family are in.*

When he got back to his house on the hill, Reiter felt as if the storm within him had died. Even the pain was different, honing his senses rather than numbing them. He felt calmer, not fretting every second, more at peace, more resigned to whatever might come.

Rudi Unterthiner

CHAPTER TWENTY

Reiter could have sworn bloodthirsty coyotes were chasing him as he hurried to the airstrip. He dreaded running into any of his friends, knowing there was no way to be himself, to pretend things were normal. And the thought of meeting Consuelo made him leap into the airplane and slam the doors. Quickly, he pointed it into the pre-dawn sky. The plane hugged the coastline as he flew north to Santa Monica.

Desperate for a reprieve from the monsters within him, he decided to head for Betty Love's mansion the moment he landed. He was anxious to reassure himself that her lip was getting better.

When he got to the mansion, he was once again escorted to her suite. Betty Love greeted him. "It's so good to see my handsome doctor." Her voice was warm and inviting and so was her smile. It was as if a thousand tons had lifted from his back when he saw her lips moving. Suddenly the sunshine streaming through the bay window was brighter, the colors of the room more suffused.

"Maria, you can leave us alone," Miss Love said to the maid without taking her eyes off Reiter. She folded her arms and drew up her knees. Two gold-rimmed hand mirrors were on the end table. She picked one up and held it in front of her face.

"I always believed things would work out," she insisted. He didn't know what to make of her faith, by all accounts much stronger than his own.

Reiter blushed. "Where could I wash my hands?"

She continued to study her image in the mirror. Finally, she looked up. Their eyes locked for a moment, and then she waved a pale hand toward a door. "In there, Dr. Reiter."

He entered a huge mirrored room. It was not like any bathroom he'd ever been in. Rows of bright lights shone around myriads of mirrors that seemed to wrap around him. He blinked in the glare. As he washed his hands, he saw his image reflected so many times it made him feel he was in a crowd.

He thought about the cantina in Puertecitos and the single light bulb that hung from the cracked ceiling. It cast a warm glow over the corner table where he and his friends spent so many hours. On damp winter nights, everyone entering the cantina cast a familiar shadow on the walls, and the shadows linked them together, as if they were all made of one piece.

He threw a quick glance in the mirror in front of him and was surprised at the lines and furrows across his forehead and around his eyes. Like on that day in the coal mine so many years ago, he seemed to look older than his years. Guilt and regret kept taking their toll. Or was it that he felt out of place here? He swallowed down the questions with bitter uncertainty.

A shrill cry brought him back to the present, and he dropped the heart-shaped bar of soap he was holding.

"Oh, my God! Get it out! Someone call Felipe!" Miss Love was screaming as if fearing for her life.

He rushed back into the bedroom and found her pale and trembling with the bedspread pulled up to her chin.

"What happened? What is it, Miss Love?"

"There's a mouse in here! Get it out!" she shrieked.

Suddenly, the room came alive with people running in from all over the place: maids in starched uniforms and little white caps, gardeners, and other servants. They hurried over to Betty Love, a glint of fear in their brown eyes. "Que paso?" They all spoke at once.

Betty Love pointed under the bed and covered her mouth with a hand. "It's under the bed." She paused and closed her eyes. "Get the damn thing." Everyone looked under the bed. Suddenly the mouse scurried out and ran along the wall. Reiter could have sworn it stopped for a moment below a painting of Mickey Mouse and looked up before disappearing behind a chest of drawers.

Reiter thought he saw Miss Love glance at the painted mouse on the wall too, and he wondered what was going through her mind. She probably had invested in the company that made Mickey Mouse famous. A mouse was okay as long as it made money.

"You let it get away, didn't you?" she quavered.

Suddenly, Felipe, the head gardener, showed up, and Miss Love quieted down.

"Buenos dias, Senora", he said, and he removed his hat. The way he spoke, curt and precise, had the ring of a general to it.

A hint of respect crept into Betty Love's voice. "There's a mouse in this room, Felipe," she said. "See what you can do."

Felipe surveyed the scene and turned to Miss Love. "What we need is the cat," he announced, and left the room. The other servants all nodded in agreement and beamed at him. Surely, Felipe would solve the problem, maybe even change their lot here? Reiter could almost feel a wave of pride in the room. Perhaps Miss Love was realizing that these people were important to running her house and taking care of her.

Instead, Miss Love seemed to ignore the servants and turned to Reiter. "Can you believe this? I never dreamed I'd live to see a mouse in my bedroom!"

Just then, Felipe strode back in the room, a fat Persian cat under his arm. It was a tranquil animal, a shiny collar glistening against perfectly groomed fur. Felipe marched up to the dresser and whispered to the animal, "Go get the mouse. I count on you, you beautiful thing." He must have added the flattery remembering how vain the cat was.

The thousand-dollar Persian cat sat on the thousand dollar Persian rug and looked up at Felipe, as if waiting for some Italian sardines.

Felipe winced. Betty Love was outraged. "I can't count on you people," she exclaimed. "First, you let a mouse in my room, and now you can't manage to catch it." She gave them all a look of disgust. "I can't stay in this room a minute longer."

The servants continued their conversation, breaking into Spanish as if she wasn't there. "What now? What are you going to do, Felipe?" one of the maids asked. "The mouse is still here."

155

"Hold on a minute," Felipe interjected. "Why catch the poor thing? I have no intention of catching the mouse." There was an accusing ring to his voice. "I'm tired of people trying to catch me. I know all about it." He paused and lowered his voice. "What makes you think anybody here is much different than that mouse? What are we in this house? To the gringos? No better than mice." His voice cracked for a second as if he hated to be blunt, but that they left him no choice. "We are worse than mice. We are illegal mice. Mice with no green cards."

Felipe knew he had their attention. "At least the mouse," he said, "can hide and is safe in some crack. No police or migra can keep it from scuttling back and forth across the border. The senora's house is like your hiding place in the wall," he added. "When she is in the right mood, she throws you some crumbs. And what if she isn't? What then?" He held back with the answer as if to make sure the question had sunk in. "She'll have the migra hunt us down and trap us."

What Felipe said next made Reiter chuckle. "And you know what? There are many nights I feed the mice." There was a collective gasp. "Why not?" And with that, Felipe picked up the cat, a mischievous glint in his eyes.

Betty Love looked bewildered, and she darted from the bed to Reiter's side. As he led her out the door, she threw the servants one last, withering look.

Walking down the hall, she turned to him, "What were they talking about back there?"

"I couldn't understand," he lied. "Probably making plans to get rid of your mice."

***

Felipe's words made Reiter think back to those miserable days when the 'migra' tried to catch him too. As he walked to the car, he recalled that cold and gloomy winter in Denver. It was his second year in America, and his Fulbright student visa had expired. The immigration officials were hot on his trail. He'd moved to Colorado by then, but the letters followed him wherever he went. They all said the same thing: He was going to be deported.

He'd tried to keep to himself, blending in as a ski instructor in the ski resorts west of Denver. He preferred a place called Berthoud Pass because it was less known and easier to hide. The job didn't pay much, but no one asked for identification papers. Most of the time he lived in a rickety car another ski instructor who'd been deported had left him. "I'll be back," were his parting words.

Reiter settled into a grueling routine so he could vanish into the crowd. He'd pick a different place to park the car each night, a schoolyard, a supermarket, or hospital parking lot where he could slip in between other cars and avoid the suspicious stares of strangers.

Nights in the car were cold and cramped, so he tried to make the evenings last as long as he could. Often he went to the public library where he practiced English by reading the newspapers, repeating words in a whisper. He hated the 'th' sounds, which he couldn't pronounce. The hushed echo of his own voice in the empty room discouraged him.

For weeks he struggled with the damn sounds until one could night at the end of October when it all seemed to fall into place. "Mo-th-er, fa-th-er, o-th-er"...Suddenly, the 'th' sounded right to him—just like an American.

His upbeat mood defied the gloom of the dreary night as he left the library and climbed into the old car. He'd already decided that the Jefferson Elementary parking lot would be a good place to spend the night. Pulling out into the street, he was blinded by a pair of bright lights in the rearview mirror. Instinctively, he speeded up and had a seeking feeling when the car behind him went faster too. He was sure it was a government car, and it was right on his tail. A cold sweat broke out on his forehead and he tightened his grip on the steering wheel.

With a start, he suddenly remembered that the licenses plates on the car were expired. He'd tried to pay the fee weeks ago, but the clerk behind the counter had eyed him suspiciously and insisted on documents he couldn't produce. He'd left the office in a hurry without getting new plates.

The worst scenario began to flash through his mind: He saw himself handcuffed and herded off to jail, accused of stealing a car, driving without a license, being an illegal alien on the run. He'd end up a criminal and spend years in the state prison.

Frantically, he searched for a side street where he could hide, but the car following him wouldn't let up. Suddenly, he heard the whistle of a train and decided it was his only chance to escape. Warning bells were clanging and red lights were flashing as he shot across the railway tracks. The crossing arm slammed down behind him, and the train thundered through, leaving the gray sedan on the other side of the tracks.

Taking a deep breath, he turned down a side street that took him to the east end of Colfax Avenue, the worst part of town. A crooked neon sign with a burned out letter S hung over a building at the far end of the street—'ILVER STAR SALOON'. The chipped plaster exterior wore a layer of soot from the railroad that gave it an air of despair. It seemed the only building on the block that hadn't been demolished or boarded up.

The alley behind the building had no streetlights, and he pulled in and turned off the engine. As he stepped out of the car, a haunting voice drifted from the building. Approaching the door, he caught the sweet smell of burning sage that reminded him of the hills of Tyrol.

It was dark inside, but a red glow bathed the walls, giving the room a cozy, warm feeling. The patrons were mere shadows lumped together around a long bar that took up most of the room. All of them wore hats that seemed too large for their faces or were meant to hide them. The place gave him a sense of comfort, an unexpected reprieve from the immigration officers on his trail. At least, that's what he hoped.

The name of the singer, Floyd Red Crow Westerman, was scrawled on a sign behind him. His deep, baritone voice drowned out any conversation, and Reiter was intrigued by the way it could rise when he wanted to add a whoop at the end of a verse. Reiter struggled to follow the words of the song and was proud of himself when he found he could understand most of them.

The singer's dark, shoulder-length hair was pulled back and held in place with a beaded clip. A partial breastplate made of bones hung over his leather shirt. His cheekbones were chiseled and bold, but the distant, far-away look in his gray eyes gave him the air of a man on the run. During his break, he sat down next to Reiter at the far end of the bar. "You're new in here," he said. "Anything special you'd like to hear during the next set?"

Reiter was startled. The last thing he wanted was for any one to notice him. He looked down and shook his head. "I like everything you sing, Sir." His accent sounded strong, and he blushed.

"So, you're not from around her," Red Crow said. "Where'd you come from?"

It had been a long time since anyone except an immigration officer was interested in him. Before he could stop himself, Reiter told Floyd Red Crow a little bit about his wanderings and how he happened to be in Denver. "But they don't want me to stay," he admitted. "I try to keep out of sight. I'm an outsider. For a while."

Floyd gave him a warm smile. "Funny thing, I'm an outsider too. But my people were here long before the white man came." Reiter's eyes widened, and the man went on. "You see, my people," and he nodded towards the others in the bar, "are not really welcome, even here."

"I read about Indians when I was a boy," Reiter said. "I know all the stories of Old Shatter Hand. Do you know about him?"

Red Crow laughed and shook his head. "I'm Lakota from the Pine Ridge Reservation in South Dakota. But it wasn't like your stories when I grew up. For many years, they wouldn't let us speak our language, sing our songs, or hold our dances. Drinking alcohol, having a driver's license, marrying a white person…everything was forbidden. We were aliens, my friend. Outsiders in our own country. Savages, they called us."

Reiter was overcome by a sense of empathy. "I know exactly what you mean. My people were forbidden by the Fascists to speak their language. But you had it worse."

Red Crow nodded. "They tried to exterminate us." He turned to Reiter. "We are brothers in pain. Mitakuye oyassin. That means all my relations and you are part of that, my friend. All creation is." He took another sip of his coke. "I have to go back now and sing like an Indian. But when I leave this bar, they want me to act like a white man."

***

One afternoon, a week later, Reiter brought up his housing dilemma to one of his students, a stuffy accountant from Denver. "You wouldn't know a place where I could stay in my car for a day or two? Just until they have an opening at the YMCA, would you?" he'd added. The minute he said it, he was gripped by shame. The last time he tried to stay at the 'Y' the clerk at the front desk had asked for a social security number. Reiter had pulled up his collar and hurried out.

The accountant must have sensed the desperation in Reiter's voice; he surprised him by this response, "Actually, you could hole up in the utility trailer sitting in our back yard." He sounded matter-of-fact, as if he was giving advice about taxes. "All we use it for is camping gear in the summer," he explained. "And it's perfect for hauling junk and dead leaves in the fall. We have no use for it other than that. You can crawl in from the tailgate. At least, it'll keep you out of the weather."

Reiter was grateful for the reprieve. He put a piece of plywood across the corrugated metal floor and threw a sleeping bag on top. As he bundled up in the darkness of the long winter nights, his mind often strayed to his homeland. More and more he missed his friends, family, and his small village. He found himself wondering if he'd ever see them again. He hadn't heard from his mother and father for months, but he knew they must be sick with worry. That tore at his conscience. But there were only a handful of phones in Sterzing, and he couldn't afford a trans-Atlantic call anyway. He'd write a letter from time to time, though he knew it took weeks to reach them, and he could never be sure he'd be in the same place when they wrote back.

As the weeks went by, he wondered if he was imagining things because he felt the accountant in the warm house started eyeing him with suspicion and trying to avoid him. After all, Reiter was just a drifter to him. The accountant couldn't know how it felt to be cut off from the world, living in fear that anything you might say or do could get you in trouble. Reiter was terrified that his accent might give him away, so he spoke very little.

He'd even become paranoid about leaving tracks in the snow. He made a habit of inching along an icy path that the accountant used when he took out the garbage. It skirted one side of the trailer, and from there he could hop inside with only one step. If there was fresh snow, he'd lean out of the trailer and use a broom to wipe the last footprint away, obliterating any sign that led to his tomb. Then he'd pull up the tailgate

Sometimes in the early morning, he'd watch the accountant's cat sneak out of the pet door and hunch down as if it was sure there was something under the snow. Its tail would twitch slowly, and then it would leap forward, striking at something that darted out of the snow. Reiter would pull his sleeping bag closer as he watched the cat fling a mouse in the air, only to catch it again when it landed. Then it would turn it loose and let it run for a second before pouncing again.

It was no different than what the immigration agents were doing to him. They' let him run for a while till he'd run out of breath, then catch up to him again. There were times when he felt as if he'd landed back in the coal mine, unable to escape. He found himself listening to every sound in the night air, and his heart would pound with fright when he thought he heard footsteps.

When he made his way out of the yard in the mornings, the hard-packed snow crunched under his shoes. Carefully he scanned the street for a gray sedan with government license plates. If the streets were clear, he'd catch the next bus to the YMCA to shower and shave.

Then one day, a gray-faced man with wire-rimmed glasses came up to him as he got off the bus. The high voice and quick movements reminded him of the cat in the yard. "Are you Paul Reiter?" the man asked, opening a brown folder.

"Yes, I am." Reiter tried to keep the answer brief to hide his accent, but he knew it was already too late.

"Can you tell me where you live?" the man wanted to know, as he got ready to scribble his answers on a pad.

Reiter hesitated. "With a friend up on Berthoud's Pass," he said. He blushed because he still had trouble pronouncing the 'th'. He wondered too late if they knew he worked there.

The man handed him a copy of a deportation order and asked him to sign it. "In the meantime you are expected to report to our office twice a week. Every Monday and Thursday at 4:00 p.m."

Even as he signed, Reiter made up his mind to gain some time by going underground again—another job in another city, another place to hide. He had to become a phantom once more.

CHAPTER TWENTY-ONE

Reiter tried to follow Beto's advice and put Linda out of his mind. Beto said to forget about time, that being apart had nothing to do with physical distance. Like the waves on the ocean, he explained, there was no beginning and no end when you truly care about someone. But it took only minutes for his good intentions to be gone, blown away by winds of self-pity. He found himself struggling with the urge to call his wife and beg forgiveness. He'd heard that she and the children were fine, which on one hand was reassuring and on the other hand was an unpleasant reminder that he wasn't indispensable. They seemed to manage without him easier than he did without them.

Glancing at his schedule one morning, he noted that there was a committee meeting at the City Hospital that night. Usually, he dreaded the boring affairs, but this time he surprised himself by almost looking forward to the meeting. Being at the hospital would take his mind off his troubles, and he could make arrangements for Jorge's surgery.

Dr. John Hassler, Chief of the Medical Staff, chaired the meeting in one of the stuffy conference rooms. He was a stout man with a paunch and unkempt gray hair that flowed over rounded shoulders. While he spoke, he tapped the table with his finger, as if demanding undivided attention. To highlight a point, he'd bang his fist on the table, and sometimes his notes would fly in the air. There seemed no end to the important points he tried to make, but after a while nobody seemed to pay much attention.

As he listened to the speech, Reiter remembered the icy stare the man had given him years ago at a staff meeting in another hospital. Reiter had just joined the staff of St. Luke's as a junior plastic surgeon and had been invited to comment on his specialty. He recalled how his heart had pounded as he'd walked to the podium. He'd clutched the microphone Dr. Hassler handed him. "Ladies and gentlemen," he began, "I'm pleased to be on the staff of this fine medical center. I'm impressed with its state-of-the-art operating theaters, diagnostic facilities, and laboratories, and with the caliber of this staff." He paused to gain composure, unsure what the reaction to his next statement would be. "On the other hand, if facilities like this are not available to every patient, then to my mind they don't serve the purpose."

"Just yesterday," he went on, "a Mexican farm worker had fallen from a palm tree he was trimming and sustained some nasty facial fractures. Because he had no insurance, his family was told to take him across the border to Mexico, a four hour drive from here." There was an eerie silence in the room as he went on. "It concerns me that modern medicine is only for those who can afford it."

His voice seemed to grow more confident as he went on he ignored the dubious looks in some of the doctor's eyes.

"I wonder if it isn't time to take a good look at the medical system in our country. There are ways to make our services available to everyone. I went to medical school in Canada, and I've seen it work. The Province of Saskatchewan, for example, has a system that insures affordable medical care to everyone." Suddenly, whispers interrupted the silence. Reiter looked out and saw his friend, Ripton Jeffers, the only black physician on staff, give him a nod and a fleeting smile.

When the meeting was over, he was aware of the disparaging looks many of his colleagues gave him. Some avoided him altogether. Dr. Hassler put a hand on Reiter's arm as he was leaving. "Maybe you should go back there and take care of every sled dog on the loose?" he sneered.

Reiter backed away, as if he was struck by a whip. Behind him was the senior plastic surgeon of the hospital, Dr. Rafael Sporks. He'd been professor of plastic surgery at a New York university and had always made a point of ignoring Reiter. Tonight, he stopped him and said with a condescending smirk, "It might be wise to tone down the rhetoric, Dr. Reiter. If you want to survive in this town, that is."

Later, when he applied to join the staff at City Hospital, he met with fierce opposition. Hassler and his friends tried to squash his application, looking desperately for any reason they could find. What hurt most was their claim that he was not a good doctor, that because he was an outsider he was not trustworthy. He kept the pain of their accusations to himself, but in his heart he knew the real reason for their animosity was that speech he'd given at St. Luke's.

"You'll run into people like this all your life," Linda tried to console him. "Like Willy in the coal mine." Still, he was almost ready to give up when he received a letter from Ripton Jeffers. It almost sounded like Beto was speaking as he advised Reiter to hang on to the rigging until the storm died down. It helped him cope with the Willys he ran across on hospital staffs, medical licensing boards, and professional associations. He often pulled it out on days when he questioned his life and was overwhelmed by the strain of it all:

"Dear Paul:

I want to tell you how much I appreciate your friendship, first of all as a human being and secondly as a fellow physician. I truly admire the way you always put the welfare of others first. During your talk at the staff meeting the other day, you suggested that we go back to the concept of the family doctor—and you are a good example, my friend—because I've seen you take care of patients whether they have money or not. It was something that needed to be said. You made the point that all the medical know-how in the world is of little use if people can't afford it.

I know you came to this country alone fought to get into medical school. I know what it takes because the odds were against me too. The difference is that I never had the guts to be so outspoken and sometimes I'm sorry for that. I like that you're not afraid to say what's on your mind. But at the same time it saddens me because I know you'll pay a price for your beliefs.

Be prepared—they'll make you pay dearly, put obstacles in your way, spread rumors about you, instigate lawsuits, keep you off hospital staffs, and influence boards and committees against you. They'll never give up. You'll be on the outside from now on, and I know it's not an easy place to be. Remember that the person who sticks his head above the crowd is the first one to be shot. Your views on medicine, and your unusual surgical abilities make you the perfect target.

I don't know how you can avoid it. All you can do is not let it get to you. Hang on and good luck.
Your friend,
Ripton Jeffers, M.D."

***

But it didn't start out this way. He thought of those merciless years in medical school when days of classes and clinics blurred with nights of study and review. He'd plowed through them relentlessly in his drive to be a medical doctor, trying to prepare for a lifetime of healing.

The seed to be a doctor had been planted long before he entered medical school. During the war, he'd seen men without limbs hobbling around, some with patches over their eyes. And the dead. Though he was only a child, he had railed against a feeling of helplessness. He thought about how he could make a difference by being a healer, a medical doctor. It became an obsession.

In the late 1950s, when he came to America, the dream of becoming a doctor was stronger than ever. When his student visa ran out, it was impossible to stay in the country and continue his schooling. Still, he knew if he left America he'd never become a doctor. That's when his battle with the Immigration Service began, their letters shadowing him everywhere. "You have thirty days to procure a proper visa", they declared, "In lieu of deportation." It was a threat he couldn't escape except by keeping on the move.

Finally, he was able to stay put long enough to attend a small, private university in the state of Washington. They let him enroll as a senior, giving credit for the European Lyceum and his year as a Fulbright scholar. To pay expenses, he worked the nightshift at the Kaiser Aluminum plant not far from the campus. Night after night, he'd guide the spigots that poured molten metal into endless rows of hollowed carbon blocks. The boring routine of the assembly line dulled his fears at being discovered. Sometimes, he'd play games in his mind, crumpling imaginary letters from Washington and tossing them in the molten steel that slid by. He also spent hours pretending he was a doctor, picturing himself in a white lab coat with a stethoscope around his neck. He smiled at the thought.

"What are you dreaming this time, boy?" The big-shouldered foreman startled him.

"Of being a doctor some day," Reiter replied as he readjusted his hard hat and wiped the steam from the protective goggles.

"No dreaming here," the foreman warned.

Toward the end of his studies, he began applying to medical schools at various state universities. It took hours and faith to fill out the lengthy questionnaires and the many requests for letters of recommendation. When he got to the part that asked for a permanent address, he always felt a cold sweat on his forehead. Nervously, he chewed on the end of his pencil as the waves of sadness spilled over him. Everybody had a home, a place they belonged to, usually the place where they were born. But not him. He was still a phantom.

The only thing he could really come up with was "General Delivery, Spokane, Washington." He scribbled it down with a trembling hand and felt ashamed there was no street or house number. But the words, "in lieu of deportation" danced in front of his eyes, and he knew he had to remain elusive.

Then came the letters of rejection. Each one was a stab in the heart. He 'wasn't eligible' they explained neatly, because most of their slots were reserved for residents of the state where the university was located. The letters were another painful reminder that he was a misfit who didn't belong, that something in him was missing. He was a lonesome drifter attached to nothing, to nobody.

If the letters were meant to discourage him, they didn't work. Instead, the lit a fire in him that made him persist. He decided to apply to private universities like Stanford, The University of Southern California, and Columbia; there was nothing to lose.

He spent days sending out applications, and then days turned into months as he waited for a response. He could remember when the first letter came. He'd looked at the envelope with Stanford University printed in the upper left hand corner and stuck it in his back pocket. For two hours, he was afraid to open it, not sure he could swallow another defeat.

Finally, sitting in the school cafeteria, he took the letter out of his pocket and with trembling hands ripped it open. He jumped up and let out a whoop when he saw the magical words "Letter of Acceptance" stamped across the top. He wanted to tell everyone in the room, "I made it," but thought better of it and sat down again. The students at the next table looked at each other and shook their heads.

When took a closer look at the letter, he saw a sentence about the "financial requirements." Immediately, his elation melted away. They needed a deposit, half of the eighteen hundred dollar tuition, immediately. Where could he come up with that kind of money?

Walking the streets later that afternoon, he felt once more like that discouraged young man in the back room at Idyllwild Airport. It was so real he could feel the heat rising in his face, remembering when the people in uniform came to get him that morning. "There is no way you can stay," they'd told him. He turned down a lonely alley that cut through the campus and raised the lapel of his worn sports coat to fend off the sudden blast of icy wind from the north.

He quickened his pace. He couldn't give up now. He headed towards the school library. Someone had once mentioned medical schools in Canada. The schools there were part of the North American Association of Medical Colleges with the same curriculum, the same examination system as the United States, and the same credentials, but tuition was only a fraction of that of private U.S.

schools. He spent the better part of the night looking up Canadian medical schools and writing applications all over again.

The responses were disappointingly similar to the state universities in the U.S. Foreign students were not often admitted; there were only a few positions reserved for them. With that slim chance in mind, he decided to visit one of the schools where he'd applied. He lost count of the coins he lost in public phone booths, pleading with clerks for an appointment. Finally, he managed to schedule an interview with an assistant dean in the admissions office of the University of Alberta. It was a school well known for its faculty and scientific curriculum, and he could drive there in a day and a half.

He arrived at the campus hours ahead of schedule and spent the time meandering through imposing buildings and hospital pavilions, pretending he was already a medical student. Finally, he sat across from the Assistant Dean, a man with fiery red hair who looked like he'd had a bad case of acne when he was young. His starched white lab coat was buttoned all the way to the top. A stethoscope dangled from his pocket like an ominous reminder that he was a doctor, while Reiter might never be one.

The Assistant Dean opened a yellow folder. Reiter strained to read the name written in the corner, but he didn't want to be obvious, and besides it wasn't easy to read the letters upside down. "Reiter is your name?" the man asked without looking up. There was a hint of mockery in his voice, as if he didn't care for the sound of the name.

Reiter squared his shoulders and hoped the man didn't notice the threadbare edges of his sports coat. Trying to come across as being at ease, he uncrossed his legs. When he saw specks of mud on his shiny shoes, he tensed up again. "Yes sir," he said self-consciously.

The gentleman kept scanning the folder. "It says here you've done rather well as an undergraduate," he remarked, as if that didn't suit him. "It also says your grades are good, and I see good recommendations." Reiter felt his heart pounding and hoping. He clasped his hands under the table. "There is only one problem." The man looked up. "We have another thousand applications like yours. Our quota for this year's class is forty-two. Do you understand what that means?"

Reiter did know what that meant and thanked him as he shuffled out of the office.

That evening in the hospital library, he pored over the admission policy of the university. In the pamphlet, he read that the final decision was up to an Admissions Committee composed of eight physicians: three full-time professors and five clinical professors who were also in private practice. He jotted down the names and addresses of those five.

Over the next several days, he trekked to the five offices, one by one. He would walk in, without an appointment and with a confidence he didn't feel, and ask to see the doctor. He knew it was crazy, but it was as if the stubborn young man sitting in the waiting rooms among the patients was a different person.

In the end, he managed to see all five of the practicing committee members. When they first spotted him in their waiting rooms, they didn't bother to conceal their displeasure and seemed ready to dismiss him. But once in their office, whatever he said made them reconsider; he got their attention. He didn't plan what to say; he let it spill out on its own. Maybe it was the way he spoke, the way his eyes came alive, the way he leaned forward to tell them what being a doctor meant to him and why nothing was going to stand in his way. He said that he'd honor them someday by being a faithful healer, always doing his best. When he started talking, some of them took off their glasses, or looked away as if they were bored or didn't know how to take him. But by the time he finished, every one of them shook his hand and walked him to the door. He could feel hope when he looked in their eyes.

Two months later, he got a letter from the University of Alberta. The Assistant Dean, the one with the red hair and the pocked face had written, "We are pleased to inform you that you have been selected for the 1961 medical class that begins in September." The signature seemed to waver, and he could imagine the Dean's surprise.

CHAPTER TWENTY-TWO

One by one, the doctors filed out of the committee meeting. At the door, Reiter ran into Ripton Jeffers. "Good to see you, Ripton," he said. "I was thinking about you earlier. Got time for a cup of coffee?"

Sitting in the cafeteria together, Reiter talked of their years of friendship. "You can't know how often I look at the letter you once wrote me. It kept me going when I had all the trouble getting on staff at City Hospital, and well," he stammered, "probably more times than I like to admit."

"Then I'm glad I wrote it," Ripton said. "But I'm sorry that so much of what I predicted has come true. The medical establishment hasn't been easy on you. You've had to survive pretty much on your own. It couldn't have been easy, but you did it."

Reiter shrugged. "Yeah, well, for one thing, it's forced me to do more cosmetic surgery than anything else. I don't have to depend on referrals this way, but sometimes, to tell you the truth, I miss what I'd hoped to do as a doctor."

"You're good at what you do; that's the most important. As far as being a family doctor, you do your share of that…in Baja and for the farm workers here in the valley. At heart you're a country doctor. But you're also plastic surgeon who's got some world-famous patients. I know it drives the docs who were against you crazy." Ripton laughed. "In the end, you're better off. But I know it can't be easy to contend with their envy. And you must have learned that envy and hate aren't far apart. You have to keep looking over your shoulder."

***

The next morning, Reiter drove to St. Luke's Hospital on the east side of town. The faded tile roof and the uneven bricks floating through the walls gave the place a cozy appearance. The parking stalls along the perimeter were dug out of the thick adobe and looked as if they had been intended for horses or ox carts not so long ago. The square bell tower in the middle of the cobblestone courtyard convinced him the structure had been a mission at one time. No one remembered when the two stained-glass windows had been added above the hand-hewn double doors, but every time he drove up they seemed to sparkle, and he was reminded of a gentle old face.

The unlined face of the administrator, Sister Superior Mary Kathryn, was also gentle, though Reiter was sure the starched linen plastered across her forehead hid some secret wrinkles. He knew that she'd managed busy hospitals for some thirty years and that she had to be in her early seventies. Years ago, after his speech at the staff meeting, they'd talked about doing more charity cases at St. Luke's, and he knew in this hospital "surgical quotas" never came up.

He was in a good frame of mind when he headed for Sister Mary Kathryn's office to discuss Jorge's skin grafts and Juanita's baby with the cleft lip. The wizened nun listened attentively when he told her the number of procedures the two children would need and the expected recovery time. Donning her wire-rimmed glasses, she thumbed through a thick, leather bound book and scheduled Jorge's first surgery for the middle of October. Juanita's baby would only need one procedure and could be done earlier. The hospital would underwrite the cost, Sister Mary Kathryn assured him as she took off her glasses and walked him to the door. "All part of God's work isn't it?" she nodded.

***

The weeks crept by slowly, one day melting into the next. Surgery and patients filled most of his days, and he retreated to his room for the nights. It was a lonely existence, but he tried to follow Beto's advice and avoid thinking about his problems. Clinica Day always brought a welcome break in his routine.

He left the Santa Monica airport early Friday morning, planning to stop in San Felipe for supplies. At the north end of San Felipe, he made a low pass to signal his friend, Juan, that he'd need a ride from the airport. After skidding to a halt on the short gravel strip, he piled out of the aircraft and stood in the shade of an old building, waiting for his ride. He squinted into the morning sun and looked impatiently down the road. There was no sign of Juan. Half an hour went by, and by then he was sure that Juan's temperamental car had refused to start or had heated up along the way.

There was nothing to do but start walking toward town. Less than a mile from the airport, he came to El Chino's junk shop. El Chino was a half-breed with slanted eyes and heavy lids that made him look almost Chinese. Because of that, they called him El Chino, the Chinaman. His graying hair, smoothly parted in the middle, was held in place by a soiled bandana. Whenever he wanted to make a point, his bristly mustache twitched and so did his eyebrows, as if they were connected somehow. His short, skinny legs seemed too fragile to support his protruding belly. He usually wore a guiavara shirt buttoned up to his neck like a loose tunic that hung over his midriff, reminding Reiter of a by-gone torero lost in a bull pen.

Reiter thought of the many times he'd been to El Chino's shop and wondered why he could never get close to the man. Perhaps it was El Chino's habit of measuring his words, as if he had an eternal secret to keep, or maybe it was the mysterious courtyard behind El Chino's shack that made Reiter feel uneasy. He would have given anything to know what was hidden there and why El Chino seemed so determined to shut it off from the world. Every time Reiter looked for an entrance, he could never find one. He remembered flying over the place, trying to steal a quick glance, but the overgrown bushes and saguaros made it impossible.

Reiter had a strange feeling as he paused at the door of the shop and wiped the sweat off his forehead. He knocked, not wanting to just burst in, respecting the mystery that surrounded the place. Cautiously, he stepped over the threshold and caught a glimpse of El

Chino standing in front of a smudged mirror in a lighted corner. He was waxing his mustache and grinning at himself.

He turned towards Reiter. "Oh, Espanto, it's you," he called out, obviously happy to see him. "Why don't we have a cold beer?" he suggested.

They sat under an overhang of dried-out palm fronds and sipped their beer, oblivious to the flies buzzing around them. Each seemed to be waiting for the other to speak first. "You don't look yourself today, Espanto," El Chino finally volunteered.

Reiter's hands went to his unshaven face. Self-consciously, he forced a half-hearted smile. "I was in a hurry to leave. Didn't have time to shave."

"No, something's wrong," El Chino went on. "It shows." His eyebrows and mustache started twitching. "The face never lies." El Chino's words were drowned out by a raspy chorus from behind the shop.

Reiter turned his head, a puzzled expression on his face. "What's that, El Chino? What's going on?"

El Chino jumped up and headed towards the back of the cluttered shack. He motioned for Reiter to follow. "Let me show you," he said with a mysterious look in his eyes.

Stacked against the back wall were several fish crates and what looked like prawn traps. Quickly, El Chino put them aside, one by one. Behind them, tattered fishnets hung over a grimy tarp. El Chino turned around as if to make sure that Reiter was still there and gave him a reassuring look. Then he pulled the tarp aside to reveal a low doorway.

Reiter felt apprehensive when they walked into the courtyard, not knowing what to expect. Suddenly, he found himself in the middle of a flock of screaming crows. Some were sitting on old fish crates stacked haphazardly around the yard; some were perched on twisted branches of a dead cottonwood tree; and some were pecking away at sunflower seeds or hopping along a wooden trough filled with water. They were the biggest crows he'd ever seen. They flapped their wings when El Chino showed up. Some of them clacked their tongues against their beaks making the weirdest chorus he'd ever heard. Either they were the happiest birds in Baja or the meanest. He couldn't decide.

Reiter's mouth dropped open. For a minute he was sure he was dreaming. He saw red, green and blue markings on the tips of the wings, and a little purple around their eyes. He remembered the fishermen in the bar in San Felipe. "They weren't so crazy after all," he said to himself.

El Chino smiled. "Didn't you know crows love colors? Let me show you." In the shade of an old cottonwood tree was a paint-spattered bench lined with cans of paint. "These are the colors I use." A few brushes stuck out of one of the larger cans, which was filled with a foul smelling liquid. "And this keeps the brushes clean," El Chino explained, twitching his eyebrows and mustache.

He picked up a crow and set it gently on the bench. It spread its wings a few times and then tilted its head at El Chino, sitting perfectly still. "This isn't the first time he's been here," El Chino explained. "He knows what he wants."

Reiter took a step closer. "I've never seen anything like this," he confessed as he stared at the bird. "They must be hungry. Or maybe thirsty. Why else would they come?" There was a serious ring to his question. "Certainly not to be painted."

El Chino bristled, and then seemed to catch himself. "You're wrong, amigo. They don't come only to be fed." He smiled. "They also want to be pretty. They like shiny colors. No different than butterflies." He paused for a moment. "Or ladies."

El Chino began to paint the bird as if it was the most natural thing to do. With bold and sure strokes he painted red rings around the eyes and steel-blue streaks on the head feathers. He dabbed yellow and green on the tips of the wings. No real pattern, just whatever came to mind. "You have to be gentle, do the feathers one at a time. You don't want to glue them together. And I paint each bird a little different. You don't want them to all look alike."

Reiter nodded, trying to conceal his amazement.

Finally, El Chino waved his big hands like open fans to dry the paint. "And you never want to overdo it. They don't want to look like freaks. Use the colors sparingly." He picked up the crow from the workbench and carried it across the yard before he turned to Reiter. "It doesn't take long for the paint to dry. The birds just wait in the sun," he explained. "They never fly until the paint is dry."

The loud chatter of another crow with shiny, preened feathers interrupted him. Like the first one, it hopped on the workbench.

"This one is new," El Chino said. "I've never painted it. But soon it will be like the rest. Los cuervos mas lindos del mundo, the most beautiful crows in the world."

"Hell, all they are is crows, even with all the colors. Cuervos pintados, that's all." Reiter couldn't resist the temptation to tease him.

El Chino wrinkled his nose and ignored him. With the back of his hand, he wiped his forehead before he started to paint the next crow. "No, amigo. They know a lot about beauty." He paused for a second. "You can see what a little paint does for the way they look." He studied them with a critical eye. "What's more important, it's good for their soul, their xenta. It makes them feel good," he insisted. "That's why they come. They keep coming even when I run out of sunflower seeds." His eyebrows and mustache kept twitching, as if he needed to make sure that Reiter understood. "Or don't you believe that it's good for them?" His eyes gleamed triumphantly as he looked at Reiter, like a proud colleague.

Reiter looked away, searching for the right answer. In his heart he wanted to believe El Chino, that the painted crows had happier souls.

The sound of a big black crow flying in caught his attention. "Here comes another one." El Chino could hardly contain his excitement. "El Grandote, The Big One I call him." He turned toward Reiter. "He shows up every week, like an old lady who's down in the dumps. He knows I can make him feel better." He shot a questioning glance at Reiter. "But you have to see for yourself. You'll see what happens."

By the time Reiter left El Chino's shack, his head was spinning with questions about El Chino and his belief in souls and beauty.

Juan met him on the outskirts of town. "Sorry, the engine got hot," he explained. Reiter asked him to wait while he picked up some supplies at the pharmacy, and he was back in the air in less than hour.

Nearing Puertecitos, Reiter remembered to avoid Beto's place at the point. He didn't want to disrupt him with the noise of the aircraft. But at the last minute he turned the plane towards the boulder where Beto always sang, as if the heart-wrenching music could somehow reach him.

By the time he landed, Martine had already seen several patients. They worked through the afternoon, but there wasn't time for much talk. Besides, Reiter's mind was stuck in El Chino's back yard with the black crows. Several times he was about to tell Martine about El Chino but thought better of it.

After they finished, he walked out to the point to see Beto. He knew he could tell him about the secret of the mysterious birds. Beto seemed to be waiting for him.

"Have you ever heard of painted crows?" he asked Beto. "Today I ran into the man who colors them." He didn't wait for an answer.

Beto nodded. "I've seen them land on my mast," he answered. "Some fishermen get scared. They think they are magic, but to me they are just beautiful birds. And they say they bring luck."

"It seems like a crazy idea…But El Chino told me the birds like it. He swears it makes them happy," Reiter said.

"Your own work isn't so different, is it?" Beto asked, without looking up. "Don't people like what you do for them? Isn't that why they come?"

Reiter didn't know how to answer. The thought of his work being like El Chino's would never have occurred to him. But the idea intrigued him; to make something more beautiful helps the soul. "I need to tell Cobo about this," he promised himself.

When he walked into the cantina that evening, he saw Cobo at the end of the bar arguing with Larry. "You're loco," he heard Cobo shriek, pointing a finger at Larry. He was still red-faced when he turned towards Reiter.

"I saw the painted crows today," Reiter said. "The same ones that fly around the fishing boats." He knew he had Cobo's attention. "El Chino paints them," he announced as if he was revealing a long-held secret. He says he does it to make them happy. And that it's good for their souls."

Cobo shrugged. "Is that supposed to change my mind about your kind of work? Besides, crows don't have to pay for their paint job. They get it for free." He looked at Reiter. "And they don't go to El Chino because they're unhappy with the way they look."

CHAPTER TWENTY-THREE

Many times after his stop at El Chino's place, Reiter caught himself staring out the office window and thinking about the painted crows. Beto's words kept surfacing in the back of his mind as well: "What you do isn't so different." But Beto didn't know about the money he made. And Cobo was right that a lot of patients were unhappy with the way they looked.

A persistent knock on the door cut into his thoughts. He ignored it at first, but the knock continued, this time much louder.

"Doctor, we're running behind." The nurse spoke emphatically as she opened the door. He acted as if he hadn't heard. "We still have a facelift, or have you forgotten?" She sounded bolder than usual. "You know how Dr. Pirro likes to stick to the schedule."

He gave her an I-don't-really-care kind of look. "Actually, I'm thinking of canceling the rest of the day," he said, trying to sound casual.

The nurse caught her breath. "Let me get this straight," she replied. "Are you talking about canceling this case?" There was a mixture of surprise and disbelief in her question.

He knew her response wasn't unreasonable. He'd never done anything like this before. But after Betty Love's complication he'd made himself a promise that if the day came again when he didn't feel he could do a reasonable job, he wouldn't operate. He remembered the vague emptiness he'd felt the morning of Betty's surgery, how he'd ignored the tightness in his chest when he walked into the operating room. He'd always wonder if it had been a mistake to go on with her surgery and had vowed he'd never do that again.

He looked up at the nurse, remembering his promise. "I'm just not myself. Something doesn't feel right, " he said as he looked down at his hands. "Let's take the afternoon off."

He was surprised at his immediate relief, as if he'd just discarded a puzzle that couldn't be solved. An euphoric feeling swept over him though he couldn't say why. He whistled as he hurried out the door.

He could hardly believe how easy this was, as if he was rehearsing a scene that got better as the camera rolled. Clambering down the nine floors of the fire stairs behind the elevator, he hurried through the parking garage and jumped in his car with no idea where he was heading or why. It felt as if he was following a script.

He traveled west on Sunset Boulevard and then turned north instead of south toward the airport. Lights turned green and there was hardly any traffic, as if an invisible policeman was clearing the way. In no time, he found himself on the freeway, snaking his way through the outlying hills towards the High Desert. If he hadn't known better, he would have sworn the car was on autopilot. Still he refused to admit that he was heading for home.

He felt a specter of shame rising in the outskirts of his consciousness. He frowned and tried to dismiss it, though he wondered whether he was breaking his word, wanting to confront her before she was ready. He tried to justify his actions and searched for excuses. He started arguing with himself, "Hell, you don't intend to just barge in on her, hombre. You just want to circle the place, take a look from a distance, and make sure they're all right."

Another wave of sadness pressed at the back of his eyes. *How did you ever let it go this far? How did you get to this point, ending up a stranger in the only place you call home? You strayed,* he reasoned, *you hurt the very person who adores you, and now you refuse to pay the price. Like Beto says, let her go. There's still time to turn around and go back to the office. Why don't you leave her alone?*

As this churned through his mind, he drove onto the nearest off ramp. He had decided to turn around, head west and back to the office. But when he reached the top of the overpass, he eyed the hills to the east, and he promptly turned in the direction of the Chaparral. Twice more, he turned off the freeway when his conscience kept biting, but each time he found himself heading east again. It was like a merry-go-round of destiny, with only one direction in the end.

It was close to sunset when he finally reached the exit that led to a hidden valley in the foothills. It was narrow and strewn with towering boulders that reflected the sun like gold-covered giants taking an afternoon nap. The place held a special meaning for him, and now he understood why he'd been drawn here. He felt tightness in his chest when he remembered the time he'd brought Linda here, before the children were born.

She'd prepared a picnic basket: chicken, cheeses, bread and wine that tasted better than anything he'd ever eaten. Afterwards, they lay on a blanket, and he'd been a little surprised that she wasn't embarrassed when he began to undress her. She must have been reading his mind.

"You think I'm embarrassed?" she'd asked, giving him a sensuous smile. "I love the caress of your eyes on me. And the caress of the sun and the wind. The only ones watching us are the birds and the trees, and they'll never tell."

Today, he stopped the car and headed towards the shady spot where they'd spread their blanket so many years before. He remembered the tender kisses and her parted lips, the hardening nipples of her breasts. He'd let his hands wander gently over her flat stomach and down her silken thighs. He'd whispered how much she meant to him, how much he loved her. Then they'd fallen into a heavenly rhythm that carried them higher and higher, where the air was pure and a thousand swallows sang.

***

He sat down under the tree and started dissecting every one of those moments, savoring the details. The glow of the late summer sun made him drowsy, and it took only minutes before he nodded off into a hazy slumber. Suddenly, strange images started floating around him. He saw a gigantic sea turtle basking on the coarse sands of a Baja beach. Its leathery head slid out of the shell and grew bigger and bigger, its beady eyes staring at him. There was something sinister and grotesque the way it contorted its mouth. "You coward," it hissed before it slipped back in the shell.

"Wait, let me explain," he found himself pleading. He looked away from the face and studied the green-brown squares on its back. For a moment, he thought the turtle was heading back into the water. Instead, it turned and its head shot back out of the shell. He caught his breath when he saw it was a different face. There was no mistaking that he was looking at Consuelo, her black hair tussled and wet like it was that night on the beach. Her eyes looked distant and empty. The sea behind her was foaming, as if ready to boil.

"Consuelo, Consuelo," he tried to scream, but his voice failed him and the words sounded muffled. "What have I done? How could it happen?"

Anger swept over her face, and her eyes flashed. "You'll find out soon enough," she said before she slid back into the shell.

His hands went to his throat as if trying to pry something out. Slowly, the turtle made its way toward him. Instinctively, he tried to get away, but his legs felt like lead. The turtle was only inches away when it poked its head out of the shell again, and Linda's face appeared. Tears were streaming down her cheeks. "Linda, Linda," he said with a trembling voice. "I can't live like this." He tried to go on, but she cut him off.

"Why have you hurt us?" She drew back her face, slowly and deliberately. "You can wait for the rest of your life." She sounded bitter and more determined than ever. "I'll never come back. Never," she emphasized before she disappeared.

"Wait, please wait," he managed to cry out before the turtle's head came back out. This time the face was craggy and lined, the eyelids droopy and circled like the fishermen who survived on the Baja shores. Instantly, he knew he was looking at Beto.

The raspy voice caught him off guard. "Hey, Espanto!" Beto sounded serious. "This is the last time I'll tell you. You have to let her go or she'll never be back." Reiter heard a thousand voices in the back of his brain, and one of them kept insisting that Beto was right. "You have to let go of the past. What happened, happened."

Reiter tried to open his eyes. "Beto, please," he cried. "I live in hell because of that night with Consuelo. Every day I'm without Linda is torture."

Beto's voice was reassuring but firm. "Don't you ever listen?" he interjected. "You're impatient again and counting the days. For you, not for her," he added. He slipped back into the shell.

Beto's face was so vivid that Reiter bolted out of his dream. He realized that hours had passed; it was already dark. He couldn't account for the time or the meaning of the dream. One thing he knew for certain was that he had to face Linda.

When he reached the ranch, he drove slowly down the dusty lane to the house, the lights from the windows drawing him nearer and nearer. The sliding doors had no drapes, and he could see into the living room clearly, but there was no sign of his family. *The children might still be at summer camp*, he thought, but he could see her car in the garage.

He parked the car a few yards from the driveway and got out. He tried not to make a sound as he walked to the door. He raised a hand to knock, but it was shaking as hard as his heart was pounding. Maybe if I could see her first, he reasoned and made his way toward the back of the house. Through the filmy curtains of the bedroom he caught a hazy image of Linda as she undressed for bed.

She seemed to be studying her reflection in the mirror while she slipped the straps of her tank top over her arms, gracefully lowering one shoulder and then the other. Reiter stared intently as her breasts spilled out, glistening and pale. The dark brown nipples were larger than those of Caucasian women, and the tan line across her chest was rather faint. She had a faraway look as she leaned forward with an undulating motion, pushing her skirt down over her concave belly. Bending over, she rolled down her panties, exposing white buttocks that seemed smaller and firmer than he remembered.

Reiter felt like a voyeur as he gazed at the body he knew so well. Still, he couldn't see all he wanted, and he moved slightly to the right, hoping to get a better view. But she turned suddenly as if to study her figure from another angle, and he could see only her back. He slid toward another window, desperate to see more clearly. His eyes were glued to a mirror that gave him a frontal view, but only down to the navel. She slowly raised one slender limb at a time as she stepped into a lace summer teddy, pausing before she pulled it up.

He felt a powerful surge of desire mixed with shame. Love and lust, or had he forgotten how to tell them apart? He hated himself for spying, for stealing her dignity, and he plodded back to the car. But he didn't feel he could leave the ranch before they had a chance to talk, so he crawled into the passenger side, adjusted the seat as far back as it would go, and struggled to chase his lusty thoughts out into the night.

At dawn, he woke with kinks in his back and aching joints. The sun was just over the horizon when he caught a glimpse of her through the kitchen window. When he saw her turn toward the window, he knew that she'd seen his car, the blue Lincoln with a dent on the right side. They'd tried to squeeze the car through that narrow road on their way to their secret valley years ago and had dented the right fender on a hidden boulder. He'd never bothered to have it fixed. "It'll always make me think of that day," he explained.

As she opened the kitchen door, he stepped away from the car. Their gazes locked, but neither of them spoke. They stood as if suspended in the moment. The sounds about them, the shrill chirps of the jays in the brush, the gentle swish of the breeze as it wound through the trees, and the drone of a million insects sounded like the prelude to the most beautiful concert.

He felt like a schoolboy as he stood there, his shoulders rounded, his hands balled in his pockets. His normal 'I'm ready to take on the world' spirit was gone, replaced by a sudden shyness.

She took a step forward, and for a moment he considered returning to the car and racing away. But then he saw the softness in her face, the corner of her mouth turning up into a dimpled and bemused smile. His shoulders squared, and the little boy faded as he walked toward her.

"What are you doing?" They both spoke at once.

She was the first to regain her composure. "Paul," she said, drawing out the name as if she didn't want to let it go. "Are you okay?"

"I'm okay," he came back. "Yes, more than okay. Now," he added. Suddenly, he was only inches away. "What have you decided?" He sounded like the boy again.

"That I love you. That being apart doesn't help me.'"

His eyes stung with tears, knowing this was a moment he wanted to relive every day of his life. Afraid to ask her again, he put his hungry lips on hers. Not in a passionate, demanding way, but as if he were kissing an orchid, tenderly, softly.

Her fingers went to the back of his head, and she twisted the strands of his hair. "I've missed you...I've missed you," she said in a muffled voice, without releasing his lips. They stood there in the shade of the eucalyptus, a gentle breeze caressing them both.

"Linda," he whispered. "Darling, I'm so sorry," he wanted to add, but the words froze in the back of his throat. For the first time he was afraid to be afraid. So he kept his lips sealed on hers to be safe. From the side of his mouth, he pushed out the question, "Can you forgive me?"

After what seemed like forever, she leaned back without letting go of his hair and looked him straight in the eyes. "Paul, I love you. I can forgive you, but we have to put this behind us."

He traced the outline of her face with the tips of his fingers and kissed her again. Tenderly, like it was the first time.

She took his hand and led him through the house to their bedroom. Her face was flushed. "Hold me," she said.

The way they made love in the morning hours would forever be part of their lives. It was not only passion, but also passion ignited by a deep, accepting love. Like a mountain brook, ripples of love flowed over sparkling pebbles, growing into an ancient love song, plunging into a stream that swept them away.

Strands of tousled hair stuck to her perspiring face. A primordial cry of pleasure came from her throat. When it was over, she traced his face with her fingers as if it was their first time.

"Welcome home," she whispered.

CHAPTER TWENTY-FOUR

He wanted the morning to last forever. He kept his hand lingering on her back even while she dressed. His lips brushed the nape of her neck as she fastened her brassiere. He locked on to the seconds watching her every move, wondering about the incongruity of it all. He prayed that he wasn't making this up, that each minute was real, that she was willing to forgive and start over. But his cautious side kept him on edge; something told him it couldn't be this easy.

He watched her purse her lips as she sipped her coffee. Suddenly, the lines around her eyes tightened behind the rim of the coffee mug. "It's not going to be easy," she said. He caught his breath. "But," she said as she looked him in the eyes, "I'm willing to give it a try."

His breathing got easier. "I know we can have a better life. I'll do whatever it takes," he said.

"Maybe better than ever, Paul. But let's never forget what being apart was like." She paused and twisted her wedding ring. "I'm willing to trust you again because I believe that we're meant to be together. And being together is more important than either of us." Her words were like a gentle warm breeze on a winter day.

In the late afternoon, they set out to pick up the children from day camp. Shane and Robin were surprised to see their father. "You've been gone a long time," his daughter said. "How could a medical conference last so long?" Reaching down to give her a hug, he looked up at Linda, grateful for whatever she'd been telling them.

"Can we go to Puertecitos?" Shane asked. "We haven't been there for a long time."

Reiter reached over to stroke the boy's head. "That's a good idea, son. I was thinking about it myself."

They flew to Baja the next weekend. The flight was strangely smooth, reminding Reiter of the way his tempestuous summer was giving way to a peaceful autumn. When they got there, he could have sworn he was landing in a new place. Not a ripple of wind passed through the empty airstrip. Even the sea was flat calm. It was as if nature had tired of sandstorms and showers.

All through the first night in Puertecitos, Reiter kept waking up and reaching for his wife, needing constant reassurance that she was really with him. When he woke the next morning, her flushed cheeks and bright eyes told him that she'd been awake for some time. Her hands were clasped behind her head as she lay in bed, her dark hair spilling on the pillow.

"Have you any idea how good it feels," he asked, "to be here with you?" He dared to finish the sentence, prompted by the sparkle in her eyes.

She blushed, "There's something about this place; it gets under your skin. I've missed it." She leaned over, brushing his arm with the back of her hand. "And you." She added. Then she turned back the covers and started to get out of bed. "Last night, Robin made me promise to take her clamming. I thought I'd take her north of town where we got all those clams the last time."

Reiter planned his morning out loud. "I'll get Shane to help me fix the barbeque pit. We can cook all those clams you'll be bringing home," he added, winking at her.

When he looked out the window, the sunlight seemed brighter and the sky a deeper blue today. Even the barren hills were more alive, dotted with golden specks of sunlight and shadow. It felt as if he were learning to live again.

After Linda and Robin left for the beach, Reiter and his son cleaned up the patio and wondered where the family might go swimming that afternoon. They were nearly finished with their morning chores when they noticed a group of small boats on the horizon. They knew they could only be fishermen's pangas, plowing through the shimmering waters on their way to shore. As the boats neared the little bay, the sound of outboard engines grew louder and louder. A trail of black smoke rose from the back of the last one, as if its motor was straining to keep up with the rest.

"Let's see what's up," Reiter said to his son, and they headed down the hill.

They arrived at the beach just as the Indian fishermen were pulling their boats on shore. Immediately, Reiter knew who they were. He'd stumbled upon one of their camps south of Black Mountain a couple of months earlier while driving along the beach.

He remembered how he'd first noticed a flock of black buzzards circling over the same spot on the shoreline. He had taken it as an ominous sign. His ears perked up when he heard a bone-chilling chant from that direction. It sounded as if a thousand souls were screaming for mercy. He dismissed an urge to see what it was and kept on driving.

He turned up the volume on the radio, determined to drown out the noise. But the chanting only got louder. It sounded macabre, and he'd sensed it had something to do with death. In the end something forced him to turn around, and he headed toward the eerie sound. Behind a crop of boulders he came upon an Indian fish camp perched on a ledge by the sea.

He jumped out of the old car and hurried toward the cluster of makeshift shacks. In the middle of a clearing he saw a man writhing in pain on the coarse sand, gasping for breath. Terror-stricken eyes bulged from his blue, swollen face and a gurgling sound came from his mouth.

Several Seris were hovering over him. The one with big shells hanging from his pierced ears and a small, round conch wedged into the flesh of his nose must have been the medicine man. He was brushing a bundle of feathers over the dying man's neck and the others followed his rhythmic screams as if on command.

Reiter sensed the urgency and knew he had to act fast. He ran back to the car for the medical bag he kept beneath the seat. He avoided the suspicious eyes bearing down on him when he returned. He dropped to his knees beside the sick man as they all stepped aside. He slipped a blood pressure cuff on the right arm and pumped it up several times. A wave of panic came over him—no blood pressure. He felt for the pulse. It was feeble and racing like crazy. There was no doubt in his mind that he was dealing with a severe allergic reaction. Anaphylactic shock. He had to act fast.

With trembling hands, he drew some epinephrine into a small syringe. He turned to one of the Indians. "Squeeze him as hard as you can up there," he said in Spanish, pointing to the upper arm. The Indian did as he was asked, though he threw a puzzled look at the medicine man.

A vein bulged on the forearm, and Reiter quickly injected the medication. Next, he plunged a second syringe of cortisone, an anti-shock medication, into the same vein. He felt the blood pound in the back of his head, as his eyes remained glued on the man, hoping, praying for the expected result. His heart pounded as his brain raced through the possible causes of the allergic reaction. It was most likely a snakebite he thought. Immediately his eyes swept over the man's limbs, searching for signs of a bite. He'd almost given up when he noticed a coconut shell on the ground. He picked it up. Inside was some black, foul-smelling stuff. "What is this?" he asked, sniffing and wrinkling his nose.

"Tintas de calamares, squid ink," one of the Seris was quick to explain.

Suddenly, Reiter saw the tattoo on the dying man's upper arm. A serpent without a head glistened in the bright afternoon sun. He brushed it gently with his hand. It was still wet, and when he drew his hand back there was a black stain on his palm. He felt a welcome measure of comfort in knowing what the problem was. The man was allergic to squid ink.

Soon, the man on the ground began to breathe more easily. The medications were taking effect. Reiter felt like shouting. The man blinked his eyes a few times and sat up. "Xeppe, Ettemavaskron Xeppeke. It's all right," he said, forcing himself to talk. "Yes, it's all right."

"Todo esta bien," Reiter replied, hoping the man also spoke Spanish. His own breathing grew easier. It had been a close call.

When there was no response, he tried a few of the words he knew in the Seri language. "Gi ipeane?" he asked, with the hint of a smile. "How about some water?"

Nobody answered, and Reiter didn't pursue it. The way he said it was bad, he decided, or perhaps they were too focused on the man to talk. They just stared at Reiter as he checked pulse and blood pressure again. This time they were normal, and he felt like a weight had slid off his shoulders. "You're going to be okay," he said as he stood up. He hoped nobody noticed the wobbling in his knees.

Suddenly, the chanting started up again. The singing followed him all the way to the car, but he had no doubt the meaning had changed.

The Seris had a simple way of life, and he'd liked them from the moment he first started coming to Baja. Small in stature, with chiseled, bony faces, they seemed suspicious and yet curious at the same time. They preferred to keep to themselves and didn't open up to outsiders, especially the white man. Martine once told him that the Seris had originally lived on the Tiburon Islands off the coast of Sonora. There were rumors that a few of the tribes were cannibals, and stories floated around that if a fisherman strayed too close to those islands, he never came back.

That's what prompted the Mexican government to send in the army and take on the Indians. They were hauled off and scattered all over Mexico, some in Baja, some on the mainland. To the Seris, it meant the end of their culture. "If you think about it," Martine said, "the government screwed them, took everything from them. They are only a shadow of what they were."

Reiter and his son watched as the fishermen unloaded their boats. "Look at the tattoo on that man," Reiter said, nudging his son. "I've seen him before." The half-finished tattoo on the Seri's arm glistened in the hazy sunshine. The black serpent didn't have a head. "That's Iguana," Reiter explained. "And that tattoo almost killed him a few months ago."

The boy listened attentively. "What happened?" he whispered as he looked at the man.

"They were using squid ink to paint a tattoo, and he had an allergic reaction to the stuff. Lucky I had some snake bite medicine with me," Reiter answered. "He came very close to dying," he added and paused when he saw Iguana flash a grin at him. "To me, he's a hero," Reiter went on. "Not many get away with it. He has to be special."

Shane's eyes widened as Iguana began pulling at his net. Something big and unwieldy was caught in it, and it was a struggle to haul it to shore. Suddenly, the bundle in the net started thrashing around, and Iguana stepped back. Shane seemed to hardly contain himself, burning to find out what it was.

Reiter tried to make light of it. "You don't suppose they caught an elephant?" He laughed.

Finally, Iguana pulled the net away and dumped what looked like a shiny boulder on the sand. From the loud thud, Reiter could have sworn it was made of steel. Hundreds of seagulls kept circling above, flapping their wings and pecking at each other as their shrill cries filled the air.

"They've caught a sea turtle!" the boy yelled. "Look at its shell," he added, looking back at his father.

Reiter turned pale as his eyes focused on the green-brown squares of the shell. Instinctively, he looked for the little face that still remained tucked inside, as if he expected to see someone he knew. He felt a damp chill on the back of his neck. "I've seen that turtle before," he said, to himself.

The boy shot a questioning look at his father.

"I've seen it before," he insisted and laid a hand on the boy's shoulder. "In a dream."

"Poor thing," Shane said, shaking his head. "Why would they catch it?"

"They're fishermen. They fish to stay alive," Reiter tried to explain.

Suddenly, the turtle starting flipping back and forth, in a desperate attempt to get back in the water. The Indians grabbed it and tied it down on a piece of plywood. The turtle waved its flippers helplessly and stuck out its head as if trying to get out of its shell. Finally, it seemed to sense it was hopeless. The Seris meant business and their ropes held.

The olive-green shell glistened in the sunlight. Shane studied its intricate grooves. "You can tell its age from these grooves," he said. "This one must be more than a hundred years old." He looked up at his father. "It's not right to kill it, Dad." There was obvious disapproval in his voice.

An uneasy feeling that the boy was right gnawed at the back of his mind. He thought of all the years the turtle must have roamed these waters. How many times over the past century had it escaped treacherous nets, gracefully swimming just near enough to see them unfurled from the pangas? It must have learned that the trick was to stay just far enough behind the nets to catch the tasty squid that escaped through the tears. At times it must have watched other turtles caught in the deadly nets, trying to keep from drowning as they struggled to escape. Today, it had ended up in that same desperate struggle, and it had lost.

The endless journeys of the turtle and its ancestors up and down the Sea of Cortez spanned eras in history. One of the ancestors must have wondered at the arrogance of the bearded Spanish explorers as they made their way up the Gulf in their proud ships and cringed at the sound of grating chains as rusty anchors plunged down with a splash. Surely, it had been surprised to see the strange men row ashore in their shiny armor, intent on ruthless conquest. Later, Jesuit missionaries in flowing black robes came off those same galleons to preach the Word of God to Indians who didn't know what to make of them.

This turtle had witnessed the Seri Indians fishing the treacherous waters in wooden skiffs, laying out deceiving nets and deadly hooks in the sea she knew so well. Many years later, shrimp fishermen from

Puerto Penasco and San Felipe invaded her world, lumbering up the bay in cumbersome boats, dragging invisible nets. In more recent times, came the deadliest threat of all, 'factory ships' from sophisticated lands far away. They came into this water illegally, without regard for life, sweeping up everything in their path, leaving the great Gulf of California depleted and tired.

"Don't get too attached, son. This isn't Disneyland," Reiter said in an attempt to end the argument. From the look on Shane's face, he knew it didn't work. He must have sounded like Willy: "This is no dreamland down here."

"Whatever you say, there's no reason to kill it," Shane argued as he edged up to the turtle. "It should be against the law." He sounded grown-up and determined.

Gradually, half of Puertecitos joined the crowd in front of the cantina. The word had spread, and it seemed that no one wanted to miss out on the catch. Papillo had been asleep on his rock when he heard the noise on the beach. He rolled over and growled a few times, smacking flies away from his face as he hauled himself up. His curiosity must have gotten the better of him, and he too waddled over to the Seri's panga. Reiter caught his grin when he spotted the turtle.

Slowly, the turtle poked its head out of the shell, as if searching for something. The shiny little eyes blinked under heavy lids. The wrinkled old face, worried and sad, seemed resigned to this fate. With a few strokes of its flippers, it tucked its head back in, too old and too wise to resist.

Iguana nodded and waved his hand in a signal for Reiter to join them. He explained that he had been the first one to notice the sudden tug of the net that morning. "I wasn't sure what it was. When I saw it was a sea turtle, I was going to turn it loose, let it go," he reasoned, more to himself than to Reiter.

But Reiter sensed that the survival instinct must have prevailed, and Iguana had done what was expected of him. For the sake of the tribe, he had hauled in the net. Now he was ready to kill. Their life was the sea. That's how it had been for centuries; the way things were meant to be. That's what Shane would have to understand.

But even as Iguana spoke, Reiter thought he could detect a trace of guilt in his voice. He didn't believe Iguana had forgotten the day when he too was pinned down on the rocky soil, struggling for life, fighting for every breath. After looking death in the eye, life— all life — had to be more precious.

A crowd gathered around the turtle—Mexican fishermen, Cat-man Dave, and a lot of the Americans in town. Even Papillo had come to life. His fleshy face quivered, and the muscles of his thick neck bulged and throbbed as he wiped his knife on a rag. The others started drinking tequila and carousing, dancing in the shadow of death.

It was different for the Seris. They didn't say anything, but it was plain they didn't like outsiders around when they had to kill something. To them, it was almost a holy act, a necessity, not a time to celebrate.

Everybody watched as the Seris picked up the plywood the turtle was strapped to and carried it towards a clearing in one of the sheltered canyons nearby. "To get out of the sun," Iguana explained to Reiter. He seemed anxious to have it over with, going about his job without showing his feelings. The lines in his face seemed to grow deeper as he shouted directions to the rest of the Seris. "Get a bucket for the entrails and a sharp wire to cut the gristle and bone."

They started a fire with dried brush gathered from the canyon, making sure it was placed in the path of the wind so the smoke would drive the flies and other insects away. They worked quickly.

Reiter's son followed them with a downcast look on his face. "I won't let them do it," he suddenly shouted, planting himself between the Seris and the turtle. He shot an angry look at his father and then at the Indians. "Take it back to the sea. Tell them, Dad. Please." He sounded like a man who knew what he wanted.

A wave of shame lapped at Reiter's conscience. Does it take a ten-year-old boy to put some sense into you?

"Hold it, Iguana. I'd like to buy it." He pointed at the turtle.

Iguana arched his eyebrows and turned to his tribesmen. Although he was the chief, by tradition each member had a voice in the decisions made. They huddled together and spoke in low voices. Finally' he turned to Reiter. "You can buy it," he said.

Reiter looked at the shiny shell. "Can you tell me what it weighs?" he asked.

Iguana glanced at the animal as if appraising it. "Not less than sixty kilos." He sounded sure of himself.

Reiter wasn't surprised by the instant response. He'd always wondered how the Indians seemed to be able to guess the weight of a catch. He'd never seen them use a scale. He remembered one of them telling him, "The white people use scales to measure the weight of things. We do it with out xenta." He'd put a fist on his chest. "Our soul. We measure everything that way…how much it bends our backs, how much sweat pours out of us." He went on. "Sometimes a thing looks like we can't lift it, but it will be as light as a feather. Something that looks like a feather will turn out to be like a whale. The only way we can tell is with our xenta."

"How about ten pesos for each kilo?" Reiter asked. "Weighed by your xenta," he added. It was a generous offer, and he reached in his pocket as if they'd agreed on the deal.

It was clear that to the Seris fishing meant survival, not a way to make money. Money didn't mean anything to them. They'd seen the white man's obsession with it and never trusted it. The only time they used it was to buy fuel for their boats or things they couldn't catch or make themselves.

Reiter counted out the pesos. Iguana looked away as he gathered up the wrinkled bills and handed them to one of the older tribesmen. Reiter knew the exchange was uncomfortable, and he waited until the money was in the other man's pocket. "Iguana," he said. "Take the turtle back to the sea."

Iguana nodded. "Atoa. To the Sea," he shouted with a wave of his hand. He pointed to a spot on the beach. "That's where the water is deeper." He cast a quick glance of approval at the young boy.

The other Seris leaped to the task. They picked up the animal as if it weighed nothing and started the trek along the rocky pathway toward the shore. The turtle must have sensed the sudden change in her fate and stuck her head out of the shell.

Cobo's loud voice as he started singing. *'La Mananitas',* stilled the noisy crowd. In an instant they joined in. "The day you were born, all the flowers bloomed." The words to the song were about the beginning of life.

Reiter turned to his son. "The turtle is going to live after all. You were right all along," he said and put his hand on the boy's shoulder. "Why should anything die on a day like this? Come on, let's go to the beach."

The boy's flushed face showed his relief. His idea had caught on. Everyone seemed to have the same thing in mind—to get the turtle back in the water. Soon half the town was there, old and young; it seemed no one wanted to be left out. The mongrels barked as they ran with the crowd. Cobo's song echoed through the canyons and floated out to sea.

"You spoke up just in time, son," Reiter said. "I'm real proud of you." The boy beamed, his face turning crimson. He nodded, but kept his eyes on the turtle.

***

The festive mood of the crowd reminded Reiter of another joyful day in his life. Ascension Day was one of the most colorful days of the year in his old hometown. He remembered how everybody in the village assembled at the church on that special Sunday morning. They formed a line behind the somber priest, some of them carrying statues of saints on heavy wooden platforms. Then the faithful set out, up and down green meadows dotted with yellow and blue flowers, meandering past weathered barns with sunlight filtering through cracks in the gray planks. Warm mountain air bathed the colorful group when it finally turned to follow the ringing bells back to the church.

The sequence of the procession was steeped in tradition. Reiter knew that he and the other altar boys in their white tunics with wide red collars would follow the priests. The men of the Volunteer Fire Department came next in brown uniforms with bright red trim and shiny brass buttons. Following the firemen was the stern-faced mayor and the village elders. Most were farmers from the surrounding valleys who couldn't dispel the earthy odor from their Sunday suits. The village band was right behind, brass instruments sparkling in the morning sun. The ladies of the village were next—many of them plump and matronly with thick long braids wrapped on top of their heads. They wore white blouses under embroidered aprons; heavy knit stockings peaked out beneath their colorful skirts. On their shoulders they carried a heavy statue of the Virgin Mary with hollow green eyes and a thinly veiled smile. The groups of tradesmen who brought up the rear carried statues of their patron saints—St. Agnes was for the miners and St. Sebastian belonged to the musicians. There was even a patron saint for beekeepers.

Even in those days, Reiter had a fascination with faces and souls. He watched the faces of the villagers and wondered about St. Sebastian's tranquil smile, even though arrows were sticking into his chest.

Back at the church, he decided to ask the priest about the statue. "Father," he'd begun, "doesn't Saint Sebastian..." He took a deep breath and tried again. "I was wondering how Saint Sebastian could smile with all those arrows in him?" He looked down at the ground as if he were afraid he'd asked the wrong thing.

The priest rolled his eyes in exasperation. "What do you think?" he said, shaking his head in disbelief. "Why such a question? You must know that saints don't feel pain. They are the closest things to God. That's why they're saints." He twisted his white collar and loosened it, as if dismayed that a six-year old boy didn't know something so obvious. "Haven't you been paying attention in your religion class?" he fumed. He buttoned his frock and straightened his shoulders.

Reiter retreated from the sacristy, more confused than before. How could he have doubted a saint? *The priest has to be right*, he thought. Saints weren't ordinary people with pain and with feelings. But he wasn't so sure about the priest.

During the procession, Reiter had stolen glimpses of peoples' faces when they weren't looking. It seemed that some of them hung on to frowns like prized possessions. Sometimes, there would be a sudden smile, or a startled look of innocence, but it never took them long to return to their somber expression. Each person seemed as weighed down by his own thoughts as by the heavy saints they carried. That's when he began to understand that each person has a choice about the face he presents to the world. In his mind he'd begun to connect faces and souls.

***

Shane seemed to sense that his father's mind was drifting. "You're not changing your mind?" he asked hesitantly. "I mean about taking the turtle back to the sea?"

"No, not at all." Reiter looked down at the boy. "I was just thinking that I've been in processions like this before." He wrinkled his brow. "Many, many years ago," he added. His words were almost drowned out be Cobo's voice. "Cobo's singing reminds me of the times when people sang and marched in the mountains where I grew up," Reiter added, smiling.

Shane tried to walk in step with his father, like a boy who had just given a turtle new life. Together they walked to the edge of the sea.

200

CHAPTER TWENTY-FIVE

Reiter was concerned about Martine's unexplainable foul mood. During the family's visit to Puertecitos, Martine had been withdrawn and even surly. It wasn't like him. Even during the procession with the turtle, Martine had stayed on his porch, alone and brooding.

"Have you ever seen an old billy goat?" Alfonso had remarked pointing to Martine. "They look at you with those yellow eyes, and then they piss all over you before they calm down."

It reminded Reiter of his own lonely wanderings. "I wonder what's wrong with Martine," he said to Linda at breakfast. "He's off by himself again this morning. Maybe he caught a dose of despair from me..."

"Why don't you take him somewhere?" Linda suggested. "Maybe all he needs is a change of scenery."

They kept an eye on Martine's house until they saw him wander back to his porch. Reiter tried to sound casual as he joined him. "I've been thinking of flying to Muleje tomorrow. How about coming along? We could check on Juanita's boy." He took a beer from the fridge. "I haven't seen old Doctor Cervantes for a while either. It would do us both good."

Martine stood in the doorway, a scowl on his face. "Maybe," he mumbled, nodding at Reiter before he plopped down on his couch, raising a cloud of dust.

Reiter pulled up a chair and sat down across from him. "You don't sound like you think it's such a good idea." He sounded concerned. "Level with me, amigo. What's wrong?"

"Nothing. Everything's just fine," Martine answered. "It's just the time of year. When harvest time comes around I'm always reminded of my farm. And my wife." He sighed. "It's been forty years, but September does this to me." .

Reiter knew that Martine's marriage had ended in divorce a long time ago, but he didn't know any details.

"The guy's name was Andy," Martine began. He seemed to be musing out loud. "Supposedly our friend."

Reiter nodded.

"Her friend." Martine's voice was deadpan, but the furrows in his forehead deepened. "Not mine."

"We'd been married almost twenty years, and then, out of the blue, one day she starts reading the Bible." He bit his lip. "Pretty soon, that's all she did, underlining verses with a thick black pen and writing them on strips of paper. Pinning them all over—by the windowsill, on the refrigerator door. I had a feeling all of them were meant to remind me of my sins."

Reiter listened sympathetically. He had never been comfortable with Bible thumpers either. He grew pensive for a moment. "You find those kind of people in every religion," he finally said.

"No, I think the Yakis and the Seris are different. They've never tried to shove their religion down my throat." Martine was emphatic.

"That's true," Reiter said. "It makes me wonder why the white man tried so hard to change them. To my way of thinking, they're the ones who could have taught us. They have a respect for nature and animals that doesn't exist in the White Man's religions. Maybe we should have tried their ways instead of destroying them."

Martine nodded and went on with his story. "She spent more and more time talking about the Bible with this Andy. He was a divorced man. The next thing, he started showing up at our place at all hours of the day, blubbering about how lonesome he was. He always carried a Bible under his arm, and pretty soon they were reading it together." He coughed dryly. "As for me, I was usually out in the fields working the farm. I guess it was just as well for them that I wasn't a good Christian, with their Bible and all." His eyes narrowed.

"The usual story." He looked down as if searching for something. "One day I came home earlier than normal." He turned his hands over and studied them. "I should have stayed in the fields. But the wind had come up in the late afternoon, and the dust was so thick I couldn't see out so I shut the combine down." Martine swallowed. "When I got to the back door, I took off my boots like I always did. Spotty, our little dog, was sitting by the door looking up at me with shiny eyes as if he'd been crying. I should've known right then that something was wrong."

Reiter wasn't sure he wanted him to go on, but he said nothing.

"I thought nobody was home, but then I heard hushed voices from our bedroom. They didn't even notice when I opened the door. The first thing I saw was a hairy rump sticking out of the sheets. It made me think of the butt of a hare. The strange thing was, I wasn't angry at first. But then Andy lifted his head, and I saw his eyes. Looked like a buck caught in a headlight." Martine leaned forward, as if staring at something. "I was too numb to come up with a word... No dirty, filthy scum, no nothing." There was contempt in Martine's eyes.

Reiter's jaw tightened. "What did you do?"

Martine didn't answer; he just looked out on the bay. Then he leaned back in his chair and placed his hands on his brow, as if he had to knead out just the right words.

"'I can see you're good Christians,' was all I could come up with. 'Must be the Good Book you're reading.' They just lay there without saying a word. She never even looked up, kept her face buried in the pillow. I swear you could hear the thump of their hearts," he continued. "I walked out the door and never went back. I figured to hell with the farm and everything else."

When Martine finished, his face was pale, drained of color. He finally looked up. And whatever he saw in Reiter's expression made him gasp. "Hey, what's with you? Did I say the wrong thing? You look like you're having a stroke."

"What would you say if I told you that your amigo here," and he pointed to himself, "is no better than that Andy guy?" He forced himself to go on. He paused and waved a finger at a roach running across he floor. He cleared his throat and looked up at Martine. "Hell, I've done the same thing."

Martine's expression made it clear he didn't want to believe him. Reiter sighed and turned his back to his friend. "And with another man's wife."

He could hear Martine breathing faster and deeper. He'd had no idea the turmoil the confession would stir up. He felt as if he'd robbed Martine of his most precious possession. He couldn't find the courage to say anymore and hunched his shoulders, waiting for an explosion.

Minutes ticked by, but neither spoke. Martine looked like a weary ghost in the shadow of dawn, his face pale, and his lips quivering. Finally, he took each finger and began to crack his knuckles, one at a time. The shrill chants of the seagulls grew louder and closer, as if they sensed the tension. It seemed like a lifetime before Martine cleared his throat. "I got to confess," he began slowly, without the slightest condemnation in his voice. "I would have sworn you were stronger than that—that you didn't have it in you." He almost swallowed the last part of the sentence.

Getting out of his chair, he stared down at Reiter. "Hell, what do you expect me to say?" There was a note of disappointment in his scratchy voice, "You've always made everyone feel you were the Rock of Gibraltar." He paused. "Some of us were surprised to find out that you were more than a good old doctor. That you were a beauty surgeon who made gobs of money." Martine cleared his throat. "But people still believed in you. They made you into a kind of saint; for them, you even acted like a saint. And you go on taking care of them, and they're convinced you're giving them your heart. But they have no idea what you can do when they're not looking." His words faltered. "For your sake and theirs, all I can say is I hope they never find out."

Reiter's shoulders slumped. "I don't know what I can say. It's not as if I planned the whole thing; I didn't want it. It was like a different me—I couldn't help myself," he stammered.

Martine looked at him. "Maybe that's the way we all are. Like stray dogs. A few minutes of humping, a few ounces of flesh, and there goes the fire…roaring out of control, raging, scorching everything in its way. Till there's nothing left."

For once Reiter had no ready answer. His eyes swept to the spot on the beach where he'd found Consuelo that night. "A few minutes of humping, a few ounces of flesh and there goes the fire, roaring out of control…" Martine's words echoed in the back of his brain.

Suddenly, he felt a big hand on his shoulder. "It just goes to show you, no matter how we look from the outside, everyone has it in him to turn into a bastard. Maybe we both need to get away from here."

***

The next day, Reiter and Martine flew into a steel blue sky that seemed to melt with the fiery red of the mid-morning sun. From Puertecitos they flew south, keeping a little off the rugged coast, skimming over islands that floated below them. After two hours, the emerald waters of Conception Bay appeared in the distance. Scorched brown hills rose gently from the white beach lining the sea. Just behind the shoreline, the village of Muleje lay nestled in a narrow valley, the spire of the old mission silhouetted against purple cliffs. The muddy stream they called the Muleje River wound its way through the town on its way to the gulf, with dense palm growth along the banks forming the only jungle in Baja.

Reiter scanned the sea for ripples that would tell him about the current and the winds. The shadow of the plane skimmed the low hills at the end of the canyon and he followed them to the hard-packed dry riverbed that served as a runway. The 'runway' carved its way from the bottom of a cactus-strewn hill, along the shore to the town's only inn, the Serenidad.

'Serenity' was a perfect name for the place. Adobe bungalows with red tile roofs scattered like clusters of mushrooms around the courtyard, which at one time must have served as an arena for bulls and mariachis. Once a rustic hacienda, the original rooms of the main house had been turned into lobbies and lounges with alcoves where people could gather to drink tequila or dine. Whitewashed adobe walls contrasted sharply with the dark shutters and bulky doors made of oak timbers. The shadowed, cobbled courtyard was always swept clean, defying the jungle-like vegetation rambling around it.

"You know that this place serves the best tortuava in Baja," Reiter said as they sat down at the rough oak bar. "Their salsa picante is the hottest I've ever tasted."

They ordered fish tacos and by the time they'd finished their meal Martine's eyes were watering. "I swear my belly is on fire," he said between bouts of coughing. "Guess I need another beer." Martine seemed more relaxed than he'd been in days. *Linda was right —the change of surroundings is good for him*, Reiter mused.

Suddenly the door of the lounge flew open. "Donde esta el medico?" A wiry young man stood at the doorway, his eyes combing the bar. "The one they call Espanto?" Then he caught sight of Reiter. "Dr. Cervantes is looking for you. He's at the hospital." Martine and Reiter turned towards him. "Mi coche esta listo. The car is ready," he said, pointing outside.

"How the hell did Cervantes know we wanted to see him?" Reiter frowned at Martine.

"I'm sure he knows your plane. Maybe he saw us fly in," Martine replied as they slid off the bar stools.

They followed the man to his car, a rusty Ford with only one door on the driver's side. The stench of rotten fish was overwhelming and both Martine and Reiter found themselves swatting at swarms of big fat flies. Martine wrinkled his nose. "Feels like we ended up in a fish crate," he said, eyeing shrimp tails strewn over the floor.

The driver studied them in his rearview mirror and must have noticed the disgust on Martine's face. "I'm sorry about the flies," he said. "It takes a lot of patience sometimes. And some heart." He slowed down to make the sharp turn in the road. "They are God's creatures too," he added, resuming speed.

Low adobe houses flanked the dusty streets. Finally, the driver came to a screeching halt in front of one of the bigger buildings. Reiter noticed that there were no windows on the street side of the adobe structure. Two hand-hewn doors opened directly from the street into a poorly lit room with tiled benches filled with downtrodden patients. Even after they entered, Martine and Reiter were surrounded by the odor of fish. "Doesn't smell like a hospital to me," Reiter said.

"Well, we're not in Beverly Hills," Martine retorted.

From behind a curtain a nurse appeared, a white cap pinned to her dark hair. "Dr. Cervantes is in the operating room. This way, por favor," she said. They followed her into a room with a high ceiling, a row of narrow windows at the top. Stretched out on a table in the middle of the room was a large-framed man, his long legs dangling over the edge. A gurgling sound escaped from his throat as he kept gasping for air. A gooseneck floor lamp was pointed at his throat. In its light they could see blood trickling from a tiny opening above the Adam's apple. It sounded as if every breath could be his last.

A bald-headed man in a smudged lab coat stood leaning over the patient, his short, pudgy fingers holding a pair of tweezers. Dr. Cervantes, Muleje's only physician, was carefully probing the bleeding hole in the neck, shiny beads of perspiration glistening on his dark face. Cervantes was all business, but he stopped his probing long enough to look up at the two men. "I'm so glad to see you, Espanto," he said, his voice trembling with relief.

Dr. Cervantes complained that his lunch had been interrupted by a call from the hospital an hour earlier. Two local fishing guides had brought in an American from one of the charter boats with a big fish hook sticking out of his neck.

"The man was struggling for breath and collapsed. I put him here on the table and gave him an injection of Valium." He made a point to sound in control. "Then one of the fishing guides said he'd seen your plane fly into town. 'Go get him,' I told him. I knew I could use an extra pair of hands."

He didn't have to say anymore because Reiter could imagine exactly what had happened next. Cervantes had obviously cut the eye of the hook off with a pair of sharp pliers. Instantly, the hook had been sucked into the neck. The old doctor must have panicked. "Chingao. Damn it. Now what?"

Cervantes stepped back, and Reiter took over. The first thing he did was inject a local anesthetic around the hole in the man's throat. The patient winced and squeezed his eyes shut. Reiter motioned for a chair. He always preferred to operate sitting down because leaning his elbows on the table helped steady his hands. Reaching for a scalpel, he cut into the edges of the wound, enlarging the opening in the man's neck. Then he peeled back layers of skin and muscle while Cervantes focused the light on the gaping wound. Using the blunt edge of the scissors, Reiter spread the tissue apart until he could see the tip of the hook sticking out of the muscle. He paused for a moment, contemplating his next move as he felt the blood pounding in his temples. The hook had punctured the windpipe below and a pulsating artery encircled one of the barbs.

Because he knew this artery was part of the intricate system that eventually snaked its way to the brain, he had to work meticulously to avoid both the artery and the nerves that ran along it. He also thought of the other nerves in this area that controlled the vocal chords. Grasping the tip of the hook, he carefully wedged a pair of forceps beneath it. He turned the hook sideways and little by little was able to slip it out. With a sigh of relief, he laid it on the table. There was dead silence in the room except for the patient's labored breathing.

Cervantes tried to make himself helpful by blotting the wound with sponges but the continuous oozing of blood from the wound kept Reiter on edge. The last thing he wanted was for a pool of blood to collect under the skin later and choke off the windpipe after he'd flown away. He clamped off several vessels and tied them with catgut, closing the hole in the trachea with a few sutures until the air stopped bubbling out. He washed down the area with a sterile solution and watched several minutes for escaping air. Only then did he start to suture the wound itself, working layer by layer with tiny stitches. At the end he applied a light dressing.

It seemed to take forever before the patient opened his eyes. "Thank you," the man said in a low, raspy voice as if testing his throat. Then he closed his eyes again and fell asleep.

Dr. Cervantes turned to Reiter. "Gracias, amigo."

Reiter nodded. "He's going to be okay." He looked up at Cervantes. "Don't forget antibiotics. And a tetanus shot."

As they rode back to the Serenidad, Martine and Reiter discussed the case as if it had been a Clinica Day. "Guess you're a saint once more, amigo. One way or the other you saved the day."

Reiter thought he detected a hint of sarcasm in Martine's voice, or maybe it was his own sense of guilt that put it there. "I don't know about sainthood," he came back. "Yesterday you sure didn't call me that." The words caught in the back of his throat. "For whatever its worth, working on this guy today was as good for me as it was for him." There was an incredulous tone to his voice. "That hook had gone clear through his windpipe. I'm glad it came out without a lot of damage."

Martine was quiet for a minute. "All the while you were working I kept thinking how a lot of us keep hooks buried inside. Sometimes all the way to the soul," he added.

Reiter looked at him and nodded.

***

Back in Puertecitos after the children were in bed, Reiter and Linda talked about the change he'd seen in Martine. "It's good you took him away," she said. "We had a good day too. Except for running into a crazy man in the afternoon. I meant to ask you about the stranger who's living at the point. Do you know about him?"

"There's fisherman name Beto holed up out there." He paused as if to gauge her response. "One night while you were away, I was down in the dumps, feeling sorry for myself when I heard him wailing out there. He sounded like he knew what it means to lose someone close to you." She looked up at him and frowned. "Something made me go out there to see him. What he told me helped a lot. 'Sooner or later you have to let go,' he said. 'You can't cling to those you love or stop them from leaving anymore than you can stop the waves on the shore from going out to sea. In the end they come back. Without any help from you.'"

Her arm suddenly went slack. "This Beto. Does he walk with a limp?" she asked, looking intently at him.

"Yes, that's the guy."

"This afternoon on the way back from the beach he was sitting on the side of the road strumming a guitar. When he saw us he almost dropped it. He stared at me as if I was a witch or something. It was eerie."

"That doesn't sound like Beto to me," Reiter insisted.

"I kept on walking, but he kept staring and then he suddenly bolted and ran out to the point." She paused, her words measured and pensive. "Something about me seemed to scare him to death."

"Men have been known to run from beautiful women," Reiter smiled, trying to make light of it.

All night long he kept turning in his bed, hardly able to wait for morning when he could ask Beto for an explanation. At dawn, while his family still slept, Reiter stole out of the house and made his way to the point. He wasn't surprised that Beto was already up. "You were right all along," Reiter said. "She's back."

Instead of smiling, Beto turned pale. "I know," he said. "I saw her on the beach." He looked at Reiter with fear in his eyes. "But now I'm not sure about you," he said gravely. "You're a medico with magic hands. You're different than El Chino. All he does is dab a little color on the birds, make them more beautiful."

Reiter couldn't understand why his friend was so distraught, but before he could say anything, Beto went on. "What you do is not like El Chino. It has nothing to do with beauty. You can change people, make one person look like another. That's magic. Or witchcraft." There was a measure of fear in his voice.

Carefully, he pulled out a small bundle hidden under some rocks, his hands trembling as he untied the string and unfolded an old scrap of canvas. With a somber expression, like a priest holding the Holy Sacrament, he lifted out a cracked, faded photograph. Bowing his head and closing his eyes he brought the picture to his lips, sobbing as he kissed the faded image of a dark-haired woman with dimples in her cheeks.

Reiter felt the blood draining from his face as he stood behind Beto and looked at the photo. He put a hand on his shoulder. "Amigo, I had no idea that our women could look so much alike."

CHAPTER TWENTY-SIX

Reiter marveled that the creosol bushes in the desert were still green. It was the end of October, but it still felt like summer. By this time of year, most of the ground squirrels normally stayed in their burrows, but today they seemed to be overrunning the landscape. He inhaled the sweet aromas of mesquite and yucca as he sat at the edge of the patio waiting for his wife.

She came up behind him, and he felt the softness of her terrycloth robe as she put her arms around him and whispered in his ear. "Good morning."

In the weeks they'd been together they'd settled into their old routines so easily that sometimes it seemed as if the months apart were just a bad dream. He struggled with a lingering sense of disbelief at how graciously she'd forgiven him. The way she came up to him in the middle of a long day to squeeze his hand, the way she touched him at night, the way she'd whisper, "I love you, Paul" when he didn't expect it, clouded his mind with confusion. He knew these gestures were meant to reassure him, yet he still had the feeling that something was amiss. He was desperate to find contentment, but something told him that until he faced Consuelo and the truth of their night together, peace for him would never come.

His face must have betrayed his concern. "You seem troubled," she said. "What is it?"

He sighed. He didn't want her to catch him roaming around in the past among guilt and regret. So he brought up a different worry: "Jack Gotts wants to see me today," he said, rolling the cup back and forth between his hands. "I'm not sure what he wants. He's not the kind who comes to the office on a whim."

"Jack Gotts...the man who worked with you on that government commission?" Linda mused. "Isn't he some kind of agent?"

"He's the one." Reiter smiled. "But I don't think this is state business."

At the office later that day, Reiter settled back in the chair behind his desk waiting for Jack Gotts to show up. Something about the man always kept him on edge. He felt as if he was on a freight train hurling into the country, wondering what was around the next bend.

At precisely three o'clock, Gotts sat across from his desk. Reiter studied Gott's gaunt face as though he was planning to get under his skin and deal with the cool detachment he presented. He wished he could go deeper and figure him out, but Gott's skin was too thick.

Gott's voice was also cold, with a bite in it. "I'm bringing a man in tomorrow. I want you to change his face so that even his mother wouldn't recognize him." He paused to let it sink in. Remove his fingerprints so he could never be identified, dead or alive. I want you to turn him into another person."

Reiter gasped as Beto's words echoed in his mind...'change people...make one person look like another.' He looked at Gott in disbelief. "You can't be serious. This sounds like something out of the Mafia. Why come to me?"

"We trust you, or I wouldn't be here. We know what you can do."

Reiter shook his head, "What do you mean 'we'?" He tapped the desk with the end of a pencil. "Who is this man?" he pressed on.

"That I can't tell you. And you won't know any more about the patient when you're finished than you do now. You will be paid, of course. You have nothing to lose."

"Why is this being done?" Reiter demanded. "And what's this about fingerprints? It must be illegal."

"Not in this instance. No one will know of this visit or the surgery. But let me assure you, it's authorized at the highest level."

"I understand." Reiter allowed his mind to wander. Was this some kind of government cover-up, a defector perhaps? Maybe the man was being sent back to his homeland, a person of stature and importance on a dangerous mission.

"What does this man look like?"

"You'll see him tomorrow. But no pictures, please. No 'before and after photos'."

Looking for a way out, Reiter said, "I can't guarantee that none of my people will talk."

"Come on, we've known each other a long time. It was me who recommended you. Our people will screen and brief everyone—assistants, anesthesiologists, nurses, what have you."

Reiter sat back for a moment and stared at the floor. "It's too bizarre…turning a person into someone else. I always know who my patients are, and what they want. And what about risks? A blood clot, infection, even death. This isn't a haircut." Reiter slowed down. "What about his medical history?"

Gotts opened a briefcase on his lap and brought out a large manila folder. "This is your man, Reiter. You'll find laboratory reports, lung and heart examinations. All done at a military hospital."

Reiter glanced at the records. Everything seemed to be in order. But there was no birth date and no name. Nothing to link the man to anyone. "No age, no educational background, nationality or family history?" He looked up from the file.

"He has no family," Gotts responded. "We like that."

Reiter studied Gotts as though he was a patient. He saw a slight tremor in his fingers that he hadn't noticed before. "I'm beginning to think you need a rest."

A flicker of doubt crossed Gott's face, but he checked it quickly. "What do you mean?" he demanded. "Let me ask you again. Is it a yes or a no?"

Reiter frowned. "Has anyone ever told you you're very persuasive? I already feel like a traitor, and I haven't moved from this chair."

***

A week later, Reiter entered his operating room in the pre-dawn hours. The patient on the table was a heavy-set man between fifty

214

and fifty-five, without distinctive features. A lump of a nose dominated a pallid face and the deep-set eyes had crows feet etched in the outer corners. He had rabbit-like teeth with a small, receding chin.

The nurse handed Reiter a scalpel. He might as well begin with the fingerprints, he thought, and, like Martine often said, "Get the distasteful stuff out of the way first." That way he could concentrate better on a face not yet visualized in his mind's eye. Like an artist conceiving a portrait, he needed some image to shape the nose and the lips, the angle of the jaw, the domed forehead as it framed the eyes and merged into the hairline. Sooner or later, it would come to him. It always did.

Miss Atkins, one of his assistants, looked at him with a puzzled gaze that made him uptight. "Is anything wrong, doctor?" she asked as if she sensed his discomfort. He shook his head and didn't bother to answer. "Let's start with the hands," he said.

She wrapped an elastic bandage around the man's arm, and it turned waxy and dry, kind of like a body in the anatomy lab. The only thing missing was the stinging smell of formaldehyde and death.

Reiter cut across the tip of the thumb, right behind the nail. The fingertip fell onto the instrument table, just like a slice of tomato. He grasped the man's fingers, one at a time and kept slicing, first the thumb, then the others. There was no bleeding. At the end, the fingertips were gone. The nurse picked them up and carefully placed them in a glass jar filled with a salt-water solution. The gray pieces of tissue with the fraying ends floated around. Later, the container would be sent to the Pathology Department and the contents incinerated.

Reiter took a marking pen and drew an ellipse on the inside of the man's upper arm. "Scalpel, please," he said to Miss Atkins and cut out an oval piece of skin along the line he had just drawn. Next, he cut it into ten small circles, each about the size of a nickel. After removing the glistening yellow fat from the back of each 'nickel', he placed them on each fingertip. He sewed them on, one by one. At the

215

end, he removed the tourniquet from the upper arm and checked for bleeding. There was very little so he was satisfied. The man's new fingertips were white and shiny, with the intricate swirls of fingerprints gone.

There was an air of the bizarre in the operating room. The talkative anesthesiologist, Dr. Pirro, was unusually quiet and subdued, like the nurses. It was as if they were hiding behind their thoughts, afraid to come out.

They changed gowns and gloves and began to work on the man's face. There would be no problem with the crow's feet, Reiter thought, and a routine facelift would take care of the heavy jowls. He picked up his scalpel and incised along the temples and in front of the ears, like he'd done on hundreds of patients. Then he separated the skin from the deeper tissue with the long shanks of his facelift scissors. After removing large blobs of fat from under the neck, he pulled the skin of the neck and the lower face upwards and backwards. There was so much loose skin that it covered the patient's ears. After putting in a suture to hold it in place, the excess skin was cut off. The face on the table looked different already.

The next thing he would change was the man's receding chin. Reiter had decided to bring the entire lower jaw forward to meet the upper teeth. That would take care of his overbite and help change his looks. He would have a chin with character. Grasping the jaw, Reiter cut through skin and muscle down to bone, prying off the muscle as he cut. With a pen he drew a line across the exposed jawbone. The nurse handed him a small electric saw, and he began to cut along the line he'd drawn. The high-pitched whine of the saw sounded like a siren. Pirro winced. Reiter made the same cut on the other side and then squirted water on the bone to wash off the dust. The whole lower jaw was freed, as if it didn't belong to the rest of the face. He grabbed it and wiggled it forward till the teeth met. The man's looks were changing right before their eyes.

Reiter was glad there was no excessive bleeding. He started stitching, first along the jaw and then the rest of the face. He knew he still had a way to go. The man needed strong cheekbones.

With the marker, he drew a fine line with his pen just below the lashes of the lower eyelid. He started at the innermost corner of the eye and ended up at the crow's feet, curving downward at the outer corners. With his gloved left hand, he gently felt the flat cheekbones and drew a circle over them where he would put the implants.

He injected the entire area with local anesthetic and adrenaline to shrink the blood vessels and minimize bleeding. With a new scalpel, he cut along the marked area just below the eyelashes, through skin and muscle all the way down to bone. Next, he grabbed the tissue with a tiny hook and placed the point of his slightly curved scissors inside. With his left hand, he followed the shanks of the scissors, gently feeling their tips as his right hand pushed and spread them right down to the bone. When he got to the circle he had marked beforehand, he stopped.

Miss Atkins handed him two cheek implants, one for the right side and one for the left. How could these strange looking things make such a difference, and give his patient a strong profile? Whatever he looked like before and whatever family traits had been passed down to him through the generations would be permanently altered in the next few seconds.

Once again, they changed gowns and gloves to work on the nose. First, Reiter cut through the lower part of the septum. Extending the incision across the lower cartilage where the nostrils flared out. He then used a sharp instrument called a Joseph's Elevator to separate the flesh from the gristle and bone of the skull. Once that was done, he asked for a chisel and held it at the base of the prominent hump. Gently, he tapped it with a silver mallet and gradually chiseled the hump away.

Pushing a hemostat through the hole in the right nostril, he grasped the loosened hump and carefully removed it. Next, he took a curved rasp and gently filed down the rougher spots on the bridge of the nose. Every so often he'd stop to make sure the bone felt smooth and to catch his breath. At the end, he placed his index finger over the new nose. It felt even, with a gentle curve. Gotts would be pleased, he knew.

"Right chisel," he said to Miss Atkins. She handed him a small instrument with a sharp edge on only one side. He slipped it in through the right nostril into the small tunnel he had just made. As he held the instrument with his right hand, his left forefinger followed its sharp tip on the outside.

"Tap it," he said. "Gently," he added without looking at Miss Atkins, who held the silver mallet. The tip of the chisel kept sliding upward while she tapped. They did the same thing on the other side of the nose. Once the nose was freed from the bones of the face, he grasped the bridge with his thumb and forefinger. With a firm squeeze, he moved it from side to side. He could mold the nose now. It would be narrow and fine.

Only the rhythmic beeps of the electrocardiogram and the hissing gasses of the anesthesia machine interrupted the silence. It was as if time stood still. Pirro cast nervous glances at Reiter every once in a while. There was a strange charge in the sterile atmosphere of the room.

Reiter's hands moved on to the lower part of the face and pulled back the lower lip. He made a cut at the edge of the gum line. With small gold-handled scissors he made a pocket just below the teeth, down to the end of the chin. He leaned over and checked for any bleeding. There was none. He then slipped a shiny, pre-shaped plastic implant into the pocket he had made and sewed up the incision on the inside of the mouth. A strong, defined chin to match his new cheekbones and bold jaw.

Finally, in the mouth he placed metal bars with little hooks that fit onto the teeth. He then wired them around each tooth with a fine silver wire and put small rubber bands from one hook to the other so the jaw would be held in its new position until it healed.

218

Suddenly, Reiter felt drained, exhausted. He looked at the man on the table and shuddered. Strange, he couldn't remember what his patient had looked like before the surgery. He roamed the labyrinth of his tired mind, but there was no way he could recall the man's features, the way he had looked a few hours before. He couldn't find that face. It was gone from his memory.

He realized that he didn't even know this man's name, and that wasn't right either. *He has to have a name*, he thought. Something to hang his frame to. So he made one up: "Pancho." Reiter looked down at his man with the new face, Pancho. He could almost see him in the cantina in Puertecitos, having a cool cervesa with his amigos.

Reiter left the operating room and headed back to his office. He flopped down on the long leather couch. Over the two-way speaker, he could hear the recovery room nurse as she moved about. He opened the walnut cabinet at the end of the couch and switched on the closed circuit TV. He could see the patient in the recovery room now, the nurse applying ice to his face to keep down the swelling. Her starched white uniform and her snow-white hair blended in with the sterile blue and white room. A square screen to the side of the bed blinked bright green numbers that told him all he needed to know about blood pressure, pulse, and respiration. Everything appeared normal. The body was reacting well to all this intrusion. Reiter would spend the night at the clinic. As he rested, he tried to justify the surgery.

All you did was work on the shell, he reassured himself and found some comfort in that. He had only rearranged the outside in order to protect the man. That's what Gotts had asked him to do.

The next morning, Reiter was eager to remove the bandages and examine his patient. Pancho had just wakened. The bandages were peeled off, and one of the nurses handed him a mirror. His hands moved to his nose. The hump was gone. His bandaged fingers stole down to his mouth and then his chin. The nose sloped down from a smooth forehead. The prominent cheekbones lent strength to the face. The chin was firm and squared. He looked puzzled, and then he smiled at the total change.

Reiter frowned. Something about the face looked vaguely familiar.

Later that morning, Gotts called. "How are things going?"

"Fine. You can pick up your man the day after tomorrow."

"No complications?"

"None. In ten days most of the sutures should be out, and chances are he can leave the area. Till then, he should have a nurse with him. And I'll need to see him daily."

Reiter tried to ignore the recurring sense of doubt that settled over him as the day progressed. Later that night, he sought refuge in Linda's arms. She sensed his profound need for love. She also knew that there was no way he could talk to her about his strange day.

CHAPTER TWENTY-SEVEN

Two weeks later, all of Poncho's stitches had been removed. It was a relief to see him reclining in the examining chair with only a hint of bruising. Gotts sat in a corner of the room, his arms folded over his chest. "Our patient is doing well," he remarked. Reiter looked at his patient and realized that he had never been alone with him and that he had never heard him utter a word.

"I'll leave you alone for a minute," Gotts said as if reading his thoughts. "I've got to attend to an important call," he added and stepped through the doorway.

Reiter cleared his throat as if ready to speak, not sure what language his patient might understand, when Pancho surprised him with perfect, though heavily accented English. "You are an excellent surgeon," he began in a voice raspy with harsh r's .

"Thank you. I didn't know you spoke English."

"I speak six languages, Dr. Reiter," he responded. "Like you."

Reiter tensed. "How did you know that?" He wanted to say, but thought better of it. Something made him hold back.

"I've also worked in a coal mine," Pancho went on. "In White Russia, not far from Minsk."

The fact that Pancho knew so much about him gave Reiter an eerie feeling. "You seem to know a lot about me," he said.

Pancho changed the subject. "I like what you did to my face. It's good." He bowed his head slightly.

Reiter felt a sense of relief and pride. He took a step back. "How do you feel?" he hesitated, not sure how to phrase it, "When you look in the mirror?"

"I'm different. I see a different me." Pancho rubbed his square chin. "But it's only the outside. My soul is the same," he added. "When I look in the mirror now I feel better." He paused and looked at Reiter. "I don't have to hide anymore."

***

The next time Reiter was in Puertecitos for Clinica Day, he found himself looking over his shoulder as if he expected to see 'Pancho' step up on the front porch. Something about the people who trickled in reminded him of the man with the new face. There were fewer patients than usual. "I guess you did a good job the last time," Martine said. "Either we're stamping out disease or Papillo's set up his own Clinica Day somewhere down the coast."

By early afternoon, they were finished. "Why don't we drive out to Speedy's fish camp for a cold beer?" Martine suggested. "I feel like a change from the cantina."

Reiter nodded without hesitating. They headed north, kicking up a trail of dust as Martine's rickety car labored over the road.

Reiter tried to sound casual when he asked Martine, "What do you hear from Pedro and Consuelo?"

"Nobody's seen much of them lately," Martine answered. "They used to show up every Friday night, but for the past few months only Pedro's been down a few times to see his dad and brother."

Reiter knew why Consuelo no longer came, but he said nothing.

The truck groaned and tilted as Martine made a quick turn around a boulder. Reiter grabbed the door handle, but nothing seemed to faze Martine. "It gets better up ahead," he hollered above the roar of the engine. "The bad stretch doesn't last forever. Like everything else in life."

The road did get smoother, and Reiter leaned back. After turning another corner, they came upon a shallow bay lined with sparkling sand. Pelicans skimmed the surface of the sapphire waters and long-legged cranes pecked for crabs on the pristine shore. On the horizon, the silhouette of a stately shrimp boat dragged through the waves. The brakes squeaked as they came to a halt in front of Speedy's shack. Martine shut the engine as Reiter eyed the place—a shack nailed together with pieces of driftwood given up by the sea. They got out of the truck and stepped under an overhang of dry palm fronds.

In the corner of the room, Speedy's wife, Magdelena, stirred a pot over an open fire. She was scrawny and short with a sharp hump on her back. Maybe it was her wrinkled black dress, or her shiny black hair, but something about her reminded Reiter of an old crow. A pair of wire-rimmed glasses from another time perched on her hawk-like nose and behind them, piercing black eyes left no doubt that she was a Seri. Her whiney voice, shrill and persistent, made him think of a noisy vendor he'd seen at the market in San Felipe arguing with anyone who would listen.

Clusters of flies gathered in the sunlight that streamed against the soiled walls. Reiter saw them head for the grease spots that Magdelena had splattered on the floor. Magdelena seemed to ignore them until they got too close to the foul-smelling soup she was stirring. Then, she raised her fly swatter. "Enough is enough, pinche moscas," she said. The flies scattered but promptly regrouped. Magdelena seemed resigned and shrugged, rolling her eyes toward the ceiling as she kept stirring the soup.

"Buenas dias, Senores." She turned toward Reiter and Martine as if she'd known they were coming. "Siente se," she went on before they could respond.

The warped plywood walls of the shack had several gaps that Speedy always insisted were windows, even though they looked more like places where he'd run out of patience or plywood. To cover most of the gaps, he'd nailed up oil-stained pieces of tarp, which had grown stiff with brine and made a brittle sound when they flapped in the wind. They headed toward the one window that had a piece of plywood hinged to the bottom instead. The unhinged edge balanced on two wobbly legs, forming a table of sorts. "La ventana del mar," Speedy called it.

They sat down, prepared to hear for the umpteenth time how Speedy had cut out a piece of plywood to exactly fit the opening and hinged the lower edge to the window frame. "When the sun shines, we drop the plywood, and it is our table," Magdalena said, edging toward the men. "Our Mesa del Mar. When the fog comes in or the wind starts howling, we swing the table up to shut the window. All it takes is two clavos and our cantina is tighter than the Mexicali jail."

Their metal chairs with 'Speedy' scrawled on the back in faded black ink. From the table, Reiter and Martine could see Speedy down by his panga. Even from far away, they couldn't miss his imposing figure with shoulders too big for the thin cotton shirts that he wore. The first time Reiter saw Speedy he'd been impressed by his neck, bulky and broad, like a grizzly's. He remembered how it swayed back and forth when he walked. And like a grizzly, Speedy would stop as if to sniff the wind for danger, and then tilt his head as if trying to discern the difference between his instincts and his physical senses. His shirt was usually open to the navel, revealing a smooth, brown chest without a single strand of hair. There was not a hint of hair on his face either, and Reiter had been told there was none on his head, though he couldn't be sure because Speedy never took off his cap.

Someone had said Speedy rode with Pancho Villa in the Mexican Revolution. Combing the Sierra's towns for women, he'd run into syphilis. That would explain why he didn't have any hair, and why his legs were bowed like curved sabers.

Speedy always wore his pants rolled up above his knees, and Reiter had never seen him wearing shoes. Still there was a dignity about the man. The way he gave orders left no doubt that he intended to get what he wanted, one way or the other. Magdelena must have known that too. With just a hint of fear and so much more affection, she did whatever he said. "Si, senor," she would sigh, with a strain in her voice, as if implying an almost welcome resignation. It probably freed her of the burden of making her own decisions.

Reiter and Martine watched Speedy beach his boat and remove a rusty anchor from its bow. He dragged the anchor up on the beach and plunked it in the wet sand. Every movement was deliberate; even routine tasks seemed important. It was as if he'd never forgotten the revolution and was always plotting the next one. He stopped for a moment as if he wanted to prolong the chore of making the boat secure. He wrestled with a rope that led to the bow, then lifted two rusty pails out of the stern while casting a quick look at his place, el campo de Speedy. Finally, he started walking toward the campo, balancing the two heavy pails, his eyes straight ahead, his face set and determined.

But Reiter was convinced that nothing escaped him…another one of his habits left over from the Revolution.

Reiter sat across from Martine, looking intently at Speedy. He was vaguely aware of a sense of uneasiness creeping over him. He groped about in his mind, trying to figure out why.

Speedy must have noticed of Reiter's curious gaze though he didn't return it. Martine noticed it too, and looked puzzled, "What's going on here?" He wanted to know. Reiter ignored him.

Setting the pails down near Magdelena's stove, Speedy walked over to the table. "Buenos dias, Espanto. Buenos, Martine," he said, as if seeing them for the first time.

"Buenos dias, hombre," Reiter replied.

"Como estas?" Martine added

Something about Speedy was disturbing to Reiter. Suddenly, like a mirror image, a face appeared in the back of his mind. He studied Speedy's heavy furrowed brow, straight nose, chiseled cheekbones and the strong, square chin. There was no doubt that he was looking at Gott's man. Pancho was standing before him.

His hand trembled as he picked up the bottle of beer. Had he subconsciously used Speedy's strong features as a model? He remembered the chisel cutting through the hump in Pancho's nose. Instead of guiding it gently inward the way he usually did, he'd let the chisel slide outward as he advanced it along the bridge of the nose. In the end there was a striking similarity to Speedy. Even their square jaws and strong chins looked the same. And the cheek implants had given Speedy's chiseled profile to Pancho. Beto's questions about changing people suddenly overwhelmed him. Had he tried to make one person into another, dabbling in something he barely understood?

"What are you staring at?" Speedy wanted to know, shaking him out of his reverie.

Reiter tried to sound casual. "You just remind me of someone," he said.

As the sun was setting, Martine and Reiter climbed back in the old truck and headed towards town. "What was all that about?" Martine sounded annoyed. "Do you have any idea how you kept staring at Speedy? You must have made him feel like a freak."

Martine pressed on the accelerator, and the truck bounced with every rock they hit. He stared through the dusty windshield with a frown on his face.

"I'm the one who should feel like a freak," Reiter mumbled. He paused and studied his hands. "I operated on some guy the other day and changed him completely. Cut off..." He stopped. He was about to say "his fingertips," but then thought about Gotts. "I worked on his forehead, his nose, his jaw...everything. When I got through, not even his mother would know him."

He had Martine's total attention now. The truck slowed to a crawl.

"What's really strange is that the guy I worked on looks almost like Speedy now. Turning someone into a different person isn't something I've ever done before."

Martine's answer was matter-of-fact. "I'm not so sure you should be concerned. Look, they do all sorts of things to people these days. They transplant hearts; they use dead people's bones and livers too. We live in a different century. I don't see why you're so uptight."

"I'm not sure you understand," Reiter interjected. "We're not talking about organs or skin grafts. I made someone look like Speedy. It's weird," he added. "As if I'd stolen Speedy's face."

Martine shook his head. "Let's suppose for a minute you could make someone look like Speedy. It still wouldn't be him. Not the way Speedy thinks and feels. Nobody can duplicate a soul. You know that."

CHAPTER TWENTY-EIGHT

When they got back to town, it was nearly dark, and the two friends settled on Martine's porch. As they sipped their beer, the old diesel generator banging away behind the cantina disrupted their conversation. Soon their words began to fade like the flickering bulb swinging from the ceiling.

The lights finally flicked off, and Martine yawned. "That's it for today," he said. It was almost as if the dark silence that followed was welcome. The only thing missing was Beto's haunting cry and the whining twang of his beat-up guitar.

"I miss Beto's singing tonight," Reiter mused. "Come to think of it, I haven't seen him all day."

"Haven't you heard?" Martine didn't sound too concerned. "He's been gone since last Tuesday."

"Any idea where he is?" There was a sudden urgency in Reiter's voice.

Martine took another swallow of beer. "Cobo and Alfonso have been looking for him. They think he hopped on one of the shrimp boats out there," he said, nodding towards the mouth of the bay. "Took the old panga that someone left on the beach."

Reiter frowned.

"He's done it before," Martine reassured him. "He'll be back before long."

***

Perhaps it was Reiter's extreme preoccupation with Beto that propelled him into one of the most realistic dreams of his life: He was sure he could hear Beto's voice, sounding more like a wail as he pulled on the strings of the guitar.

"Please answer me, my love, precious queen of my life." In his dream he could see Beto cock back his head as if to let the words gather strength in the back of his throat before they spilled out.

"Where are you, my love? Tell me, tell me, I beg you—where are you?" He yanked at the strings—twang, twang, twang. Suddenly he stopped singing and started shaking like a man caught between desperation and fury. "Don't you know that I saw you walking on the beach? There were children with you. Our children? Has your ghost come back to live as someone else?" A flood of anger contorted his face as he smashed the guitar on the rocks and thrust his hands toward the sky.

A sudden burst of wind blew across the sea, churning up the waters into a frenzy of foam. The wind became a roar as his voice rose another pitch. "Forgive me, light of my life." Tears streamed down his face. "Please, please let me come to you," he cried in a final, drawn-out wail. "I want you back. I don't care who you are."

He grabbed the piece of driftwood he used as a cane and a small bundle wrapped with a string before he started down the hill. He headed to the leaky panga beached on the sand, pain etched in his face. It seemed to take all his strength to drag the boat to the water.

Still sobbing, he made the sign of the cross and threw the cane over the stern. Then he wedged his body against the boat as if uncoiling a spring and pushed it into the water. When the current caught the panga, he hoisted himself over the side. The oars sliced through the water as moonlight streamed across his haunted face. Plunging into the fury, Beto rowed as if he could outrun the storm.

Reiter cried out in his sleep as Beto clung to the bow, struggling to balance himself. The waves had turned into a sea of black mountains that buried the prow of the boat. "Answer me, my love. I beg you one last time," were the last words Beto uttered.

When Reiter woke from the unsettling dream, dawn was breaking. As he fumbled for his clothes and walked down the hill, a flicker of sunlight spilled over the horizon. He was determined to discover some sign of Beto but found only shadows and a relentless breeze blowing in from the sea. The high-pitched whine of the wind sounded as though someone was wailing. Reiter crouched down beside the boulder in front of Beto's place and looked up at the rose-tinged sky.

He thought he heard the shrill cry of some seagulls in the distance, but when he looked around he couldn't see them. It was unusual for them to be flying at this hour. They sounded restless and sad.

He searched in every direction for some sign of the panga as he walked along the beach, trying to reassure himself that Beto was just out fishing. He could remember that months ago he'd seen Beto row along the steep cliffs outside the bay. With binoculars, he'd watched him cut a big sea bass into strips and toss it into a bucket before heading back to shore.

The sun climbed over the horizon, and the sky mottled. Suddenly, he had the feeling there was someone behind him. Turning around, he saw Papillo shuffling across the rocks like a walrus. He was out of breath when he caught up to Reiter.

"I came out here looking for Beto," Reiter said. "Have you seen him?"

"He took the old panga the other night." Papillo's eyes were fixed on the sea. "I saw him rowing into the storm. The waves were like mountains." He shook his head. "I kept shouting for him to come back." He looked at Reiter as if riddled with guilt. "I waited for hours till the chubasco blew over. The next morning, I came across some Seris who had pulled their pangas into the bay. They said the current was too strong to make it back to their camp." Papillo pointed south and held up two fingers. "Two of their own were lost in the storm."

Papillo and Reiter kept combing the shore. On the far side of the bay, they finally came upon ribs of a panga floating in the water.

Papillo was grave. "These ribs are rotten. I'm sure they belong to the old panga Beto took."

A piece of driftwood with a knobby end swirled around in the foamy waves. It looked strangely familiar. Reiter waded into water up to his hips and shivered. He was unsteady and cold as he reached for the driftwood then waded back to shore. As the sunlight bounced across the waves, he knew he was holding Beto's cane

When they got back to town, Papillo waddled over to his rock by the cantina, and Reiter walked to Martine's place to tell Martine and Cobo what he'd learned. Pale-faced, the three friends lingered on the porch, unable to find comfort in conversation.

Looking toward the beach, Reiter noticed that Papillo had left his rock and stood on the small strip of sand in front of the cantina. His arms were stretched out with his palms turned up toward the sky like two cups trying to catch the rays of the sun. Then he bent forward and back again on the balls of his feet. With his fist he kept thumping his chest and landed back on his heels. He shot forward again, digging in with his toes. He kept doing this over and over again, lost in a trance as if he were the only person on earth.

Martine's eyes narrowed, as if he were seeing a mirage. He turned towards Cobo. "He's done this before. Wasn't it when his brother disappeared?"

"Yes, I remember. They thought that Chimalon had drowned or been killed by a shark," Cobo answered. "The Yakis do that dance when somebody dies. I think it's how they let go of their pain," he said. "They never use the word 'death'. They believe that when soul leaves the body it floats in the air, like a handful of dust. And when they do the dance, they reach out to the spirit."

"Remember when Hector's baby died?" Martine added. "When he took the body to the desert, they said he did the same dance. They believe only the body is gone, not the soul. They dance to the soul that's part of the sun and the moon and the winds."

Papillo kept dancing; the others watched in silence.

"They say they can stop the sun from shining when they dance with the dead," Cobo said cautiously.

They looked up. At first the sky was clear and blue, then suddenly a bank of dark clouds came out of nowhere and swallowed the sun. "I have a feeling he's caught up with the spirit," Martine said slowly, his eyes still fixed on Papillo. "That's exactly what happened when Chimalon disappeared." One thing was certain; there was power in this ritual.

Finally, Papillo stopped and headed toward the cantina and the huge boulder that was embedded in cement a few feet from the door. The boulder had been too heavy to move when Don Rafael built the cantina so he'd made it a part of the building. It was Papillo's favorite place and over time the people in the village had named it piedra de Papillo, Papillo's rock.

Papillo flopped down, drained by his dance. The hours crept by, slowly and heavily. He seemed to be studying the colors of the afternoon as they became muted and softened by the setting sun.

Word of Beto's death spread, and the people of the town began to gather on Martine's porch. Dave, the Cat Man, was one of the first to arrive. "Good evening, Espanto," he said with a long face. "I just heard about our friend out there at the point."

"Yes, amigo," Reiter said, putting a hand on Dave's back. "I'm afraid he's gone for good."

Dave glanced at Reiter quizzically. "I was out at his place before he disappeared. He sounded like he was mad at you. He wasn't himself, kept blabbering something about faces. All worked up about your turning one face into another." Dave paused, scratching his unshaven chin. "You know I don't speak his lingo like you, but one way or the other I figured out what he was trying to say. Mostly what I did was listen."

"What did he say?" Reiter interrupted impatiently

"He kept wanting to know if you were magic or something. He called you a Brujo." Nervously, Dave bit off a piece of the twig that dangled from the corner of his mouth. He seemed to be having trouble going on with the story. "Finally, he pulled a bundle from under a rock and shoved a faded photograph under my nose. It wasn't real clear, but it sure looked like your wife to me. He said that only brujos could mess with faces and souls. Then he started to cry. I left him alone, didn't want to be rude."

"I know he's gone," Reiter said, his eyes fixed on Beto's driftwood cane.

He could hear the despair in the old man's voice as the tears trickled down his face. "I guess I should have known that I'd never see him again."

CHAPTER TWENTY-NINE

Like relentless drizzle of sadness, a dull sense of loss hovered around Reiter's daily routine. Then, on the last day of the busy month as he stepped out of the shower, his wife came up to him with a mischievous look in her eyes. She started to dry him off with a terry towel, then dropped it and wrapped her arms around him. She leaned her head against his damp chest. "Are you up to being a father again?" she whispered.

His eyes widened, and his heart started pounding. She was trying to sound casual, but there was warmth in her voice, and he could see the dimples flashing on her cheeks. She put the flat of her hand on his chest, as if feeling for the heartbeat.

He inhaled the fragrance that made him think of wild flowers high in the mountains, and he let her words sift through his mind for a minute. A slight breeze from the ceiling fan felt like a blast of cold air, and her words swirled through the dimly lit room. Then she took his hand and placed it on her stomach. Her skin felt warm and moist, and he thought he felt a late quiver of passion within her. "Let me draw you a picture." Slowly, she started to trace something on his chest with her finger. "About the birds and the bees. About the stork."

"You're pregnant?" He drew her face into his hands. It doesn't surprise me."

"And why is that?"

"I've thought a thousand times about the day you forgave me." He pulled her closer. "In my heart I knew that morning would live forever."

She blushed. "If the baby in me…" She smiled, touching her stomach. "is a measure of our love, it will be the happiest child."

He took her hand and brushed it with his lips. "I understand what you mean," he whispered. "The way I see it, this baby is a special gift." The words faded as he struggled to keep from being swallowed up by the knowledge that their passion had turned their love into a new life. *You're the luckiest man in the world*, he said to himself as he took her in his arms.

***

Maybe it was the unusually smooth flight to Puertecitos that put Reiter in a soul-searching mood. He kept asking himself if others could see the change in him. One thing was certain; something within was different. He wondered if it all started when Linda told him about the new life coming into their family. Or maybe it began during the months of separation, during the long nights filled with guilt and remorse. Whatever it was, something had put a brake on his impetuous side. He felt that he was more patient with the children, hopefully more thoughtful in the way he treated his staff. It was as if the rough parts of him were gradually being ground away.

As he was pondering the ins and outs of his life, he folded down the plane's visor and gazed at the familiar photograph clipped to it. The image of his wife smiled at him. "If there's one thing you've taught me," he said directly to her picture, "is that we never know what's around the next corner. Or do we?" He could imagine a warm glow radiating from the dark eyes. "Whatever it is, you make me want to be a better person."

By the time he landed, a sudden strong wind had blown in from the sea and sand was hurling down the runway. There wasn't a soul to be seen, as if the place was deserted. Then, out of nowhere, Cobo ran up to the plane, one arm shielding his face from the biting sand as he leaned into the wind. He'd never seen him so anxious to help. He grabbed a chain and swiftly pulled it through the loops under the wings. Reiter thought he noted a smirk on Cobo's half-hidden face.

"What's going on?" he yelled over the howling wind as they made their way toward the cantina. Cobo ignored him.

They finally ducked behind an old trailer for shelter, and Cobo leaned towards him. "Hey, hombre, you want to hear some good 'noose?" he asked. You won't believe it. I saw her yesterday;

Consuelo, I mean," he went on, and his grin got wider. Reiter's jaw tightened. "The first time in months," he added. "She was all by herself, and she headed straight for her trailer. She picked up a few things, and then she was gone."

Cobo was sounding more and more mysterious. "You should have seen her stomach," he confided as he cupped his hand caressing an imaginary pumpkin in front of his belly. "He finally did it. That weasel of a husband made sure she had to eat her words about him being sterile. I guess he finally showed her, that sly son-of-a-bitch." There was an unmistakable sound of triumph in his voice. "And it was no watermelon she was carrying around. No sir. The way she was blown up it wouldn't surprise me if she has twins. Or maybe triplets," he added and broke out in laughter.

Reiter hoped his face didn't show the panic he felt. "'I'm happy for them." It was all he could manage to say. His vision blurred, and he forced his eyes to focus on the few fishermen waiting for him near Martine's porch.

It took all of his strength to hold himself together as he went through the motions of the long Clinica Day. As they worked, Martine seemed troubled by the distant look in Reiter's eyes. "What seems to be your problem today?" he finally asked.

"Nothing, amigo, nothing at all," Reiter snapped.

Martine shook his head. "There are times we get all caught up in ourselves, kind of like a spider spinning webs, fretting about our own problems and forgetting all about how lucky we really are. Some of the things we see here on this porch are like a stab in the belly, and you're forced to say to yourself, 'Hold it, boy, there's a lot more to life than your own little game.'"

Reiter nodded, and then winced as Beto's words echoed in the back of his mind. "Think about somebody who's about to drown in waves even bigger than yours."

Martine nodded toward an approaching truck. "I think that's Capi. He's been havin' a lot of trouble these past couple of weeks. I don't know what to tell him. Maybe you can figure him out."

Reiter gripped the arms of his chair. The last thing he needed was to look Consuelo's father-in-law in the eye.

***

"Capi" was short for Capitan, and over the years, in his own quirky way, he had become the policeman of Puertecitos. It was true that the work he'd done up north for thirty years was with the Department of Agriculture, not the police, but to the people of the town, he was still a 'Federale.' They looked on him as someone who stood for a mystical part of Mexico that evoked fear and respect. His presence lent a certain air of authority to the town, like a tentacle of government that kept its grip on the people.

Capi's starched uniform with the wide epaulettes and golden government emblems created the impression that he was much bigger than he was. The holster of a long-barreled pistol with its mother-of-pearl handle reached halfway down his leg. When he puffed up his chest and squared his shoulders, he was the only person Reiter knew who could look as if he was standing at attention even when sitting on a couch.

Capi lived in a shanty at the entrance of town, and much of the time he sat in his doorway as if guarding the village. There seemed to be no logic as to why he would stop certain people as they drove by. Maybe they had disturbed his mid-afternoon nap…a noisy muffler or a guilty look was all it took. According to him, they were breaking the law.

"Did you ever hear of someone fooling a Federale?" was his standard reply if anyone questioned him. He always insisted on a multa, a fine, and no one ever protested; they just handed over the money. With one quick movement, he stuffed it in a crumpled envelope with a fancy government insignia stamped on it.

Everyone in the village knew that Capi had his own heartache. It was his retarded son, Israel, who'd lived for years with relatives in Mexicali. He'd been in and out of mental hospitals most of his life.

Capi had never talked much about him. But now Israel was almost a man, and recently he'd been coming to Puertecitos with Pedro and Consuelo, spending more and more time with his father.

At first, Israel seemed perfectly well behaved under his father's benevolent eye. But in the past weeks he'd been seen wearing Capi's uniform around town, and Martine told Reiter that Israel had threatened an American tourist the other day. Apparently, the American had been speeding and ignored Israel when he stepped out in the road and held up a hand.

"When the gringo got to town, he drove to my place, and I could tell the man was all shook up. Told me about a crazy Federale on the loose at the north end of town. I guess Israel pulled a gun on him," Martine said.

"The next day, on my way back from hauling water, I stopped by Capi's hut to talk to him. He told me Israel was at the beach keeping an eye on the place. When I told him about the gringo and the gun, Capi seemed to know all about it. But," Martine continued, "he didn't seem to know what to do with his boy, how to stop him."

As Martine told him about Capi's problem with Israel, Reiter felt the cold perspiration of remorse trickling down his back. Capi was not only struggling with a retarded son, but he might have to worry about Pedro and his marriage. By the time Capi stopped the truck and got out, Reiter wasn't sure he could even look at the man.

"How are things, my friend?" Reiter finally asked, knowing he didn't really sound casual.

"Not good, not good," Capi replied, looking out to sea. For the longest time, they both were quiet. The angry white caps seemed to break up the tension, making it easier to talk. "The sea spills over our feelings and cools down the soul," Beto once said. So they sat in silence and waited for a sign from the sea.

Capi's words slipped into the stillness when the winds died down. "My son, Israel, has a problem." He paused and straightened his tie. "He has been sick for a long, long time. He threatened a gringo with my gun the last week."

Martine nodded toward the pistol. "You know, Capi, Israel isn't well. Pedro's told you a million times that he needs a doctor," he added with compassion.

"Pedro is all wrapped up with that woman," Capi responded. "He doesn't pay much attention to Israel and me."

Even while Capi looked at Martine, his thoughts seemed far away. "Israel was never like his brothers and sisters. He didn't go to school, always stayed a loner. But worse than that, his illness drove a wedge between me and my wife." He glanced at Reiter and went on. "One time when I was still working for the Forestry Department, I had to be away for a week. When I came home, my wife met me at the door crying. Israel had taken one of my pistols and shot the neighbor's dog. For no reason at all. The police took him to a hospital for the insane. Not long after that she died. Of heartache, I think."

Reiter avoided looking at Capi until he'd dried the tears that trickled down his cheeks. "Capi, listen to me. You can't let Israel wear your uniform or take your gun anymore." He was sympathetic but firm.

"I get scared when his body starts shaking all over and nothing can stop it. Then he is quiet as if nothing happened and he sleeps all day." Capi blew his nose before he spoke again. "Pedro and my other children are not much help. Nobody can help."

Reiter felt compassion welling up inside him as he looked at Capi. "What we have to do, Capi, is get Israel to a specialist who can give him the right medicine to stop the seizures," he said. "I know a good one at the University Hospital in Los Angeles. He'll know what to do." Reiter tried to be reassuring. "I'll take you there. Israel can get better," he said without being as certain as he sounded.

Capi straightened his shoulders and adjusted his tie, a grateful look in his eyes. "Thank you, thank you," Capi nodded humbly. "I hope you're right." Then he paused and his eyes lit up for a brief moment. "There is one good thing that I forgot to tell you, my friend. I'm going to be a grandfather soon. Consuelo is going to have my first grandchild."

Reiter shut his eyes. The porch started spinning around him as Capi's words kept ringing in his ears. "Consuelo is going to have my first grandchild."

***

Far into the night, Reiter agonized over Capi and his family. Suddenly, the distant sound of footsteps hurrying toward him interrupted the stillness. Martine's face, deathly white and drawn, emerged from the shadows.

"Amigo, come with me," he said. "It's Capi."

Reiter followed Martine to Capi's shack. It was enveloped in the night's blackness.

"I can't believe it!" Martine said woodenly, pointing to Capi's battered chair. Reiter's eyes widened, and his chest constricted at what he saw. Capi sat, his head bowed, cradling his son in his arms. Both seemed asleep in tender repose. Both were dead.

"My God, No!" Reiter gasped as he peered closer at the bodies and the blood that had pooled beneath the chair.

Martine words caught in his throat. "The drunk gringo in the dune buggy came back to town looking for Israel. They fought. Israel shot him with his father's gun. They say the guy was dead before he hit the ground."

"But, why...why this?" Reiter struggled to make sense of it.

"I think Capi knew they'd put Israel away in prison. I'm sure he couldn't bear the thought of the boy ending up behind bars for the rest of his life. So he dug a grave behind the house and brought Israel here..." Martine's voice trailed off.

Reiter knew instinctively what must have happened next. Distraught, Israel may have suffered another seizure. Perhaps Capi took him in his arms, as he had so often, intent on soothing away the boy's demons. And when he was quiet, Capi placed his revolver against his son's heart and pulled the trigger. Then, clutching Israel to him, he turned the pistol into his own chest to end his sorrow.

"He dug a grave for both of them," Martine whispered.

***

As they lowered the bodies into the grave and began shoveling dirt on them, Reiter felt himself choking back tears. He knew that he needed to cry not just for Capi and Israel, but for himself as well, for Consuelo and the unborn child.

Martine was silent, giving his benediction to the loss he buried and to the Phantom's pain he could not understand.

Reiter methodically started filling the grave. Smoothing the earth on top with his hand, Reiter was overcome by the tenderness of Capi's ultimate sacrifice. While trying to make sense of the desperation that must have driven Capi, Reiter was struck by the thought that nothing is absolute. Not love, not hate. Not life, not death. Not even the Hippocratic Oath, which had always been so sacred to him. Capi had stepped outside of it all, had done what it took for the good of his son. Tonight, alone in the darkness with a steady wind howling at sea, Reiter knelt on the rocky ground and let the cold earth sift through his hands as he sensed his own life spiraling out of control. The last vestige of his old self was gone. He wept.

CHAPTER THIRTY

All through the flight back to California, Reiter struggled to stay focused as hundreds of questions kept racing through his mind. How could he deal with the earthquakes of the past week that had torn through so many lives: the loss of Beto, the deaths of Capi and his son, the news of Consuelo's baby? For so many years he had tried to pretend that the part of him that others perceived as a phantom— unattached and aloof— did not exist. Now the idea that this shadow side, the rogue phantom, had fathered a child that night on the beach rattled through his mind like an ice-cold wind in the middle of August.

He wanted to seek refuge in Beto's words, but Beto was gone now. It was as if he was drifting in the middle of an ocean, cut off from the world, unable to confide in anyone. And the one person he wanted to share with everything in his life— the one person he didn't want to perceive him as a phantom— was Linda. He felt now that being completely open with her was impossible. He'd floated out too far to get back to shore. Consuelo's child would have to be his secret forever.

It seemed now as if his life was spent trying to stay out of the winds that blew him in a hundred directions. One minute, he was in heaven, caressing his wife's growing stomach and feeling for new life. The next minute, he was crashing into a pit of despair thinking of Consuelo and the baby she was carrying. He didn't know if there would ever be a way to find peace.

***

Weeks went by before he was in Puertecitos again. When his airplane touched down, he was surprised to find Dave the Cat Man, and the reclusive Larry waiting with Alfonso at the cement pad. As he tied down the plane, he eyed them with suspicion, wondering what was on their minds. Then Alfonoso came up and effusively threw his arms around him, slapping him on the back. "I guess you heard the news."

"What the hell are you talking about?" Reiter snapped as he drew back, his face flushed.

"Pedro is going to be a father," Dave said. "It's all over the village."

Alfonso looked at him. "Why are you so touchy?" he asked.

Instinctively, Reiter groped for an excuse. "Sorry. I've had a rough week." He tried to dismiss what he imagined to be a smirk playing at the corners of Alfonso's mouth. "I'll see you guys at the Cantina in a little while," he added, surprised that it was becoming so easy to lie to his friends.

He headed instead for the beach, to the spot where his troubles began. Maybe this was the place to find answers. Sitting on the sand, he could imagine his wife walking towards him, her dark hair waving in the breeze. If she found out about Consuelo's child, would she turn and walk the other way? Had he destroyed their dream of growing old together? The thought cut through his mind like an ice-cold wind.

He wandered out to the point where Beto had lived and crouched down at the foot of the boulder. Looking out to sea, he was painfully aware how the loss of Beto had created a great void in his life. If Beto were here, he would have listened to his pain without judging, without comment. The tormented fisherman would have soothed him with stories of the sea.

After a while, he couldn't take any more of the turmoil, and he headed to his house on the hill, avoiding the Cantina and the usual gathering of friends.

***

Stepping on Martine's porch the next morning, he had the unsettling feeling that this Clinica Day would be different. He felt strange, disconnected, as if he was playing a role. And he was afraid that these simple people could see through him.

Jorge was among those waiting to see him, and Reiter was pleased that the skin graft he'd done on his nose had completely healed. He talked to the parents, Nacho and Maria, about the upcoming surgeries, and they agreed to bring Jorge to California in the spring. In spite of his efforts to stay focused, his thoughts kept floating away. Not even Jorge was enough to rein in his wandering mind.

It took a fisherman staggering in with a cane, holding up a fragile woman with a tattered black rag wrapped around her face to shake Reiter out of his personal gloom. The fisherman was thin, as if his skin was stretched too taut over his bones. Lovingly, he unwound the rag from the woman's head and looked at Reiter. Yellowish discharge clouded her eyes.

"Creo que es ciega. I think she's going blind," the fisherman explained. "She's been bumping into walls for months."

It was a malady that was all too familiar in this desert. Years of sunlight reflecting off the endless expanses of sand had done irreparable harm to the retina. Reiter knew that it wouldn't be long before she would lose her eyesight completely. As he meticulously washed out her eyes with a sterile solution, he sensed that somehow they accepted the fact that there wasn't much more he could do. He was grateful for that.

The old woman, with a feeble voice, turned toward the man. "My sight is fading, but I will always be able to see you, mi amor," she said, tears welling in her eyes.

Reiter felt awed by the power that came from her soul, and he watched the old couple make their way to a waiting panga, the man's arm wrapped around the old woman's shoulder.

The afternoon shadows cast a sad light over the town as he sat down to visit with Martine at the end of the day. He tried to make the question sound casual. "Any news of Consuelo and Pedro? "

Martine looked over at him and nodded, making him wonder whether he'd been waiting for this. "They came down after Capi and Israel died to close up the house," Martine responded. "But nobody's seen either of them since." He shook his head. "Alfonso thinks they moved down south. Oahaca, I guess. To be closer to her family. With Capi and Israel gone there's nothing for them here." He seemed to avoid Reiter's uncomfortable gaze.

Reiter was spared a response when he saw a familiar van driving in from the north. He tightened his grip on the armrest and tried to swallow his surprise. It was Linda and the children.

"Looks like you've got visitors," Martine pointed out. "I thought you said that the washed-out road would be too hard on her. That she wouldn't be down here till after the baby comes."

Reiter's flushed face showed his embarrassment. He didn't know what to make of this decision to come to Baja. "I guess she decided to surprise me," he said feebly.

"Or check on you," Martine quipped.

Reiter got up. "Ill see you later," he said as he headed toward the stairs.

He reached the house before Linda climbed out of the van. He knew right away that something was wrong. He'd never seen her so pale and unsteady. Her eyes told him she was frightened, but she smiled when she saw him. He held on to her hand and turned to hug the children. They were too excited to notice something amiss. "Let's go to the beach!" they both said at once.

"Don't forget your towels, and stay in front of the cantina," Linda said. Her voice sounded weak.

"What made you drive down here now, darling? I wasn't expecting you," Reiter said, planting a kiss on her cheek. Her skin felt clammy.

"The kids begged to come down. They have a long weekend. We wanted to surprise you so we left right after school yesterday," she said, looking in his eyes. "It's probably the last trip before the baby comes," she added. "It's still a long drive, and I'm a little light-headed from all that bouncing around." She grabbed his arm with both hands. "Flying down here, you wouldn't know about that. But it does feel like a washboard sometimes." She tried to steady herself.

He didn't have time to reply before he felt her go limp in his arms. Quickly, he picked her up and carried her to the children's bedroom. It took all his effort to get hold of his fear. He took two pillows and placed them under her feet. He saw how pale her face was, and he was struck by the way it clashed with the darkness of her hair. The long lavender dress she wore had small black buttons down the front. As he loosened the top buttons and turned on the fan, she stirred and opened her eyes.

"Just give me a minute," she said as the breeze from the fan tousled her hair.

"I'll get a cold cloth," he said, and hurried to the kitchen. His hands trembled as he grabbed a bowl and filled it with water, then pried some ice cubes from a tray and threw them into the bowl. When he got back to the bedroom, he yanked open several drawers, searching for a clean cloth. He plunged a cloth into the bowl, wrung it out, and laid it on her forehead.

"That feels better," she whispered.

He leaned over her and instinctively touched the bulging part of her stomach. Turning his head sideways, he placed an ear on her navel to listen for life. "And how is our baby?" he started to ask, but the question froze in the back of his throat as his eyes shot down the buttons of her dress' and he saw a spot of bright red blood at the triangle between her legs. For a second, he prayed he was dreaming. *'Please, God, tell me I'm making this up.'*

Quickly, logic took over and he placed a hand on her chest to feel for her heartbeat. He looked at his wristwatch and counted the rate without saying a word. It had to be over ninety. He made a supreme effort to sound in control. "When did this all start?"

"We spent the night in Mexicali. My stomach started acting up this morning when we left. Maybe it's something I ate."

Reiter watched in horror as the bright red spot on the lavender dress got larger. He was determined not to alarm her and spoke calmly, "Didn't you see Dr. Alder last Monday?" He trusted her obstetrician as a meticulous man.

"Yes," she said, though she must have detected the concern in his voice. "He said everything was okay."

"Tell me again about your stomach acting up," he persisted. "Any cramps down below? Maybe in your back?" He stopped, annoyed at himself, remembering that one should never ask leading questions but let the patient tell her own story. He was straddling an invisible fence between lover and physician.

During the first trimester, the most likely cause of bleeding was either a threatened abortion or an ectopic pregnancy, he reasoned. "The first thing we have to do is figure out why you're bleeding," he said, emphasizing the word 'we', as if the communality of the task made it easier. He brought her hand to his lips. "I know it's nothing, but I still need to check." He lowered his eyes. He thought of Beto and what he'd said about love being unselfish, and about people who waste too much time hoping instead of believing. If there ever was a time to believe instead of hope, this was it.

He unbuttoned her dress right above the small bulge of her stomach. He leaned over and placed his lips on her forehead, like a priest kissing the rim of a chalice. Then he released the rest of the buttons, and the bloodstained dress fell open.

"Let me get a pair of gloves. When you're pregnant, we need to be extra careful. Don't want to risk an infection."

He hurried out the front door and towards the stairs that led down the hill. Spotting Martine at the back of his house, he cupped his hands and shouted. "I need a pair of surgical gloves." He was surprised that Martine seemed to understand right away, despite his poor hearing. He disappeared into the house.

Reiter headed back to the sink in the kitchen and was still scrubbing his hands when Martine came in the door with a package of surgical gloves in his hand. Reiter looked up in disbelief. "You ran up all those stairs, and you're hardly out of breath."

Martine ignored him. "Is Linda okay?" He demanded.

"I hope so. I'm going to find out."

"I'll be down on my porch. Holler if you need me." Martine put a hand on his shoulder.

Back in the bedroom, Reiter pulled on the gloves as he neared the bed. Then he bent Linda's legs and slowly spread them apart, positioning heel against heel. He noticed that there was only a small spot of blood on the sheet beneath her. He took it as a good omen.

"I'm not going to hurt you. You know that, don't you?"

"Yes, I do," she said as she opened her eyes.

Physician or husband? Or could he be both? Suddenly, the physician took over, tossing aside any feelings of doubt. He gently parted her labia and slid two fingers inside her, placing his other hand on top of her stomach. Meticulously, he probed the birth canal and felt for the opening of the womb. He closed his eyes and turned his head sideways, as if trying to imagine what his fingers were feeling, hoping the opening was closed and that there was no sign of tissue protruding. He breathed a long sigh of relief when he realized everything was intact.

Next, he felt along the lower part of the womb for any swelling or tenderness on the sides. That could mean a tubal pregnancy. If the baby was growing in the fallopian tubes, the situation could be life threatening, and it would mean the end of the pregnancy. But everything felt normal. Slowly, he removed his hand, but the crimson glove was a sober reminder that the situation was still serious. What unnerved him was that he had no control over it. "Please God, don't let this be happening," he prayed. "I know I've screwed up, betrayed her. I know I deserve it. But why her? Why our innocent baby?"

He moved her to the other bed with a clean sheet and put a pillow under her knees again. "You'll be all right," he said as he covered her with a bedspread.

"I know." She sounded confident. He studied her face. The worry lines faded as she drifted to sleep.

He sat next to her on the edge of the bed with one hand on the bulge of her stomach, the fingers spread apart, as if protecting the struggling life underneath. He could almost see the delicate arms crossed against a tiny rib cage, the legs tucked up underneath. How could it forget the ride on that road, when it was bouncing all over? It must have been frightened at the prospect of being thrown out of the warm and cozy womb it was in. "Don't worry, precious little thing. So help me God, I won't let anything happen to you," Reiter whispered.

He had no idea how much time went by before Linda woke up. He must have dozed off himself. Suddenly, they heard the sound of the children's laughter at the bottom of the stairs. Linda stirred. "Let me fix something to eat," she said. "The children will be hungry."

"No, darling, you have to rest. I'll get Chana to feed them."

For the next twenty-four hours, Reiter stayed by his wife's side. Somehow, everything and everyone fell into place. Cobo took the children fishing the next morning, and when they got back, they took the fish to the cantina where they were cleaned and cooked. Like the others in the village, Cobo somehow knew that Reiter and his wife needed to be by themselves, and it was late in the afternoon before he brought the children back to the house.

When Reiter walked out to meet them, he looked up at a sky radiant with the golden glow of sunset. A family of seagulls flew low over the darkened sea, calling to each other. A brisk wind swept down from the canyons with a cheerful whooshing sound, strong enough to whip up a few white caps. Even the distant howls of the coyotes seemed to be a song of hope. His eyes swept out to the boulder where Beto had lived. "Wherever you are, Beto, I need you. Say a prayer for me. I know I don't deserve it, but do it anyway."

"It'll be all right. Everything's going to be all right," was the answer given by the wind and the seagulls.

He checked on his wife again and was pleased that she was sleeping peacefully. He shot a quick glance at the spot between her legs and noted that the bleeding had stopped. He sighed with relief.

She startled him when, without opening her eyes, she reached for his hand. "I'm okay; you don't have to worry anymore." She said it with the most reassuring voice in the world, as if there was absolutely no doubt.

"I know, I know," he answered gratefully, and kissed her forehead.

"Go look after the children." She tightened her hold on his hand, as if to confirm that her strength was back.

By the next morning, he knew that the crisis was over. Her color was back, and there were no signs of bleeding. He glanced at the children sleeping in the next bed.

As he made his way down the stairs toward Martine's porch, he found himself praying. "Thank you, my God. Thank you for looking after my love, for helping us through this dark time." Just as he reached the foot of the stairs, unexpectedly, his thoughts went to Consuelo. He felt a stab of guilt as he pictured her with a swollen belly. Was there anyone to protect her and her baby? Had Linda's threatened abortion been a retribution for his reckless ways? And had God, in his mysterious mercy, spared him the ultimate pain of losing a child?

Martine met him at the porch steps. He fidgeted as he handed Reiter a cup of steaming coffee.

"Linda and the baby are going to be fine," Reiter said quickly, knowing he had to put him at ease.

"I had a hunch it would turn out okay," Martine said in his raspy voice. He glanced at Reiter. "This town has a lot of heart, amigo."

"I know."

While they sat down, Martine kept talking. "Do you have any idea how much they all care for you both? The word got around that you had a problem up there. Every minute, someone dropped by wanting to know how things were going, if there was anything they could do. It went on all afternoon."

Reiter tried to look calm, but he couldn't hide his emotion.

"I can't remember a time when so many candles were lit. Everyone seemed to be praying. I could hear Chana saying her rosary over and over, and for once Alfonso didn't tell her to shut up. Even the waterman sat here in his truck for hours without saying a word. Maybe he was praying too."

"How do you suppose they all knew?" Reiter swallowed hard.

"They wanted to know why you never came off the hill. I could see that they sensed something was wrong, so I told them. I said that Linda was sick." There was a hint of guilt in his voice, as if he'd reneged on a promise. "But that's all I said. It was like Clinica Day, but this time you were the patient," Martine finally said.

"What can I do to thank them?"

"You're asking me?" Martine sounded incredulous. "Do what you always did. Be yourself. Quit avoiding people. Quit being a phantom." Then Martine lowered his voice. "One more thing... about Consuelo...there are rumors floating around. Could be that people are more nosey than they should be, or that they're making things up."

"What are you talking about?" Reiter stammered.

"Man, what's the matter with you? Maybe most of these people haven't gone beyond grade school, but don't ever think they're dummies. Or that they're blind. Don't you suppose they've seen how you've been acting lately? Roaming around town all by yourself, listening to voices and talking to the birds and the fish out there on the beach." He pointed to the beach and his voice suddenly became accusing. "There are rumors. It's as simple as that."

Reiter gasped, any answer stuck in the back of his throat.

CHAPTER THIRTY-ONE

Over the next few months, they settled into halfway predictable routines that were somehow reassuring. Then one day toward the end of May, he walked out of the operating room, relieved that a complicated case had gone well. He stepped into his office at the end of the hall with the intention of calling his wife.

As the door closed behind him, he winced at a deafening roar that rattled the windows behind his desk. A flash of lightning and claps of thunder stirred dark memories and late night fears lingering just below the surface of his mind. With a shattering roar, a sheet of rain struck the window and water streamed off the glass. He placed a hand on the pane as if to make sure it would hold and instinctively closed his eyes. Another clap of thunder seemed to shake the whole building. The silence that followed was like an eerie reprieve before a momentous event. Earlier that morning, the sky had been blue, and he wondered what this sudden change in the atmosphere might mean. A persistent knock on the door added to his discomfort.

"Come on in." He turned to the door and attempted a smile. His secretary handed him a manila envelope. "I think this is for you," she said politely and left the room.

He studied the wrinkled envelope and the row of red and green stamps along the top margin. "Estados Unidos Mexicanos" was stamped across them. He strained his eyes and flipped the envelope around, trying to read the smudged postmark. He felt his jaw tighten. The only thing he could decipher was the year and the month, but not the town from which it was mailed. It had taken months to reach him. The envelope was frayed at the edges, and there were grease spots splattered across the back. He shifted it around in his trembling hands as if he could gauge its importance by weighing it. The handwriting with his name and address was graceful and neat with precisely styled letters. All the S's and C's ended in gentle drawn-out curves like delicate flowers.

Methodically, he opened the drawer of his desk and searched for a letter opener. When he found one, he slashed open one side of the envelope. The first thing that fell out was the neatly folded page of a newspaper. He glanced at the headline, "Typhoon Swallows Baja Sur." It was the daily paper of La Paz, the capital of southern Baja. He searched for a date—December 30[h]. Inside the newspaper was a letter written on ivory stationery with Consuelo's signature at the bottom. The handwriting was smudged and not easy to read:

"*Espanto,*" it began. "*Months ago you changed my life. First with your haunting eyes that stirred feelings within me I thought had died. They told me I was beautiful and desirable. Pedro's eyes no longer said that.*" He felt a pounding in his temples as he held the letter.

"*That midnight,*" he read, "*when we met on the beach I knew it was no accident. I was sure God had sent you to show me about true love. When I finally realized that what we did had nothing to do with love, it was too late.*" The next sentence had a thick ink mark streaking across it, like she had changed her mind about something. Frantically, he held the letter against the light from the desk lamp, but when he couldn't read what she had crossed out, he read on.

"*I was ashamed of myself, hating every bit of me for betraying the man whose love never failed me. When I returned to Pedro's arms and the love that waited for me, I couldn't look him in the eyes.*

Espanto, I am pregnant after all these years of marriage. But what we did have robbed me of the joy I should feel. It is swallowed up by the guilt of that night.

Do you have any idea what it is for a woman to carry a life, not knowing who the father is? I curse you for that. And myself. Every day that goes by is a day of anguish and pain.

Last night I thought it was the end of the world when a storm crashed over the city. I felt that the thundering winds and towering waves were God's wrath for what we had done. I sank to my knees on the cold stone of my room and prayed that the storm would end my life and sweep me into the ocean. This morning, when I woke up, I thanked God for sparing my life, for I'm not just me anymore.

*Why should an unborn child pay for our sin? You and I have to pay. I know
that as surely as the sun is shining again today.*

*Do not ask about me, ever, and don't try to find me. We are with friends in
the south, and I will stay here to raise the child, either with Pedro or alone."*

Consuelo

Her signature faded, and with the back of his hand he brushed
away the tears.

The storm wouldn't let up and battered him and Beverly Hills
for the rest of the day. When he finally drove along the water-
drenched highway toward the ranch, he fought relentless waves of
despair. He tried to open the windows, turn on the heater, then put
on some music, but nothing seemed to help. Finally, he pulled over
to the shoulder somewhere along the highway and bolted out of the
car into the torrential rain. Dry heaves almost ripped out his stomach.
His clothes drenched and his hair disheveled, he finally climbed back
in the car and decided to return to the clinic. The winds raged, and
the night turned a rusty black as if fomenting the thoughts that raced
through his mind. He called home. "I think I'll stay at the office
tonight. I'm sure the storm will ease off by morning."

"I was sure you wouldn't drive in this weather," Linda answered.

***

The weeks that followed, Consuelo's letter kept grinding against
his conscience like a million pebbles of stirred up sand. There were
days when the heat in his stomach felt as if molten lead was swishing
around. Day after day, he struggled to dampen the heartache and
plod through the hours as if nothing was wrong, both at home and in
the clinic. He was obsessed by the calendar, adding up the months
and days, reluctantly comparing them to his wife's pregnancy. He
knew Consuelo's child would be born any day, or had already been
born.

Thoughts of the child kept resurfacing at the most improbable
times—in the middle of surgery, or when he was examining a patient,

253

or even playing soccer with his son. All it took was a careless word, and without intending to, he'd find himself comparing love and lust. Beto had talked about love living on forever, while lust, he said, fades away like the fog. There was no doubt that the day Linda had forgiven him they had sealed their love with a new life. But what about the night with Consuelo?

Every time he'd steal glances at his wife's bulging stomach, he hoped she couldn't detect the guilt in his face. *Please*, he'd implore, *let Consuelo's husband be the father of her child, let it be his love that lives on.*

***

A few days later, when he thought the workday had finally ground to an end, one of the nurses came running after him as he was leaving the office. His instinct told him to just keep on walking, but the nurse was faster. "Mr. Love is on the phone. He says it's urgent."

Reiter nodded and turned back to the desk. He sat down before he picked up the receiver. Love spoke in a rush. "Betty has a problem. A serious problem. Her ring finger is swollen like a sausage and the ring is cutting off the circulation. She's in a lot of pain." His voice rose higher with every word.

With all the doctors in this town, why does he have to call me, Reiter wondered. Any one of them would have been pleased to accommodate Betty Love. On the other hand, maybe he should be glad for the distraction.

As if reading his thoughts, Love persisted, "You're the only one she wants. We're in the emergency room at City Hospital." Then he paused, as if groping for words. "She won't let anyone else touch her."

"Okay, I'll be right there," he replied and hurried to the hospital.

Reaching the emergency department, Reiter found Miss Love waiting in an examining room, the odor of her expensive perfume floating through the air. She was sobbing dramatically, surrounded by

254

fawning technicians and nurses. He could see that her finger was swollen grotesquely, and when he touched it, the skin felt like it was ready to burst. The many diamonds in the ring were biting into in the purple flesh of the finger.

"We were at a party at Jeff Clancy's, and I felt this tingling in my hand. When I tried to take off the ring, my finger started swelling," she explained between sobs. "I asked Edmund to take me home, but it only got worse." Her breathing was hard and heavy, and she kept looking at her left hand resting on a stand by the bed. The nurse had placed it in a bowl and was packing ice around it.

Reiter remembered the fuss over that ring when he'd worked on her face. Even then she'd been adamant about not taking it off. He'd never forget her anguished look or the way her eyes had followed the nurse when she finally gave in and allowed them to remove it.

There was one thing he knew right away; this time it was going to be much more difficult. He tried to turn it just a little, but it wouldn't budge. Betty Love winced in pain. Without waiting for instructions, a nurse brought him a pair of surgical pliers and placed them on a tray by the gurney.

"What is that ghastly looking thing?" Miss Love wanted to know, arching her eyebrows.

"It's called a ring cutter," Reiter answered, skipping quickly over the last word when he saw her reaction.

She gasped, "Nobody's going to use that on my ring." She stared at the glittering piece of jewelry. "It's worth over a million dollars," she explained between sobs. "A gift from my husband." She shot a questioning look at Edmund, who blushed slightly.

Reiter just let her talk while he gently lifted her hand out of the ice tray. "First, I'll try to remove it the simplest way. We'll wind a tight tape around your finger just above the ring and squeeze out the fluid and blood." He started the process as he was talking. "Next, we'll coat it with this oily stuff here and see if we can get the ring to slip over the tape. If that works, we won't have to cut it." With his gloved hand, he applied ointment from the jar on the table.

"I'd rather cut off my finger than damage even one of those diamonds," she moaned, sounding melodramatic.

That would be one way to get the ring off, he thought, but reined in his sarcasm and tried to look sympathetic.

Miss Love glanced over at her husband before she turned to Reiter. "I guess you have to do what you have to do," she said, as if resigned to her fate.

Reiter turned to the nurse standing at the side of the gurney. "Give me five milligrams of Valium," he said casually.

A sudden tap on his shoulder made him turn. It was Mr. Love. "May I talk to you for a minute?" he whispered. "It's important," he added.

Reiter felt a twinge of annoyance. "I'll be with you in a minute," he said and injected the medication in Betty Love's arm. "Let's wait a few minutes till the medication works." He headed toward the door.

Outside the room, Edmund Love seemed to be fumbling for words. He looked like a man with a great weight on his conscience. His right hand kept clutching his chin, and his left hand groped through his pocket, as if searching for loose change.

"I don't want you to worry," Reiter said reassuringly. "You'll see. She's going to be okay."

"No, no, that's not the problem." Love sounded embarrassed. "I'm not sure how to tell you," he stammered, his eyes studying his short, chewed off nails. His hands were trembling. "It's not worth hurting her in any way." Then he paused for a second as if to gain some composure. "The ring's a fake," he blurted out and looked at the floor. "There isn't a single diamond in that ring." He went on. "Haven't you ever been in love and wanted to impress someone?" His eyes seemed to be begging for a partner in crime. "I bought the ring, and let her believe it was set with diamonds. The truth is, they're zirconium. It's hard to tell the difference these days. I always meant to replace them with the real thing, but time has a way of slipping by.

Besides, she really liked it." He sighed. "In the end, it's all about love, isn't it? And diamonds are only stones." The flush of color on his cheeks deepened as he spoke.

Reiter found himself thinking of Beto. "Love is no different than the sun rising over the sea. Always there, whether you see it or not."

"Don't worry," Reiter said. "You know I wouldn't hurt her." He turned and headed for the door.

Edmund Love ran after him. "Promise me you won't tell her. Nobody needs to know about this." His voice trailed with a desperate note. Then he shuffled back to a couch in the waiting room and sat down.

When Reiter returned to the examining room, the Valium had calmed Miss Love, and she was quiet. He re-wrapped the tape around the swollen finger to get out the rest of the blood. Minutes later, he was able to slip the ring over the tape coated with more soap. The old home remedy worked like a charm. He held up the ring and handed it to the idol of his youth.

Tears came to her eyes and there was a quiver in her voice. "Thank you. Thank you. I knew I could count on you."

"Sometimes we get lucky," he replied with a nod. "To tell you the truth, I wasn't sure it would work. That finger was pretty swollen."

She sat up and lowered her voice. Let me guess what my husband said to you out there." Reiter's eyes widened, and she paused for a moment as if to make sure he was listening. "Didn't he tell you the ring is a phony? I knew it all along." She made no attempt to wipe the tears from her eyes. "Not long after Edmund gave it to me, I met a famous jewelry designer from Paris. He was the one who told me that Edmund's ring was an imitation. I was lonesome at the time. And desperate for attention. I fell for his charm."

She looked at Reiter as if pleading for his understanding. "We became lovers, and he replaced the fake stones with real diamonds. We were going to get married, but the studio was against it. Another divorce wouldn't be good for my image, they insisted." She turned the ring sideways. "It turned out he was only after my money anyway. He didn't know a thing about love. I'm so grateful now that I stayed with my husband."

Reiter found himself thinking about Consuelo. And about betrayal and commitment.

CHAPTER THIRTY-TWO

Consuelo's letter fanned a renewed determination in him to find out what had happened to her. He ignored her request to leave her alone and instead called friends, judges, and fishermen on both sides of the border to ask about her. He couldn't help himself, even phoning the governors of three Mexican states, disguising his questions behind the veneer of inquiring about patients.

On the last Friday of the month, he left for Puertecitos. But instead of landing there, an uncontrollable urge kept him flying on to La Paz. Four hours later, he was at the tip of the Baja peninsula. From a distance, he saw the long bay that led him to the airport in La Paz. He hurriedly tied down the plane and waved at the yawning guard who tipped his hat. His eyes combed over the few waiting cars until he spotted a taxi. Urging the driver on, they drove to the main market near the town square. He combed through the noisy crowds that mingled in the old plaza, but saw no sign of Consuelo.

It was late morning when he happened upon an old adobe church near the market. He knelt in a pew behind a young couple who were trying to quiet their five noisy children, but walked out halfway through the sermon when the portly priest seemed to be pointing a finger at him as he talked about the sanctity of the family and the role God planned for mothers and fathers.

He spent the next few hours making inquiries and checking with hospitals that had maternity wards, but there were no records of Consuelo or her baby. It was as if they had been swallowed by the sea or carried off by the hurricane that had destroyed so much of the city months ago.

***

Back in California, it was a constant struggle to keep thoughts of Consuelo from spilling into his everyday life. He tried to act normally, but it wasn't easy, and there were many nights he lay awake, worrying about the fatherless child.

When Jeff Clancy called him at the clinic late one afternoon, he was grateful for the distraction. "I'm giving a party for the cast next month," Jeff said in his matter-of-fact-like voice, halfway between an order and an invitation. "Why don't you plan on coming over to meet some of the crowd?" Before Reiter could answer, he added, "You need to show your face for a change. A lot of people are beginning to wonder if you really exist."

"What do you tell them?" Reiter laughed.

Jeff lowered his voice and sounded slightly annoyed. "Don't tell me you have to go on one of your mysterious jaunts. What's the name of that place south of the border?"

Reiter was surprised by how much the call lifted his mood. He and Jeff had developed a special relationship. Despite his worldwide notoriety, there was a noble streak in the famous actor that Reiter had come to admire. From what he could see, Jeff was a happy family man, extremely close to his wife and children.

"Tell you what," Reiter took a chance. "Let's make a deal. You fly with me to that place south of the border this weekend, and I'll come to your party next month."

Jeff hesitated for only a moment. "You're on." He sounded pleased. "I have a tennis game with one of the big shots at Warner Brothers Saturday. You just gave me the way out. But I'll hold you to it. Don't forget to show up at the party.'"

"A deal is a deal," Reiter replied, smiling to himself.

***

The morning he and Jeff met at the Santa Monica airport, the sky was a flat, monotone gray. The family had driven with him from the ranch. After stowing his bags in the airplane, Reiter turned to kiss his wife and the children good-bye. She leaned her swollen stomach against him. "Be careful," she whispered. She had the contented radiance of a new mother. As they climbed into the aircraft, she called out, "Jeff, take care of your friend. New fathers are nervous. Know what I mean?"

Reiter smiled weakly, and for a minute felt an impulse to cancel the flight and stay home with her. Instead, he leaned over to check the door handle. "Let's go," he said as he watched his wife heading back to the car.

Jeff nodded and adjusted his seat belt. "Is everything okay?" he suddenly wanted to know. "I mean with you and Linda?

Reiter lowered his eyes and turned his head sideways, as if listening to the engine. "What's that supposed to mean?" he finally responded.

"I don't know. You just don't act like yourself. Are you feeling all right?"

Reiter pretended he hadn't heard him, and scanned the instruments. He adjusted some dials but his expression remained distant. He couldn't tell Jeff the reason he wasn't sleeping at night, that his wife's pregnancy was a daily reminder of another woman and the baby she was carrying or perhaps nursing by now.

Jeff went on, unaware of Reiter's turmoil. "Linda looks great, by the way. Pregnancy agrees with her. But something tells me you don't appreciate what she's going through. I remember how Evelyn needed lots of reassurance when she was pregnant. Every woman does." He looked out the window as they taxied by the tower. "You've got to learn the finer points to make a woman feel like a goddess. There isn't a day that goes by that I don't make sure Evelyn knows how special she is. Sometimes I call her out of the blue just to tell her that." He paused. "In fact, I'll call her the minute we land."

How could any man be so attentive after all those years of marriage, Reiter wondered, almost out loud. Especially, a famous Hollywood star. Husbands like Jeff are one in a million, he decided. I could never measure up to him. On the other hand, Jeff doesn't have to worry about a fatherless child. He shook his head. "Jeff, sometimes I wonder if you're real."

"What's the big deal? Why shouldn't I call Evelyn? "

The way he said that it sounded like he was reading a movie script. But the expression on his face was genuine, as if connected to a noble soul. When he looked into Jeff's eyes, he saw the sparkle of truth with no secret children to hide, no sins to be forgiven, no phantom lurking around.

As they flew south, Reiter tried to diminish the nagging guilt that clung to him. He started thinking instead about the meeting between Jeff and his Puertecitos friends. It had often crossed his mind to take one of his celebrity friends down to the amigos in Baja. For years he'd toyed with the idea of connecting the two worlds, but as they approached the Mexican border, he grew tense. A million questions flooded his mind. How would Jeff react to the stench of rotten fish? Would the millions of flies drive him crazy, the heat wear him out, and the Indians frighten him? And how would the people in Puertecitos react when they saw a big shot movie star like Jeff Clancy? Would they be shy? Would they resent him? He'd seen it before, growing up in a land where there was a fierce clash of cultures. Without a common bridge, the two worlds could remain separated forever.

He knew Jeff had traveled all over the world to the most exotic places. But the context were always strictly controlled, with props and sets and 'advance people' to mold events and provide Jeff with all the cues. Wherever he went, everything was planned and rehearsed and scripted and budgeted. Nothing left to chance. How would Jeff react when he ran into Papillo and Speedy? These were real hombres from a primitive land, with no props and no scripts. Their only cues were their schemes of survival.

He stole another look at Jeff's handsome features, his strong profile, those deep-set eyes and well-styled hair, a face known all over the globe. Reiter shuddered and hoped his instincts were right. People are people, here and everywhere, he told himself as he grasped for a little reassurance. All one can do is get them together and stand back for a while and hope for the best.

From the plane, he could see the familiar buttes of San Felipe, sleeping volcanoes jutting out of the sea like two rounded breasts with the deepest of cleavage. The approach to the old airport used to be between the two buttes.

Reiter turned to Jeff. "Did you really mean it?" He studied his friend. "I mean about calling your wife?"

"Yes, I'd like to do that."

"That means we're going to have to land here. San Felipe has the last phone for the next five hundred miles," Reiter said as he started a gentle descent.

"On the other hand, I'm getting real hungry," Jeff interjected. "What about some of those shrimps you keep bragging about? I can already taste 'em." He paused and turned to Reiter. "Maybe we should keep on flying. I can always call Evelyn on our way back."

Reiter frowned, re-applied power, and the aircraft started to climb. "Just make up your mind. We can head for Puertecitos right now and land in San Felipe tomorrow on our way home."

Jeff raised an eyebrow and put a hand on Reiter's shoulder. "The more I think about this, you're the one who should be calling your wife. I mean today. She's the one who's pregnant."

He sounded emphatic, and Reiter shrugged. "Okay. Maybe that's not a bad idea. We can land long enough to call the girls and be back in the air in no time."

Jeff must have sensed that he'd stirred Reiter's conscience. "I think you'll be glad you did. It's a known fact that when women are pregnant they're kind of fragile. There's nothing wrong with being extra attentive." He looked out the window.

Reiter's face softened. He tried to picture how Linda would react to an unexpected phone call from San Felipe. He felt a familiar wave of guilt rising in the back of his conscience. He clapped Jeff on his shoulder. "You're a better husband than I'll ever be."

"I try my best," Jeff bubbled. "Like I said, it's important to remind her how much you love her. I'm thinking of getting Evelyn some Mexican jewelry while we're here. Maybe a silver necklace, or one of those shell bracelets layered with topaz. I'm no cheapo, you know."

Reiter didn't answer, his eyes fixed on the horizon. They were right over San Felipe.

Jeff craned to get a better view of the sandy, white beach that came into view. "Look at all the people down there on the beach." He turned to Reiter with a smile. "I can picture the muchachas under the umbrellas. It's youth, my man, youth in tiny bikinis."

They made another pass over the north side of town with its small houses and shacks on the beach and looked for the brightly painted shack that was Juan's. For years, Juan had been driving Reiter around town in his old, junky car. He was also one of the town policemen; at least, that's what he claimed. Reiter buzzed Juan's house twice to let him know they were going to land. Then he headed for the airport miles from town. He circled the strip and studied the familiar windsock. It was hanging limp, so he landed from the west and taxied to a tie down. By the time the last knot was tied, he saw Juan drive up.

Barefoot children ran out from a nearby shack, picked up some big rocks, and wedged them against the tires of the plane. Then they ran up to Reiter, who gave them some coins. All the while they kept eyeing Jeff and grinning. They must have known who he was because Reiter heard them giggle to each other. "El Charro Americano de las Peliculas. The American cowboy from the movies." Their big eyes almost popped out of their heads.

With a beaming smile, Jeff pointed his forefingers like guns in the air. "Boom, boom," he laughed. "Hallo, muchachos,"

Juan looked puzzled, but not impressed. "Buenos dias, Senor. A sus ordenes," he said, giving Reiter a long, quizzical look.

"We need a telephone, amigo," Reiter explained.

They headed for the Cortez Hotel on the beach. It had the only telephone in town.

"I sure hope they don't recognize me," Jeff said, taking off his sunglasses and lifting the pointed brim of his world-famous hat.

At the Cortez Hotel, there was a palm-thatched cabana on the beach with a long bar wrapped all the way around it. A sizable crowd of tourists milled around in their swimsuits. "I feel like a cool margarita," Jeff said, eyeing the beach and the bikinis.

They walked up to the bar, and Jeff took off his hat. He grinned that broad grin that had gone around the world, the smile for which he was famous. It seemed to achieve its intended response. People began staring and crowding around him, gushing. Jeff kept on smiling, his cowboy hat in his hand. Everybody wanted autographs and pictures. They all seemed to have a camera. Even Guillermo, the mayor of the town, came running. "I'm the mayor of the city," he kept repeating until he caught Jeff's attention.

Jeff grinned broadly. It looked like he had no intention of leaving anytime soon. He drank one margarita and then another. He seemed to have forgotten about calling his wife as he smiled for the cameras and gave autographs. It took most of the morning.

"It's time to go," Reiter finally insisted.

Once they were in the air, Jeff turned to him. "We didn't call our ladies. That friend of yours never took me to a phone," he complained. "That's a Mexican for you. Manana, manana, everything manana."

Reiter furrowed his brow. 'Mexican manana' reminded him of an unpleasant side of people that he'd seen in his childhood—a fierce loyalty to a race or a religion that made men turn against anyone who was different.

"Did I say something wrong?" Jeff interrupted his thoughts.

Reiter was inclined to suppress his displeasure, but thought better of it. "I don't like what you said about Juan being a lazy Mexican, or the thing about manana." He paused and adjusted a dial. "It makes me wonder what you think of me. After all, I'm not your All-American boy."

Jeff waved that away. "Don't take things so seriously, hombre," he urged him. "What I said was just a figure of speech."

But Reiter didn't want to let it go so easily. "Juan's not the kind to tell you what to do. Besides, the way you were carrying on with the ladies, not even God could have dragged you to a phone."

Jeff grinned. "Calm down, man. Calm down. You seem to forget that it all goes with the territory. The studio pays me a ton of money to show my face, to be nice to the ladies. It's all part of my job. I can't let them down. But it isn't always easy." His voice dropped. "What I said about Juan—let me take it back. I'm sorry."

Feeling somewhat mollified, Reiter perked up when he saw the outline of the horseshoe bay in the distance. He pulled up gently on the yoke and reduced the RPMs. Then he reached for the switch that let down the flaps. When they got closer, he searched for the windsock and lowered the landing gear, hugging the coastline as he swept above the purple-blue bay.

"Where are we going to land?" Jeff asked apprehensively.

"Down there, by the beach, on the other side of those shacks."

Jeff scanned the narrow strip of land below, and he wrinkled his forehead. "There's no way. That looks more like a postage stamp. No one can land there." He took off his tinted glasses and stared in disbelief as they flew over the little shack at the end of what looked like a gravel road with a sharp hump in the middle.

Seagulls scattered out of the way. The airplane touched down and raised a cloud of dust. "What do you think of this one, amigo?" Reiter smiled as he gently tapped on the brakes.

Jeff studied the little shacks scattered along the runway and around the beach. A couple of junked boats and a few rusty cars dotted the arid landscape nearby. "Are you sure we didn't land on the moon?" he joked.

Reiter had never thought about it; maybe it did look a little like the moon. But one thing was certain; it was a moon full of life, precious life at the edge of time, standing still in a world by itself, waiting to catch up with the other world some day. For a rare moment, Reiter forgot his troubles and felt a sudden tingling of anticipation and excitement as they taxied back to the other end of the runway. Children and dogs trotted along the sides of the airstrip, waving and barking. Several men had gathered on a cement pad just off the end of the dirt strip, each with a bottle of beer in his hand.

They stopped at the end of the runway, and Reiter sensed there was something different in the way Jeff was grinning. It was hard to figure out if he was letting down his guard or if he was feeling totally out of place. *Well, this is where we'll find out,* he said to himself.

When they climbed out of the plane, the greetings were the same as always. Hugs and back slapping and shouting seemed to take hours. It was an old ritual that had gone on for years. Reiter noticed that Jeff looked a little dazed, the famous grin slowly fading. Not one soul seemed to know who he was. It was as if he were suddenly stripped of the trimmings of his name and his fame. Reiter kept glancing at his friend, trying to pry into his mind. He was probably telling himself that surely someone here had seen his TV shows or his movies. After all, they'd been shown everywhere on the planet. But maybe not here on the moon.

"Let's get this airplane off the runway." Martine sounded concerned.

Together, they pushed the plane toward a slab of cement on the west side of the runway. Reiter tired to ignore the crudely chipped letters in the cement: 'Esparto.' Right above it was written 'Privada porperti' in uneven letters. An uneasy feeling came over him, just like the first time he saw this parking spot. After all, when his friends poured the cement, they did it to surprise him. And before the slab was dry some drunk must have scratched in his name with a stick, half in Spanish and half in English. He always imagined it was Cobo. He remembered thanking them profusely that first day, but when he walked by the airplane a few weeks later he winced when he overheard two American pilots talking as they pushed their plane next to the slab, "Must be another crude California big shot," one of them said.

The friend was quick to respond, "Someone told me he's some ass-hole doctor insisting on a private pad for his airplane."

Today, he shot a disparaging look at Cobo. Parking his aircraft on the gravel like everyone else would be just as easy. But obviously his friends didn't agree. Perhaps they saw it as a way to cement their friendship, something permanent, and something that lasted a lifetime or two, like a tombstone. Most things on earth were built to be bought and sold or blown away by the wind. But not tombstones or cement pads in Puertecitos with 'Espanto' written on them.

As they pushed the plane, Pablo looked over at Jeff. "Hey man, don't just stand there. This thing's heavy. Can't you give us a hand?" He sounded outright annoyed.

Suddenly, a huge, bear-like figure lumbered over. Jeff straightened up and forced on his smile, as if ready to greet someone who finally wanted his autograph. But Papillo, the lumbering bear, plodded right by him as if he didn't exist. Jeff looked over at Reiter and smiled weakly.

In the last rays of the Puertecitos sunset, Jeff seemed unusually quiet. The lunar landscape, with the stench of rotten fish heads and the strange collection of people was having the same effect on Jeff as everyone else. Puertecitos had a way of cutting every one down to size. Fame and stature meant nothing. Jeff Clancy was just another hombre here, settling down like the rest in the dusty trenches of everyday life.

"I can tell already, you'll like this place," Martine laughed. "Why not have a cervesa?" And he slapped Jeff on the back.

CHAPTER THIRTY-THREE

Behind the bar in the Cantina, Rafael studied Jeff Clancy's neatly styled hair-do that seemed to defy the breeze from the squeaking fan on the ceiling. His eyes wandered over the purple shirt open to mid-chest and the starched, pressed jeans held up by a wide belt with a silver buckle. The embroidered leather snake boots had such pointed toes that Rafael must have wondered how a man's foot could fit into them. He squinted at the rings that sparkled on Jeff's fingers.

The stranger must have looked familiar, but Rafael didn't seem to be able to place him. As if trying to hide his confusion, he turned and started to pull beer bottles from an open ice chest behind the bar. Then, apparently shrugging it off, he made his way over to Reiter and Martine. He threw his arms around them while glancing sideways at Jeff. "Welcome, amigos," he said with a hesitancy in his voice. "Who is your friend?" he whispered.

Reiter quickly relieved his doubts. "Rafael, I'm sure you recognize this cowboy here." He smiled as he put a hand on Jeff's shoulder. "From the movies and television." Don Rafael's face lit up, and Reiter added, "Jeff Clancy, the famous artista."

Jeff flashed a smile that put Rafael at ease. "Oh, yes! I knew right away you were a famous man. I'm your servidor. It's an honor to meet you," Rafael said and immediately shook Jeff's hand. "Welcome! Welcome to Puertecitos, Senor," he exclaimed with a mixture of pride and surprise in his voice.

Suddenly, Jeff slipped into his role as the familiar 'master' working the crowd. His voice and laughter bounced through the room, confident and strong. Reiter could imagine the wheels spinning in his brain: "Of course they know me. Everybody knows me from the movies."

Martine stepped up to the bar. "Cervesas for everybody," he ordered. In no time and out of nowhere, Simon and several guys with guitars began to set up in a corner of the room while many of the town folk trickled into the cantina.

Pablo joined Reiter and Martine at the bar. Several beers later, he leaned closer to Reiter and whispered, "Whatever you say, this Jeff Clancy comes across as a real prima donna to me." He cleared his throat as if to tone down the remark. "Just look at that hairdo." He nodded toward Jeff. "I swear it's glued to his skull," he added. A loud twang from a guitar drowned the rest of his words.

Reiter swallowed to fend off a sudden dryness in the back of his throat. Maybe the whole thing about getting Hollywood and Puertecitos together had been a crazy idea. Maybe famous actors and half-breed fishermen were too different after all. Had he let his nutty ideas sweep common logic under the rug? Or was his ego trying to take over, thinking he could control and distort the facts?

Finally, he looked at Pablo and decided to give it one more try. "You don't even know him," he said. "You have no idea that he's really a nice guy. Besides, if you think about it, his life isn't that easy." When Pablo looked annoyed, Reiter pressed on, "Don't you know the man has to live in a fishbowl? How would you like not being able to walk out the door and take a leak like everyone else? Always having to look over your shoulder?"

"Have you ever thought that he might like it that way? No one's forcing him." Pablo shrugged.

"Come one, give the guy a break," Reiter insisted. "I've heard you say a hundred times that people are more alike than they are different."

A boisterous exchange at the other end of the bar caught their attention. Jeff was sitting with Cobo and Alfonso, his new friends, and something he said had them howling with laughter. They kept toasting each other as they lifted glasses filled with tequila. Jeff was leaning back in a rickety chair, a wide grin across his face. Reiter couldn't remember seeing him so at ease, as if he were suddenly freed from the shackles of fame. This was one place where he wasn't forced to smile or shake hands.

"So tell me, what do you think of the place?" Reiter finally asked Jeff as he joined the small group.

"I got to admit I couldn't imagine anything like this on earth," Jeff said. "Never in all my life" he insisted, scooping a fly out of his drink and flicking it in the air. "But then, it's one place I've never been—to the moon." And he took a long swallow of tequila.

***

The next morning, Reiter pried open his eyes just as the fiery sun was climbing out of the sea. He wandered to the back of the house where Jeff had spent the night and hesitated at the door, thinking it might be too early to knock. But he heard a rustling inside, and Jeff opened the door before he raised his hand.

"I didn't sleep all that well," Jeff was quick to remark as his eyes swept up the hill. "It was teeming with coyotes up there. All night long." He shuddered. "I swear, they never stopped howling. Gave me the jitters."

Suddenly, his eyes shifted to a mirror hanging beside the door, and in an instant he seemed to forget about coyotes. He was studying his face, tracing his jaw with his fingertips and touching his taut neck and his temples where the crow's feet had been smoothed out by the facelift. He walked his fingers around his ears. "There isn't a trace of a scar, Reiter. There isn't anybody who has a clue that I've had surgery," Jeff beamed.

"What difference does it make?" Reiter was quick to reply. "Your fans are crazy about you anyway." He paused. "Facelift or not."

"You think so?" Jeff sounded grateful. "I keep asking myself if they like the young Jeff Clancy with the facelift or the Jeff Clancy who's getting older." He sighed. "It's all about what I look like, Paul. Not what I feel like."

They moved to the patio, and Reiter brought out fresh coffee. Jeff took a sip and looked down at the village. "You've got to admit, you have some weird friends in this town."

Reiter thought for a moment. It was true. Puertecitos attracted unusual people. It wasn't for everyone, especially for someone whose life was chained to the mood of his fans. How could he be expected to blend in with howling coyotes and half-breed fishermen who didn't speak English? He put a hand on Jeff's shoulder and smiled.

"But the place is perfect for a movie," Jeff interjected, as if a light had been turned on in his brain. "You don't run into natural sets very often. And the extras are already here. We could cook up a hell of a story and come up with a screenplay in no time." He was gesturing wildly, hardly able to contain his excitement. "I've been thinking about that Papillo guy. With the right lighting and the right lens, those beady little eyes in that fleshy flat face…we could make him look like a killer."

"I'm not sure he'd go along with any of that," Reiter objected. "I've seen him get furious when some tourists wanted to take pictures of him as if he were an ape in a zoo. They seem to forget that he's a human being. You can't treat him like a weirdo."

"Calm down, man. You make it sound as if he were your cousin. It's not my fault the guy looks the way he does," Jeff said. A shadow of annoyance swept over Reiter's face, and Jeff backed off. "I keep forgetting you're not in show business. You'd make some director," he added, a hint of sarcasm in his voice.

Reiter had no intention to get into that discussion. He realized Jeff lived in a different world. Realizing they were getting nowhere, he decided to change the subject. "Why don't you come down to Martine's with me?" he suggested. "Today's Clinica Day. Let me show you what goes on."

As they made their way down the steps, they could see Martine shuffling back and forth between his bedroom and the front porch. "Martine's getting ready. There are a lot of sick people here today," Reiter added. "This is what being a doctor is all about. It's what makes the years in medical school worthwhile."

"More material for a movie," Jeff said, seeming pleased with himself.

The fishermen and their families perched on the rocks waiting their turn reminded Reiter of tired seagulls at the end of a long flight. Reiter and Jeff stepped on to the porch just as Martine finished wiping the table and was ticking off the medical supplies that he'd brought out: bandages, instruments, alcohol bottles. He was all business. "Good morning, fellows." He finally turned to Reiter. "Everything's ready, I think."

"It looks like we have more patients than usual this morning. This may take longer than I thought," Reiter said, turning to Jeff. "Maybe you'd rather go down to the beach and work on your tan."

Jeff's reply caught him off guard. "Me? No! I'd like to help you guys," he offered. "When I was in college, all I dreamed about was becoming a doctor. I'd made up my mind to go to medical school." His voice took on a hint of regret. "But all that studying…it just wasn't for me."

Reiter proceeded to wash his hands in the chipped bowl of boiled water that Martine had set out. "Well, I suppose we could always use an extra pair of hands," he finally said. He held up his dripping hands and shook off some of the water. Grabbing a clean cloth, he dried each finger carefully, one by one. "Just promise me one thing, forget about movies for a while." He put the towel aside. "Okay, let's get to work."

Martine nodded. "We're already behind schedule."

A young woman with a crying baby in her arms was the first person to step on the porch. She brushed a long strand of black hair off her face, and Reiter could see the worry etched across her forehead. Bending over the child, he moved his stethoscope across the chest. Then he gently opened the infant's mouth and examined the throat. "His tonsils are swollen and red. Give him a shot of penicillin," he said to Martine. Martine was already holding a syringe and immediately plunged it into the baby's behind. The child's whimper turned into a shriek of protest.

Jeff went out of his way to make himself helpful, and he smiled as he gently stroked the child on the back of its head. He walked with the mother to the edge of the porch. "Your baby esta mucho bien, senora," he tried to reassure her in broken Spanish. The mother seemed to understand, and smiled as she made her way towards North Beach.

Reiter beamed when he saw Juanita and her husband making their way to the porch. Their baby slept in Juanita's arms, a clean rag draped across its face. The surgery on the cleft lip had been done in California months ago. Juanita carefully removed the rag and propped up the child's head. Her eyes sparkled as she kissed the toddler. The upper lip was neatly joined where the huge hole had been, and there was barely a scar.

Reiter gently rolled the boy's lip outward, trying not to wake him. He could hardly contain the pride pounding in his chest. Juanita's, "Muchas gracias, Espanto. Que Dios te bendiga" put a lump in his throat. He knew what he'd done would change the little boy's life. "I see, Juanita. Everything is fine," he finally said, knowing for a brief moment the meaning of joy.

As the afternoon wore on, Reiter was touched by the love and attention Jeff gave to every patient. He made happy faces at the children, and put his arm around worried mothers and uneasy fathers.

When they were finished, Martine, Reiter, Jeff and Cobo sat in the shade of the porch. "I think you should have stuck to your college dream, Jeff. You would have made a fine doctor," Martine volunteered. "You ought to come down here more often. We sure could use you."

Jeff's face lit up. It was as if the Hollywood veneer was melting away, baring a kind and loving soul. "Now I know where you are when you hide out and don't show up at Hollywood parties," he teased Reiter. "You have no idea how often we wondered where you were hiding." He stood up and cast a look at the Indians and the Mexicanos winding their way out to North Beach and south toward Black Mountain, some of them pushing their pangas into the bay. "You guys do a lot of good down here. But I can see you've got your hands full." He looked concerned for a minute. "Who pays for all the medicines and supplies?"

"Who do you think?" Martine snorted, looking at Reiter. "But that doesn't mean we couldn't use some extra money. More and more people seem to be showing up. Hell, they come from all over." He looked at the sea. "Juanita and her husband made their way by boat from Muleje. Took them days. We should have Clinicas like this up and down the coast."

Jeff seemed lost in thought. "Help me do this right," he finally said. "I know the brass at most of the networks and studios. I bet they'd come up with some money. It's good publicity...look real good in the papers."

Martine and Reiter glanced at each other.

"And I can help with the antibiotics and medical supplies right now," Jeff insisted as he rummaged for his checkbook in the pocket of his jeans. He scribbled on it and handed a check to Martine. "This is a start." It was made out for ten thousand dollars.

Martine stared at it with an incredulous grin. He turned to Reiter, unsure what to say. He blushed for a moment as dignity and pride collided within him. "I never thought the day would come when we'd see this kind of money for our little clinic." He waved the bottle of beer in his hands toward the mainland. "This could be the seed money for other Clinica days in Baja. Maybe even over in Puerto Penasco." He turned to Jeff. "Thank you. Thank you, sir."

Jeff looked pleased and pointed a finger at Reiter. "And don't forget you promised to come to my party."

"I haven't forgotten," Reiter responded. Then he nodded toward the others. "What would you say if Martine and Pablo came along? Maybe Cobo too." He paused when he saw the look of surprise on Jeff Clancy's face. "Maybe they could help raise money for Clinica Day," he added.

Jeff thought for a moment. "I think that's a great idea. I can round up some of the big shots in showbiz," he beamed, "Let's do it right and turn it into a big charity event."

Martine wrinkled his nose, and Reiter knew right away what must have been going through his mind. Martine wasn't the type to go to big parties in Hollywood. But maybe, just maybe, the idea of money for Clinica Day sounded enticing to him because his expression softened and a mischievous smile crossed his face. "Guess we could take you up on it. I've always wondered what it was like to be in the movies."

Jeff beamed. Something told Reiter that the connection between his two worlds was beginning to take shape and that Jeff's visit had been a good idea after all.

When they took off that afternoon, Jeff looked at the ramshackle village below. "Right now if someone asked me about Baja, I wouldn't know what to tell them. It's a world I had no idea existed," he said. "It's strange, but I hate to leave this place. These people have a way of drawing you in," he added. He turned his head for a last look at the bay behind them.

"You'll see them again soon," Reiter assured him. "Remember, some of them will be at your party."

CHAPTER THIRTY-FOUR

Over the next few weeks, Reiter kept thinking about Jeff's party, dreaming up all kinds of scenarios for his Puertecitos friends and wondering how they would cope with the traffic jams and the celebrities of Hollywood. Two days before the party, he flew to Puertecitos to make sure they hadn't changed their minds.

As soon as he landed, he headed for the cantina. A stiff wind was blowing down the canyon, whipping the crest of waves into boiling white foam. He pried open the door of the cantina and was startled by the loud screech of its rusty hinges as he steadied it against the howling wind. Instinctively, he scanned the crowd, forgetting about the sand blowing in until he saw the disparaging looks from the Seri fishermen sprawled around the bar.

"Haven't you ever heard of a door?" an angry voice bellowed from a corner. "Or don't they close them where you come from?"

Quickly, he slammed the door and searched for the person who'd made the cutting remark. He could hardly see through the thick smoke. Most of the fishermen had oddly shaped cigarettes in their gnarled hands, and he wondered if they were just smoking cheap tobacco, or if they'd added ground up bits of saguaro to make it go further. Or did the strange smell come from the scraps of moldy newspaper they'd used as wrapping? It reminded him of the way his father rolled homemade cigarettes at the end of the war. He'd mix a pinch of cheap tobacco with some dried out hay leaves on a scrap of paper, roll it tight and lick the edge to seal it. Reiter hadn't known then that puffing those cigarettes helped ease his father's hunger pangs, but he did remember the pungent smell of the smoke as it drifted through the room.

He didn't think the Seris had hunger pangs, but they seemed to be all puffing at the same time, as if one of them was giving a signal. Then they leaned back, slowly exhaling black clouds of smoke and watching it as it rose slowly to the soot-caked ceiling.

Cobo sat at the far end of the bar staring at the bare light bulb that hung above him. Reiter joined him. "Espanto, I've been theenking." Cobo's voice startled him. The inflection and the way he pulled out the 'eee's was a sign that he'd been 'theenking' for some time. He continued to stare at the light, but seemed aware that Reiter was looking at him.

"Thinking about what?" Reiter felt impatient.

"About going up north. About the fiesta at the house of—what's the guy's name?" He wrinkled his forehead as he glanced at the black rims of his fingernails, which seemed to provide the perfect excuse for forgetting the name. "Jesus Chavez," he finally ventured, skimming over the name real quick.

"You mean Jeff Clancy."

"Yes, that's who I mean, Jess Clan zee," Cobo replied. There were flies swarming around his shadow on the peeling plaster of the cantina wall. "Why not take Alfonso to the party instead? And forget about me." He plunked down his beer bottle and began to head for the door.

Reiter was right behind him. "You can't back out now," he almost pleaded. "A promise is a promise. You said so yourself." He thought he caught a smirk on the Seris' faces.

Cobo turned around. "And what about the migra at the border?" he wanted to know. "You," he stammered as he pointed to the ceiling, "You're always in your plane. You never cross the border like the rest of the people."

"Okay, okay." Reiter tried to appease him, but Cobo's sour look persisted. "What if I ride up with you guys in Martine's van?" Reiter said. "I can get a ride back and pick up my plane later."

Cobo seemed to like that better. "Let me finish my drink," he said. He wiped a dribble of beer from his chin with the back of his hairy wrist and returned to the bar.

***

The next morning, Reiter found himself bumping northward over the dusty road with his friends. He began to regret his decision to ride along. Martine looked like he felt crowded and tight, and Cobo's bad mood had returned. Cobo said very little, his eyes fixed on the road ahead. He'd never been north of San Felipe, and today they were traveling nearly two hundred miles beyond the border. He kept staring out the window as Martine's squeaking van labored over the winding dirt road that was littered with rocks.

Reiter had always abhorred the idea of the border between California and Baja. It just never felt right. And he knew that for someone like Cobo the border's fences and border guards must be a constant reminder that his people were not welcome. After all, the border, or 'la linea' as they called it, was meant to keep Mexicans out, even though California had once been their land.

Cobo's silence irritated Martine, who kept pursing his lips and wiping a spot on the windshield over and over again. Finally, Cobo spoke up. "Do you think we could run into a problem at the border?"

"Why would you ask that?" Martine demanded impatiently. "You know damn well what to tell them. We've gone over it a thousand times, haven't we? If anyone wants to know why you're traveling up north all you have to tell them is that you're having your hemorrhoids operated on in California." He sounded impatient. "No, better than that, why don't you tell them the Phantom is going to cut out your tongue?"

"Okay, okay. I know you want me to make up a story," Cobo came back, skipping over Martine's sarcasm. Reiter could only guess what Cobo was thinking *'Why should I have to come up with some crazy excuse just to drive across the linea?'*

Reiter sensed the uneasiness in their conversation and searched for an excuse to change the subject. He caught a glimpse of Pablo in the rear view mirror, slumped against the rusty door. The Baja heat and dust had lulled him to sleep. There was no need to wake him, but Reiter couldn't miss the chance to try a little humor. He nudged

Martine. "Look at our friend Pablo," he said, motioning toward the back seat. "He doesn't look too worried about anything." Pablo's mouth was half-open, his nostrils flaring with each burst of air.

Martine shook his head and grinned. "One thing's for sure," he muttered out of the corner of his mouth, "he'll never win a beauty contest."

Two hours later, they reached Mexicali and pulled the van in line with the rest of the cars waiting to cross the border. Reiter knew this was the part Cobo dreaded the most.

"I never liked borders." Cobo started the argument all over again, making it sound as if he'd crossed hundreds of times.

"What d'ya mean, you never liked borders?" Martine was quick to reply. "How is a country supposed to protect itself—keep out the riff-raff—if it don't have a border?"

Reiter leaned ahead, frowning. "What do you call riff-raff?" he countered, doing his most to keep his annoyance in check. "Besides, California used to be Mexico. There hasn't always been a border here." He felt a tinge of anger that he had to defend that point. "Hell, half of the cities and streets still have Spanish names. What about food—tacos, salsa? What about Cinco de Mayo and mariachis?"

Martine listened and puckered his lips. "Now wait just a minute," he argued. "It's not Mexico now, hombre. We're talking about two different countries today." He glared at Reiter. "And what's wrong with a border?" He shifted gears and the engine briefly howled.

Reiter's face tightened as he thought of the borders in his homeland. "I have to agree with Cobo. To me a border is like an ugly scar on the land. It keeps friends apart." He sounded sad. "And usually it's in the wrong place for all the wrong reasons. Like a scar on a face that keeps someone from smiling."

"Now you're getting carried away with yourself," Martine insisted. "You don't make much sense."

Reiter leaned back, suddenly tired. In the back seat Cobo sat up. "Why do we need a border? To me, California will always be Alte

280

California. And the flavor of Mexico will never go away from here, border or no border. What I will never understand is how they treat us when we do come across." He nodded knowingly. "I've heard the stories a hundred times from my friends."

The whole conversation was troubling, like the unfriendly border up ahead. A twenty-foot chain-link fence, reinforced by steel girders, separated the cities of Calexico and Mexicali. Barbed wire wound around the top on the California side and armed guards in green trucks patrolled it like a war zone. Wild stories about the dangers on the American side were every-day talk in the towns below the border. To Cobo, from the looks of the heavily armored trucks, the stories he'd heard were probably true. He brushed his mustache with the back of his arm. "I can tell right away they don't like Mexicanos here," he whispered, as if he was afraid they might hear him.

The van inched along with the rest of the cars. Cobo leaned forward and pointed. "Look! Look how they hassle the Mexicans walking across!" he said indignantly. "What have they done?"

Reiter was about to recount his own run-in years ago with the immigration people in New York and Denver, but Martine cut him off. "Those immigration officers are just doing their job. That's all they're doing. Their job." He leaned heavily on the last part of his sentence, 'their job', as though he was trying to end the discussion.

A few minutes ticked by, and Cobo seemed inclined to let the remark pass. Then his eyes strayed across the lanes of traffic to the opposite side of the border where cars were heading south into Mexico. There was no line-up over there. The cars just drove right through without delay. The placid Mexican guards only smiled and waved them across.

Martine almost jumped out of his seat when Cobo gave him a sharp nudge in the back. "I don't see Mexican policemen searching through cars or making people get out. Does that mean they're not doing their job? Or does it mean that they have bigger hearts?"

It seemed clear that Martine was feeling outnumbered. He raised one eyebrow as he always did before losing his patience. "Can't you guys put it through your heads that the border is a symbol, a sign where a country's laws and customs begin."

"Or where they end," Cobo shot back. "Besides, what do you make of a symbol with barbed wire on it. A border should be like a beautiful park where neighbors get together and have a fiesta and celebrate with good tequila and mariachis. Not a place to make people feel like criminals." It was plain to Reiter that Cobo made more sense than politicians. How could anyone explain why friendship and good will should end with a chain link fence?

When they finally got to the border checkpoint, the lanky immigration officer recognized Martine right away. He broke out in a smile when he saw the craggy face of his friend. "Hey! How are you, you old buzzard? You're back for that doctor supply stuff again?" He smiled condescendingly and waved them through.

"Well, what do you know about that? And without mordita? No bribe?" Cobo shook his head in disbelief. "You probably could bring whole truck loads of reef raff across and the migra would even help you." He looked at Reiter. "Reeff raff," he repeated, as if tasting the words. "I guess that means trash. That's what they must think of Mexicans," he added. And he was strangely quiet for the rest of the trip.

After another three hours of driving, they finally reached the Chaparral. It was near sunset, but Reiter's home immediately improved everyone's mood, even Cobo's. It looked like a piece of Old Mexico. The thick adobe walls and rough-hewn timbers jutting out from the roof might just as well have been on the Mexican side of the border. There was even an old mission bell hanging above the entrance. No sign of migra here, just Linda and the children waiting for them.

For a special moment, Reiter and Linda seemed oblivious of the others. He put his hand on her swollen belly, ignoring the commotion around them. Then Linda turned towards her guests. "I'm so glad you're here. We were beginning to wonder if you'd make it before dark."

Martine and Pablo greeted Linda and the children with laughter and small talk. Cobo tipped his hat and gave a slight bow. "Buenos dias, Senora," he said. He stood erect, and there was respect in his voice. It was clear that he had a special affection for her. Inconspicuously, he leaned towards Martine. "I always said Espanto's wife is no gringa," he whispered.

"I already told you that," Martine answered. "She's got Indian blood in her veins."

"I've always thought she looks like a half-breed. Even Papillo is convinced she's part Yaki," Cobo replied, lowering his voice. "Just look at her black hair and the sharp bones in her face. What about the color of her skin? Her dark eyes? To me she never looked like a white woman." Martine just shook his head.

Reiter smiled to himself. He'd always been proud that many of the Mexicans and Indians showed a special kinship for his wife. They treated her differently from the other American women who periodically showed up in Puertecitos. Without knowing it, she helped Reiter reach out to his other world. He was grateful for that.

Cobo unpacked a box and brought out some abalone shells. "These are from the cliffs near Black Mountain," he said as he handed them to Linda. "They're the biggest you can find in all of Baja."

"Cobo, thank you. I've always loved these beautiful shells," Linda said with a gracious smile.

After dinner, they all gathered in the library. Cobo kept eyeing the rows and rows of books stacked on the dark wooden shelves. Reiter could imagine what was going through his mind: 'Too much knowledge in those dusty pages.' But to Reiter, the books gave the room a warm feeling, and he liked it. They drank cervesas that Shane served from a bar in the corner. He kept asking if the beer was cold enough, and he tried to make sure that no one was ever without one, just as he'd seen Don Rafael do in the Puertecitos cantina.

Reiter eyed the clock and saw it was getting late. "Amigos, we've got to go into town in the morning and rent tuxedos for the party," he reminded them. "Better turn in."

***

The next day, they all piled into Reiter's Jeep and drove to the special store that rented formal clothing. Fitting the tuxedos turned into a long, boring affair. All the measuring, trying on different pants, shirts, coats and shoes seemed to go on forever. As they paraded in front of the tall mirror, Reiter was reminded of frustrated crows. Even Martine seemed out of place. "This thing feels strange," Martine said as he fiddled with a bow tie. "The last time I wore one of these it got me into a lot of trouble," Martine said as he unbuttoned his shirt.

"How's that?" Reiter wanted to know.

"It was the day I got married," Martine scowled.

CHAPTER THIRTY-FIVE

Everybody seemed conspicuously quiet as they all piled into Reiter's van early that evening. Brian drove them to Beverly Hills through a dreary June fog. When they arrived at Jeff's mansion in Beverly Hills, they found the entrance studded with photographers and television crews. Even Reiter and Linda seemed taken aback by the bright lights flashing in their faces. Walking on a plush burgundy carpet, celebrities and their guests crossed a barricade of onlookers, smiling and waving. It reminded Reiter of the way kings and queens must have been greeted a long time ago. But tonight the adoration was for the faces of Hollywood. The photographers seemed to instantly sense the status of each new arrival, and their cameras flashed accordingly.

When Cobo stepped on the carpet, everyone turned and for a moment, they were quiet. Something about him seemed to have taken them by surprise, but it wasn't long before they recovered and the whispers began. "I think its Juan Castana," Reiter overheard someone say. "You know who I mean...the new star from south of the border. I've heard he's up for some big nomination," the bystander insisted.

"Sure looks the part," his companion agreed. "The guy must spend half his life in a gym." The comments went on and on.

Cobo seemed to enjoy the attention. He kept looking over his shoulder as if to make sure the others were still behind him, flashing an occasional smile at Martine and Pablo. They didn't smile back, and from the way they looked at each other, Reiter concluded they were more embarrassed than envious.

Martine walked stiff and erect, his silver hair reflected in the flashing camera bulbs. His face was taut, his right eye clamped down as if he was determined to ignore the crowd. Pablo walked next to Martine, with a limp in his gait and a sour look on his face. His huge midriff was constrained by his tuxedo, and the shiny buttons seemed ready to pop. Drops of sweat glistened on his purple nose, and he kept wiping them away with the palm of his hand. He made no effort to hide his discomfort.

Reiter and Linda weren't far behind. Reiter was scanning the crowd, looking for Jeff, when he heard a voice behind him, "I think that guy is a plastic surgeon. The one who does all the stars." There was a long pause. "This is the first time I've seen him at a party like this." Reiter felt tightness in his chest and looked in the direction of the voice, but the lights were so bright it was useless.

Linda must have seen the uncomfortable look on his face, and she leaned closer and squeezed his arm. "At least they don't think you're a stunt man," she teased him in a whisper.

Jeff Clancy was standing in the doorway flashing his world-renown smile. His face lit up when he saw Reiter and Martine, and without hesitating, he broke loose from the crowd to greet them the way he'd seen them do in Puertecitos, clutching each one to his chest and slapping them on their backs. "I knew you'd come, never had a doubt." But even while he spoke, he kept scanning the crowd, reminding Reiter of a director in charge, making sure that the show went on without a hitch. The cameras kept clicking, and the lights kept on flashing.

Martine didn't even try to pretend he liked all the commotion. "I'm not sure about all this horse shit," he grumbled to Reiter. "Now I know why you like Puertecitos. No wonder you fly down there every chance you get."

"You're right," Reiter said to himself. Puertecitos has soul; Hollywood's more about faces. He'd hoped Martine would be gracious, even though these people were different. "Just don't forget why we're here, amigo." Reiter reminded him. "It's all about Clinica Day."

A raspy voice startled him. "Dr. Reiter, it's been ages. How wonderful to see you." Reiter's pasted on a quick smile and turned to greet Betty Love and her husband.

Linda was the first to speak. "I'm so happy to finally meet you, Miss Love."

286

Betty Love gushed, "Mrs. Reiter, I've heard so much about you from your husband. He's a remarkable man."

Reiter turned to introduce his friends. "Miss Love, these are our guests from Mexico: Martine Flemmer, Paul Nielson, and Cobo..." At that instant, Reiter felt a stab of guilt that he didn't know Cobo's last name. Someone in the crowd had said, 'Castana' and that sounded fine, he quickly decided.

Betty Love studied Cobo's features and spoke as if she was thinking out loud. "Castana...Yes, Cobo Castana. You must be the great actor from Mexico we've heard so much about." There was a hint of uncertainty in her voice. She turned to her husband for reassurance. "Don't you remember, darling?"

He nodded dutifully. "Mr. Castana is a wonderful performer," he said sheepishly.

"Yes, Mr. Castana does excellent work," Reiter confirmed.

Something in the way he said it made Betty Love frown and throw him a questioning glance. He made it appear that he had to translate for Cobo as he turned to him. "She thinks you're a famous movie star," he said in Spanish.

Cobo's expression indicated that he didn't see any problem with that. "I know what I'm doing," he reassured Reiter and straightened his tie.

The flimsy fantasy, like a runaway echo, seemed to career through the crowd. Cobo's grin grew smug and sure. Before long, the name Castana was on every one's lips. They managed to come up with movies and plays they'd seen him in, and actresses he'd been romantically linked with. He kept them guessing all evening.

In Hollywood, Reiter had learned that a sprinkle of fantasy mixed in with a few wild rumors could create a new hero any day. So why should he be surprised that tonight the bubbling champagne and the imagination floating through the party would make Cobo into the next Ricardo Montalban?

Cobo kept eyeing Jeff and then Reiter before he turned to the crowd, glowing with contentment. Short-skirted waitresses kept filling his glass with champagne. He must have sensed that soon it would be all over, but for the moment he seemed content to make the most of it.

"I've never seen anything like this," he whispered to Reiter as he bit into a skewered sardine. He pointed at Jeff. "What's he scribbling on all those papers they keep sticking in front of his nose?"

"He's signing autographs," Reiter explained. "People always get excited when they see someone famous and so they ask for their signature, their poderosa."

Suddenly, an excited lady waved a piece of paper in Cobo's face. "Just write down your name," Reiter urged him. "Like Jeff does."

"But I don't know how to write!" Cobo protested, a wave of panic sweeping over his face.

"That doesn't matter!" Reiter reassured him quickly. "You don't have to know how to write. Just scratch something down like a chicken." When Cobo still looked dubious, he added, "Nobody ever reads it."

That did the trick, and Cobo breathed a sigh of relief. Soon he was scribbling and smiling just like Jeff. "Como patas de pollos," he muttered self-assuredly, "Like chicken scratches." The more he scribbled, the more people wanted his autograph.

"And why are they taking all those photographs?" Cobo asked. But this time, instead of waiting for an answer, he put his arm around people's shoulders and smiled into the bright flashes. "I'm Cobo. I live in Puertecitos," he kept saying in Spanish. The word Puertecitos was twisted in all kinds of ways that boisterous night…Puerto Vallarta, Puerto Escondido, Puerto Perdito…But the important thing was that people paid attention.

Martine and Pablo weren't having such an easy time of it. As the evening wore on, they settled onto a couch in an out-of-the way corner and watched all the fuss. Reiter began to have doubts about the two worlds getting closer.

"I've always said the guy is a genius at making a fool of himself," he overheard Martine grumble.

Reiter's response was cut off by Jeff's voice booming over the loudspeaker. "Ladies and gentlemen, I have a surprise for you tonight." He paused as if to let his announcement sink in. There was absolute silence in the room. Jeff's eyes combed through the crowd until he found Reiter. "There is a man here that a few of you know." He pointed at Reiter. "Some of you call him the Phantom because he is rather elusive." A powerful beam of light swept across the room and focused on Reiter. "Allow me to introduce Dr. Paul Reiter, ladies and gentlemen. Recently, I had the privilege of spending a weekend with him in the little village of Puertecitos on the coast of Baja. Dr. Reiter spends many weekends and holidays down there taking care of sick people who have nowhere to turn. I've seen with my own eyes the dedication, the care, the love that he and his friends—some of whom are with him tonight—bring to those people." Reiter was uncomfortable with the attention, but Jeff went on. "They've come up with the idea of holding a Clinica Day once a month. You should have seen the tears in the eyes of the mothers as they saw their children snatched from the clutches of death!" Jeff stopped and scanned the crowd. Their attention was riveted on him.

"There's so much suffering down there," he continued. "Babies dying, deadly diseases, fishermen slashed by sharks, hurricanes ripping out entire villages and earthquakes carving up the coastline." His voice kept rising with plea ding staccatos, "Not to mention the thousands who are starving every day." He rose on his toes as if leading a chorus. A few sighs rose from the crowd before he set his heels back on the ground.

Reiter could feel an air of gloom settling over the ballroom, and Jeff's voice fanned it masterfully. "The situation is critical. But Dr. Reiter and his friends in Puertecitos are working hard to put together more clinics, bring doctors, nurses, and medicine to these isolated area. But they need our help." He paused again strategically. "We've never forgotten about the sick and less fortunate, have we? You have a big heart, always ready to give when you hear the call of the needy." He hammered on. "The ladies at the table by the doore will help you fill out your checks. Please make them out to 'The Clinica Days.'" Then his voice changed. "Let me humbly suggest, ladies and gentlemen, and it's only a suggestion, that you make this night count. I think a minimum of five hundred dollars would be in order."

A rustle at the back of the room interrupted Jeff Clancy's last words. Everyone turned towards Betty Love, who was making her way toward the podium, her husband at her heels. Her face was red, and she kept dabbing at her eyes with a facial tissue that Edmund handed her.

Betty reached for the microphone held tightly in Jeff's hands. "I've seldom been so moved. It's hard to imagine all the suffering that goes on in the world. How fortunate we are that Dr. Reiter, Mr. Castana, and others are trying to do something about it." She looked at the crowd. "And tonight we have an opportunity to show our solidarity." Her moist eyes focused on Reiter. "I have no words, Dr. Reiter, to tell you how proud I am to know you." She struggled to go on. "So proud," she repeated.

Reiter tried to duck the bright beam of light hitting his face. He wished he could disappear. His heart beat faster and faster, and his wife's hand gripped his arm a little tighter.

Thrusting the microphone back at Jeff Clancy, Betty Love walked toward Reiter and hugged him. "Thank you, my dear, wonderful Doctor. Edmund will prepare a check tonight," she gushed, looking at her husband warmly. She turned to Cobo. "And thank you too, Mr. Castana."

Betty Love's donation was only the beginning. People seemed overwhelmed, and they were generous. The shimmering face of show business was connecting with the soul of Puertecitos by lending a helping hand. Reiter beamed; *the two worlds weren't so far apart after all,* he thought. Before the evening was over thousands of dollars were collected for Martine's Clinica Days. And there were pledges for more.

***

Later, on their way back to the Chaparral, Cobo complained of a terrible headache. He tried to contain the waves of champagne-smelling burps, and he was strangely pale.

"Amigo, you did great," Reiter said, wishing that his words could take away the hangover.

"Did you ever have any doubt?" Cobo shot back. Then he yawned, leaned back, and fell asleep.

As the van pulled into the driveway, Reiter's eyes strayed to the yucca trees and the tops of the palms in his pool. "Yes, I think they're getting closer," he said.

Martine looked at him. "I'm not sure what you mean."

"Hollywood and Puertecitos is what I mean," Reiter said. "Like a face and a soul."

***

The next evening after the family had gone to bed, Reiter and his Puertecitos friends found themselves in the library again. Reiter turned to Martine and Pablo sprawled in the lounge chairs across from his desk. "I have to leave for Beverly Hills early in the morning," he began. "I'll probably be gone before you guys get up."

Cobo, who was sitting on the floor with his back against the couch, seemed sympathetic. "I feel sorry for you," he said. "How do you stand it day in and day out with those locos up here?" It didn't really sound like a question. Cobo pulled himself off the floor and seemed about to deliver some profound insight, then obviously thought better of it and slid back down.

The minutes ticked by, and Cobo propped up his knees and wrapped his arms around them. "Yesterday at Jesse Clanzee's palacio, with all the noise and lights and music…" He glanced at his friends before he continued. "I kept asking myself what these people do all day long? I wondered if they wouldn't be better off fishing," he sighed. "And that senora, the one you said is known all over the world. I looked in her eyes when she was talking." He paused as if trying to find just the right words. "And I could see nothing, like she was empty, like life had blown out of her. Like the short man beside her."

"You've got to remember…" Reiter answered. She's had a much different life than the rest of us."

Martine cut into the conversation. "I think you talk too much, Cobo." His speech slowed down, and his tone was critical. "Besides, if you ask me, it looked like you fit right in with the bull shit. You seemed to be having a good time pretending to be one of them big shots. If it was all a game, you sure didn't mind it." He leaned towards Cobo.

Cobo shrugged. "What are you talking about?"

"I tell you what I'm talking about," Martine shot back. "Those people are crazy. They're different, that's all. Being different doesn't make them crazy. But maybe you wanted to be like them. That's what bothers me," Martine said, looking at him directly. "Why not give up fishing," he added. "You'd make one hell of an actor."

"Which goes to prove everyone is a little loco at times," Reiter put in, hoping to stop the two from arguing. "No, amigos, Martine's right. The people here aren't crazy, just different." He shot a look at Martine. "But maybe not so different from us when you get right down to it."

Martine nodded. "I've been thinking about that for days, ever since you brought Jeff to Puertecitos. Maybe Hollywood people aren't all phonies. Sure, they make a lot of money, but in the end they make movies to help people forget their own troubles for a while."

"You have something there," Reiter agreed. "Actors make people laugh and forget themselves. It reminds me of what El Chino said about making living things happier when he paints crows." He turned to Cobo. "You do the same when you take people out fishing, don't you? You help them forget their troubles for a few hours, no different than Jeff Clancy or El Chino." He almost seemed to be talking to himself as he rambled on. "Making living things happier…I hope I do the same thing. I've learned—and it took years—that people feel better when they look better."

Martine mused, "The Hollywood crowd may look as if they stake their life on what they look like on the outside, but all I care about is that everyone at Jeff's party gave money for Clinica Days. And it'll make a big difference in the lives of people they don't even know. They gave with their hearts, fancy hair-dos and all."

That was the end of the Sunday night session. One at a time the amigos left for the guesthouse to sleep a few hours. Reiter was the last to leave. He sneaked into his bedroom and slid under the sheet, trying not to wake his sleeping wife. He was startled when she took his hand and placed it on her swollen belly. "I love you," she said.

CHAPTER THIRTY-SIX

R eiter's eyes lingered on his wife's round belly as she stepped out of the shower and patted herself dry with a towel. She was in the last month of her pregnancy. The time had flown by, but he never missed a chance to savor what he looked upon as nature's way of sealing her forgiveness. He moved toward her side of the bed as if to get a better look at her bulging stomach. "It doesn't really show," he said with an approving look in his eyes.

Her black hair was shiny and wet, and she struggled with a hairpin to gather it together at the nape of her neck. "What doesn't show?"

"That you're nine months pregnant. Believe me, you don't look it. No one could tell," he added.

His eyes wandered to the slight sway of her swollen breasts with the dark, shiny nipples. She walked over to him and slowly turned around. With a mischievous smile she placed his hands on her stomach. "I'm sure you can tell," she said. "Can't you?"

He leaned towards her and put an ear on her belly. "Not really," he teased. "But I think I can hear something," he whispered and with a finger he traced the midline of the bulging curve down towards the dark triangle. "Most women would be huge by now, huffing and puffing, barely able to take a step. You're as agile as ever."

She lay on the bed next to him and adjusted the pillows. He saw that she was making an effort to stay awake and smiled when she fell asleep immediately.

Watching his wife over the past nine months, he had to wonder what pregnancy had been like for Consuelo. He tried to imagine what she looked like, how she felt, where Pedro fit into the picture.

He was desperate for sleep, but his eyes were glued to the glowing hands of the clock by his bedside. It read four o'clock when Linda stirred and opened her eyes. "There's something going on," she said. "Feel for yourself." She guided his hands to the small of her back. "Right here," she said calmly.

There was an unmistakable wave of tension in the lower part of her back, he thought, as if many forces were flowing together. "Yes, I think it's time," he said.

In his mind, he'd rehearsed this moment hundreds of times: He'd call Dr. Alder, then pile Linda and the children into the car and drive them all to the hospital. But this time it was no rehearsal, and it surprised him that he wasn't as calm as he'd intended to be. The children were reluctant to wake up, and he nearly drove off without Linda's suitcase.

When they got the hospital and the nurses took his wife down the brightly lit halls, his mind slipped away to that night in Calamuje Canyon when he'd delivered Alicia's baby. He could still hear the wind rattling the shack; in a strange way he missed it. He remembered the dirt floor and the look of terror in Alicia's eyes when her water broke. He'd never forget his own fear and the burden of knowing that everyone was depending on him. He didn't miss that.

It's different tonight, he thought; yet he couldn't dismiss the thought that every delivery involves some risk. This time, he let the coward within him prevail, and he stayed out of the delivery room, hunkering down in the doctor's lounge with Shane and Robin. The children fell asleep with their heads in his lap. His eyes followed the lines between the spotless white tiles to the door that led to the delivery room, wondering whether a son or a daughter would be born behind those doors. They'd already decided on a name for a girl.

He smiled to himself when he looked at the calendar and realized it was the twelfth of October. He remembered an argument not long ago in the cantina of Puertecitos. Rafael's daughter in Mexicali had just given birth to a little girl, and they'd radioed the news to Puertecitos. "They should name her Guadalupe," Cobo had commented.

"No," Rafael said. "I told my daughter if she had a girl she should be called Pilar." He looked back at the calendar hanging behind the bar. "Too bad it's only the twelfth of August. October twelfth is called El Dia de la Pilar in Spain. If she'd waited a few months, she could have had the right birthday. My grandfather celebrated it as a Holy Day even after he came to Mexico."

"But Mexico's important Feast is the Virgin of Guadalupe," Cobo insisted. "Her name should be Guadalupe."

That had been the end of the discussion, but the name 'Pilar' stuck in Reiter's mind, and he brought it up to his family the next day. He'd told them how the vision of the Holy Virgin had appeared on a pillar in the city of Zaragoza on October twelfth. "The Spaniards have a national holiday in honor of the event," he said.

"Pilar is a pretty name," Linda agreed. "If we have another daughter."

"You have a little girl, Reiter." The hoarse voice of Dr. Alder jerked him out of his reverie. "Congratulations," he added and patted Reiter on the shoulder. He rubbed his eyes and tried to stifle a tired yawn. "Everything went very well. Give them a few minutes to get the baby ready, and you can all go to her room. Mother and child are fine."

Reiter breathed a sigh of relief. "Your mom and Pilar are waiting to see us," he whispered to the sleepy children.

CHAPTER THIRTY-SEVEN

Over the course of the next few years, Reiter came to believe more than ever in Beto's words, that only real love had the power to create new life. All he had to do was to take a look at their youngest child to know Beto had been right. Love had forged itself into their daily life in the form of a brown-eyed baby with dark hair like her mother's. Pilar seemed to bring the family closer, breathing new energy into the daily routine. Shane and Robin were suddenly the 'older' children at nine and ten, and they always seemed anxious to help care for their little sister. The trips to Puertecitos continued, but   diaper bags and a portable crib were added to the baggage stowed in the back of the plane. All in all, they were good years, despite Reiter's nagging guilt that perhaps Consuelo's baby wasn't as fortunate as theirs.

On the weekend of Pilar's fifth birthday, Reiter went to bed late. Linda had been asleep for hours, and he snuggled in beside her, trying not to wake her. He let his hands wander slowly over her breasts, touching them gently as if for the first time. Her breasts are real, he mused. She has no implants, no scars. But they aren't as firm or as full as they used to be. Maybe she should consider having them lifted a bit. As he considered this thought, he felt ashamed of himself.

He sensed a fleeting tension in her body. Maybe she had picked up the change in his touch. "Is this supposed to be some sort of examination?" she asked sleepily. But he could tell she was smiling.

He felt a flush of embarrassment. Had the tenderness of the moment been lost? He'd been at this crossroads before—when he'd done her physical exam in Montana, and when she'd nearly lost the baby in Mexico—and he remembered his struggle to remain professional and detached. Both times he'd had the strange sensation that the probing hands of a doctor could easily become the hands of a lover.

"Don't tell me you're thinking I need a breast lift or something." She surprised him, as if reading his mind. "After three children, what do you expect?"

"Of course not," he answered, trying to sound convincing. *After all these years, she knows me too well*, he thought. Still, wasn't easy to separate the professional and personal sides.

She put an end to his thoughts by sliding out of bed and tiptoeing to the mirror. He followed her through half-open eyes. Her movements were graceful, making him think of the day they'd met, when she'd reminded him of a shy doe on a secret mountain meadow. It gave him a warm feeling.

Standing in front of the mirror, she placed her palms on the sides of her face. Then she turned sideways a bit, moving her fingers across her cheeks, sliding the skin upward and backwards. She cast a quick glance at him and their eyes met in the mirror. "Tell me," she asked. "What could you do about this?"

She said it as if she already knew what his answer would be. It isn't every day that a naked woman stands in front of a mirror asking her husband to operate on her face. He knew she caught the puzzled look in his eyes because she went on to explain. "There are mornings when I take Pilar to kindergarten and feel like all the other mothers look twenty years younger. I feel uncomfortable at times and think they must wonder if I'm her grandmother." She leaned closer to the mirror. "What I'm thinking is that maybe you could help. I know I'd feel better, that's all."

At first he thought he hadn't heard right. "What's gotten into you? What are you trying to tell me?" His voice couldn't mask his irritation.

"What's wrong with having surgery if it would make me feel better about myself, get rid of my tired expression?" She came back to bed without waiting for an answer.

"I don't think you need it," he shot back. To me you look fine." He drew her towards him and looked in her eyes. "Believe me, you look fine."

298

She didn't reply, but pulled away, adjusting her pillow as if she couldn't find the proper support for her back. Then she leaned against it and stared at the ceiling.

He tried to make light of it. "Come on, honey, you know you can run circles around any of those mothers. You don't need a facelift for that." He attempted a smile, and then he leaned over to kiss her.

But she turned her face away. "Why won't you do it?" she asked with more determination. He sat up straighter, ready to explain. But she kept on talking. "You mean to tell me that when you operate on people you don't believe in what you're doing? That you think they shouldn't be having surgery?" She sat up and looked him straight in the eye. "Doesn't it matter how they feel?" Her tone shamed him. A reproachful look crossed her face. "Or is it just for the money like that English journalist said?" She stopped to adjust her pillows again. "I thought I knew you better than that."

He lay back down and rested his flushed cheek in his hand.

"This would only be for myself. It has nothing to do with anyone else. Not even you," she argued as she pulled up the sheet. There was silence in the room, except for the whirling noise of the fan on the ceiling. She looked over at him. "No different than a little make up or a new dress. I think it would be good for me." It sounded like a modest request, but he couldn't dismiss the misgiving he felt in the back of his mind that by operating on her face he might do something to her soul. The old dilemma came back, but this time it was too personal.

***

For weeks, Reiter kept turning the idea of surgery on Linda over and over in his mind. Ironically, he found it unpleasant. The thought of invading the delicate tissue beneath her skin was revolting to him. It seemed a perversion to operate for no other reason than to erase the lines that time and experience had imprinted on her face. Why obliterate any of her pasts, unless they were signs of the pain he had caused? Just the thought of approaching the lips that he'd kissed so many times with the menacing blades of his surgical scissors evoked a sudden sense of panic. How could he disrupt the familiar lines on her neck that he'd traced with the tips of his fingers, or cut the strands beneath her dimples or interfere with the soft shadows below her brown eyes?

She didn't bring it up again. But he'd surprised her more than once in front of a mirror, pulling back on her face with the palms of her hands and studying her image. It was obvious that it was still on her mind.

He decided to ask Martine about it the next time he was in Puertecitos. After a busy Clinica Day, Reiter turned to his friend, "You won't believe this, but Linda's talking about a facelift. She says she looks like the oldest mother at the kindergarten." He settled more deeply in the chair, shaking his head. "But I'm not too crazy about the idea, to tell you the truth."

Martine didn't answer at first; he kept rubbing his forehead like his mind had grown blank. Just when Reiter had decided to change the subject, Martine got up and started pacing the floor. Then he stopped right in front of Reiter. "You know, you're not talking about some stranger; you're talking about your wife. The woman gave you three children." He pointed a finger at Reiter. "Maybe what she wants has nothing to do with you. Why should you decide what she can or can't have?" He headed towards the refrigerator. Before he opened the door, he turned back to Reiter. "Besides, I'm sure you're not the only one who knows how to do it. There are other good surgeons in town. Maybe she should go to somebody else."

Stubbornly, Martine went on. "I mean, all she wants is to feel better about herself. Isn't that the point of these operations? At least that's what I understand." He hauled a coke out of the refrigerator and slammed the door. "If you think about it, the only reason you come into it is that you happen to know how to do it. And I know you do it for other people, so you must think the operation is safe."

He paused and started pacing again. "And if it's okay for everyone else, then why not for your wife? Look, you can't have it both ways."

Reiter reached for the cigar in his pocket. He tried to take it out of its wrapping without interrupting Martine. He held it under his nose and slowly slid it back and forth, savoring the aroma. He bit off a tiny piece of its tip and without taking his eyes off Martine, spat it out over the side of the porch. Martine settled into his squeaky chair as if signaling the end of the discussion.

They didn't talk about it again, but on his flight home, Reiter decided to land in San Felipe and drop in on El Chino. His answer too was simple. "All I can tell you is the painted crows seem happier than the plain ones. That's what I see. Don't tell me that after all these years you don't know that's what your patients want too—to feel better about themselves, be happier." He lifted his eyebrows along with his mustache as he always did when he expected no argument. "Somewhere deep down you must know why you do this kind of work. For the same reason I color the crows."

"El Chino. Let me ask you a question: If you were me, would you work on your wife?" Reiter persisted.

El Chino looked annoyed "And why not, if that would make her feel better?" He leaned over and picked up a crow that had dabs of fresh paint on the face and gently caressed it. "Sometimes I get the impression that you turn your nose up at me. That you think I'm beneath you because I work with the crows and you work with people." He squinted his eyes as if he didn't like the comparison and brushed his mustache with a finger. "But to me they might as well be wives. The important thing is why we do it." He'd put the crow down on a fish crate and watched it fly off. "The way I see it, if you just insist on your own way, it's a selfish road that leads nowhere. Why don't you forget about yourself and think about other people for a change?"

He gave Reiter a knowing look. "The more of God's creatures you make happy, the better you feel." When their eyes met, they both smiled. "And that includes your wife."

***

Months went by as Reiter waited for Linda to bring up the subject of a facelift again. Martine and El Chino were right; it was her decision, not his. But she said nothing; she didn't bring it up. It was as if she'd forgotten it entirely.

It was getting close to the end of the year when he sat waiting one afternoon for the last consultation of the day. He wasn't sure what aroused his curiosity and made him leaf through the appointment book to find that the patient he was about to see had flown in from England. He couldn't make out the name, but suddenly a tall, blonde woman was ushered through the door, and he caught his breath. He had no doubt he was looking at an older version of Deborah Townsend.

Instantly, he felt like his face was on fire, and he was afraid he was turning as red as the scarf she was wearing. It was hard to believe how much she'd changed since he'd seen her with her husband in Puertecitos. Her face looked drawn, and there was a waxy pallor to her skin. The vibrant colors he remembered were gone. Her lips were thinner, almost shriveled, and her cheeks had sagged into the beginning of jowls. Her eyes didn't have the old luster, that piercing look of desire. She glanced nervously around the room, as if searching for something she'd lost. Her hair, which he remembered as thick and lustrous when she'd stepped out of the airplane, now hung limply to her shoulders, strands of gray scattered throughout. Her body was pounds lighter, and the full bosom he had once dreamed about seemed to have melted away. The black dress she was wearing made him think of a widow in mourning.

He pursed his lips and furrowed his brow as he studied her, trying to add up the years since he'd last seen her. "It's been more than eight years," she admitted, as if reading his mind. "And they've been hard ones." She fingered the scarf around her neck and straightened her black jacket.

He wanted to be gentle. "Has it been that long?" he asked, putting all the emphasis on the word 'that'. "Won't you sit down?" he asked. He started to say, "How have you been?" but it was self-evident, so he changed it to "What brings you here?" He promised himself to steer clear of any personal questions.

To him she looked beaten down, harmless. Not the roaring waterfall that had once tossed him around in his dream.

"I want a facelift, Doctor Reiter," she said flatly. "That's the only reason I'm here."

There was no question that Deborah had been ill, and his first reaction was an absolute 'no'. It was more than a simple matter of discouraging her as he'd done to his wife; he sensed there was more to her request and that it wouldn't be easy to dissuade her. He puzzled over it, but answers eluded him and made him uneasy. He didn't respond.

Deborah appeared distracted by a sound at the window. Tiny raindrops, like tears, drizzling from the sky, struck the panes ever so softly. Her hand went to her throat, as if she needed more air. "There is something else," she said. "But what I want is an absolute promise that regardless, you'll do the facelift for me." She gave him no time to reflect on her request. "Doctor Reiter, it's as simple as this; I have leukemia." Her voice dropped off to a whisper as she skipped over the last word. She must have to see the alarm in his eyes. "The specialists assure me it's not the fast-growing kind," she added, as if that would soften the blow.

He tried to control his reaction with an understanding nod, directing his attention to her chart. According to the patient information sheet she'd filled out, she was presently in good health, no illness, no medications, and no problems. Everything was perfect according to her notes. He felt betrayed. "I'm sorry. I can't do it," he said without looking up.

Her eyes hardened. "I should have known. You're no different than the rest of them," she said scornfully. "No compassion, no feeling, no heart. All for yourself." She pulled a piece of lint from her dress and threw it on the floor. "For a moment during the interview that day on the Mexican beach, I thought you had a heart. Didn't you know that I saw you peeling off my bikini with your eyes, with that holier-than-thou look while you pretended to be smiling at your wife? At least, I thought you were human, like a red-blooded man that get caught up in his lust," she added, tightening her grip on her purse. "But I can see I was wrong. It takes guts to be human." It sounded as if she was at a crossroads between resignation and anger.

"Let me spell it out," she said evenly. Her expression grew more somber. "Don't you think I know that my days are numbered? But during the time I have left, I intend to live every minute of every day to the fullest. And I the first thing is I intend to be beautiful again." Suddenly, she was pleading, all her defenses down. "I want to look like I did when you devoured me with your eyes."

He felt as if something was twisting his insides around, stirring up the deepest compassion. At the same time, he was desperate to cling to his professional side. *You just can't go around giving facelifts to women one step from the grave*, he argued. His fingers beat a new rhythm on the desk as he tried to grapple with the dissonance that had begun to stir the even stream of his logic. "But it's life we're talking about," he pointed out. "Your life. Not just wrinkles and jowls," He walked around the desk and put a hand on her shoulder hoping to make her understand. She pushed it away.

For a moment, his pity turned to resentment. He was determined than ever to change her mind. He would play it safe, but keep his conscience clear. "Please listen to me. The last thing you need at this time is an operation. It could set you back. Concentrate on getting well." He sounded a little sanctimonious, even to himself, but he wanted her to understand this. "There are cases where people end up beating this disease. That would be the time to do the surgery. When you're well."

"That's not my luck," she said flatly. "The chances are that this time next year I might be dead." She smiled remorsefully. "And uglier."

He was already feeling like a coward, taking the easy way out. Here was a chance to help some one through a nightmare, and he was pushing her away. Maybe she was right. Maybe he'd become too smug and complacent in his certainties, unwilling to go the extra mile.

She stood up and touched his sleeve. "Please, Doctor Reiter."

He had to ask. "What does your husband think?"

" Gordon? We've been separated since he found out about the disease," she answered, pretending to readjust her blouse. "He never liked being around sick people." She sounded bitter. "But my oncologist told me I should do whatever makes me happy at this point."

It was as if a light turned on in the back of his mind. *There might be a way to help her after all,* he thought. "All right," he said after a long pause. "I'll make you a deal. We'll consult a second oncologist, and if he thinks you can handle it, I'll do the facelift. Otherwise, you can't risk it," he added. "And neither can I."

Her face brightened. "Thank you. Thank you, Phantom. I appreciate that more than I can say." She looked almost beautiful.

Reiter smiled, a professional, reassuring smile. She walked around the desk and threw her arms around him. He could feel her heart beat against his chest. They walked to the door. He would stand by her, he promised himself.

After the door closed, he walked to the window and looked up at the darkening sky. The wail of a siren put his thoughts on hold, and he searched the traffic far below. Ambulance? Police? Or was it an omen? He shook the thought out of his mind. *It's just coincidence, hombre,* he said to himself. A distant memory of the storm the night he met Consuelo on the beach careened through his mind.

***

The next time Deborah came to the office, she had a copy of her latest lab report from the professor of hematology at the University

Medical Center. "He says it's okay. I knew it would be," she said as she laid the letter on his desk.

Reiter had already seen the letter. The oncologist had sent it the day before, and he'd phoned the doctor to discuss the case. The specialist confirmed that Deborah Townsend's condition presented no additional risk for surgery at this time. The leukemia was in remission, at least for now.

Reiter wondered whether she had actually been cured, or if this was another example of the triumph of the human will. What she wanted was something more than life. She wanted beauty, even in the face of death— beauty that would go on forever, at least in her mind. And maybe that wish was stronger than death, perhaps even stronger than the cancer that had invaded her blood.

CHAPTER THIRTY-EIGHT

Early on the morning of Deborah' surgery, as he flew into Santa Monica Airport, Reiter was surprised when he ran into a fog bank. The forecast had been for a clear, cloudless sky. It made him wonder why so many times destiny interfered with the best-laid plans.

As he guided the plane lower, the fog got thicker, and at six hundred feet, the minimum safe altitude, he was still in the clouds. Instinctively, he lifted the nose of the airplane until he was back in the clear. He had no choice but to switch to an instrument-controlled landing. Since Santa Monica wasn't set up for that, the closest place was Los Angeles International Airport, another ten miles to the south.

Adjusting the backrest, he resigned himself to a more complicated approach and began to bank left. He bit his lip as he searched for the LAX approach charts and calculated that the change would delay the morning's schedule by more than an hour. He picked up the mike to advise air traffic control when suddenly the rays of the sun blinded him. In those few seconds, the fog had disappeared. He shook his head and laughed. Destiny was fickle. Didn't it always end up shuffling his cards?

"Santa Monica tower I'm four miles out," he quipped into the mike.

His spirit rose with the clouds as he headed toward the runway. No sooner was he on the ground than the fog, like a heavy black curtain, rolled in again. He tapped the rudders back and forth to keep the plane on the yellow line that led to the parking ramp. He knew that Brian, the guy who had taught him to fly helicopters, would be waiting there. He caught sight of blinking headlights at the far end of the taxiway.

"That's what I call luck," Brian said as they tied down the plane. "For a while, I didn't think you could make it."

"Luck's been good to me lately," Reiter agreed, climbing into the car. They headed to the clinic on Sunset Boulevard.

Deborah Townsend was the only patient on his schedule that morning. Since she was in total remission, he didn't expect this surgery to be any different than the hundreds of other facelifts he'd done. He picked up the scalpel and let his bolder side take over, his movements swift but precise. Instinctively, he knew when to slow down and be more cautious.

The surgery went exactly as he'd hoped. No excess bleeding, no surprises. Cutting through the tissue, freeing layer after layer, gently draping back the skin and then stitching the edges together was routine. When it was over, Deborah was moved to the recovery suite and during the long afternoon, between appointments, he kept checking on her progress. She looked serene and comfortable as she slept. That's what they look like in death too, he thought, serene and comfortable. It made his stomach lurch.

He pondered on life and death and how close they were, as if on opposite sides of a canyon. One side was vibrant and bright, but not far away, on the other side, there was silence and darkness. He thought of Iguana, the Seri Indian whose life he had saved. "Every breath we take, we're hanging between life and death and don't even think about it," Iguana had said. "What you call dying is "ktaol" to us. It means dreaming," he continued. "Because the soul never dies. It can drift from this earth slow and gentle like a dream or it can rush out like a blast of cold air."

Reiter was reminded of a sad day in El Chino's courtyard. One of the crows was sick and had perched on a crate against the wall where the sun shone all day and the winds couldn't reach it. Chino had painted it with the brightest of colors, fiery red around the eyes and deep green behind the beak. He remembered El Chino picking it up and cuddling it in the tuck of his elbow. With his right hand, he stroked its back. The crow kept uttering strange sounds and blinking at Chino.

"Esta muriendo, pobrecito. The poor thing will be gone soon," El Chino said without raising his eyes. The bird seemed content. "But you can see for yourself, amigo, what a little color can do.

Especially when they know they're dying." The crow stretched its neck as if it understood, and El Chino petted it gently. "When the time comes, this one will be happy to die as the best looking crow in Mexico." He put it back down.

Reiter looked down again at the sleeping Deborah, silent and peaceful. He walked back down the hall to his office. He had decided to spend the night at the clinic, but every hour he got up and walked back to the recovery room. He ignored the nurse by the bedside as he checked Deborah's vital signs. Everything seemed to be fine, yet it turned into one of the longest nights of his life.

When morning finally arrived, he helped the nurse remove the bulky dressings. He was pleased with the way Deborah looked but reminded himself that the results were always more obvious the first few hours after the operation, before swelling and discoloration had time to set in.

Deborah asked for a mirror. She turned her head from side to side as if she couldn't believe what she saw. Wide-eyed, she studied the contrast. Where was her tired, angry expression? The jowls were gone; the neck was smooth and tight. Her eyes were bigger and more open. She reached for Reiter's hand with a grateful smile, and a tear trickled down her cheek. "I am beautiful again," she said solemnly. "It's as if I've gone back in time."

Reiter studied her face, and his mind shot back to that distant night in the coal mine when he caught a glimpse of his reflection in the lid of the water canteen. He remembered catching his breath when he seemed to be looking at a ravaged old man. Deborah must have thought the same thing—that the deadly disease was changing more than her face and her body. She had pleaded for this surgery; it was as if by changing the effects of the disease she could change the disease itself. The certainty that her days were charted must have endowed her with a sense of eternity. Like Beto, she wanted to make the final journey in her own way, and like El Chino's sick crow, she would be beautiful when she made it.

Now she had what she wanted. She would be beautiful for the rest of her life.

He felt a measure of pride that he'd been able to erase the lines that the cancer had carved in her face. He hoped it would help make her final journey more peaceful.

Deborah put the mirror aside for a moment. "You've given me back my youth," she said softly. "More than that, you've given me back life.

***

"Will you promise to let me know how you're doing?" Reiter asked Deborah several weeks later. She was at the clinic for a final check up before leaving for England. He was relieved that she'd healed so well and proud that the scars inside and behind her ears were barely visible. But what surprised him was her renewed will to live.

"Of course I'll call you," she replied, reaching for his hand. He was startled when she brushed it gently with her lips and closed her eyes. "I love these hands," she whispered, ignoring the nurse standing nearby. "And I love you," she added as she looked at him. "And not just for what you did to my face."

He felt himself tense up as he detected a flicker of passion in her voice. He was taken aback by the moment and fumbled for a response. "Thank you," he finally said.

She let go of his hand. "Love is more important than life. Or death for that matter," she added. "Love, life, death. They're inseparable. Always connected in one way or the other." She was halfway through the door when she turned to him. "I'll call you every month for the rest of my life."

After Deborah was gone, Reiter turned to his nurse. "I admire her courage," he said, trying to make conversation. "Do you think she'll make it?"

"'Spontaneous remission' is what you doctors always say," the nurse came back. "But haven't you heard of miracles?"

***

Weeks later, on a sunny Sunday afternoon, Reiter and his wife sat on a familiar knoll at the east end of the Chaparral. They'd been talking about Deborah and her stubborn hold on life. "It wasn't and easy decision," he said. When Linda said nothing, he continued. "Look, it's a big operation. Anything could have happened— bleeding, a severed nerve, infection—who knows what else."

"Are you trying to tell me something?" she asked. "If so, why don't you just come out and say it?"

"Of course not," he said, but it didn't ring true, and he knew it. "All I'm trying to say is that surgery is hard on the body. It can be risky. Especially for someone who's sick to begin with."

"But I'm not sick," she reminded him. Then, sensing he was troubled, she looked him in the eyes. "If it's my facelift you're worried about," she went on, "I can live without it." She wrapped her arms around her drawn-up knees and looked down at the desert sand. "I know I look older than most kindergarten moms, but I'm getting used to it. It's not such a big deal. Let's forget the whole thing." She might as well have said, "I know you won't do it for me."

He turned back toward her. "Do you have any idea what you mean to me?" he asked in a raspy, low voice, pleading for her understanding. "You see, operating on you..." he stammered, lowering his eyes, reluctant to face her. "That's getting too personal; I just don't know if I could do it."

She drew several circles with a twig on the ground. "I L Y," she wrote in one of them with big, wavy letters. She ran out of space after the Y so she looked at him and said it instead, "I love you anyway."

Several moments went by, and he asked himself why he was so selfish. Martine and El Chino were right. She wanted this for herself.

Faces, Souls, and Painted Crows

It was her journey. "Pick a date, Linda," he said as he turned to her. "I'll do it whenever you want."

CHAPTER THIRTY-NINE

Linda's surgery was scheduled on a day that arrived with a merciless wind bending and twisting every tree and branch in its way. It reminded Reiter of the fog bank he'd run into the morning of Deborah's surgery. Like that day, he felt torn in a thousand directions. On one hand, he was relieved that the day had finally come; on the other hand, he was a bundle of nerves thinking about operating on the person he loved more than anyone else.

Sitting at his desk, he kept looking at the clock on the wall. The hands pointed to twenty minutes before six. The operation was scheduled for six, the early part of the day when his brain and hands worked best. He could picture her on the operating room table being scrubbed and prepared for surgery. He glanced at the clouds that seemed to be rolling right through the window and wondered whether it was another ominous sign. Shivering, he dismissed the idea and headed for the operating room.

Linda had spent the night in town and was already asleep on the surgical table when he walked in. He could hear the bleeps of her life ticking away and see it displayed in flashing green numbers on the electronic screens in the room...pulse, blood pressure, breathing, and the amount of oxygen in her blood.

The first thing that caught his eye was the troubled expression of his anesthesiologist, Dr. Pirro. Pirro was usually upbeat and gung-ho. "Are you sure you want to do this?" Pirro asked. "It's not something you do every day, a facelift on your wife. I'd like to know what the American College of Surgeons says about this."

Reiter tried to wave off the uncomfortable atmosphere as he dried his hands. He wasn't quite sure what to say, and Pirro pressed on. "Didn't you tell me once that you'd never operate on your family?" he asked without looking up. He re-adjusted a dial on his anesthesia machine. "What I want to know is, was it her idea to do this?"

"Look, Pirro, we have a job to do," Reiter admonished, trying to put an end to the unpleasant discussion. "It's a simple facelift like dozens we've done." He slipped on his gloves with the help of the nurse. "As for whose idea it was, that shouldn't be your concern," he said curtly. Pirro didn't respond. "I'm sorry about your doubts, Pirro, but if you want to know the truth, I wasn't really ready for this. But it means a lot to Linda, and you know what she means to me," Reiter said.

"Okay, okay," Pirro came back.

Reiter felt relieved that cutting into Linda's face didn't make him squeamish after all. He put in a sharp hook under her skin and lifted it the way he always did. Then he started to separate the skin from fat and muscle below with the long scissors that the assistant handed him.

It took only seconds to discover that something about her skin was different. The shanks of the scissors ran into a network of fibers that tethered the skin to the muscles beneath it. Gently, he probed the plane between the layers of skin and muscle, but the scissors balked as if a wall pushed them back. Aware that all eyes were following his hands, he made a point of hiding his surprise. He'd seen this type of skin only on patients from the Orient and when he operated on Linda's aunt. He remembered how tediously he had to cut through each one of the fibers. *Fibrous septa* was the medical term for those strands.

He'd once asked a Canadian plastic surgeon about it. The doctor had come up with a quick answer. "You see that type of skin in Orientals and North American Indians. I've operated on several of them, and they have a particular type of skin that acts like it's glued to the fascia below. That's what keeps their skin from sagging and why you rarely see jowls on elderly Natives. If you think about it, they don't have drooping necks like white people do. Their skin get weathered and wrinkled, but those fibers keep it tight against the muscle." It was because of those fibers that Linda's surgery took longer than usual. It crossed Reiter's mind that the others in the operating room might be thinking he was taking extra care because the patient was his wife.

"She's going to have a real good result," Dr. Pirro said at one point. "Your results are always good," he added as if trying to make up for his earlier remarks.

"Thanks, Pirro," Reiter responded. "Maybe you won't believe me, but if anyone would ask me right this minute about this patient, I'd swear I've forgotten who she is. But I will add this: She's the only wife I'll ever do."

He kept threading the shiny needle and the hair-like suture in and out of the flesh, trying hard not to disturb it. To him the patient beneath the sterile blue sheet, whose heart kept bleeping on the monitors, was no different than any other case right now. He was doing his best. When the surgery was over, she would look the same to him as when he started.

***

A few days later, he drove Linda home from the city. There was no doubt the children had missed her, but Reiter was puzzled to see them keep their distance at first. Pilar ran to her mother and wrapped her arms around her waist, but the two teenagers were unusually quiet and reserved.

Shane was shy anyway and usually kept his feelings to himself. Finally, he spoke up. "I'm glad you're back home, Mom." Then he wandered over to his father. "To me she doesn't look any different," he whispered, stealing another look. Before Reiter could answer, the boy was out the door. So that's what it was, Reiter thought. All week they must have worried that their mother would look like a different person when she came home. They seemed relieved that she hadn't changed. In fact, the more he tried to see a difference, the more it eluded him. He wondered why she'd gone to all the trouble. What was the point of having surgery?

315

A few days later, as they were getting ready for bed, she turned to him. "I love what you've done for me," she said with a quiet certainty in her voice as she leaned towards the mirror in the bathroom. He stood behind her, and she must have noticed his puzzled expression. When he didn't respond, she turned and slid an arm around his waist. "What's wrong?"

"Nothing, nothing at all," he finally answered and caressed her hair.

It didn't take long before Reiter did sense something different about her, but it wasn't her face. She seemed bubblier and more assertive somehow. It showed in many ways.

He heard her respond to a phone call one morning, and what caught his attention was that she sounded so sure of herself, like she knew exactly what she wanted. "I know he'd be delighted to come." He wasn't sure how to take that. It was something new; she was speaking for him. "Of course we'll be there, Esther. Eight o'clock sounds perfect."

There was no question the facelift had given her something he hadn't planned on. In one way, it was reassuring; in another way, he felt threatened. He made a point to dismiss the latter, and instead reasoned that the surgery had changed the way she felt about herself.

The party invitation she had accepted was at the home of Raymond Kerz, the prominent producer who was Jeff Clancy's close friend. It was Raymond's birthday, and all of Hollywood had been invited. Reiter had been reluctant, but Linda had insisted. When she said she wanted to go, he'd given in even though it wasn't like him.

Throughout the evening, he had the feeling that all eyes were on Linda. Only half-listening to the conversations around him, Reiter kept watching her out of the corner of his eye. At one point, she sat on an overstuffed couch in a corner of the room with their suave host standing in front of her. Her lips parted slightly as she looked up at Raymond Kerz with a confident smile.

A strange feeling crept over Reiter. He wasn't sure what was wrong, but he felt a flush in his face and tightness in his chest. Kerz had a reputation as a lady-killer. "They all turn into jell-o around Raymond. No woman can resist him." Jeff Clancy had said once. Thinking of that, Reiter realized the unfamiliar feeling in his chest was jealousy.

Suddenly, he got up and headed towards his wife, just in time to catch Kerz saying, "Life is meant to be enjoyed, my dear, every day and every night."

As Reiter joined them, Linda turned to him, "It's a wonderful party, isn't it, Paul?"

"Very nice, Raymond," Reiter responded as the producer walked away.

Driving back to the Chaparral after the party, rain pelted the windshield so hard Reiter had to strain his eyes to see through the fast-moving wipers. It got so bad he had to pull off the road. He was unusually quiet as they sat there on the shoulder of the highway waiting for the storm to let up.

Linda broke the silence. "What's wrong? You don't seem yourself."

"Nothing's wrong," he insisted, peering through the relentless rain. "Nothing at all."

"Ever since you did my facelift, you've been acting kind of uptight," she said, and put a hand on his knee. "Don't you like the way I look? Don't you like the result?" She crossed her long legs.

"You don't look any different to me. You look like you always did," he finally said, slightly annoyed.

"Is that it? It didn't turn out like you expected. Not a good result as you would say?"

He heard her irritation, and that unnerved him. He shrugged. "No, it's not that. That's not the issue." He turned back onto the highway even though the rain hadn't let up. He kept his mind on the road until finally, he turned into their driveway.

Now she sounded exasperated. "So why don't you tell me? What's the issue?"

"You looked good to me before, and to tell you the truth, I'm not so sure it was worth it. In a way, I'm sorry I did it."

Her reply was sharp, high-pitched. "Just like you were sorry about what you did for Deborah Townsend? You told me she was happy with the result, but in your opinion she shouldn't have done it." She pulled her hand from his knee. "What about her feelings? What about mine? Or don't you care?" Her voice trembled. "I don't understand you. First you give me something that makes me happy. Then you want to take it back. I could have lived without it, but I like what I see when I look in the mirror now. Why would you resent that?"

He frowned and opened the window a little, as if trying to clear the stale air. He hadn't heard her like that before she was a smoldering fire about to ignite. And she wasn't finished yet.

"It really makes me wonder why you keep doing this work if you honestly don't think it's meant to help people." She said it fiercely, almost angrily. "I know it can't just be the money. Or can it?" she added.

They were out of the car before he spoke. "Those were harsh words. You hit below the belt."

She sounded unrepentant. "I didn't mean to hurt you, but we need to get it out in the open. You've got to give other people's feelings more value. And more value to your work." She frowned.

The argument ended, but he felt on edge when they went to bed. He was hoping for a peaceful sleep. Instead he plunged into a strange nightmare.

He dreamed he was caressing Linda, but that it felt as if she were two different people. One side of her face felt tight, with a barely perceptible but definite scar by her ear and up into the temple. There was no hint of a wrinkle; her neck was firm and tight. His wandering hands moved to her breasts, which felt firm and round and pointed up. Then he let his hand wander back up and across to the other side of her body. He felt for the scar around her face. There was none. But he could feel the familiar crow's feet at the corner of her eyes and the skin of her neck was lax and drooping a little. On that same side her breast was sagging and felt a bit smaller. That side of her body hadn't been touched. He kept going back and forth between the two Lindas. Even her smile was different from one side to the other. He woke up in a sweat, relieved to see her sleeping peacefully and looking normal.

***

The next day Jeff Clancy telephoned. "I'm sure glad you and Linda came to the party last night," he began. "Your wife is the talk of the town. She looks terrific; she really does."

"Thanks," Reiter said, swallowing his guilt. "I'm sure she'll be happy to hear that."

"You're the one who should be happy. You did a number one job. And without changing her." There was only static on the line. Reiter was quiet. "Can you hear me?" Jeff's voice boomed. "What's eating you?"

"Sorry, Jeff" Reiter finally responded. "But I can't see any real difference in her face, and it's not because I haven't tried. In most patients, I can see some difference right away. But with Linda I have the feeling she went through all this for nothing. That I didn't do her much good."

"If you can't see it, then you must be blind," Jeff scolded. "But don't they say that love is blind? Like any fool in love, you didn't really notice her getting older. That's why she hasn't changed in your eyes."

CHAPTER FORTY

As the months passed, there were times when the routine of his days felt as predictable as a clock. And yet no matter how evenly life moved along, a vague awareness that something was amiss kept stirring his conscience. Often when he looked at his youngest child, he would wonder what had happened to Consuelo's baby. The child would be in school now, not an easy time for a youngster without a father.

His surgery schedule frequently included reconstructive procedures on Jorge, the burned child from the fish camp. Over the years, he and the team at St. Elizabeth's had performed a total of sixteen operations on the boy, taxing Reiter's skill and Jorge's courage. It had been a difficult road for Jorge's parents too. Nacho and Maria traveled to California with Jorge, keeping the family together, living in a small guesthouse at Reiter's ranch and helping out with various odd jobs. They had put their trust in Reiter, but each time they must have wondered how the surgery would turn out, how much longer it would take.

Each operation brought some improvement. Scarred tissue had been replaced by healthy tissue and gradually Jorge's face took on features: the shape of a bulky nose, eyelids that almost closed, ears that looked human. Methodically, Reiter molded Jorge's cheeks and forehead, grafting skin and bone to brow and nose. But every time he tried to repair the lower lip, he felt like he'd run into a brick wall. Beneath Jorge's lip there was an opening, or fistula, and every time he tried to close it surgically, thick cords of 'proud flesh' would eventually form, pulling Jorge's lip down again, exposing gums that had become red and swollen. Rivulets of foamy saliva dribbled down his chin and kept the gaping hole from healing.

Reiter puzzled over the problem, rifling through books on reconstructive surgery and conferring with some truly great surgeons. But the thundering, "Nothing much can be done," rang often in his ears. The experts' opinions were vague, and their advice was sparse.

He felt more and more lonely, with recurring doubts blowing through mind like icy winds in the mountains.

Another surgery was scheduled for the end of March. The only date available was the 20th, and Reiter wondered if destiny had played a part in making it coincide with his birthday. The night before surgery, he felt a sudden urge to pray. "Help me find the answer to the hole in Jorge's face. That would be the best birthday present of my life."

The next morning, he walked into the waiting room and found Jorge's mother and father waiting for him. "Buenos dias, Doctor," they said with hope in their voices. He felt a new resolve. "I promise you that this time I'll be able to fix the lower lip. It will stay exactly where it belongs," he vowed.

Even as he spoke, he realized that in his eagerness to lift their spirits, he'd made an unreasonable promise, one he wasn't sure he could fulfill. He tried to look more confident than he felt and smiled at Maria. Deep down in her eyes, he saw the steady flame of love. He was her only hope. He felt like a phony.

"Jorge is in your hands," she interrupted his thoughts. "May the Eternal Father bless them today," she said as she reached for them. Suddenly, her face became serene as her eyes reflected her faith in him.

Reiter walked to the surgeon's dressing room more slowly than usual. He felt clammy and cold, like a condemned man on the way to the gallows. He was alone once again, no one left but him and his God. He felt crushed by an unbearable weight.

After he'd changed into operating clothes, he sat down for a minute and held his face in his hands, trying to once more think of an answer, to formulate a plan for the surgery. But nothing new occurred to him, and after a few more minutes, he got up and made his way to the scrub sinks outside the operating room.

Over the sinks was a set of brightly lit mirrors. He'd never liked them. They revealed everything and had a way of reminding him of how flawed and imperfect he was. Usually he made a point to avoid looking at his reflection. He kept his eyes on his hands as he scrubbed them. But today, he glanced up and what he saw caught his attention. Like the night in the coalmine, he was shocked at his own reflection. He saw deep furrows in the middle of his forehead, and a downward pull at the mouth. The marks of guilt…past guilt about Consuelo's child, the pain he'd caused his wife, and now guilt about the promise he'd made to Juan and Maria. Like the night in the mine, he had to wonder if his face reflected a withering soul.

Maybe I just need a facelift, he thought trying to make light of it. He stopped scrubbing and pushed his surgical cap down over his forehead and tightened the mask up under his eyes, hiding as much of his face as he could. But it didn't help. It was as if the mirror was looking into his soul. He ran the brush over his hands, faster and faster. Finally, he walked into the operating room with his heart pounding.

"Happy Birthday," Dr. Pirro said, looking up and turning a dial on the anesthesia machine. Even under Prior's mask, Reiter could see him stifling a yawn, as if he was already bored.

"Happy Birthday, Doctor," Miss Evans, the assistant, echoed before Reiter could respond.

There was a subtle hesitation before Reiter replied. "Thank you. Thank you." He sat down at the head of the operating table. "Okay, let's get started." As he picked up his marking pen, Maria's words echoed through his mind, "Jorge is in your hands. May the Eternal Father bless them today."

Reiter's eyes focused on the boy's chin. Deliberately, he took a pen and drew a line around the scarred flesh that kept pulling down the lip and keeping the wound open. He planned to excise it completely. With a scalpel, he swiftly cut along the lines he'd drawn, and with the shanks of the scissors, he probed around the bothersome scar and removed it. The lip was finally released and slid up and into place. He smiled but knew the most difficult part was to close the gaping hole that he'd created. He was aware that everyone in the operating room was waiting for his next move, and he tried to

portray a confidence he didn't feel. Staring at the open wound and
the glistening bone underneath, he hesitated, not sure what to do
next. Finally, he decided to do something different and swallow his
pride. "I'm not sure how to close this," he admitted.

"If I know you, you'll figure it out," Pirro said as he readjusted
his mask. "Too bad you can't use some other skin," he added as he
nodded towards the neck.

Reiter looked down at the boy's neck. The skin there was
smooth and unscarred. Pirro was right. Why not use that skin to
cover the big hole? Why hadn't he thought of it before?

It made perfect sense. A normal skin graft would be difficult and
unsightly, but if he kept the skin from the neck attached, there would
be no need for a lot of stitches. The wound would be covered and
when it healed there wouldn't be the 'pull' on the lip that made it
look so grotesque. *Yes, Maria and Nacho*, he told himself, *this time I'm
going to make it work.*

With long sweeps of the knife, he cut two straight lines across
the throat, one below the chin and one at the base of the neck. Bright
red blood trickled down the pale skin. Miss Evans kept blotting it.
Next, he freed the wide strip of skin between the incisions by slipping
the shanks of his scissors under it and then prying it loose with his
fingertips. It was a slow process to work the skin upwards, but he
finally managed to cover the hole. The smooth skin moved all in one
piece, like one of those visors he'd seen on ancient armor in medieval
castles. He forced Jorge's mouth open to see how the 'visor' fit when
he moved his jaw up and down. There was still a slight pull on the
lip. He freed more skin at the sides of the neck with his scissors and
tried again. The tissue, the 'visor', fit better. It covered the defect, and
the lip that was finally freed from the scar moved easily into place. It
looked normal and covered the gums that had been sore and exposed
for so long. It all worked perfectly.

The only thing left to do was close the wide opening in the neck
area. Fortunately, slight tension in this area wasn't anything to worry
about. He could loosen the skin right below the wound by cutting a

series of zigzags in it and then easing it upward. Patiently, he cut and sewed, cut and sewed.

He felt his spirit soar. Nothing could stop him now. "Jorge is in your hands. May God bless them today." He heard Maria's words echo through his mind, and the stale air of the operating room came alive. The anesthesia machine hissed with more vigor, the bleeps of the monitors seemed louder. It felt as if the room was charged with creation and hope.

He looked down at Jorge to reassure him that the problem was solved. The contorted lip that used to make him look like a snarling dog was gone. Jorge would be able to smile now. He was no longer a boy without a face. His soul was free to express itself in his new face. Now he had a mouth to smile and to kiss and a nose to wrinkle in mischief or disgust. Like everyone else.

Reiter felt as if he had helped to complete the connection between Jorge's face and his soul, the connection between how he felt and how he looked.

After putting the last suture in the neck, he gently cleansed the new face with swabs of sterile water. "I think it's going to be okay this time," he said half-aloud. "We've done enough for today." He got up and smiled at Dr. Pirro and the nurses. Miss Evan's eyes glistened with tears. "Thank you." That's all Reiter said.

The staff looked at each other and nodded. Pirro started to wake Jorge up.

In the doctor's dressing room, Reiter flopped down on the couch like a tired climber on the ledge of a mountain. For a minute, he wasn't sure where he was and why he'd climbed up so high. He studied his hands. God had really blessed them today. Maria's prayers had been heard.

His operating clothes were bloody so he took them off, first the shirt and then the pants. Then he headed for the showers. Right by the doorway were those mirrors, and again his reflection caught his eye. But something was different this time. The tired look that he'd seen earlier was gone. The deep frown that had been there since the nights in the coal mine was gone. These mirrors told a different story. The story of another face. A face that looked younger…like after a facelift.

Look, hombre, come to your senses, he argued. *You're seeing things. Face it: you're getting old and beat up like everyone else. The years are slipping by and so is your mind. The wrinkles get deeper; the jowls are getting heavier. Why should you be different than the rest?* The mirror is playing tricks. With just the right lighting, mirrors and cameras can do wonders, Jeff Clancy always said.

He jumped in the shower and hoped the warm water could wash away the confusion. It seemed his mind cleared as he considered the irony of it all. For years he'd had a strong yearning to know more about how the soul etched each face with unique wrinkles that came only with life itself—pain and laughter, sorrow and joy. There were times when the face and the soul didn't seem connected, when genes caused the face to age prematurely, or ravaged by despair or bad memories or by whiskey. Sometimes an earthquake, the damage of a fire or a deadly machine could turn a man into a monster. That's when his work could change a life.

A myriad of faces appeared in his mind, and he remembered the changes he'd made in each life. There was Deborah, who would be beautiful for the rest of her life now. And he could see Pancho, the man with the new face who looked more like Speedy than a government spy. He even saw Miss Love, the idol of his youth. And finally, Linda—happy and confident.

Yet in spite of surgical skills, deeper down in the soul, the marks of time still took their toll. The wrinkles of life. He knew that no matter how deft his hands had become at removing sagging skin and wrinkles on the outside, only God could touch the soul.

He went into the waiting room. Maria and Nacho got out of their chairs with slow, cautious movements. Their anxious eyes met his like old friends at the end of a journey. Reiter cut the tension like a thunderclap after the lightning.

"Jorge is fine. His lip is okay. He has a new face. He'll heal soon, God willing."

Maria's voice quivered as she reached for his hand and kissed it. "Thank you, Doctor. Thank you forever."

She turned to gaze at her husband who was wiping tears from his eyes. "Today is Jorge's cumpleano," he said. "You have given him the most beautiful regalo."

CHAPTER FORTY-ONE

There were many times during the following years when Reiter's mind wandered back to the day when he'd operated on Jorge and changed his life. His own life had been affected as well. When things got out of hand at the office or at home, when he ran into a difficult patient, when unexpected gusts of wind interfered with a landing or his mind strayed into bitter times of the past, all he had to do was think of Jorge, and a smile would cross his face. He'd heard that Jorge worked with his father on a fishing trawler in the summer and attended high school in La Paz the rest of the year. It pleased him that the boy was leading a normal life.

Reiter was alone in his office on his birthday, exactly ten years after Jorge's last surgery. He leaned back in his chair and put his feet up on the desk, one at a time. It wasn't proper, he reminded himself, but it was late in the day, and he had a right to be tired. Maybe he could catch a quick nap before his wife joined him for a quiet birthday dinner.

The phone in the office interrupted his plans. He picked up the receiver. "Hello. Hello...Who is it?" he asked several times, holding the cord of the telephone as if he could squeeze out a voice.

"Espanto, Espanto," a voice droned through the static. Instinctively, Reiter leaned into the receiver. He hadn't heard Jorge's voice for a long time. He swung his feet off the desk and winced when another burst of static garbled the voice on the other end of the line.

"Espanto, Espanto. Me escuces. Do you hear me?"

Reiter smiled broadly. "Si," he responded warmly. "I don't hear so good any more. You've got to speak up."

The conversation continued in Spanish. "Do you know who this is?" The voice was persistent, like the heavy static.

"Si, of course," Reiter insisted, repositioning himself in the chair. "Jorge, como estas?"

"Felize cumpleano, Espanto." Jorge's voice was clear and manly, befitting his eighteen years.

Reiter felt rising warmth in his chest. "Felize cumpleano a te. Where are you, my friend?" he asked as the line went dead. He tapped for an operator. "Jorge, Jorge," he persisted.

He asked his secretary to re-establish the line, but there was no use. Jorge must have called him from some out of the way phone strapped to a light pole near a fish camp. Placing the call must have cost a day's wages and there was only enough time to wish the man who had rebuilt his face a happy birthday.

Reiter felt alternate waves of frustration and joy wash over him. He was reminded of how quickly the years were passing. He unlaced his fingers and held them in front of him. The soft light of his desk lamp illuminated the backs of his hands. He was momentarily taken aback at the bulging veins that snaked their way, like purple-blue rain worms, under his age-spotted skin. It surprised him how worn-out they looked. It had to be from all the scrubbing with sterile solutions and the surgical gloves he wore for hours at a time, he reasoned. And long before that, in the coalmine, hanging on to rattling jackhammers every night for a year. Then it struck him that the real explanation was that today he was nearly sixty years old.

Not wishing to dwell on what had seemed a morbid reminder of time, he flipped his hands over and studied the palms. They still appeared soft pink, and he thought of the many times over the years they had caressed his wife. He never tired of loving her, and he had a special feeling in his heart for their youngest child, Pilar, whom he had come to think of as their child of forgiveness. The older children were out of the house and starting careers of their own, but Pilar was still a teenager, and she kept them both young.

Of course, when he strayed into memories, he had to face his conscience and the event that loomed above everything else. Often, when he looked at Pilar, he would think of the child of Consuelo. After Consuelo's letter years ago, questions and speculations had ground away at his soul, layer by layer, leaving him vulnerable and exposed.

Had he fathered a child who was alone in the world? He believed that every child needed both a father and a mother to nurture it as a reminder of their love. That's the way it should be. But what happens to a child not created by love, he asked himself? What happens to sorrow's child?

When the voice of the nurse tore him away from painful memories, he was almost grateful. "Are you up to seeing one more patient today?" He didn't answer right away. "She says it's important. Her name is Consuelo."

He felt the blood draining from his face as he bolted upright. "Consuelo?" He hoped the nurse didn't catch the terror in his eyes. "Tell her to come in," he managed to say.

As if in a dream, Consuelo appeared in his office and sat down across from him. When she lowered her eyelids with their long lashes, it was as if fifteen years melted away in a heartbeat. She had the same sultry look as that night on the beach. Her sensuous lips were slightly parted, revealing white and even teeth; her eyebrows were arched and well defined. The only thing different was that her black hair was now peppered with gray and was neatly pulled back in a bun. She wore a crimson blouse with the top buttons opened, giving a generous view of the cleavage he remembered so well. She crossed her legs discretely, and he noticed the fishnet black stockings. With a graceful motion, she loosened the white scarf that draped around her neck. His eyes shot to the wedding ring that was still on her slender hand. He found that reassuring.

"You haven't changed, Consuelo."

"Neither have you," she responded.

As if reading his mind, she cleared some of the confusion for him. "Thank you for not contacting us," she said as she twisted the ring on her finger. "You haven't bothered me or the child, and I'm grateful." She looked him straight in the eyes. He caught a calculated tone in her voice.

"It's been hard; I've always wondered..." he stammered. "I'm glad you came to see me..."

She cut him short. "That's not why I came. I came here with the boy because I want you to help him."

Reiter merely stared at her. She shifted in the chair as if she wanted to avoid his gaze. "What happened, Consuelo? What happened that night?" he whispered. "Please. I have to know."

His pleading seemed to make her more indignant. "You were there," she snapped. "Weren't you? Besides, I'm sure you got my letter."

"Yes, I got your letter. But it didn't answer any questions."

"What do you mean?"

"Consuelo, I can't remember that night." He closed his eyes before he added, "Just tell me the truth, whatever it is. How much more can it hurt?"

She must have sensed his dilemma was genuine because she seemed suddenly inclined to shed light on that night. "It was a night when I thought the world had blown up. I have no idea how it started—the way you looked at me, or what you said to me, but before I knew it, every last bit of me was on fire, a fire that kept getting hotter and hotter. There was no more thinking, no turning back, just wanting. And I wasn't the only one. Don't you remember rolling in the sand at the edge of the sea, splashing in the shallow waves? You didn't have to tear off my clothes; I did it for you. But you," she pointed a finger at him, "you turned into a raging bull."

"Consuelo, stop," he wanted to say. But he didn't move.

"But in a flash it was over," she said. "Because...or maybe you don't want to know." Her voice rose a pitch. Lines of anger were etched on her face. "You called out a name over and over again. I tried to strangle you. I begged you to stop. You ignored me and then it was too late." She paused and then whispered as if she didn't want to hear her own words. "Don't remember what you called me?" Her eyes were wide, welling up with tears.

He shook his head in disbelief.

Her eyes flashed at him. "Linda, Linda you kept screaming into the night as your body twitched, and you spewed life into me. Then the earthquake was over, and we sank back into the sand." Her voice became brittle, "I knew then that you had the wrong woman." She looked at the floor. "I felt like a whore." He saw the pain in her eyes as she went on. "It was as if you'd torn out my heart. I wrung out my dress and put it back on. I thought I would die from the humiliation, the shame. I ran back to my husband—to Pedro." Her blazing eyes shot toward the door. "And you will see how it ended."

She got up and smoothed her skirt as she stood in front of his desk. "I think you owe me this one last favor. Take a look at the boy."

Reiter regretted that she could see the perspiration on his forehead and the fright in his eyes. "Why don't you have him come in?" he said and was relieved that at least his voice sounded steady. He wondered why he hadn't just asked for the boy over the intercom. But nothing made sense.

She seemed to take all the time in the world leaving the office, as if to let him squirm, make him pay.

While she was gone, he buried his face in his hands. "You fool," he said aloud. "Did you think this day would never come?" The seconds ticked by on the clock behind him.

His thoughts were interrupted by a boy's high-pitched voice. "Con permiso? May I come in?"

Quickly, Reiter straightened up. He struggled to compose himself, trying to look like a concerned professional.

A young man, wearing a white guaivara shirt and neatly pressed trousers, stood at the door. His dark hair curled down and nearly brushed his shoulders. Reiter felt the heat rising in his face. He was looking at a younger version of Pedro, Consuelo's husband. He had to press his lips together to keep the relief from exploding.

There could be no mistake. Pedrito's face was just like his father's, round and chubby. Reiter could picture Pedro in the smoky cantina, his pudgy fingers ready to pluck the guitar. But what he remembered most were his big, floppy ears. Instantly, he saw that the boy standing in front of him had exactly the same type of ears. He wanted to embrace the young man, clasp him to his chest and kiss him on both cheeks. "You marvelous miracle you," he wanted to scream. Instead, he crossed his legs and gripped the arm of the chair as he let his eyes wander over the young man's face. Young Pedro even had a mustache like his father and grandfather, or at least the beginning of one. But his dark eyes and long lashes were pure Consuelo.

"I'm sure you can see why I don't like my ears. They're big and kind of floppy," the young man blurted out, raising his hair and turning sideways. "For years, they have been making fun of me at school."

Pedrito spoke hesitantly in heavily accented English. Every sound that came from his mouth sounded exactly like his father. Pedro's tenor voice had always been slightly off-key and usually lagged behind the rest of the band. Capi always chuckled about it. But today Reiter thought it was the most beautiful music he'd ever heard.

He answered the boy in Spanish. "Let's take a closer look." He felt his heart pounding in his chest, but made every effort to keep his voice level.

It wasn't the usual examination, he knew, as he let his fingers slide over the ears. He wanted desperately to believe that this was truly happening. "I'm sure I can help you," he said. "We can make the ears lie flat and even make them smaller." As if to show Pedrito what he meant, he grasped the upper part of the ear and gently folded it backward.

The boy nodded and looked down at the intricate embroidery on his pointed cowboy boots. Then he raised his eyes and smiled at Reiter. "You are a friend of my father aren't you?" he beamed. "He said you're the best." There was no hesitation in his voice.

"Yes, your father is my friend." Reiter answered, as much for his own benefit as the boy's. "And I knew your grandfather." As he spoke he felt the familiar stab of guilt. "I think I can do something for your ears, make them look the way you want," he said with as much reassurance as he could muster. "Why don't I talk to your mother now?" He pressed the intercom. "Send in Miss Consuelo." He walked over to Pedro Jr. and put an arm on his shoulder. "Let your mother and me work out the details."

The young man got up. "Thank you, Doctor," he said with a barely perceptible sigh of relief. "I'll wait outside," he said, and walked out the door, the heels of his cowboy boots clicking across the oak floor.

Consuelo came back in and looked at him a long time before she spoke. "You can see he's so much like his father. The ears might be a problem for him, but when he was born, and I saw those funny little ears sticking out, I thought my heart would leap out of my chest. They were the most beautiful ears I'd ever seen."

Reiter nodded, knowing the joy and relief she must have felt.

"Pedro and I have had a good life with our son. But Pedrito has been embarrassed by his ears for a long time, and when his father said he knew of someone who could change them, I didn't want to argue." She went on, "I would be grateful if you could help him. Whatever it costs, correct little Pedro's ears."

Reiter gazed at her distractedly still trying to take it all in. "Consuelo, can you forgive me?"

"Forgive you?" she repeated as if she wasn't sure she had heard him. She thought about it for a moment. "Yes. Yes, I can. The question is 'Have you forgiven yourself?'"

***

Reiter was buffeted around by a thousand mixed emotions after Consuelo left the room, but he decided not to share them with Linda over dinner. It was something too intimate. He struggled through the sad/happy birthday dinner to keep his feelings hidden, but it must have been the way he fidgeted when he tried to extract the lobster from its shell, the way he looked at her across the table or his subdued tone of voice that alerted her.

Finally, she asked him outright, "You seem different tonight. Has something happened?"

"What makes you think so?" he stammered as he wadded up his starched napkin.

"I know you, Paul. I can feel there's something unusual. Something I should know."

"I'll tell you later. Please, let's talk at the house," he said and reached across the table to touch her hand.

When they finally got back to the Chaparral, Reiter waited until they were in bed before telling Consuelo's story, sparing no details. "Linda, can you forgive me?" He finally asked, like a penitent sinner in the most important confession of his life.

She let him finish before turning to him. "Paul, I forgave you a long time ago. But what's more important," she said, "have you forgiven yourself?" She brushed a strand of hair off her face.

He let her words sift through his mind, realizing that it was the same question Consuelo had asked him. He felt a sudden throbbing behind his eyes knowing that he still didn't have an answer.

She answered for him. "I don't think so. What you're telling me about Consuelo and her boy, and about the guilt and hurt in your heart…I don't think you've ever stopped beating yourself up." She sounded sad and reached for his trembling hand. "Those months we lived apart never really ended, did they? The separation remained in little ways," she continued. "I could feel an invisible wall between us. Now it all makes sense."

He tried to swallow the lump in his throat, knowing she was right. He'd been hiding behind that wall of remorse, building it thicker and thicker over time.

She looked into his eyes. "I'll never forget my own pain, and the anger I felt that day in Puertecitos when I found the letter in your pocket." She shot a warm glance at him. "Forgiving you was the last thing on my mind. I told you that I wanted to, but I didn't know how hard it would be." Her words faltered. "But then I got tired of the bitter woman I kept seeing in the mirror."

The moonlight streamed through the open window and bathed their faces in its silvery glow. "Paul, I was sick when I saw what I was becoming. I realized I had to forgive you and then forgive myself for what seemed to be weakness." She frowned as she looked at him again. " Do I make any sense? I finally realized that in the end I needed to forgive you for my own sake."

He looked down, knowing she wasn't finished. "But nobody can just say 'I forgive you' and think it's over and done with. You have to live it every day of your life until it becomes a part of you, of the way you talk, the way you look at your children, the way you see every thing that happens around you." She hesitated and shook her head. "Without true forgiveness life can't go on."

"I remember what holding on to old hurts did to Martine," Reiter mused. "He couldn't forgive his wife, and for years he kept wallowing in that night when he caught her in bed with their neighbor. It took almost a lifetime before he finally let go, but when he did, he told me it was as if a hook had been pulled out of his soul."

The whirring of the blades on the ceiling fan seemed to keep time with her next words. "I can understand that. The day I let go, it was as if I became a new person, as if I started to live all over again." She nodded as if to strengthen her point. "But forgiving another person is much easier than forgiving yourself."

Reiter nodded. "I never thought of it that way. But I can tell you a lot about guilt, how it turns into despair, churns your insides and sneaks into your soul like a cancer." He glanced at her. "And all along I thought that no one could see it, that I was hiding it. But I guess people could tell. Like El Chino says, the face never lies."

"That makes me think about Beto too," Linda said. "I remember the day I ran into him on the path. When I looked at his face I could see a troubled soul."

Reiter studied her silhouette in the moonlight, awed by her insight. "It's true. He could never get out of that storm that shattered his boat and drowned his wife. He felt it was his fault and for years the guilt tortured him," he said.

He looked at the ceiling, thinking about Beto and all the comfort his broken-hearted friend had given him. "I had no idea how the guilt was crushing his soul. He waded around in it night after night, crying and wailing. In the end it destroyed him."

Linda wrapped her arms around him as if warding off a chill. "Please don't let it happen to you, Paul." The moon slid behind a bank of clouds, and her words spilled through the darkened room. "What happened between you and Consuelo was a long time ago. You tell me that she and Pedro have been a happy family all these years. I'm sure it couldn't have been easy for her to forgive you or to forgive herself. But I'm also sure that without forgiveness there couldn't have been all that love in her family. And there wouldn't be a little Pedro."

Before he could respond, she went on. "In the end, I think forgiving yourself might be even more important than forgiving someone else. It's the only way to open your soul." She sat up and leaned forward, her hands on the silken sheets. "So let go of your guilt, Paul. It's time. Don't let it destroy us too."

He got up and walked to the open window. The smell of sage drifted through the night air, and he heard the reassuring sound of crickets as he searched the face of the moon. He realized the choice was his. He could waste away in the prison he'd built or break out in the same way he'd walked out of the mine so many years ago.

Going to her side of the bed, he flipped on the night lamp. Taking her face in his hands, he spoke softly, "I'm done with my secrets, done with my guilt, done with the phantom."

She ran a finger down his profile. "You don't have to tell me," she smiled. "It shows in your face."

EPILOGUE

He should have known from the muffled tones of the trombone and from the way the wiry Indian who played it kept stumbling through the rocky desert, that the funeral was going to be a disaster. Reiter frowned as this thought went through his mind.

With his fleshy lips wrapped around the mouthpiece, the Indian puffed out his cheeks, forcing the sounds from the trombone like gasps from an ancient cow on the way to slaughter. In a stubborn attempt to defy the troublesome winds that blew down the canyon and threatened his balance, he tightened his grip on the instrument and leaned slightly into the wind. Next to him, a boy played a beat-up accordion, his stringy black hair held in place by a bandanna. Behind him a younger boy kept striking a drum with the stump of an arm.

Reiter winced every time the musicians' naked feet struck the jagged rocks as they skirted bushes and boulders on the road north of town. The merciless mid-day sun beat down on the ragged procession.

Reiter kept an eye on the box balanced on the shoulders of the pallbearers up front. The casket was made of fish crates with two large branches from a cactus nailed to each side. The priest walking behind it kept brushing the dust off his cassock with one hand while the other held up the hem to keep from stepping on it. A triangular hat was pushed down low on his forehead so that the wind wouldn't blow it away along with any semblance of ceremonial demeanor. His face was somber.

The sea pounded at the shore as they continued their march. Above, dozens of crows above flapped their wings, cawing in time with the music.

Reiter was grateful that his son, by now taller than his father, walked by his side.

***

The call from the head of the San Felipe Police had come to the Chaparral, his California ranch, early Tuesday morning. The officer's voice had been oddly crisp over the static of the telephone line. The epitaph was brief: "He didn't turn off the gas. He must have fallen asleep." He paused and cleared his throat. "That's right, he blew out the flame, but forgot the damn gas." There was another burst of static on the line. "If you ask me, the guy was stupid. That Cobo," the officer added, leaving the name to the last.

Reiter groped for a seat. "So?" he argued. "That's happened before, even to me."

"Yeah, as long as the windows are open," the officer pointed out meaningfully. Reiter sensed gravity in the man's voice.

"What are you trying to tell me?" Was this about Cobo dying? He struggled with the suspicion that rose in the back of his brain.

"I know you were friends." The officer's words sounded distant. "He often bragged about you."

Reiter was assailed by a wave of sadness. They're all dying on me, my hombres, he thought to himself. He bit down on his lip. During the last five years Jeff Clancy had a heart attack, Martine had died of cancer, Pablo had a stroke, Papillo had wandered into a canyon and never come back, and Alfonso had fallen off a roof and broken his neck. Now Cobo.

"They are going to bury him by the old well north of town," the police officer said. "On Thursday, I think." And he'd hung up.

***

The ragged musicians following the fishermen seemed stuck on the same tune. It took a while before Reiter recognized it, even though his son kept humming the melody. He'd always loved the somber song. It was also Cobo's favorite. *A Fistful of Sand.* "The day I pass on," he remembered the words, "I will remember the good times, the good friends along the way. My soul has always been free, like a seagull, hopping from one rock to another, flying along he shores. The only thing I'll take with me when it's all over, my friend, are memories…and a fist full of sand." The words gripped his soul, and he felt like singing with them.

Finally, the musicians ran out of air. They took a deep breath and the music faded into the hills. The priest began to chant.

Big black birds perched on the crosses of the cemetery, their red hoods bobbing behind curved yellow beaks. They were vultures, Reiter knew, waiting to devour the remnants of death. They seemed oblivious to the approaching procession, but at the last minute they loosened their claws and, slowly flapping their wings, rose into the sky.

The priest registered his annoyance as he rushed up to the grave. "In Nomine Patris, Filli, Et Spiriti Sancti, Amen," he began and made the sign of the cross. Nervously, he eyed several crows that had dropped onto the mound of dirt at the edge of the grave. They kept cawing and cawing and cawing, as if in anticipation.

Once they got to the graveside, the pallbearers placed the box on the ground and looked at the priest for further directions. He motioned for them to move closer. Then he must have decided that they were in the wrong place and nodded toward the other side of the grave. They picked up the fish crate and started to move around a pile of rotting fish heads with empty sockets where the eyes had been.

Kicking the fish heads out of the way, they'd almost made it to the other side of the grave when the first pallbearer, who was holding down the lid, lost his balance and let go of the coffin. The others were caught by surprise and the fish crate came crashing down, striking the side of the grave with a thud. The lid flew off, and a wide-eyed Cobo flipped out of the coffin, staring sightlessly at the mourners. Someone had put a bottle of tequila in his hand, and he held it tight, rigor mortis having set in for some time.

The mourners gasped collectively as Cobo landed near the edge of the grave raising a cloud of dust. He came to rest face down, his arms spread out and his legs dangling in the grave. With a bang, the lid careened off into the desert, picked up by the wind. It reminded Reiter of his own life as it bounced off unyielding boulders. Meanwhile, Cobo's rigid hands clung to the side of the grave without letting go of the bottle of tequila.

The grimace on the priest's purple face spelled out his frustration. "Useless imbeciles. Can't even put a coffin together. Then don't bother to nail it shut. Sacrilegious misfits. You can't even walk." His shoulders drooped, and he motioned first to the corpse and then to the grave. "Finish him off," he seemed to be saying, though words failed him.

One of the musicians put down his accordion and started to lift one of Cobo's hands. Gravity took over, and Reiter winced as he saw the rest of Cobo slide into the grave. There was something darkly comic in the final act that dispatched Cobo from the earth, Reiter thought. A ray of humor piercing all the sadness.

Reiter felt his son's hand tighten on his forearm, and without a word, the boy looked down at his father. His moist eyes spoke clearly: "I know you loved Cobo, Dad," they assured him. "Look at it this way, he gave you something to laugh at while you cry." His eyes returned to Cobo. "Let's remember him as he was."

The trombone started up again, its blare muffled as the accordion once more took up the melody of *A Fistful of Sand*. They kept playing it over and over.

The fishermen started shoveling the mound of dirt into the hole. The priest bit his lip and held up a hand to stop them. "Dust to Dust," he started to read from a book, his face turning peaceful, openly grateful that the accident had cut short the ceremony.

Reiter watched the crows, as if on command, suddenly head for the clouds, their shrill cries sounding the death knell.

It may have been exhaustion that shaped Reiter's dream that night. He followed the brightly colored birds as they flew higher and higher. He couldn't make out what flew in their midst, but had a feeling they were escorting an invisible companion. He thought he could hear Cobo's whining voice, "Where are we going? I'm not ready to go."

If it was heaven where the flock finally landed, it looked familiar. Reiter saw the old tower of his hometown rising from cobblestone streets, ancient houses with pointed steeples lined up at its feet. The Dolomite Mountains sparkling under an azure sky appeared in the distance. On the other side of the walled tower lay the shacks of Puertecitos, laundry flapping in the breeze. The emerald green of the Sea of Cortez shimmered in the background. There were dozens of musicians walking the streets—Mexicans with sombreros and shiny suits studded with buttons, Tyroleans in green hats with the brim folded down on one side, and Indians in colorful headgear beating on drums. Everything he'd ever loved blended in one place.

Martine, Pablo, Papillo, Don Rafael, Beto, El Chino and Jeff Clancy were sitting around a table. Capi laughed robustly at a clever joke told in a confident voice by Israel. Everyone was smiling. Then Cobo appeared. He didn't seem to know where he was.

A turtle showed up and poked its head out of its shell. "You are with the souls of your friends," the turtle tried to reassure him. "Don't you remember when you put me back in the water?"

Cobo's face reflected his continuing confusion as he looked around. He turned toward Alfonso and seemed startled by his youthful appearance. Gone were the lines of worry on his face. Pablo and the rest also looked like men in the prime of life. Cobo backed up, shaking his head in disbelief. He seemed determined to leave.

"Why be in a hurry?" Beto suddenly spoke up. "You are in a place that's only for souls," he explained. "It has nothing to do with time."

Cobo reluctantly walked up to the table and was about to sit down. "That chair is for the Phantom," Martine said.

"The Espanto?" Cobo smiled wryly. "I think he has other plans." He pointed to the chair. "I don't think he'll be needing that," he said with an all-knowing look "Not for a long, long time."

341

Everyone smiled as the musicians marched down the cobblestone street and around the shacks. Tyroleans, Americans, Mexicans, Indians, "A Fistful of Sand" echoed into the sky like a million guitars, this time in tune. Then all together they yodeled like Tyroleans and whooped like Indians.

Reiter woke up and caught his reflection in the window beside him.

This time he was more than a face and a body.

The journey was over.

Printed in the United States
119776LV00001B/157-192/P